to jill g...
with a[p],
your enthusiasm,
susan storer clark
november 2017

THE MONK WOMAN'S DAUGHTER

Praise for The Monk Woman's Daughter

The Monk Woman's Daughter is a brawling, lusty novel about brawling, lusty America in the middle of the nineteenth century. The story will grab you by the lapels and haul you along with the cursed, blessed, resourceful, and fascinating Vera St. John as she navigates a world that grants little opportunity— or even regard—for women so unwise as to be born without advantages. Enduring waves of misogyny, political turmoil, and religious and ethnic hatred, Vera survives it all and then some. A terrific read!

DAVID O. STEWART, author of *The Lincoln Deception*

A young woman's story of survival, this meticulously researched novel brings to life an era when women wore bonnets and steered a narrow course between the roles of wife, widow, maid, and "parlor girl." The driving force behind this riveting tale is the mystery of Vera's birth, which contains the essence of the fierce conflict between Protestant and Catholic in nineteenth-century America.

SOLVEIG EGGERZ, author of *Seal Woman*

The Monk Woman's Daughter takes us back to an era when Irish gangs ran whole chunks of Manhattan and pigs rooted in the muddy streets. You'll meet low-lifes and high livers, con men and saints, union leaders and union busters, as you race through history with Vera on a quest to unscramble the mystery of the woman who gave her birth.

FRANK JOSEPH, author of *To Love Mercy*

The Monk Woman's Daughter

by

SUSAN STORER CLARK

PORTLAND • OREGON
INKWATERPRESS.COM

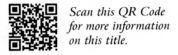
Copyright © 2017 by Susan Storer Clark

Edited by Andrew Durkin
Cover layout and interior design by Masha Shubin
Front cover design by Nick Bowen
Baltimore Maryland in 1870s. by Rev Samuel Manning © Shutterstock.com

Publisher: Inkwater Press | www.inkwaterpress.com

Paperback ISBN-13 978-1-62901-490-6 | ISBN-10 1-62901-490-7
Kindle   ISBN-13 978-1-62901-491-3 | ISBN-10 1-62901-491-5

Printed in the U.S.A.

1 3 5 7 9 10 8 6 4 2

With grateful thanks to the Holey Road Writers, Ann McLaughlin, and archivists and librarians everywhere.

CHAPTER 1

M Y MOTHER SAID SHE WAS A NUN. THAT MIGHT HAVE been a lie. Her story made her famous, but it was always hard for me to tell how much of it was true. She was also a whore, and she might have been a thief. I learned more about my mother's history from strangers than I ever learned from her. I was often ashamed of her, but I always loved her.

I loved the freedom of city streets when I was a child, and I love that freedom even now, though city streets can be dangerous for girls and for women. We lived on Goerck Street until 1846, when I was ten. Pigs ran free in the streets; little girls did not—except for me and my sister Lizzie. Many mothers kept their daughters close. Our mother only came looking for us if she wanted us to read to her or take a bucket to fetch her beer.

The streets were filled with people who, it seemed, came from everywhere except New York. More black folk lived there in those days, and plenty of Germans, along with some Jews and ever-increasing numbers of Irish. Entertainment was everywhere: dog fights, street vendors crying their wares, drovers bringing cattle through for slaughter, pigs everywhere. The streets themselves were pitted, dank, and filthy with the

1

contents of refuse pails and chamber pots. We did have privies, but they were usually full, and they always stank. Children assigned to empty the chamber pots took the easy course of dumping the contents in the street. So did adults, when they thought nobody was looking.

Lizzie and I often went to glean bits of wood or coal from the docks, where the steamboats spewed cinders that could still be burned. The great sailing ships were exciting to watch, and the sailors were often jolly, telling us stories and making us laugh.

I have always loved to dance. I still do, even though I am now thirty years of age. When I was ten, I was fast-footed and light. I could earn a few pennies dancing for the sailors or outside one of the saloons—especially if I was dancing with someone else, and most especially if I were dancing with one of the black boys. I'd start by clogging, as the Irish do—rapping my feet on stone or brick and leaping very high. The black children would dance low to the ground, with snaky, sinuous movements I would imitate. Then they'd imitate me. Even when there was no fiddler about and we had to make our own mouth music, we'd be entertained, and so would passersby. If all other entertainments failed, we always had the pigs.

Pigs were everywhere in those days. I understand they still are, twenty years later. Some of the more provident women of the neighborhood would catch and mark the pigs as their own by cutting notches in their ears. The pigs disapproved of this idea, and would squeal mightily and try to run—sometimes dragging the women along the ground, and almost always gushing spectacularly with blood. Those of us who saw would laugh and applaud.

Disputed ownership could provide even better entertainment. The Irish women didn't always honor the German women's marks, and vice versa. A female punch-up often brought the men out of the saloon to watch. The women would feed their pigs and maybe find some country boy to slaughter them in the alley or the street when the time came. Meat was scarce for poor folk, especially fresh meat.

Salt pork could be had from the barrel at the grocer's, or at the saloon. That is, while it was sold as "salt *pork*," people claimed if you listened closely enough, you could hear it whinny or bray or bark or meow—or maybe say the Lord's Prayer.

My friend Ziprah Carvalho hardly ever got to eat meat at all. She and her family were Jews from Portugal, and Mrs. Carvalho said they didn't eat pork, even when they were sure that's what it was. She certainly wasn't going to feed her family anything that came to Goerck Street in a dirty barrel. They lived closer to the saloon than anyone else, except the Chayevskis. Mrs. Chayevski thought all redheaded people were evil and unlucky. Unfortunately for her, she lived next to the saloon in an Irish neighborhood. Every time Mrs. Chayevski saw someone with red hair, she would cross herself three times and spit. She seemed to spend all her time crossing herself and scowling, and she looked like giving out all that spit had dried her right up. It might not have been the spit alone. Maybe having eight children had something to do with her shriveled face.

It was especially unfortunate for her to live near the McGonagles, since the mister, the missus, and all six children had blazing ginger hair. Mrs. Chayevski might have been happier if she'd tried to get along with Mrs. McGonagle—a big, strong, capable woman who had marked several pigs, and scared off any possible poachers.

I was dancing in front of the saloon one late-summer day when I saw Mrs. McGonagle spread out some potato peelings and rotted vegetables. Her biggest pig trotted up, and her six children quietly surrounded it as a big Negro stood by with a butchering knife. One of the children moved too quickly, and the pig bolted, knocking Mrs. McGonagle down. Her oldest boy Tommy tried to run after it, but he slipped on some chamber pot filth and fell. I stopped dancing to watch, and the crowd by the saloon door laughed and shouted. Two of the younger children trapped the pig by a wagon wheel, and Mrs. McGonagle strode up to tie three of its legs together. She must have been rattled by her fall, because she didn't tie the legs properly, and when the Negro stuck the big knife into the pig's neck, it thrashed free, spurting blood into the Negro's face and running toward the front of the saloon, heading straight for the horse and wagon standing in front of it.

All seven McGonagles tore after the pig, with the Negro roaring after them—a bellowing, bloody apparition. The frightened horse started plunging away from them with the wagon, bringing the driver out of the saloon, shouting and cursing. The pig doubled back, knocking down three of the children and running straight into Mrs. McGonagle, who grabbed it up and started to tie it again, right in front of the Carvalhos. The bellowing Negro began hacking at the pig in a blind fury, with Mrs. Carvalho starting to shriek as the unclean blood and entrails of the pig gushed over her family's doorstep.

The drinkers began pointing and guffawing. "Sure, and she should have had a sober man do the butcherin' of it."

"Sober? Any sober man here?"

Laughter.

The laughter made Mrs. Carvalho shriek louder, and Mrs. McGonagle began shouting in her thick Kerry accent at the Negro, who was still hacking at the pig's carcass. "I won't be payin' for this, ye spalpeen. This is no proper butcherin' job."

The Negro turned and threatened Mrs. McGonagle with the butchering knife. The drinkers began taking bets—about half of them on Mrs. McGonagle, even though she faced an armed and angry man who was already covered with blood.

Behind Mrs. McGonagle's back, Mrs. Chayevski tiptoed through the mess to grab a large piece of meat.

"Ma!" yelled Tommy. "Thief, thief!"

Mrs. McGonagle whirled around and fetched Mrs.

Chayevski a cuff on the ear, knocking her down and bringing a cheer from the saloon audience. She stood there a moment, breathing hard but making it clear she'd fight the whole neighborhood for the remains of her pig. She paid the Negro, who dragged the carcass into the street, silently cut it into pieces, gave one nod, and got up and shouldered his way into the saloon, still covered with blood. Some of the drinkers followed him in, knowing the show was over and hoping perhaps he would stand them a treat.

Mrs. McGonagle and her children gathered up the large pieces and the guts, leaving some of the entrails in the street. Those of us in the street were laughing and joking when suddenly I heard everyone go silent, and saw people start to move away.

I knew without looking that my mother had come out of our house. I knew she'd been drinking already, and I didn't have to look at her to know her boots were untidily laced, her dress disheveled, her hair askew. She had a large, empty bottle in her hand. "Vera," she called to me. "Dearest child, come here."

She wanted me to take the bottle and get more beer. I wished I were invisible.

Maeve McGonagle stopped in front of me, carrying bloody hunks of flesh. She was my age—but half a head taller, and mean as a fighting rat. She narrowed her eyes and stuck her face in mine. "Your ma's a drunk." I looked away, but that didn't stop her. "My mother says she's an evil woman and you're going to be just like her."

Ziprah came to my rescue. "What will your ma say when she sees you talking to the likes of us, when you're supposed to be helping her?"

"She'll strip the hide from your backside," I jeered. Ziprah and I started to chant, "She'll strip the hide from your backside! She'll strip the hide from your backside!"

Maeve gave us a sneer and walked off.

My mother stood glassy-eyed, swaying slightly, still holding the bottle in her hand. The remaining saloon drinkers looked at her, muttered to each other, and went back indoors. Stray dogs and pigs moved forward to make a meal of the entrails in the street. I went to my mother.

"Sweet child." She put a hand on my head. "Please take the bottle and get me a drink."

"I won't, Mother. You know I won't." I waited a minute and said, "Let's go inside. I'll read to you."

She liked having me read to her: the Bible, newspapers, anything we had. I hoped if I read to her, she would fall asleep, and wouldn't slap us or rage at us.

It hadn't always been like this. There was a time when she would read to me, or I to her, and we would sit contented in each other's arms until we fell asleep.

I didn't know why our neighbors treated our mother the way they did. I had once tried to ask her, and she had slapped me and burst into tears, so I didn't ask her again.

I remembered visits from well-dressed, dignified men who would talk to her kindly, and listen to me read. Sometimes they would give Lizzie and me money, or even leave another book in the house. I know now they were Protestant clergymen—maybe even the ones who made my mother famous, or infamous. One of those men might even have been my real father. But none of them had visited for a long time.

We'd also had paintings in the house—bright and beautiful, featuring dramatic scenes from the Bible, usually involving virtuous women in danger or difficulty. My favorite was Susannah's trial, with Susannah's pale, noble face glowing in a beam of light, while dark, bearded men stared menacingly from the shadows. Susannah looked different from the women on Goerck Street. She was clean. Her hair shone and her hands were soft-looking and white. Even Ruth, gleaning in the fields, knelt in the soil in what looked like perfectly clean garments, with the same lovely light upon her face. The paintings were gone by the time I was ten, and I know now that my mother sold these paintings to buy her drink.

When the neighbors talked about her, they didn't call her "Mrs. St. John" or even "Maria," but "Maria Monk." Both names. They stopped talking whenever they realized I was nearby, listening.

They made me feel ashamed, outcast, unclean, and I didn't really know why. I wondered what my mother had done. And I thought, as children do, that I must somehow be responsible. I loved her, for children often love even the most unworthy of parents. I knew that she loved me.

I have been fortunate, I suppose, to have survived at all. If I had stayed in Goerck Street, I could easily have died as a child, or been crushed under the wheels of a cart, or forced into whoring.

I didn't know what my surname should have been, or who my real father was. The name I had came to me from the man I knew as my mother's husband. He was as good to me as any father can be to a child. My name was Vera St. John.

CHAPTER 2

M Y MOTHER SOMETIMES TOLD ME MY FATHER HAD BEEN a Catholic priest. She also told me at various times that my father was either the Monkey King, Cardinal Richelieu, a Welsh laborer she called "Lovely Davy," or Satan himself. I didn't know what to believe, and finally decided I couldn't necessarily believe anything she told me.

After we'd seen the pig slaughtered, when my mother was weepy and woozy with drink, I read to her from the newspaper. There was a dreadful story about some children who drowned in the river. She cried and moaned about the poor babies, and then talked about Lizzie and me as though we had drowned. Finally, she fell asleep, still catching her breath in sobs.

Lizzie came into the house quietly, just at dark, with some bread she had foraged in the street, and I suddenly realized I hadn't eaten that day. Our father came in a few minutes later, with a loaf of bread and some sausage. The bread was welcome. The sausage was an unexpected treat.

"Where is your mother?"

"She's asleep."

He sighed. "I suppose that's better than drunk."

She was both, but I knew what he meant. At least she wasn't

in the saloon. It occurred to me that he had not been drunk for quite a while. That was a change.

"Here," he said. "Let us share some supper. We have something important to do tomorrow."

Lizzie and I didn't care what we had to do tomorrow. Hunger made a feast of bread and sausage, and our relief that there would be no noisy argument that night made it easy to swallow. Our parents' arguments were loud and terrifying. Sometimes my mother hit my father or threw things at him. Lizzie and I would usually huddle in a corner, as far away from them as we could get and still be in the house. We were still afraid to go out on the streets late at night. And besides, there was an awful fascination hearing him call her a drunken whore, and hearing her bellow back that he had no money and no manhood. He'd had money once; he came from a wealthy family. But that was all we knew.

That night, he went out and got washing water for us from the street pump. "Here," he said, "make your hands and faces and feet clean before you go to bed." He watched as we did, and said, almost as if he were talking to himself, "You two don't stand a chance here. If you don't get run over by a cart or poisoned by what you have to eat, you'll be sold for whores before you're twelve."

He stopped and rubbed his eyebrows as though his head hurt. "As soon as anyone finds out who your mother is, they'll want nothing to do with you."

Lizzie and I looked at each other and gave little shrugs. We knew what our mother was like. We were also used to odd behavior, and going to bed clean and fed was agreeable enough that we weren't going to make a fuss.

Even as we began to stir in the morning, the two of them were arguing. My mother shouted that he was just trying to take her babies away from her, and she would make sure he couldn't. She stamped her way out of the house, probably headed for the saloon.

If she was afraid of losing us, why was she leaving? It didn't make sense to me, but there was no point in trying to figure out what my mother did.

After a few minutes, our father called us to get up. "We're going somewhere important today," he said.

He combed our hair—carefully but clumsily—and told us to put on our "best clothes." That was confusing. We had few clothes to choose from, and no "best." We did what we could, and put on our shoes, which we hadn't worn since spring. They were too small.

We walked with him out of Goerck Street and up toward Wall Street. He explained to us that an uncle of his had died and left him an income—money that was his—and his children could inherit, as long as they were legitimate. This did not make a great deal of sense to me—although the idea of a bit of money sounded good, especially if it would buy more sausage and larger shoes. We went with him to a law office, where he talked to the clerk, signed some papers, put up his right hand, and swore we were both his lawful children.

As we walked back to Goerck Street, he talked about how much better our lives would be now that he had stopped drinking and come into some money.

Our mother was home when we got there, and when she found out what our father had done, she began to rage. "You stinking maggot." She stormed. "You did that to take my babies away."

He tried to explain, said he'd done this to get money for all of us. "Vera is not your child," she snarled. "What do you care about her? You just want to take my babies from me. Well, you won't. I'll show you."

She stalked out of the house, out into Goerck Street, and toward Wall Street, with our father behind her, and us panting and limping after them in our tight shoes. She stalked into an office and bellowed for the clerk, saying she was not Mr. St. John's lawful wife.

The clerk looked baffled, as well he might. "This is most unusual," he began. "Usually, under these circumstances, well ..." His voice trailed off. He looked at my father. "Mr. St. John, can you produce a marriage certificate?"

"Well, I, um ... That's hardly the sort of thing one carries about."

"Indeed," answered the clerk. For a moment, there was silence. The clerk spoke again. "Were you married in New York City? We can verify this through the town hall."

"Yes. Yes, we were." My father glanced triumphantly at my mother.

"Good, good," said the clerk, picking up a pencil. "What was your wife's maiden name?"

Silence. My father turned pale and closed his eyes. My mother smiled a nasty, gloating smile and folded her arms.

What is she doing? I wondered. It didn't make any sense to me.

Until it did. I thought, *She thinks he's going to take us away if he can prove we're his children. And he doesn't want to tell anyone he is married to Maria Monk.* But I didn't understand why. What had she done that was so horrible?

I thought for a moment my father was going to cry. He did not, but his face crumpled, and he left the clerk's office, defeated and pale.

Lizzie and I followed. "Sir," the clerk called after us, "even without a marriage, you still ..."

His voice trailed off as the door closed behind us. My father walked through the streets looking dazed. When we got home, he kissed us each on the forehead, and left without a word. My mother had not come with us. Lizzie and I took off our shoes and went out into the street.

We came home at dark to an empty house, confused and wondering what to do next. Very late that night, our mother staggered home, drunk, and fell into the bed. She was snoring early the next morning when Lizzie and I quietly got up and went out looking for something to eat.

We went into the saloon, where there was usually some food. But it was too early, although there were a few men there drinking. The place was dark and smelt of old beer, bad tobacco, and unwashed bodies.

Mr. Luehring, the tall, thin German who ran the saloon, recognized us. "Poor *kinder*. Nothing to eat? Sit, have bread." He found us some bread and some cheese, and he watered down some beer.

"Don't tell the others," he said, although it sounded like "udders." He gave us a wink and a sad smile. "I'll have all the little ones in here."

"Oh, there you are, my sweet children. I've been looking everywhere for you." My mother's voice—with its sweet, wheedling tone—struck terror into me in a way her shrieking never could. I looked into her face; the corners of her mouth turned up, but her dark eyes were vacant and hard. "Do get dressed in your best, my darlings, and Mama will take you for a walk along the river."

My mother never took us anywhere, and hearing her call us "darlings" made the hairs on my neck stand up.

"Oh, dear, kind Mr. Luehring, let me pay you for your generosity to my girls."

His mouth hardened into a thin line, and he shook his head.

She wheedled. "Perhaps I could have a bit of your fine drink."

He shook his head again, and started to wipe the counter. "Too early," he said.

"Well, then," she said, "I'll just sit here with my babies."

She turned that vacant smile on us. I had been hungry, but now I felt as though a cold stone had dropped into my belly and filled it.

"Mother," I said, taking Lizzie's hand and edging toward the door, "Lizzie and I will go get ready for our walk."

I pulled Lizzie outside, but once we were on the street, she jerked away from me. "I don't want to go on a walk with *her*." Lizzie never referred to our mother by a name or title, just as *she* or *her*. "She wants to drown us."

"I don't want to go, either," I said. "I just wanted to get away from her."

Lizzie started to wail. I put my arms around her.

"Lizzie, hush. We won't go anywhere. She won't go anywhere, either. She'll just stay here and drink. Let's go home with our food. We can hide if she comes."

We walked in the door to find our father there. He was dressed in a smart new hat and coat, and had bundles with him. "Good, good," he said. "There you are. Here, girls, these are for you. Where is your mother?"

We were afraid to answer.

"Is she in the saloon?"

We looked at our feet. Lizzie nodded.

"Good," he said. That surprised us, especially since it was so early. "Here, I've brought you some new clothes. Please go put them on."

New clothes? It wasn't even Christmas. The bundles he brought had a new frock for each of us, plus a hat, a coat, and shoes. The shoes were a bit large, but that was better than too small. When we were dressed, we thought we looked as fine as any little girls we'd ever seen.

When we came into the front room, dressed, my father hardly glanced at us. He was holding the door open just a crack, looking out nervously. "Oh, good, you're ready. Um—you look quite nice, both of you. We're going to the country."

The country? Our walk to Wall Street the day before had taken us about as far from Goerck Street as we had ever been.

"Please, gather your things together. Take your other clothes. Here, I have a bag for you to put them in."

That didn't take long. We had a few underclothes, plus the shoes and clothes we had stood up in only minutes before. Lizzie put in some of her prized toys, I put in my three books, and we were ready to go.

"There is no need to say goodbye to your mother. I'm sure she's busy. Just come with me."

That was odd, but there had been many odd things happening, and we were afraid of our mother. Off we went, down Goerck Street, past the saloon. I glanced in and could see her with her back to us—her hair disordered, her dress dirty, her voice already rising and loud. When I think of her now, this is the picture I see.

We walked quietly toward the river landings. When Lizzie realized this, she pulled on my arm, giving me a glance of alarm and whispering, "Is *he* going to drown us?"

I shook my head no, and we walked on without saying a word.

As we went, my father began to talk.

"I think you'll enjoy this, girls. We'll be taking a river boat across to Brooklyn, and from there we'll take the new omnibus to Flatbush. We'll be visiting my cousin..." His talk washed around us, the place names meaning nothing. He said the money from his uncle had come at a perfect time—just as he had decided he would never drink again. He had loved our mother and tried to save her, but he couldn't—and now he would try to save us. We must remember not to empty the chamber pot into the street, nor to eat with our hands. I wondered briefly how we could eat without our hands.

He stopped. We stopped. He turned to us and put his hands on our shoulders, looking into our eyes. He barely spoke above a whisper. "One thing you *must* remember. You must never tell anyone who your mother is. She was wicked, and many, many people know she was wicked.

14

"Things will go very hard for you if people know you are her daughters. I am going to tell my cousin your mother is dead, do you understand?"

We nodded mutely.

"Promise me you will never tell anyone her name. Do you promise?"

"Yes," we answered, our voices very small and uncertain.

"Good," he said. "Never tell anyone. Ever."

CHAPTER 3

*I*T WAS A SHORT WALK TO THE FERRY DOCK AT FULTON Street, and we crossed the busy river. So much was wonderful and new to me—the sheer novelty of being on a boat, the deep blast of the whistle, the mighty belches of steam and smoke from the stack, and the way the sky opened up as we stood on the deck. I had never seen so much sky before—every place I had ever been was rimmed by buildings. It was a dazzling early autumn day. The river sparkled, and the sky arched over us, never-ending and blue. I was tempted to spread my arms just to see if I could fly.

When we landed at Brooklyn, we walked toward a handsome new omnibus—brightly painted, and drawn by handsome horses, with room for at least twenty people.

"This is our 'bus,'" said our father, and I'm sure my jaw dropped.

There were plenty of omnibuses on city streets, but we'd never had the fare. My father paid, and we climbed up and sat on red-cushioned seats. In a few minutes, the vehicle was full, with an elderly couple, a mother with small children, and some working men sitting on benches to the side. The driver clucked to the horses, and we rolled forward onto the plank road to Flatbush.

Trees lined the road, arching over it in a sort of canopy, and

the breeze stirred their leaves to a noisy rustle. I was fascinated—I'd never been so close to so many trees. When we broke
out into the sunshine, our father pointed out shimmering fields
of gold, telling us which was barley and which was rye. We saw
trees with apples growing on them, and fat cattle grazing in the
green fields. I had never been so conscious of the sunshine, or
smelled air so sweet and crisp.

We were the only people left on the omnibus when the
horses clopped to a halt and the driver said, "Flatbush, sir. End
of the line."

"Oh!" said my father, looking around. "I didn't recognize it.
I was looking for the courthouse."

The driver gave him an amused look and said, "Courthouse
burned more'n ten years ago."

"Oh. I see. Well, step down, girls. I think it's only a short walk
to Cousin Julia's."

"The Widow Van Deventer?" asked the driver. "Down that
way, on the edge of the Van Deventer farm, past that fine new
house of Mr. Lott's."

We walked past several houses that were neat and fine—all
with clean, white fences bordering the road. In front of most of
them were tidy sidewalks, neatly graveled and leveled. A short
distance down the road was a plain, old farmhouse, covered
with cedar shakes, and with a long, low porch in the front. A
woman sat there smoking a pipe. When she saw us coming, she
stood, knocked out the pipe, and smiled at us.

"Miles! It's a good thing you got here before dark."

"Yes, indeed," he answered. "Vera St. John, Elizabeth St.
John—this is your cousin, Mrs. Julia Van Deventer. May they
call you Miss Julia?"

"They may."

We had never been formally introduced to anyone before,
so we stood there dumb, looking at her. She was a thin, dark-
haired country woman. She could have been anywhere from

five-and-twenty to fifty years old. She had a kind smile but tobacco-stained teeth, and handsome eyes—although one of them wandered a little bit.

"Girls," prompted our father. "Say, 'how do you do?'" We mumbled the phrase without any conviction or enthusiasm.

"Hmp," Miss Julia returned. "I'm as well as could be expected. Would you like some lemonade?"

Again, we stood dumb, staring up at her. We didn't know if we wanted lemonade, because we'd never had any.

"Girls," said our father—a little exasperated, but still patient. "Say, 'Yes, please.'"

"Yes, please," we said, barely audible.

"Sit," Miss Julia said, with a slight smile. "I'll fetch it."

Our father sat in one of the two chairs, and we sat on a low wooden bench. He whispered to us, "When she brings the lemonade, say, 'Thank you.'"

She brought the lemonade, and we mumbled our thanks. She sat, and the two adults began to talk. Lizzie and I looked at each other, holding the cold metal cups in our hands. Lizzie shrugged and tried her lemonade, then looked at me, licked her lips, and grinned. I tried it. I had never tasted anything so wonderful in my life.

I'd never had any drink with any flavor. Our drinks had been mostly stale beer or weak tea. Lizzie had often taken water from the street pump—not because she liked it, but because adults told her it was dangerous to drink. Lemonade—cold, sweet, and sour all at once—was delicious on my tongue, and refreshed me as nothing ever had. I have loved it ever since.

I leaned against the wall of the house and took a deep breath, listening to the sounds of dusk rather than the adult talk. The sun was low; the shadows were getting long and deep. Over the rustle of the leaves, I heard the lowing of cattle and the drowsy clucking of nearby chickens. They were strange sounds to me, but they were soothing.

Miss Julia's sharp voice brought me out of my reverie. "Miles, I'll set the girls to shelling peas while we talk. They do know how to shell peas?"

"I don't think so. We, ah, we don't get many fresh vegetables in the city."

That was not quite true. Farmers came in to sell their fruit and vegetables near Goerck Street. We just didn't buy any.

"Well, they'll need to learn. I just picked these." She brought us a big bowl of peas, with a smaller bowl to put the shelled peas in. She sat right down on the porch to show us how to split the pods and gently work out the shining green spheres with our fingers. She watched as we tried, waiting patiently while we clumsily shredded pods and squashed a few peas. Then she showed us again, and when we'd acquired some skill, she said, "Take it slow. No need to be quick, just careful." Then she went and sat down, resuming her conversation with our father.

Lizzie whispered to me, "This is stupid. These things rub my fingers."

"Don't be in such a hurry," I whispered back. "Don't tear them like that. Just split them with your thumb. Like this, see?"

"I don't want to do this. I want to go home."

"We can't go home, Lizzie. We don't know the way, and even if we did, our mother would hurt us. We have to do what Miss Julia says."

"I don't care."

"Lizzie, please. If she doesn't like us, we'll have no place to go."

She looked angry, like she was about to cry, but she stayed silent. I continued shelling the peas and started listening to the conversation.

"Julia, I must say I didn't recognize Flatbush, with all the new fine houses and the courthouse gone. I understand it burned?"

"It did," she answered, knocking out her pipe. "And a pip of a story that is. You remember Ophelia, the sheriff's daughter?"

"Can't say I do."

"Hmp. Not many would. Homely as a she-toad. Well, one night they arrested a handsome young fellow named Richard Fenton. Came here on the stagecoach, back in the days when it still ran. He was a gambler, and the sheriff put him in jail and charged him with murder."

She stopped to clean out and relight her pipe. "I don't think anybody knew whether he did the murder, but we all figgered he would hang for it. He started sweet-talking Ophelia, who'd probably never had a man talk to her before in her life, and she got him out of jail, and set it afire to keep the town busy while they escaped."

"Did it work?"

"Oh, it worked. Ophelia was clever. She knew they had to ring the bell on the old Dutch church to get the fire company—and to ring the bell, they had to find the sexton. That was old Jim Huygens. He was deaf as doomsday. She knew he'd be out digging a grave the night she set the fire. They hallooed all over town, looking for him. All the time, he was out back of the church.

"By the time they got him to ringing the bell and getting the men together, the courthouse was cinders and the two of them gone. We heard stories about where they went—probably out west, on the Conestoga wagons or the Erie Canal. Who knows?" she reflected, gazing at the sunset. "You girls done with those peas?"

We were. She put us all to work, getting my father to draw water for us all to wash up, and enough for Lizzie and me to bathe later. She had Lizzie get bowls and spoons from the sideboard and set the table. I sliced bread and fetched the butter. Supper was cold ham, bread, butter, and the peas we had just shelled, along with cold buttermilk.

The evening seemed very long. We worked together to wash and dry the dishes, and then put them away. Lizzie made faces at me to show how much she hated being ordered about. I liked putting the things in order, but we had to wait for the bath water to heat, and Miss Julia slathered our heads with a foul liquid to kill lice. When she asked if we had nightgowns, we produced our old raggedy shifts.

"Rags," she said, and she tore them up. "You can sleep in Jakob's old shirts."

"Who's Jakob?" Lizzie asked.

"He was my husband."

I nudged Lizzie to keep quiet.

By the time we were clean, dry, and clad in old shirts, we were exhausted. We dragged up a ladder into the loft and lay on a bed of clean straw. I put my arms around Lizzie, and she fell asleep almost immediately. I lay awake listening as Julia and our father talked.

"Miles, they're street urchins. I don't see how I can take them. I a'nt some fine lady. Jakob's brother only lets me live here on his tolerance, and if there's any trouble, I'm out on my ear."

"They'll fit in," he said, reassuringly. "The little bit I can give you each month will help. They can both read. Can they go to school here?"

"They may take Elizabeth," Miss Julia answered. "Vera's too old. They don't have school for girls older than eight. I can make sure they can read, write, and figure. Even girls ought to know that."

"Vera reads well," he answered. "Her mother taught her. Elizabeth can read a little, but she wasn't so close to her mother."

"Vera's well-spoken," Miss Julia remarked. "Sounds like a lady."

"As does her mother," answered my father. "I mean, her mother was well-spoken."

"But your family don't approve," said Miss Julia.

"No."

Silence. He was letting her think my mother was dead. He said that's what we needed to do, but hearing him talk about her as though she were dead made me feel very small and sad ...

21

and very alone. I held myself close to Lizzie. I felt like crying, but I didn't. Soon I fell asleep.

⌇

THE SUN WOKE ME THE next morning, and I lay in the soft, warm straw, smelling the clean shirt, and the sweet scent of the straw.

Miss Julia called us. "Up! And up! No sleeping 'til the sun is high! The hens are waiting."

What did that mean? What did hens wait for? I climbed down the ladder into the kitchen, pulled off the old shirt, and put on my frock. Miss Julia stood there with a basket. "If you want eggs for breakfast, you'll have to go get them."

The henhouse was dark, with a heavy, sweetish smell. The hens were mostly silent, watching us vacantly, giving the occasional lazy cluck.

"Be gentle," said Miss Julia, "or you'll get yourself pecked." She showed me how to slide my hand gently under the hens. The nests were warm, and their feathers were soft.

And the eggs! Fresh eggs have a taste that is full and sweet, and by the time Lizzie and our father awoke, I had cooked and eaten three of them with bread toasted over the kitchen fire.

Our father left that morning, promising to be back in a month. Lizzie cried and clung to him as he kissed us goodbye. I felt sad and afraid, too—but I hung back because I didn't want to hurt Miss Julia's feelings.

⌇

DAYS WITH MISS JULIA BEGAN with a trip to the henhouse and milking the cow. Then we worked in the vegetable garden or "put up" vegetables or fruit from the apple trees. We cleaned the root cellar and learned to keep the Dutch tiles around the fireplace gleaming, putting whitewash on them and rubbing it away. We churned butter; we made bread and cakes and pickles. In the afternoons, we did the housework—the laundry or the ironing or the bed-freshening—and lessons. In the evenings, we finished our lessons and read to each other while Miss Julia smoked her pipe.

It was dull. True, it was easier than living with our mother. There were no slaps or loud arguments, the food was good, and Miss Julia didn't get drunk or sell the furniture while we slept.

Lizzie hated it. She didn't like having to sit and sew, or do lessons, or work so much, or ask permission to go out. Before the month was out, Lizzie had made it clear she did not want to get along or fit in: she threw apples down the well, emptied the chamber pot out the front door, and crushed eggs that were to be hatched.

When our father returned, Miss Julia met him before he came to the front door and said, "Miles, Elizabeth a'nt staying here."

He took a step backward. "Julia. Can we at least discuss it?"

"We can, but you won't want to hear it. It's a long litany of bad behavior and disrespect. Come in and eat. And when you leave, take her with you."

He came in and kissed us both. Lizzie clung to him and said, "I want to go. Please, take me with you." He pulled her arms from around his neck.

It was an uncomfortable supper. He said he could take Lizzie upstate to his sisters' in Amenia, but I couldn't go. They would only take Lizzie.

Lizzie burst out, "Anywhere is better than here."

"Elizabeth," said Miss Julia. "That's enough. Leave the table and go to bed."

Lizzie glared at her, stamped away, and flounced up the ladder to the loft.

I helped clear away and tidy up in the tense silence, and asked if I could be excused to go to bed. Miss Julia nodded.

I climbed up into the loft and slipped out of my frock and into the old shirt. I lay down beside Lizzie, who was lying with her back turned to me.

"Lizzie," I said, starting to cry, "can't you say you're sorry? You're going to be taken away, and I can't go with you."

"I don't care."

"I do. I can't go with you. Please say you're sorry so you can stay."

She flopped over onto her back and looked at me in the half darkness. Angry tears glistened in her eyes.

"I don't want to stay here. I hate Miss Julia. I want to go anywhere but here."

"Do you want to go back to Goerck Street? You hated Mother."

"I miss her!" Lizzie started to sob. "I want to be anywhere but here!"

"Lizzie, I can't go anywhere but here. Father will only take you to his sisters, and he won't take me."

"Beg him. He'll give in to you."

"I don't think so."

She turned her back to me again.

"Lizzie, don't you understand? You're his child. I'm not.

"He acts like you are."

"I know. But I'm not. And his sisters won't take me. I know it. They won't take me because of my mother."

"She's my mother, too, and they'll take me."

I sighed. This was going in circles. I didn't understand, but I knew there was nothing I could do.

"I hate Miss Julia," said Lizzie. "She's ugly and she's mean."

"She's not mean. You just want to go home," I said, trying to put an arm around her.

She angrily pushed me away and flopped down with her back to me. She sobbed and hiccupped until she fell asleep.

The next morning, she refused to speak to me, pulling away angrily when I tried to embrace her. As she rode away with our father, she looked back over her shoulder, stuck out her tongue, and crossed her eyes.

I was alone with Miss Julia.

CHAPTER 4

I WAS LEFT IN FLATBUSH WITH A STRANGER, WITHOUT anyone I loved. I had to appear to be someone I was not, without the least idea how to do it. Sometimes I felt I had to be nobody at all. I received a monthly letter from my father and sometimes a little letter from Lizzie. I wondered why my mother didn't come looking for me and decided she just didn't want me. I was angry with Lizzie, who acted like a hellion to get taken away from me. I was also angry because she was good enough to go someplace else, while I was not. Most nights I cried.

I knew what to expect with Miss Julia, but she was odd—though I was just ten years old, I could still see that. She said "a'nt" to mean "ain't" or "aren't," and some of the other expressions she used were very strange. I liked the good food and the clean clothes, the shoes that fit, and the supply of dry wood that meant we didn't have to scrounge for fuel to keep us warm. But I was a city child, accustomed to the roil of life on city streets—with dancing, rat fights, pigs, drunkards, and brawlers for entertainment. Flatbush was just a village in those days. It was dull, and I did not belong there.

The other girls in the village did not play with me. In fact, girls my age played very little, because they were expected to stay home and learn housekeeping from their mothers.

Miss Julia was a widow. We lived on the edge of the village, and we were not Dutch. The neighbors tolerated her because she had married Jakob Van Deventer, who was much respected in the community. After he died, his land passed to his brother. Miss Julia was allowed to stay in a little house, have a garden, and keep hens and a cow—but she was not allowed to cause talk or trouble. Worse for her, she could read and write and figure and think, and she had *opinions*. None of this was considered desirable or useful in a woman. A girl who knew her alphabet knew as much as she needed, as far as our neighbors were concerned. One of their favorite sayings was, "A pinch of patience is worth a bushel of brains"—and that went for everybody.

All the Dutch folk went to the Old Reformed Church for services on Sunday, morning and afternoon. We went, too. In the morning, there were only white people there; in the afternoons, the black folk—who were servants for the white folk—were allowed to attend, but they had to sit in the balcony.

Miss Julia actually waited a month or so, I think, before taking me to church. It was a cold, bright autumn day when we walked to the middle of the village, to a square, gray stone church with a graceful white spire reaching up into the deep blue of the sky. Inside, the pulpit was in the center of the room, which seemed a little odd because it meant the pastor had his back turned to part of his audience whenever he was preaching. But Miss Julia told me it was in the center, along with the Bible, to show that preaching and the Bible were at the center of their faith. The people closest to the center were the wealthy ones, who paid rent for their fine pews. Miss Julia's brother-in-law and his family occupied one of them, and they gave us grave nods when we entered. We sat in the back, on benches. Miss Julia helped me follow the service in a prayer book—although, of course, I had no idea how to sing the Psalms or hymns. Other people did, and they sang loudly and fast.

I had never heard sober people singing. The singing I'd heard had been in a saloon, the songs coarse or sentimental, the notes slurred and sometimes accompanied by sobs. These church people marched the words out clearly, and one man near me sang so forcefully it was like hearing a mule bray. When I heard that, I started, staring at him. Miss Julia touched my shoulder, shook her head, and pointed to the open prayer book. I understood there were only two acceptable things to look at: the prayer book and the pastor.

Pastor Ruysdael had a sweet, cherubic, round face, and he preached in a high, resonant voice about nothing much—or so it seemed to me. Part of that first sermon, though, seemed to be directed right at Miss Julia. Why he might do that, I could not fathom.

"You know," he said, "there are some people—and they seem to be perfectly fine people—who will tell you there is no such thing as damnation. They will tell you God loves all of us and so would not send any of us into a lake of brimstone to burn for eternity. No—God so loved the world that he sent his only son to save us. To save us from perdition. And since the beginning of time, the Lord has known who would accept his love and who would not. But some people don't believe that. They think everybody's good!"

This produced a ripple of knowing laughter from the few people who were listening.

"They say about someone who commits the most horrible crimes that he's just *in pain*." Here Pastor Ruysdael minced out his words in a girlish voice and put his hand over his heart, mimicking these poor fools. He was looking straight at Miss Julia, who sat calmly, looking back at him. "These *Universalists* would have you believe there are no sinners. Just think how dangerous that is! We are practical people." He spread his arms

28

to include all his flock. "And we know that many people are kept from wickedness only by their fear of God. We know good people are God-*fearing* people."

I was puzzled. Why was he looking at us? I started to feel ashamed, just as I did when people talked about my mother.

As we were leaving, one woman stopped Miss Julia to say, "We have missed you in our little congregation. I am so glad to see you back. And whose little girl is this?"

"My name is Vera," I piped up. Miss Julia put her hand on my shoulder, and I understood I was not supposed to speak. "This is my cousin Miles's child," she said. "Her mother has passed on, and Miles brought her to me. Vera, this is Mrs. Van Vliet."

I started to say, "How do you do?" but Mrs. Van Vliet talked right over me.

"What did you think of Pastor's sermon?"

Miss Julia gave a sort of smile, her lips closed in a straight line. "Pastor's sermons are as good as ever," she answered. "Come, Vera, we must be going."

We walked quickly away from the church. A few people nodded a greeting in our direction, and Miss Julia nodded back. But we did not stop to speak to anyone else.

"Miss Julia," I said in a half-whisper when we were well away. "Is Mrs. Van Vliet a friend of yours?"

"Hmp. Hanneke Van Vliet is a ninny."

"Why does she want to talk to you about the sermon?"

"She don't. She just wanted to make sure I heard it."

"Why? I don't understand."

"Because I hold with the Universalists, and everyone in Flatbush knows it."

I must have looked confused. She slowed our pace a little and said, "I get *The Universalist* newspaper. Everybody knows who gets what in the post."

"So he was talking right at you, in front of everyone."

She nodded. "Hmp. This afternoon, he will single out someone else for something else, but you can be sure it won't be any of the folk in the pews—just those of us on the benches. Pastor knows where his bread's buttered, and it a'nt on our slice."

So she had to keep her mouth shut, too, just as I did.

"Oh, it a'nt as bad as I make it sound," Miss Julia continued. "Folks here are kind enough. They don't hold much with thinking, but they don't much care what you think as long as you don't mention it."

∞

EARLY IN THE SPRING, I was out for a walk. The weather had cleared for the first time in weeks, and Miss Julia had sent me on some little errand. I was glad to get out of the house. It was a pinched time of year, with most of the vegetables in the root cellar starting to rot, the cow giving less milk because there was less for her to eat, the cured meat running low. The house smelled musty, and I was restless, so I was glad to be outside with the sun shining, no matter how cold and blustery it was.

Suddenly, Pieter Huygens was blocking my way. Pieter was one of the numerous Huygens children of the multiple Huygens families. He was bigger than I was, but still, in Goerck Street, his attempt at bullying me would have earned him a stiff arm in the belly. Here, I just tried to walk around him.

He smirked and blocked me again. "You live with the Widow Van Deventer."

That was true, of course, but the way he said it sounded like an insult.

I tried politeness. "My name is Vera."

He pushed his face within a few inches of mine. "She's a crank," he sneered, "and you're a bastard. My mother says so."

He pushed me. I pushed him back. He pushed me harder, and I fell down into a cold mud puddle, and he laughed. Fury swept me up. I punched him in the chest and kneed him where it would hurt the most. When he doubled over, I kicked his behind—three times. Then I ran home and hid in the henhouse.

Soon, I heard people approaching the house and Mrs. Huygens calling for "Mrs. Van Deventer." I heard the women's voices and Pieter's angry bawling, and I heard Miss Julia call out the back door.

"Vera. I know you can hear me. Come in now."

I obeyed, with my insides trembling, because I didn't know what she would do. This was surely worse than what Lizzie had done, and I didn't know what would happen to me or where I would go. I wanted to cry. But the minute I saw Pieter's defiant face, I decided I wouldn't. I just wouldn't.

Mrs. Huygens clenched a fist and declared, "That little hellion attacked my boy."

Miss Julia said, quietly, "Vera, what happened?"

"He called me a nasty name, and he called you a nasty name, and he pushed me. He pushed me down, and I ... I fought him."

"Hmp," said Miss Julia, glancing at Mrs. Huygens. "What were the nasty names?"

I stood up straight and looked her in the eye. "He called you a crank, and he called me a bastard," I answered clearly. "He said his mother called us that, too."

Pieter shut his mouth and opened his eyes wide. His mother gaped and her face flushed scarlet.

"Well!" she sputtered, "A decent girl wouldn't speak such words."

Miss Julia looked at her levelly. "Heard 'em from Pieter."

Mrs. Huygens grabbed Pieter by the ear and marched him, bawling, out of the house and down the lane.

"Serves him right," I muttered.

"Could be," said Miss Julia, getting out her pipe and filling it. "It don't put things right, though. They're embarrassed, and when they've thought it over, they'll blame you."

"Why? That's not fair!"

"No." She agreed. "T'ant fair."

"I never did anything to him! Before, I mean," I protested.

"He'll still say those things when you're not around, which will be most of the time. Nobody around here will say any different."

"Why not?"

"Well, there's more of them than there is of us. And I *am* a crank."

I stared at her. She lit her pipe and shrugged. In a moment, she went on. "I don't think the way they think, and they know it. They only let me be because of my late husband, and because they think I don't do 'em no harm. As for what he called you, do you know what that means?"

Of course I knew. She could see in my face that I knew.

"It just means a child's parents wa'nt married. Lots of folk think that means the child's bad, but it a'nt the child's fault. It's true for you, though, a'nt it?"

Well, yes, it was, but I didn't want to say so. She could see I had no answer I wanted to give.

She watched me for a minute, smoking her pipe. "About seven years ago, I heard my cousin Miles had taken up with a woman his family thought was trash. Never heard whether he married her or not. So after seven years, he comes to me with a ten-year-old child." She paused and let that sink in. "Don't know a thing about your mother because Miles wants it that way. He's told me she's dead, but I'm beginning to wonder if I should believe that." She watched my face.

I looked down at the floor.

"Sit down," she said gently. "There's more to this than nasty names."

I sat on the little stool near her chair. "Most of the houses in Flatbush are large, a'nt they?" she asked. I nodded, and she continued. "Who lives in the small ones?"

"Well ..." I began. "There are the Negroes over past the center of town." She nodded, and I went on. "There's Simple John, over by Pastor's. A few others, the Widow Troost. And us."

"That's right. You ever think how Widow Troost manages to live?" I shook my head no.

She took another draw on her pipe. "She gives to some of the men in this area comfort and affection they should be getting from their wives. Do you understand me?"

I did. She was saying Widow Troost was a whore. She talked on. "Now, I don't condemn Katrine Troost for doing what she can. She has to stay alive, and she don't have the wits God gave a daisy, so that's about all she can do."

She took another draw on her pipe and continued. "Some people figure I do the same thing."

That surprised me so much that my jaw actually dropped.

She looked at my startled face and held up a hand. "And some don't know if they believe that or not, but they keep their distance anyway." She rocked and smoked for a few more minutes. She put down her pipe and held out her arms. "Let me hug you, girl." I let her hold me in her arms. I clung to her, my throat hurting and my eyes stinging.

"They don't much care for me," she said. "I *am* a crank, but I'd a sight rather be a crank than a fool. Maybe they won't ever much care for either one of us. It don't matter to me who your mother was or what she did, but it does matter to them. It can be lonely here, and I am mighty glad of you."

I began to cry. She stroked my hair. "Fighting about it a'nt going to improve things." She held me for a few more minutes and said, "Though it may improve Pieter." And I began to laugh. She did, too, and we both laughed until we were gasping for breath.

"Oh," she said through her gasps, "that did a world of good.

Here, take off your skirt and petticoat and we'll rinse 'em out. We'll have some tea and a walk. Wash your face first."

I took off my petticoat and my skirt and changed to my other skirt. As I washed my face, I wondered if I should tell her who my mother was. But I didn't tell her. Not then.

❦

LIZZIE WAS NOT AS LUCKY as I was. In Amenia, they knew whose child she was. Her letter to me was confusing and sad.

> Thay called me munkey girl and thrue mud at me. I ran home and cryed. Ant Betsy said it was my fault they were meen to me becuase I am a child of sin. The skool said it mite be better if I stayed home. I had to memmerize Bible verses about Job.

I didn't quite understand all of this, but I didn't want to ask Miss Julia. It would have meant telling her who my mother was, and she might be as unforgiving as Aunt Betsy.

I think Miss Julia was better liked than she gave herself credit for. Some people actually appreciated her, or at least her useful skills. She was skilled with bees, and we always had honey. She was also a skilled plaiter of rye straw, and she taught me how to make hats. Country people always needed straw hats. Men and women alike wore them, from planting through harvest, for work in the fields. Sunday best hats for spring and summer were also made from straw.

Many made their own hats, but they'd do it from a continuous braid of straw stitched in a spiral. Miss Julia made the braids, and she taught me to make them, too. Rye straw was the best. I loved walking out with her on summer days to see which of the farmers' fields held rye. All they wanted was the grain, and if we asked before threshing and got there right after, we could have the straw just for picking it up. I can still close my eyes and see the shimmer of grain fields in the sunshine—just the memory of the sight lifts my heart.

Miss Julia knew many different kinds of braiding, and her plaits remained firm and handsome for many years. Many of the neighbors bought them from her, and some of the wealthier folk even had her make their hats.

She had a way with bees, too—almost magical. Bees were valuable, but many people simply took the honey and didn't properly tend the insects, so their hives might leave or even die. Miss Julia knew how to make new hives, cutting the comb precisely from a living hive to create a new queen. She showed people how to build bee boxes with movable combs, so the keeper could remove honey without disturbing the bees. These had to be measured and built precisely: bees make honeycomb an inch wide, with exactly three-eighths of an inch between combs. Bees are fussy, Miss Julia told me, and if a farmer was sloppy in measuring, they'd leave. The men of Flatbush didn't listen to women much, but when it came to bees, they listened to her.

Our neighbors believed that when a family member died, the bees had to be told, or they'd leave. When I asked Miss Julia if she believed that, she laughed. "Yes and no. If a hive a'nt tended, the bees leave or they die. That happens when a body is dying, or when the family's grieving."

"So doesn't it trouble you that you have to go to a house where someone's died and do something foolish like talk to the bees?"

"Don't mind. It comforts 'em and gives me a place here. You seem to notice when we get ham or a slab of bacon or a piece of new cloth."

I did notice. The only animals we kept were chickens and the milk cow, and we had very little cash money—so bacon and ham had to be gifts.

There was a lecture, though, that always made me feel like

rolling my eyes. I can repeat it from memory. "You'll need to learn to support yourself just like a man does," Miss Julia would say. "Girls think if they're pretty enough and sweet enough, all they have to do is sit and wait, and some handsome, rich man will come along and fall in love with them and make them happy forever. That's piffle, girl. And a pretty girl who gets a rich man a'nt always happy."

Since then, I've heard other women say such things—but they're sometimes the ones who think women should vote, and other crazy things. It wasn't what I wanted to hear. I wanted to think that I'd be swept away to a beautiful place where no one would dare disapprove of me, where they would all love me because of my great beauty and superior virtue, and no one would ever, ever think of sending me away.

I have to laugh as I write this, because I realize, now that I'm thirty, I sometimes sound a lot like Miss Julia.

CHAPTER 5

I HAD LIVED WITH MISS JULIA FOR MORE THAN A YEAR WHEN I found out why my mother was scandalous. I got used to life in the country, but I missed my mother and father and sister, and I often felt very small and sad and alone. That was the way I felt on a Sunday I'll never forget.

The preacher that morning was not the cherubic little Mr. Ruysdael, but the Reverend Mr. Oosterhuis—a famous preacher noted for his learning. He was a small, thin man, and his booming voice startled me. He read a verse of the Bible and, within a minute or two, was warning us about the tortures of the fires of hell, how sinners would be cast down into a lake of brimstone. This time, though, it wasn't the Universalists who would be burning; it was the Catholics. Still, I thought I knew what to expect, and I settled back for another morning thinking of brimstone, and suffering, and consigning people I didn't like to hell.

The beast of the apocalypse, Reverend Oosterhuis thundered, was threatening us with its evil—it was threatening the very life of the American Republic. I didn't know what he was talking about, but many around me nodded their heads in agreement. "It is that evil beast of the venal city of Rome."

And his voice began to rise. "It is the Roman Catholic Church! And at its head—the ANTI-CHRIST! The Pope!" He made me jump, he was so loud.

"The BEAST is reaching its pernicious claws into our beloved country, sending its evil spawn day after day, in wave after wave upon our shores. The sons and daughters of IRE-LAND"—he paused, then began again with a whisper—"of *Ireland*, are here to put the mark of the beast upon the foreheads of everyone they can reach. And everyone they reach will be cast with them into the lake of fire on that last great day, there to burn in fiery torment forever."

The McGonagles were Irish. I thought of them writhing in a lake of fire. I squirmed a little, myself.

The pastor's voice rose again. "And the spawn of the beast will reach out and overwhelm you and your children. They will chant their evil mumbo-jumbo and spray their scented smoke to cover up the stench of their wickedness. Even now, Romish priests are trying to keep schoolchildren from reading the Bible! And remember. REMEMBER! The awful disclosures of MARIA MONK!"

It was like I'd been slapped. I stopped squirming and sat frozen, terrified of what might happen next.

"Remember that poor young woman, enslaved to the min-ions of Babylon! Made a NUN, forced to renounce a normal life, sent to a nunnery where priests hold absolute sway over young women—young women who must obey them in ALL THINGS!"

He paused, and then whispered, for emphasis, *"In all things."*

Another dramatic pause.

"Could there be a greater outrage upon decency, a more determined assault against the decency of young women? And this young woman was forced to bear a child of shame!"

The child of shame was sitting right in front of him. Did he know, somehow? Was he going to charge toward the benches and point at me?

"This poor young woman, made a mother by a priest, was forced to flee from this convent of evil—a place called the BLACK Nunnery—forced to flee hundreds of miles, alone, unaided, to protect the life of her child. Only God's protection brought that poor young woman out of the darkness, away from the land of her bondage—away from Montreal to New York City. And she is only one of many—one of the lucky few who escaped to tell her story.

"But remember, that was not the worst of it! Remember, at this nunnery, at this Black Nunnery in Montreal, Maria Monk was most soundly beaten for reading the Bible." He thumped the pulpit, no doubt to help us all feel the beating she received.

"BEATEN! For READING THE BIBLE!"

Now I was really lost. Why would anyone be beaten for reading the Bible? And was this why our neighbors on Goerck Street avoided my mother, and talked about her behind her back?

"They forced this pathetic young woman into a life of the vilest sin and depravity. At the Black Nunnery, what they considered to be the blackest of sins was the reading of God's holy word. They forced these young women into vile unions with priests, made them perform unspeakable acts and monstrous couplings, and would not let them read the Bible! That is the true intention of the black-robed servants of Satan—to corrupt us, to violate our children, and to take from us the light of the Holy Bible.

"These are not comfortable things to hear about," he concluded. "But we must know the evil that confronts us."

I sat unmoving, hardly breathing, hearing only the thumping of blood in my ears as my heart pounded. I was barely conscious of what was going on around me. The reverend did not mention my mother's name again.

When we emerged into the Sunday morning sunshine, I was still so frightened that Miss Julia had to call my name several times. We were to stop, as usual, to chat with some of the neighborhood women—several of whose voices were already rising in an animated conversation.

"I certainly remember her," said Mrs. Van Vliet. "We went into New York to hear one of her lectures—and very touching she was, too. I quite wept to hear her story." She dramatically laid a hand over her bosom. "She was a sweet little thing, with an innocent face in her nun's habit, her baby in her arms. And what she had to say was, of course, quite shocking, but not appropriate to repeat now." She arched her eyebrows and smirked at me.

"Vera and I must be going," said Miss Julia quickly, moving me away.

"Why do people know so much about this Maria Monk?" I asked, hoping not to seem too interested. "Was she famous?"

"You heard what Mrs. Van Vliet said," she answered shortly. "Yes, Maria Monk was famous. We still hear about her whenever the preachers think we need a good scare." She did not look pleased.

"The pastor said it makes people uncomfortable to hear about her."

"Some people like it. Hanneke Van Vliet is one of them."

"What do you know about Maria Monk?"

"Hmp. You heard the pastor say she was a nun, and you understand she had a child?"

"Yes."

"And you understand nuns are not supposed to do that."

"I understand now."

"She said a priest was the father of her child. Priests are not supposed to become fathers."

I had so many questions but was becoming afraid to ask them.

After a few minutes, she went on. "She told people that the priests forced the nuns to ... to lie with them, as wives lie with their husbands. And there was more to it—tales that men and women shouldn't hear, let alone girls of eleven. You heard Mrs.

Van Vliet talk about her lectures. I'm sure many people went just to hear every titillating detail.

"Mistress Monk wrote her tales in a book, and they were also published in the newspapers. *The Sun* made a serial of her whole book, and so did *The Protestant Vindicator*, which silly people in this village read. What the pastor failed to mention today is that Maria Monk's tales were most likely lies."

"Why do you say that?"

"Well, for one thing, she had another child a couple years later, and she still wa'nt married. So a newspaperman went to Montreal to find out if what she said was true. What they found was she had never been a nun, as she claimed, but a way-ward girl who was already with child when the nuns took her in. Her own mother said she'd never been right in the head."

"What do you think?"

Miss Julia heaved a loud sigh. "I think she was a poor, sad crea-ture, badly used by people who knew better. The preachers who write the *Vindicator* helped her because they want to stir up folks against Catholics. It worked. That story's more than ten years old, and people still tell it like it's gospel. Every now and then, there's a mob burns a convent, and they're still talking about Maria Monk. Some people don't have the sense God gave a grape."

So my mother had written a book and had become famous and had help from Protestant ministers! That would explain the visits from ministers in our Goerck Street house, and perhaps even the paintings I remembered. *I* was that child of shame. I felt so dazed it's a wonder I didn't stumble and fall flat on my face.

What would happen if people knew who I was? Would they hurt me? "What happened to her?" I asked. "What happened to her baby?"

"Don't know. Dead, maybe. Living in a grand house with ser-vants for all I know. More likely, though, she's poor. Her baby?" She shook her head. "Poor child probably don't stand a chance."

Will people figure out who I am? I felt fear crawl up through my chest. *At least,* I thought, *I don't look like her.* She was small and plump, with dark eyes and dark hair; I have gray eyes and fair hair and have always been thin. I wanted to hide, to be invisible, but I had to know.

"Why wouldn't they let her read the Bible? Don't Catholics believe in it?"

"They wouldn't let her read the Bible we read. The Bible didn't start out as a book written in English, you understand; it started out in Hebrew and Greek. The people who did the translation we read thought very much like the people in the Dutch church, and it shows in the way they translated things. Catholics don't like it, so they don't let people read the King James Bible. The pastor conveniently left out that little detail."

"And why," she continued, "do you want to know all this?"

I shrugged and was silent.

That afternoon, it was my turn to read the Bible as we sat and knitted. We usually read some from the Bible and some from *The Universalist.*

The Universalist had a children's section, which usually featured a story about dear, kindly Uncle Jacob, who was often the victim of some slander from his neighbor Mrs. Bigotry. She complained he had no religion, and kept telling him he would burn in hell.

"Do you think Maria Monk will go to hell?" I asked.

"You know I don't," Miss Julia answered sharply. "I don't think anybody's going." She put down the sock she was knitting and looked at me for a long moment. "Why are you so interested in that Monk woman?"

I sat looking at my hands. *Should I tell her?* I wanted to tell her. My father had made me promise. But he wasn't really my father, was he, and I really wanted to tell someone, and maybe I really wanted to think that what the preacher had said that day wasn't the truth—that there was some other explanation, or maybe two Maria Monks.

"I think I knew her where we lived before."

"Hmp." Miss Julia picked up her knitting again. "What was she like?"

"She was sad. She drank too much, even in the morning. She had two girls, and sometimes she slapped them and screamed at them. The neighbors gossiped about her, but I didn't hear much of what they said."

"Do you think she was evil?" asked Miss Julia. "Or just sad?"

"I don't know. It was awful when she hit us and screamed at—I mean, it was awful when she hit her children and screamed at them."

I sat still for a moment, frozen, looking at my hands, afraid to talk any more, frightened by what I'd said, and hoping Miss Julia hadn't heard. When I looked up, she was watching me closely.

"You mean she hit you and your sister, don't you?" she said.

I wanted to deny it. I wanted to tell her. I wanted all the awfulness to go away, but I knew it wouldn't. Finally, I gave a sob and choked out, "Yes."

She sat looking at me for another long moment. "Your mother was Maria Monk," she said, as if she couldn't get herself to believe it.

I nodded, the tears beginning to stream.

"Oh, my dear God," she said. "No wonder Miles was so closemouthed. He told me not to ask you about your mother because her death had upset you so."

"She isn't dead!" I blurted. "He took us away from her."

Miss Julia closed her eyes and sighed. "Why didn't you tell—" She started, then gave her head a quick shake. "Well, of course I know why. Trying to keep trouble away. Come to me, child."

I got up obediently and went to her, wiping my eyes and nose with my hand.

She got out a handkerchief and had me blow my nose. She pulled me onto her lap, and put her arms around me. "Oh dear, oh Lord," she said. "What a secret for a child to have to keep."

After a few minutes, she said, "Do you have any good memories of your mother?"

"Oh, yes," I answered. "When I was little, before she drank so much, we used to cuddle, and she would tell me stories. She taught me to read, and I loved reading to her. She loved me, I know she loved me, but I couldn't make her happy. That's why she had to drink." I started to cry.

"Hush, child, hush." Miss Julia stroked my hair and my back. "That a'nt so. She was so sad nobody could have helped her."

"She's still alive," I said. "I know she is."

"That's as may be," said Miss Julia. "It's late now and time for bed. You can write to her in the morning."

That made me feel better, at least at first.

I lay awake, looking through the little loft window out into the night sky, thinking how lovely it would be to see my mother again. She loved me. Maybe she had stopped drinking. Maybe she was even now looking for me, and maybe I could have a life like I did here in Flatbush, with clean clothes and good food, but with my mother here to love me. I drifted happily to sleep.

CHAPTER 6

I WAS UP EARLY THE NEXT MORNING, AND MISS JULIA HELPED me write a short letter telling my mother I was well and that I loved her. I wanted to invite her to come live with us, but Miss Julia pulled me up short.

"I'm doing well to keep you here," she said. "I a'nt taking in Maria Monk."

That discouraged me a little, but I still felt hopeful as I wrote my little letter. We talked about whether I should address it to Maria Monk. If I did, I could be sure the postmaster for Goerck Street would know who she was, but the postmaster in Flatbush would also spread around that we were writing to Maria Monk. I addressed the letter to Mistress Maria St. John, Goerck Street, New York City, and took it in to the post office.

My brain buzzed for the next few weeks with hopeful plans for me and my mother. She could live here. Miss Julia would like her and tell people she was another cousin. We would care for the hens together. She would be so pleased to see how well I could knit and sew and read. We would all be so happy.

That ended when the letter came back with "Whereabouts Unknown" scrawled on it. Miss Julia explained to me what that meant: the letter had gone to Goerck Street, but my mother was no longer there, and nobody knew where she had gone.

The little bubble of hope that had buoyed me for weeks now burst. I probably moped around for weeks more before Miss Julia said we would start taking trips into the city next spring, and perhaps we would look for my mother then.

Spring seemed a long way off. I wrote to Lizzie about my attempt to find our mother, and let her know that Miss Julia now knew who our mother was. Lizzie wrote back that she was enjoying "ise skatting" and didn't care if she never saw our mother again.

I was getting better at braiding straw and making hats, so we were selling more of them in the village. I kept up my lessons, learning multiplication tables and reading from Foxe's *Book of Martyrs*. Miss Julia said she privately considered it "rubbish," but all educated people had to know about the sufferings of William Tyndale and Anne Askew. She also had me learn a little bit of Latin—enough to discover that my name meant "real" or "true."

"Why would my mother name me that?" I asked when I found this out.

"Folks said she was a liar. They called her 'the infamous Maria Monk,'" Miss Julia answered. "Maybe she wanted to tell them she wa'nt a liar."

∽

WHEN WE FINALLY MADE THE trip to the city in March, I was so excited I chattered all the way in, although I have no idea now what I talked about. We were going there to hear a great Universalist preacher and to look for possible places for future employment for me. We took hats and honey to sell, but as far as I was concerned, our primary purpose was to look for my mother. I still nursed a little bit of hope. Maybe if I'd addressed the letter to Maria Monk, they'd have found her. Maybe she was still there.

We walked to Goerck Street first—along streets far smellier and more crowded than I remembered—shouldering our way through sailors, hawkers, and whores of all descriptions. Goerck Street was smaller, narrower, and shabbier than I remembered, but the saloon was in the same place. I walked right in, as I had many times before, but I noticed Miss Julia looked uncomfortable when I did.

It's morning, I thought. *Nobody's going to think anything of this.*

I was wrong. The bartender, a youngish man with greasy light-brown hair, looked at me as though I had two heads and said, "And what do you want?"

"I'm looking for someone," I said. "A woman. Mrs. Maria St. John. She used to live in this neighborhood." I spoke with such confidence that I surprised myself, because my knees were beginning to shake a little.

"Don't know her." The young man looked away from me and started to wipe the counter.

"Mr. Luehring does. Is he here?"

"Mr. Luehring died last summer."

There was a young woman cleaning up at the bar, and she looked at me while whispering something to the young man. He stared at me again and asked, "You mean Maria Monk?"

"Yes." If I wanted to find her, I had to admit it.

"She went off. Don't know where. Probably Five Points."

He and the young woman gave me a final look and turned away. Miss Julia and I retreated out into the street.

"Well," she said, as though she were just finding her voice. "Will we be going into every saloon in the city?"

"No," I replied. "I'm sorry. I just thought they'd know where she was. Please let me try some of the neighbors."

I knocked at the Chayevskis' door, next to the saloon, but

the toothless man there told me the Chayevskis had gone, too—and, no, he didn't know where. It was the same story where the Carvalhos used to live, where a tangle-haired young girl with dull eyes answered our questions and closed the door quickly. The building where the McGonagles had lived wasn't even there any more.

"I think we need to be heading uptown," Miss Julia said. "I know you want to find her, but the Lyles are expecting us, and I a'nt walking through Five Points."

I nodded, and we set off toward Greenwich Village, where the streets were a little more open—although not much cleaner.

The Lyles were a family of three—father, mother, and grown daughter Jerusha. They greeted us kindly and gave us a straw pallet in their attic room to share for the night. Miss Julia fell asleep quickly, and I lay next to her, listening to her light snoring, wondering if I would ever see my mother again.

It was a busy time. We sold out of our hats and honey at the market on Saturday, spent Sunday listening to the great preacher and singing with the Universalists, and, Monday, went with a group of Universalist women to visit the prison on Black-well's Island. I was a little afraid to go to a prison, but Jerusha Lyle told me on the way there was really nothing to be afraid of.

"The women we see are in the almshouse. They're not the murderers and such. They may be there for debt or stealing from a customer. Most of them are whores."

"Jerusha," murmured her mother. "Not so coarse."

"Well, they are." The young woman continued. "Nothing illegal about that, until they steal something. They're supposed to learn sewing and such in the almshouse, so they won't have to sell themselves. But whoring pays a deal better than sewing."

We were taking them clothes—particularly clean undergarments—and bread, because they would have had to pay for any clothes and anything better than gruel to eat. The differences between rich and poor mattered, even in prison. Rich people had bedding, food, clothing, even money to bribe the guards. Poor prisoners ate gruel, wore rags, and slept on the floor—or, if they were lucky, a board held up by chains. There were many more poor prisoners than rich ones.

The Blackwell's Island prison building was long, low, and dark. Inside, there were a few dozen women in a long room, most of them sitting on benches, a few of them stitching, some staring blankly into space. Some slept on the floor, and others flirted with the guards.

We put down our gifts near the women sewing. Some thanked us. Most did not. Some of the visitors sat and chatted with the women, but I felt uncomfortable and suddenly wondered if my mother was there. I walked quietly around, looking at all the women's faces. But I did not see her.

We left Blackwell's Island, took our leave of the Universalist women, and started toward the ferry to Brooklyn. We stopped in a little shop run by a Chinaman to spend some of our hat and honey earnings on cheese and currant buns. He also sold books and newspapers. On the rack outside, I saw two copies of the little book, *The Awful Disclosures of Maria Monk*.

I stopped short. My mother's book. My mother's story. Maybe my story.

"Miss Julia," I said urgently. "Look."

She stopped and looked and then turned to me. "I see it."

"Could you buy it for me?"

"We've spent a deal of money already."

"I know. But we still have some, and this is important to me."

She gave me the money. As I handed it to the Chinaman, gave me an odd look—one that made my insides cringe. I wanted to run away, but I didn't. I gave him a tight smile and a little nod, and we left.

"He looked as though we shouldn't be buying that book," I said to Miss Julia.

"Hmp. Perhaps he shouldn't be selling it."

♥

WE WERE SILENT FOR THE ferryboat ride to Brooklyn and the omnibus ride home. I kept my mother's book in my pocket because I didn't want to take it out with so many people about.

The sun was setting, and the heat of the August day was cooling as we walked toward home. *It won't be my home for much longer,* I thought, and that made me sad.

We had a supper of apples and cheese, with the currant buns from the Chinaman's shop, and water from our well, which was sweet and refreshing after several days in the city.

As we dried our dishes, Miss Julia broke our long silence. "When do you want to read that book?"

"Well ..." I began. "I don't know." I was afraid, but twitching with curiosity. I looked at Miss Julia and took a deep breath. "I'd like to start tonight."

She nodded. "Do you want us to read it together?"

"I don't know," I said, in a very small voice. "Yes. Maybe I won't be so afraid."

She lit a lamp and picked up her mending. I sat looking at the little book for a minute, turning it over. It was one hundred fifty-two pages long, with a red paper cover, and on the front it had a drawing of a horrified-looking woman in a nun's habit. It had been printed in London in 1847. That meant it was printed only a year earlier, when I was eleven. If she wrote this book around the time I was born, that meant people were still printing it out more than ten years after my mother first wrote it. I took another deep breath and started reading it aloud.

The beginning of the book told me a few things I didn't know about my mother—harmless things, things any child should know. She was from Canada. "My parents were both from Scotland," she wrote. They would be my grandparents. She wrote that they "had been resident in the Lower Canada

50

some time before their marriage." Were they still there? She was born in 1816, which made her thirty-three. I had never thought about how old she was. She was young to have as much gray hair as she did the last time I saw her. She described a childhood education in a neighborhood school, and wrote that her parents enrolled her in the convent so she could learn French.

"Miles said she was well spoken, like she had an education," said Miss Julia, snipping off a thread. "Now I know why. You are, too. Always wondered about that."

Mother wrote that she learned nothing at the convent except some catechism in French, and remarked frequently that much of the instruction was directed against the reading of "the Protestant Bible." Soon, she began describing horrors she'd heard about.

> I will only say here that when quite a child, I heard from the mouths of priests at confession what I cannot repeat, with treatment corresponding; and several females in Canada have assured me that they have repeatedly, and indeed regularly, been required to answer the same and other like questions, many of which present to the mind deeds which the most iniquitous and corrupt heart could hardly invent.

I had never heard her speak in such a flowery way. I began to wonder if she really wrote this herself.

"Hmp," said Miss Julia. "A high-falutin' way to write, I'd say."

"Yes." I agreed. "That's not the way she speaks."

The rest of the story didn't sound the way she talked, but it was the way she thought, strange and disconnected. I had heard so many wild stories from her, and I'd never been sure if they were true, or products of her imagination, or a combination of both.

Her book said she was forced to take a nun's vows, and the

Mother Superior told her that she must obey the priests in all things. She wrote: "This I soon learnt, to my utter astonishment and horror, was to live in the practice of criminal intercourse with them."

She named names:

> Father Dufresne called me out, saying he wished to speak with me. I feared what was his intention, but I dared not disobey. In a private apartment, he treated me in a brutal manner; and, from two other priests, I afterwards received similar usage that evening. Father Dufresne afterwards appeared again, and I was compelled to remain in company with him until morning.

Had I been conceived on that first awful night? Wait, no. This was when she was a novice. She said she spent seven years in the convent—five as a novice and two as a nun. So she would have been about my age on that night ... if what she said happened at all.

"Horrible," said Miss Julia. She sighed and looked at me for a long moment. "Well, it's late, and I'm tired."

"I'm not sure I can sleep."

Miss Julia looked at me sharply. "It a'nt going to get better. This is a mountain to climb, and I need rest. You do, too. The lamp's going out."

No choice, then. It was too dark to read without the lamp. I lay awake for a while, feeling confused. I slept fitfully, with disturbed, dark dreams.

We let some of the chores go by in the morning, and started reading again. This time she read while I sewed. We read the book over several days, taking turns.

My mother wrote that the other nuns whispered their sympathy to her, but told her some of the nuns had borne children. "Infants were sometimes born in the Convent," she wrote, "but they were always baptized and immediately strangled." She believed she had discovered where the babies were buried, and she had a list of nuns who had borne children: a dozen of them in three months. She also said she knew these children would not have been left alive.

That was horrifying, certainly, but—what about *me*? That was what I really wanted to know.

She did not say how or when she discovered she would have a child. She never really told a specific thing that happened to her She did say she was forced to watch as three nuns and three priests bound and gagged a young nun called Saint Francis, and smothered her under a mattress, laughing and joking the whole time and saying she made a fine Catholic martyr. Of her first confession after taking the veil, she wrote, "I found abundant evidence that the priests did not treat even that ceremony, which is called a solemn sacrament, with respect enough to lay aside the shameless character they so often showed on other occasions."

She never wrote exactly what went on, but wrote: "I cannot persuade myself to speak plainly on such a subject, as I must offend the virtuous ear."

I thought she'd already said plenty to offend a virtuous ear.

Hers was a tortured and tortuous tale. She said that while she was out teaching as a novice, she met a young man who proposed marriage. "Young and foolish as I was," she wrote, "I heard his offers with favor and hastily married him." She regretted it soon after and returned to the convent, never telling the nuns of her marriage.

Was this my father? Well, if this was the truth, probably not. She said she spent two years as a nun after this. How could she do that if she'd had a child?

"I thought nuns weren't supposed to marry," I said.

"They a'nt," answered Miss Julia.

All right, so that didn't make sense either. So far, it was

exactly the kind of tale my mother would tell, except she wouldn't put it in such flowery language.

She also wrote that they hated the English Bible: "Several have remarked to me at different times that if it were not for that book, Catholics would never be led to renounce their own faith." I didn't remember hearing her say anything about that. I was more confused than ever.

She also wrote that this was part of a catechism she had to learn.

Q: Why are men not to read the New Testament?
A: Because the mind of man is too limited and weak
to understand what God has written.

In that case, I thought crossly, *why have a New Testament at all?*
She told how she treasured a single leaf of the Bible that had been smuggled in and how she had committed it to memory. I recognized the passage she named from the Gospel according to Matthew. It was a passage I had often heard her repeat from memory, but since it was the description of the birth of Jesus, it was one many people could recite. I had never thought that was important, but now I didn't know what to think.

Only toward the end of her tale of her time in the convent did she mention she was with child. But she never said who my father was. I went over the pages again and again. She had confessed to a priest that she wished to escape. He told her she was possessed by evil spirits, and gave her a potion to get rid of them.

She wrote, "My desire of escape was partly excited by the fear of bringing an infant to the murderous hands of my companions or of taking a potion whose violent effects I too well knew." She did not say what those violent effects were—whether this potion would kill her or cause her to miscarry. She didn't even say how she escaped.

The last chapter was written in New York City, and she said

she would deliver herself of her tales before she was delivered of her child. And then, finally, something to tell me about who I was. She wrote that her baby daughter was the child of Father Phelan of the parish church of Montreal.

Father Phelan? Who was he? This was the first time she'd mentioned a Father Phelan. What was he like?

She also wrote, "I had now that infant to think for, whose life I had happily saved by my timely escape from the Nunnery; what its fate might be, in case it should ever fall into the power of the priests, I could not tell."

I couldn't tell either. Would they have strangled me? Would they strangle me now if they knew who I was?

She ended by urging her readers to read the scriptures, a powerful truth the priests would deny them. Reading the scriptures would keep people from becoming Catholic or believing what the priests told them. Because the good people of the United States read the Bible, she wrote, "The children from the United States were the most difficult to be converted, and it was thought a great triumph when one of them was brought over to the true faith ... Search the Scriptures."

I was the last one to read, and when I finished, I sat with the book in my lap for a minute. When I looked up, I saw Miss Julia had stopped sewing and was looking at me.

"Quite a tale," she said.

I sighed. "Yes. And there's more."

There were yellowed newspaper clippings tucked into the back of the book. The first—dated January 18th, 1836—was the first installment of *The Awful Disclosures*, on the first page of the *New York Sun*.

A small clipping announced the birth of a child, a daughter, to Maria Monk. My birth. It was silly, perhaps, but my heart leapt at that. Something that told me a little of who I was. The date told me I was born on the day her story went out to the world. There was another clipping from January 20.

The Sun noted another newspaper was cautioning the public against buying *The Awful Disclosures*, calling it "lies from beginning to end." The newspaper appealed for information. "Let it be proved true or false without delay." A clipping from the same day showed they ran a third installment of her story that day. So they printed an installment, announced my birth, and printed two more installments.

There were also clippings from the *Protestant Vindicator*. "It is indubitable that the monastic system is one of the most depraved and anti-republican departments among all the machinations of Popery," began one. "Nunneries have, for a series of years, been mere schools for licentiousness, and, like other dangerous institutions, particularly of a secret nature, they have endeavored to hide their deformities with a cloak of pretended charity. The convent in Montreal could, if walls could speak, unfold a tale of licentiousness and crime which would astonish the most depraved."

"Well, *The Vindicator's* rubbish," said Miss Julia. "The only thing worse is that *Downfall of Babylon*."

"There's a newspaper called the *Downfall of Babylon*?"

"There is. Claims priests in Cuba grind up little Negro boys to make sausage."

I sat looking at the book in my lap.

"So what do you think?" asked Miss Julia.

"I don't know what to think."

"I don't either," she said. "She could have made it all up."

"She could have," I admitted.

"But then again, people who are shamefully used sometimes lose their wits. And whenever people have power over others, some of 'em will abuse it. 'Specially if they can do it behind closed doors, no questions asked."

My throat started to hurt. "This is awful," I burst out. "I don't know if my mother was some ... some what? A poor creature who was shamefully used? Or the worst liar who ever moved a tongue? It's all horrible! I wish I hadn't begged for this book! I wish I didn't know this! I don't know what to do." And I started to sob.

Miss Julia put her arms around me for a few minutes until I stopped sobbing so hard. Then she went and got me a dipper of water.

The cold water helped a little, but it sat high in my stomach, which was too filled with horror and confusion to let anything else in.

"There's more," she said, gently. "I hope it may help you sort things out. I've been sorting out in my mind what I remember.

"Her writings were a big sensation. For years, you could see this book everywhere. Plenty of silly folk bought it. You remember that ninny Mrs. Van Vliet said she went to see her lecture. You remember she spoke in a nun's habit with you in her arms."

I closed my eyes and nodded. This wasn't helping me feel better.

She continued. "There was a newspaper man, Mr. Stone, who went to Montreal to see about whether this was true or not. He searched the Hotel Dieu; he even found Maria's mother. She said Maria was with child when the nuns took her in. There were no babies buried. Her own mother said she'd never been right in the head.

"You said yourself it seemed like someone else wrote her book. Could'a been some preachers helped her put her book out. Then there's that *Vindicator.* Mr. Stone even hinted maybe one of those fine preachers was your father. Now they kept a'goin' with her story, but a couple years later, she was with child again, and she still w'ant married. Folks lost interest pretty fast after that."

So that meant Lizzie and I were both bastards. But whose?

"Now, while she was out saying these things, mobs of people attacked Catholic churches and nunneries. They burned one in Boston, I think it was. There was a big riot in New York. Some drunks attacked the Catholic cathedral, and some Irishmen armed themselves to protect it. They tore the cobblestones out of the streets and threw them. People were killed. I don't remember how many."

"So she really is a monster," I whispered.

"Don't know that," responded Miss Julia. "I think somebody, somewhere, somehow did her great harm. I think she tells strange tales, but I don't think we can say for sure they a'nt true."

CHAPTER 7

J GREW RAPIDLY OVER THE NEXT FEW MONTHS. WE HAD TO start changing the way we made my clothes. Miss Julia told me I should soon expect a flow of blood every month and that I shouldn't be frightened when it happened. Of course I didn't pay attention until it happened—and then I was terrified. I thought I was going to die an agonizing death because I was a child of such horrible sin. I started screaming and crying hysterically, but Miss Julia came to me, reminded me of what she'd said, showed me where the clean rags were, and told me to call her Julia from now on.

That summer, we were making regular trips into the city, partly to sell our hats and honey, partly to go to the Universalist Society, and partly to find a place that might hire or apprentice me when I turned fourteen.

I didn't want to do it. It was dull in Flatbush, but I was afraid to leave. I certainly didn't want to go into the crowded, stinking city, live among strangers, and work all day. I protested. I cried. I argued. It did no good.

She'd say, "Tell me how you'll live when I'm gone? Or when I can't live here? You'll end up being the hired girl on some farm. They'll beat you if they feel like it, and you'll sleep on the kitchen floor. If some farm boy gets a child on you, they'll blame you and send you away. I a'nt having it. Be sensible, girl, and stop talking twaddle."

I had seen the poor hired girls draggling into market and did not wish to be one. What else could I do? I could sell something I made, or I could sell myself. Those were my choices. I had seen some of the women who sold themselves—they were everywhere along the waterfront. Some were pretty, but some were wrecks—gaunt and toothless. I had to do what Julia said.

There were a few surprises for her, too. She had the idea I could be engaged for a formal apprenticeship, which was the way things were done when she was young. But things had changed in twenty years, and real apprenticeships were rapidly disappearing. We went to many places in the city, always wearing our country-women's bonnets as samples of my work. Most places we went, we were wildly, conspicuously out of place. Some shop owners only used pieceworkers. There were bigger places they called "factories": dim, crowded rooms with dozens of girls and women toiling in poor light, and breathing the stench from the privies outside. Usually, they sewed slops— the clothes the sailors wore—or did other poor work.

The thought of living and working there made me cry— and Julia, for once, was sympathetic. "No, of course you a'nt going there. Most of those poor women probably have to ply two trades just to live. There has to be someplace better."

The better places were north of Bleecker Street, in elegant establishments. But they were not interested in employing a country girl or someone who was not yet a proper milliner. One dismissed our bonnets as, "Neat, but hardly elegant." Even Julia became discouraged. As usual, though, she tried to find some hope. "We a'nt desperate, and we a'nt starving yet," she said, sighing. "Two more addresses today. One is on Bleecker Street."

Well, that was a possibility. Bleecker Street, after all,

divided the rich section of the city from the poor. We'd had no luck in either section. We might as well try in the middle.

We came in off the steamy street to the cool dimness of a small shop. Julia rang the little bell on the counter, and a stern-looking woman emerged from the back. She had wiry gray hair that frizzed in the front, and wide, dark-gray, appraising eyes. "Good morning," she said.

"Good morning," Julia said. "Mrs. O'Hanrahan?"

Mrs. O'Hanrahan nodded.

"I'm Mrs. Van Deventer, from Flatbush. I've come to enquire about possible employment for my ward."

"I've nothing," Mrs. O'Hanrahan said. "'Tis only myself and my three daughters in this establishment."

"Well, she don't need it right away. She's only thirteen. Your shop has an excellent reputation."

If Mrs. O'Hanrahan was pleased at this comment, her face did not betray it. Abruptly, she asked, "Who made your bonnets?"

"My ward did. Would you like to take a close look?"

Mrs. O'Hanrahan held out a hand to me. "Let's see yours." I took it off and handed it to her, and she immediately looked inside to see if I'd put in a muslin strip to keep the shape. I had. "Seven-braid plait, nice and firm," she said, appraisingly. "These little ribbon roses suit a young girl." She handed it back to me with no change in her expression and held out a hand to Julia, who obligingly unpinned her own bonnet and handed it over.

Mrs. O'Hanrahan gave a cursory look for the ribbon and went to the flowers. "These look French, but they're not silk. Neat-handed copies."

"My ward made those," said Julia.

"I knew they had to be copies, because you can only get the French silk from a jobber." She then looked at me, her expression betraying nothing of what she thought. "What about you? What have you to say for yourself?"

"Please, ma'am, my name is Vera St. John, and ..."

She snorted. "Oh, such a very aristocratic name to be sure!"

I was disconcerted by this, but Julia had given me a little speech to make. "I am neat-handed and observant," I said. "I already know how to read and write and figure. I could easily learn to do books and wait upon customers."

"Humph."

I waited for a long pause, trying not to fidget. Then she said, "Well, you're certainly well-spoken."

She stood and looked at me for a long moment, and then said, "I won't need her 'til my Mary goes, and I don't know when that will be."

Julia answered, "That suits us. We want a good situation for her, and we can wait."

"I won't pay her wages for the first year. She'd work for room and board, and live with us."

"That's fair."

"She'd have Sundays off, but she'd have to go to mass."

"She can do that, although we are not Catholic."

"She could take instruction, if the priests notice her at all. I'd still be wanting her to go to mass. All my girls go."

"Well then, she would go."

"My oldest is gone seventeen, and I expect she'll be away within the year. Come into the workroom and meet the girls."

The workroom in back was cluttered but clean. The three young women, who had been chattering and giggling, stopped when we came in. Mary looked like a young version of her mother, with the same grave expression and thick, shiny black hair. But when Bridget and Kathleen looked at me, and I at them, there was something like recognition.

They looked like me. We looked as though we could all be sisters. They were slim, with light hair and eyes. Bridget was fifteen, Kathleen a year younger. I looked at Mrs. O'Hanrahan and saw a slight smile. I knew then that she would take me. I looked the part.

Bridget showed me how they were stitching flowers onto straw hats while Mary blocked a felt hat a customer wanted remade. Soon, Kathleen and I were chatting away like old friends, while she showed me the containers for the shop with all the laces, the readymade French flowers, and the silk organza that would go into the copies they made.

"About half our work is remaking, reblocking, retrimming old bonnets for ladies who can't afford new," explained Mrs. O'Hanrahan.

"Or whose husbands are too stingy to pay!" said Kathleen in an undertone.

"That will do, Kathleen. We keep very long hours on Fridays and Saturdays because many ladies want their hats for Sunday. Many shops, you know, lay off their girls the first three days of the week. I do not. We keep busy here, making flowers or plaiting new straw."

Soon, we were taking our leave, and Mrs. O'Hanrahan said she would send for me when the time came. Meanwhile, she said she would like a "character" for me. Julia gave her the name of the Lyles. They lived only a few streets away. Mrs. O'Hanrahan said she knew them, and she nodded, satisfied.

Julia was pleased and relieved when we left the shop. I felt only a little better than I had before. I liked Kathleen and her sisters, but I would have to be on my guard all the time. I didn't look forward to guarding everything I said or did.

⤜⤐

THE NEXT DAY, WE WENT again to the women's prison. We'd been there so much, I was easier with the women and knew some of their stories. I still kept a tiny hope that I would see my mother there. I didn't care how grim it was. I just wanted to find her, to see her, to ask her again where I had come from and who I was.

Sometimes I would write a letter for a poor woman to send to a relative or lover. Sometimes I would read to them while they sat looking into space. On our third visit, I approached a little woman who sat on a bench near the back of the large holding room and sat down next to her. I don't know why I sat next to her, for there was nothing familiar about her back.

Then I looked at her face.

She was my mother.

My wish had been granted all of a sudden, without fanfare or notice. I was too shocked to speak.

She was smaller than I remembered, and thinner. Her hair was gray and wild. Her face was lined, and her eyes were blank. She stared at me, blinking dazedly, for a few minutes.

I looked around. No one was close by. "Mother?" I whispered.

She stared at me, trying to focus on my face.

"Mother?" I said, very softly. "Mother, it's Vera."

"Vera," she murmured, looking blank. Then a dim comprehension began to light her sunken eyes. "Vera! Where's Vera?"

I took her hand. "Mother, it's me. It's Vera."

She stared at me, and then touched my face. She stroked my hair. Then she burst into tears. I put my arms around her. I looked around warily, but that wasn't necessary: such a scene was so common in that place that nobody even looked up.

"Do you know my children?" she sobbed. "Do you know when I will see them again? Why did they leave me?"

"Sh-sh." I clumsily patted her as I kept her in my embrace. I hoped she wouldn't make too much of a scene, but she went on sobbing.

"I've tried so hard to be good. No one to help me. No one would give me so much as a crust of bread. No one."

After a few minutes, she suddenly sat back and looked at me. "Vera?"

"Yes, Mother," I said, very low. "It's Vera."

This brought a fresh bout of sobbing, louder now. "Oh, my dearest child, my dearest Vera. Why did you leave me?"

Now people were beginning to look in our direction. I put my arms around her again and said, "Sh-sh," and she quieted a little.

She told me tearfully she had searched for us everywhere—far beyond Goerck Street—and couldn't find us, or anyone who knew where we had gone. She said she had sold everything she owned, in order to buy food (and, I suspected, drink), and she had lived on the streets until she found a place in Five Points. So she ended up as a whore in Five Points, among the robbers and cutpurses, where bawds plied their trade day and night. I listened to her rambling tale for well over an hour, until it was time to go. When I got up to leave, she asked me to bring her beer.

"Mother," I said, "I won't do that. You know I won't do that." This was exactly the way we often talked on Goerck Street.

As I went to go, a guard stopped me. "She seems to know you."

"Yes." I was not about to say any more.

"She's a sorry one. Been here before. She's in for picking the pockets of her customers." He snorted. "Five Points."

I said little as we went back. Julia remarked that it looked as though the conversation had been difficult.

"It was." I hoped very hard that she wouldn't say any more.

She gave me a penetrating look but nothing more.

∽

WE RETURNED TO GREENWICH VILLAGE to spend another night with the Lyles. Their daughter Jerusha, a sharp-nosed spinster of about thirty, said to Julia, "You know we're quite concerned over your plans for Vera."

"We are not *all* concerned, Jerusha," said her father, mildly. "You are."

"Well, I think we should all be concerned. We understand you plan to place Vera with some Irish."

"Yes, I do. Nearby, on Bleecker Street."

"We know. The O'Hanrahans. They're Catholic, you know."

"Many people are," said Julia, evenly. She let a silence settle, and then added, "And Vera will have to go to mass."

"You will allow this?"

"A little smoke and Latin a'nt going to hurt her."

"What about men in skirts, chanting mumbo-jumbo, and planning God knows what in their little dark confessionals? Aren't you even the least bit concerned they may force her into a convent? Or worse?"

"I don't think that's likely."

There was an uncomfortable silence, and then Mr. Lyle quietly changed the subject by mentioning that Mr. Hosea Ballou would be preaching next month. He hoped we would return and hear him. The rest of the evening passed in uneasy silence, and we retired early.

We had a little, low attic room to sleep in, where we settled into a straw mattress under a couple of quilts. As soon as we blew out the candle, Julia said, quietly, "What were you talking about with that woman on Blackwell's Island?"

I didn't want to lie to Julia, but I didn't want to tell her the truth, either.

"She was telling me she'd lost her children."

There was silence between us—but a tumbling, roaring of scrambling thoughts in my mind.

"Anything else?" Julia asked.

I didn't know how to start.

"Julia. She—I ... That woman is my mother."

"What?"

I didn't answer her. I knew she wasn't asking a question. "She's my mother."

Silence.

"Well. Wish you'd spoken up a mite sooner."

"I know, but—"

"But what?" she said, sharply.

Now she's angry, I thought. I started to cry.

"Hush, hush. I a'nt mad, just surprised. Let me think about what to do. We'll sleep on it."

⁓

WHEN I AWOKE THE NEXT morning, my head ached, and I felt as though a heavy weight was on my chest.

Julia lay watching me. "I think we'll go back to Blackwell's this morning," she said. "We'll get some decent things and take them to your mother. It's only right."

⁓

THE GUARD AT THE PRISON recognized me. "She's still in the same place," he said, watching as Julia and I went over to where she was sitting on the bench.

"Mother," I said, softly. She was again sitting in the corner, her back to the rest of the room. "Mother, it's me. It's Vera."

Again, she took a few minutes to realize who I was. We gave her the food and the clean undergarments. "Mother, there are some things I have to ask you." She looked at me and looked away, starting to eat some of the dried apples we'd brought her. "Mother? The book you wrote. About being a nun and being in the convent."

"Lies," she mumbled. "All lies."

And then silence. Julia nodded at me and moved quietly away, leaving us alone together.

"Mother, are you from Canada?"

She nodded.

"Were your parents from Scotland?"

Again, she nodded.

"Who was my father?" She shook her head. "Was it Father Phelan?" She shook her head again and took another piece of dried apple.

"Who was my father?" I asked again, and again, she shook her head. I saw a tear start down her cheek. I decided I wouldn't get an answer to that just yet, so I asked something else.

"Did you take nun's vows?"

She started to speak rapidly. "I believed what those girls told me. I thought they told me the truth," she said.

I went on with my questions. Had the priests ever done what she said they had?

"The girls said there were babies buried under the convent," she replied.

"What girls? I don't understand any of this. Did those awful things happen to you?" My voice was starting to rise, and I caught a glance from the guard. "Mother," I whispered, "What happened to you? And how did you get here?" She said, "That nice man brought me to New York. The other nice men said they would give me money for my stories."

"What nice men? Those ministers who used to visit the house?"

She nodded.

"Mother, was one of them my father?"

"Who was your father?" she asked.

"I'm asking you. Was it one of those men who said they'd give you money? Who was my father?"

She began to cry. "I thought they were good men. They gave me money and told me to read the scriptures. They wrote down everything I said, and they said I was a good girl. Nobody else ever told me I was a good girl."

I put my arms around her. She sobbed harder. "Mother, it's all right," I told her. "Please don't cry, Mother. It's all right."

She cried for a good while and then looked up at me. "Vera, would you be a good girl and get me a bottle?"

The old sick feeling returned. "No, Mother, I won't. You know I won't."

I got up to leave, and moved across the room to where Julia was. She gave my face a searching look, but said nothing. She let me be silent most of the way as we picked our way through the filthy streets to the dock at Fulton Street. When we were nearly there, she said, "That can't have been easy."

"It wasn't."

"Did she tell you what you needed to know?"

"She told me nothing that made any sense."

Julia did not press me. We were silent for the ferryboat ride to Brooklyn and the omnibus ride home.

When we were walking from the omnibus, I said, "I want to go see her again."

Julia nodded. "You should." She sighed. "But I can't go with you."

I felt the blood drain from my face. "Why not?"

"Well, think, girl! There's the fare on the omnibus and the fare on the ferry and the fare on the boat to Blackwell's Island. That's all cash money. They a'nt goin' to take eggs. We don't have that much cash money. And I have to pay that neighbor boy to milk the cow and check on the chickens when we're gone, and I can't keep paying him. You're thirteen now, old enough to go alone, and that's what you'll have to do."

∽

A WEEK LATER, I STARTED the trip alone, taking some eggs and honey, and some more clean linen.

As Julia walked with me to the omnibus, she said, "Hope she's got a place to go when she gets out. I a'nt thinking about taking her in here. Hmp. One thing at a time. You take care, and I'll see you tonight."

"Julia. Maybe I shouldn't go."

"You can't not go. She's your mother."

That was true enough. It was one reason I was afraid.

∽

IT WAS A LONG TRIP to the city without Julia. The air was deliciously cool. The September sky was a clear deep blue, and the grain fields a shimmering gold—but the beauty of the day only made me feel lonelier.

I felt sad on the ferry across the river, and sadder still on the walk through the docks toward the ferry for Blackwell's. By the time we reached the dock, I felt overwhelmingly desolate and doomed.

The guard who let me in recognized me. He said, bluntly, "She's dead."

What? I couldn't believe I'd heard him right.

"I beg your pardon?"

"That old whore you visited is dead."

I was speechless. I thought wildly that this must be some cruel joke.

"Someone brought her some good food and some soft linen. She traded them for drink. She's dead."

CHAPTER 8

*M*Y MOTHER DRANK HERSELF TO DEATH. THE GUARD HAD found her dead one morning in her cell.

I stammered out questions.

"Did they tell her family?"

"Don't think she had any. Only people who ever visited were you church women."

"Has she been buried?"

"Yes, in a pit in the potter's field." So even now, the quick-lime was eating her flesh.

"Did she leave any possessions, any keepsakes?"

"No."

Her clothes had been given away. Nothing was left. It was like she had never existed. There was nothing I could do to recover her body, lay her at rest, or honor her memory. Her short, sad life was over, and there was nothing I could do.

I kept the honey and eggs and clean linen. We needed them, and there was no reason to bribe the guard with them now. I left, feeling so dazed I wasn't sure I could walk.

My thoughts whirled. She wouldn't be dead if I hadn't tried to help her. If I hadn't left her, she might not have had such a hard life. Maybe she wouldn't have turned to whoring and living

71

in Five Points. Tears slipped out, and I couldn't stop them. I stared damp-eyed at the river, at the town on the Brooklyn side, at the darkening fields as they went by. There were few people on the omnibus, and nobody noticed.

She's gone, I thought. *She's gone. I'll never see her again. She's gone, and nobody cares.*

Julia was waiting for me when the omnibus got to Flatbush, standing and smoking her pipe. When she saw my face, her mouth dropped open, and she snatched the pipe away. We walked quickly out of earshot of the others getting off the bus, and she said quietly, "What happened?"

I stopped and covered my face with my hands and then began to sob. "Julia, she's dead. She's gone."

"Let's get you home."

WE WALKED AS RAPIDLY AS we could through the deepening twilight, with me sobbing and gulping for air. When we got back, Julia made tea for us both, and I lit the lamp. I told her what the guard had told me.

She closed her eyes and shook her head.

"Julia, it's my fault! If I hadn't left her, if I hadn't given her something to trade, if I had looked for her earlier, if I had told you—if I'd just done anything right, she wouldn't be dead!"

I started to cry again.

Julia put her arms around me. "Ta'nt so. She was set on her drink, and that's what killed her." She smoothed my hair back from my face and gave me a fresh handkerchief.

I don't think I really believed what Julia was saying. But hearing it made me feel a little better.

"I know you don't believe that now. But there wa'nt a thing you could do."

I wiped my tears and blew my nose.

Julia, of course, went immediately to what had to be done. "You'll want to write your father and your sister. Tonight or tomorrow?"

"Tomorrow."

∽

I WROTE TO MY FATHER first. I couldn't waste paper, and I couldn't be too direct about what had happened because I didn't know who else might see a letter. I just said it might interest him to know that Maria Monk had died in prison.

Writing to Lizzie was even harder because I knew her aunts read her letters. Even though they knew who our mother was, they didn't need to know she died in prison. Whenever I thought about what Lizzie's feelings would be, I thought about mine and started to cry again. I wrote that I had visited the prison with the ladies of the church, and I had met someone we would both remember from Goerck Street. I wrote that this person had been in a pathetic condition, desiring drink so much that it meant the end of her. I wrote that I had learned important things in her past that would excuse her conduct. "Dearest sister," I wrote, "please look upon this woman kindly."

I needn't have been so tight-lipped. My mother's death was in the newspapers. One said, "The infamous Maria Monk died Friday last, in the women's almshouse on Blackwell's Island. Police had arrested her for picking the pocket of a paramour near a den she inhabited on the Five Points."

A few days later, I received a short note from my father, thanking me for the information I had given. A few days after that, there was a letter from Lizzie, saying she was not sorry "this person" had died. "She was allways drunck and meen. She was unnatcheral." That hurt, too, although I understood. When

73

Lizzie knew her, she *was* drunk and mean. But I loved her and didn't want her to die. She was my mother, and I had deserted her. I felt I had killed her.

About a month after my mother's death, Julia and I received a letter from my father's brother, explaining that Miles St. John had died in "very unfortunate circumstances." Julia read over the letter carefully and gently explained it looked as though he had killed himself. There was a mention of a "deathbed note" asking his brother to "take care of Vera." The brother noted with some disapproval that "the decedent" had not mentioned his other daughter Elizabeth, but, as his heir, he felt bound to send something to each daughter. He enclosed what he called a "small sum." It was a large sum to us. He wrote that we could not expect to inherit any more, and that we should not attempt to get in touch with any of the St. John family.

That letter made me feel very sad and forlorn. While I was no more alone than I had been for years, my cherished little hopes— that somehow my parents would arrive in some unspecified magnificent fashion, sweeping me away to a glorified existence in which we would be together and be happy—were smashed.

For a while, I held out hope that they were not really dead, that there had been some dreadful mistake. As the truth sank in, I felt emptied, limp.

It helped when Julia suggested we invite Lizzie for a visit. I hadn't seen her in three years. Julia and I wrote to Lizzie's Aunt Betsy, who wrote back that a visit to Flatbush would be delayed because she would be going to Miles's funeral, without Lizzie. It was several weeks after that when Betsy and Lizzie alighted from the omnibus in Flatbush.

Lizzie was taller, nearly eleven—but she was still the wild Lizzie I knew. Her bonnet was askew, and the laces flapped from both boots as she ran to hug me. "How's Julia?" she asked mischievously. "Still cross-eyed?"

I couldn't help giggling. I was so relieved to see her. Then my eyes welled up. "Oh, Lizzie, I have missed you. Come for a walk and we'll talk."

We went for a long walk about the village while she told me of her life in Amenia.

"Aunt Betsy tells me often she knows my mother was a wicked woman, and she will not have me turn out as she did." Lizzie spent as much time as she could outdoors, in the woods and by the ponds. Did she read much? "As little as possible." She giggled. She'd had to read the Bible, of course, but was much more interested in anything Aunt Betsy disapproved of, which was why she'd read an entire book of Greek myths. She even managed to find some grotesque stories by a man named Poe.

That night, as we shared a bed for the first time in three years, we talked in the dark about our mother and father. She adored our father; she said she still could not forgive our mother. I told her about our mother's book. She surprised me by saying, "Oh, I know all about her book. I've never read it, of course, but they talk about it and about our mother in Amenia all the time. I've tried to find a copy of it, but I can't. Aunt Betsy would have a fit. I can see her now, threatening syncope."

"Syncope?"

"Fainting. She says it all the time, but she never does it. If she caught me reading that book, though, she probably would. But people in Amenia are forever telling their girls these stories to keep them home and make sure they don't run off with some Irish b'hoy."

She snuggled down closer to me and went on.

"But our mother was such a liar. Do you believe all those things happened to her?"

"Lizzie, I don't know what to believe."

"Oh, Vera, she made them up. She was forever telling lies. Do you think she even wrote her own stories? I don't remember her writing anything. She didn't even read much besides newspapers, and half the time, she had you read them to her."

"Maybe someone else wrote down her words. Sometimes they seem like hers. Sometimes they're just flowery and fancy. And even if they're only partly true, what she went through was terrible."

"I don't think she went through anything. I think she probably had herself some adventures, and that's why she turned out a whore."

"Lizzie! She was your mother, and she's gone."

"You know it's probably true."

"And what does that make me?" My throat hurt as I tried to hold back tears. I didn't tell her she probably was, too. "At least you know who your father was." I didn't add *maybe*.

"Oh, Vera, I'm sorry. You know he loved you. He cared more about you than he did about me." She put her arms around me. "But I still love you."

I hugged her close and said, "I love you, too, Lizzie." We drifted toward sleep with our arms around each other.

∽

THAT SPRING AND SUMMER WERE beautiful—filled with sunshine and flowers and an abundant harvest. But the beauty just made me feel sadder. The rye fields still shimmered in the sunlight, and the twilights were still balmy and filled with singing songs or telling stories. But I moved through those days as a sleepwalker, the dread in my stomach weighing me down. I knew these were probably my last days with Julia. Soon, I would have to be on my guard always, pleasing people I didn't even know.

I brought up my worries with Julia only once. She replied testily that she had done the best she could to help me, and she really didn't know what else there was. And, no, I couldn't stay with her, and without I had a better idea, I should keep quiet about it.

So I kept quiet. But I was still afraid, and I thought about it often. What could I do, really, except make pretty flowers and firm plaits for summer hats? *I am building a life on straw*, I thought bitterly. *It's a choice I don't like, but every other choice is worse.*

CHAPTER 9

*J*ULIA WARNED ME REPEATEDLY TO KEEP QUIET ABOUT MY mother—as if I needed warnings. She harped on the subject at some unusual times. One afternoon, we had churned butter and were shaping and salting it, and I was looking forward to a cool drink of buttermilk—and she abruptly brought it up again.

"Miles was right, you know. You can't tell anyone. Not a peep to those O'Hanrahans. That missus will have you out on your elbows."

"Well, I can see how I can't tell Catholics, but what about people who aren't Catholic? And it didn't make any difference to you once you knew."

"I'm different."

Everyone knows that, I thought sourly.

"I knew you," she went on. "And I think things through. Most folks don't."

"What would they have to think about? My mother was a victim. You said so. She was either a victim of priests or a victim of some people who used her and her lies."

"Well, that's it, isn't it?"

We took our little drinks of buttermilk out onto the porch

78

and sat down. I took a big mouthful of the cool, sour-ish liquid, leaned back, and swallowed it a little at a time. I let out a sigh.

After a minute, I asked, "What do you mean that's it? I don't understand at all."

"Folks are superstitious," she replied. "Or at least what I call superstitious. Make up their minds about things before they think about 'em. When folks get robbed or hurt—and 'specially if a woman's violated—most folks start thinking those who got hurt must'a done something to deserve it. Must've been careless or loose with their morals. It's folks' way of saying to themselves those awful things couldn't happen to them, because they would never be careless or loose. Makes 'em feel safe. You tell folks about your mother, they'll figure you're just like her—or at least you'll make them think about her, and they won't like that. They won't want to have anything to do with you."

I looked down and sighed.

"It a'nt that hard," she said. "You took your time telling me."

"You didn't ask me. Other people are going to ask me."

"Just say both your parents are dead. It's true."

I knew she was right, but the thought that I would have to keep a mask up all the time weighed on me whenever I thought about it—which was often.

I got better at making hats—reworking hats for the women of the farm and the village, and studying *Godey's Lady's Book* whenever someone gave us a copy, to see what I could understand and copy in the latest fashions. I became good at making little flowers and rosebuds from calico, and even other decorations from homespun—which, to my mind, always looked coarse and clumsy, although some women liked them. Every now and then, I would do some piecework for Mrs. O'Hanrahan. And when I was fourteen, she sent for me.

Julia and I spent time in the evenings talking wistfully about how we would miss each other. But we both knew I had to go. We put my clothes and other belongings into a large carpetbag, and my hat-making materials into a box. She rode with me to the city, and we walked quietly together to the shop on Bleecker Street. Julia assured Mrs. O'Hanrahan that I would be a good girl and a hard worker. We kissed and hugged one another. She blinked back tears as she said she'd miss me at Christmas, but we'd see each other in February. Then she was gone.

I put my bag and box in an upstairs room, took off my hat, and got to work. There was no awkwardness with Bridget and Kathleen. They had me start right away using some of my straw plait to make a bonnet for a young woman, who wanted it to carry soft piles of flowers.

There was so much to learn.

About half the customers—and only about a quarter of our money—came from what Mrs. O'Hanrahan called "the Irish trade." These were poor, respectable women who usually needed their one old bonnet remade so they could wear it to church. We had a few treasured customers from above Bleecker—ladies who arrived in carriages with maids in tow. They required the utmost attention and provided us with strangely little income. We kept hoping they would tell their friends where they had found a clever milliner. Maybe they did, sometimes. Kathleen said it was more likely that they told their elegant friends they got their bonnets in Paris, and nobody was going to be looking for the likes of us.

The third sort of customer came to us from the neighborhood around us, Greenwich Village. They were wives and daughters of tradesmen or clerks. Some of these women drove us to distraction, haggling over the cost of every lace and every stitch.

It was the women from Houston Street who were the most fun, and the most interesting to me; they were also the ones who spent by far the most money. Houston Street was lined with parlor houses, the high-class brothels frequented by gentlemen of means. The women were pretty, and many of them had musical talent and would play piano or sing. Parlor houses were elegant places to eat, too, with fine wines and oysters any time of day or night. The "entertainers" wanted to look their best, and they were willing to spend to do it, even on hats.

The tradesmen's wives and the poor Irish women came in early in the day, the grand ladies later in the morning.

"They sleep late," Kathleen said of the great ladies, "and then they take half the morning getting dressed. But they must be away, don't you know, to make their calls or have their 'at-homes' in the afternoon."

I learned the first week that having a rich and pretentious appearance didn't keep a great lady from crying poor. A lady dressed in silk came to the shop in a fine carriage, and, while her maid waited at the door, she looked at all our bonnets and said to Kathleen, "I like your styles, but I cannot afford your prices."

Kathleen moved closer to her, took the lady's elegantly-gloved hand, and said very softly, "I am so sorry. You must be trying very hard to keep up appearances. We never turn away the needy. If you haven't the means to make yourself tidy for church, we can surely make up a little chip bonnet and only charge you for materials."

That changed the conversation. Madame drew herself up, with blood in her cheeks and fire in her eyes, and proceeded to demonstrate she was not needy by purchasing three of the most expensive bonnets in the place.

As she swept out, with her maid dancing after her, carrying three hatboxes, Kathleen sang out, "Good day!" and we all burst into giggles. Kathleen, Bridget, and I must have spent half an hour prancing about imitating her, until Mrs. O'Hanrahan made us go back to work.

The parlor girls would come late in the afternoon, and went back to work by nightfall. They fascinated me—some just because they were so beautiful. There were two farm girls—sisters with curly golden hair, wide blue eyes, and skin like marble. Some girls were mulattos or creoles, with coffee-and-milk skin and exotic accents, from New Orleans or the Caribbean. Some were from France, some from Germany, some from Ireland. I don't remember anyone who grew up in the city, but when they talked about being in "the life," they all agreed that it was better than anything else they might be doing. They figured their only other choices were to be hired girls on a farm or maids in a city, and they'd have to gratify a master and not get paid for it. Why not get paid, do well, and sleep late?

Sometimes, though, their voices lowered and they talked of Helen Jewett. Everyone knew the story of the beautiful whore who had been axed to death. Her paramour killed her in her grand mahogany bed and set it on fire. The parlor house burned, and her corpse baked in her silken sheets. A young man from a good family was accused of killing her, and there was plenty of evidence to show he had. The judge told the jury to ignore the testimony of the women in the house because it came from a polluted source. The young man went free. Helen's story was used to warn young girls away from whoring, as well as against other activities they thought would lead to whoring. Reading novels, for example, was a sure road to ruin.

Nonetheless, these young women laughed and seemed happy. They wore silk dresses and Italian boots and bought the best bonnets we could make. They were not welcome at elegant milliners above Bleecker Street, but they came to us in groups, chattering and laughing like little flocks of bright birds.

Customers didn't notice me much because I looked like the other two girls in the shop. To ourselves, of course, we all looked very different. Bridget was the fairest, with a sweet, heart-shaped face, gentle blue eyes, and wavy blonde hair. She bargained gently but very deftly with the tradesmen's wives, and was kind and efficient with the "Irish trade." Kathleen's hair had a slight reddish tint to it, and she had springing curls and gray eyes. In fact, her eyes were much like her mother's, except her mother's were a somber hue and Kathleen's the shifting gray-green of a sunlit sea.

Kathleen and I shared one pallet in the upstairs room. Bridget and her mother shared the other. Kathleen and I shared some whispers and giggles—as sisters would, I suppose—but there was always my secret, which was a wall between us.

And Mrs. O'Hanrahan certainly never treated me like a daughter. I don't mean she was cruel or that she beat me, although there was the occasional slap. But Kathleen was allowed to be pert with the customers. I was not. Mrs. O'Hanrahan's typical manner was dour with me, although she was less so with customers. She had done an apprenticeship the old way, with an indenture and having to present samples of her work to move up in her standing. She was proud of what she knew, and she valued talent, which was why she had agreed to take me on. I had been working with her for several weeks before I saw her smile even once. When she did, it was amazing. Her smile lit up her whole face like a sunrise.

I learned from her how to please a customer, and about making any lady look her best. She was gifted at putting a customer in front of a mirror and positioning a rosebud or changing the color of a ribbon to create the most becoming headgear. I watched her and her girls closely, and learned how to flatter a thin face or a long nose, and how colors could make a face come alive.

Kathleen had her mother's smile, and she used it more often. She had a positive genius for copying fashion. I learned from her how to tell French silk flowers from domestic ones at a glance, how to judge the quality of lace and ribbon, and what was different about a new shape that made a hat fashionable.

I still loved being out in the city streets. Kathleen did, too, and we went out walking as much as we could. Broadway could be a parade of finery, and that first autumn, I laughed at Kathleen's snide critiques, and I learned what to look for. Ladies rode by in carriages and smart buggies. Others seemed to be in a procession, attended by their husbands or their beaus or their maids, smiling and bowing to those they knew. They wore silks, prints, embroidery, lace, dainty gloves, and such confections on their heads as I had rarely seen. It amazed me to think such bonnets were made of straw and buckram, wire and silk, lace and cotton. Many wore such huge skirts that they could not walk two abreast and stay out of the street.

Two very handsome women rode by in a trim buggy. Their dresses were of silk—one dark gray, one light gray, and so beautifully cut and gracefully draped they could have been made of water. The older woman's bonnet curved up one side of her head, snowy egret feathers and black-and-white ostrich plumes flowing from it to make a dramatic frame for her face. The younger woman's bonnet had delicate flowers inside the brim in the latest Parisian fashion, framing her lovely face and setting off her porcelain skin.

"Don't gawp." Kathleen hit my ribs with her elbow. "They'll think the drovers brought you in with the cows."

"Mooooo," I said, and we both giggled.

"Now," she went on. "Do try not to stare when you look at that lady in black walking toward us. She's wearing a copy of that plumed hat."

"How can you tell it's a copy?"

"Look at it. It's got goose feathers on it, silly goose," she punctuated "goose" with an elbow to my ribs. "And it's got a few swan feathers, and that's supposed to make them look like egret. But now, can you see how the whites don't match? And that poor ostrich either died of old age, or of humiliation at having scraggly feathers."

I smothered a giggle—but obviously didn't smother it well enough, because the lady in question gave us a cold stare.

Kathleen dipped a quick curtsy and said, "Oh, madam, we didn't mean to be impertinent. We were admiring your bonnet. Is it French?"

"Oh," said the lady and paused, still staring coldly at me. "Yes, it is. Monsieur Henri is a *modiste* for the Duchess of Burgundy."

"Thank you, ma'am," we chorused and walked on, with Kathleen muttering to me, "I think the duchess had too much Burgundy. If that hat's from Paris, I lay golden eggs." We lowered our heads and snickered.

"We can't copy the feathered hats very well," she said. "You need the right feathers, and we can't make feathers. But we can make flowers, and we can copy shapes. See that little chip hat with the flowers? We can do that. And see, there's another one of those high, curved brims with the flowers next to the face. See? They're silk ribbon roses."

"It would take forever to make so many," I said.

"Oh, it does! But there are four of us now, and you make them beautifully. And we know people who pay handsomely for such things, don't we?"

∞

BACK AT THE WORKROOM, KATHLEEN spent most of a week experimenting with buckram to get the exact curve of the bonnet brim. I sat and made silk ribbon roses until my eyes smarted and my fingers ached. We could have bought them readymade, but there would have been no profit. As it was, within a few weeks, we had the first such bonnet on a stand in our window, and for the next few months, we sold them as fast as we could make them.

Kathleen was so good at this part of our work, and so persuasive, that she soon talked her mother into letting us walk out of a weekday afternoon to visit Mr. Stewart's store on Broadway. "It isn't open on Sunday, Ma. And there's so much we need to see!"

"Well …" Mrs. O'Hanrahan hesitated. "Go on, then. Mind you stick to the Broadway."

"We will, Ma," answered Kathleen, pinning on her bonnet. "Vera, don't stand there like a hitching post! Come on!"

Mr. Stewart's store was unlike anything else in the city in those days, although I understand he has since built a larger one farther up the Broadway. He had failed repeatedly at business, or at least had frequently liquidated his stock by announcing he was "Going out of Business." Kathleen and I visited his amazing place at the corner of Broadway and Chambers Street. Part of the attraction for us was that the prices of the goods were marked right on them. That was something no one else did. For us, it was a wonderful opportunity to find out prices without having to ask—for we surely would have been escorted out of such a store had they known we were just hat-shop girls. Such girls often steal.

The walk down Broadway was crowded with ordinary mortals like ourselves, until we got close to the store. Suddenly, we were watching a fascinating parade of fashionable women. We stood for a few minutes, and Kathleen said, "Look sharp. We'll go in behind this group of ladies."

"Go in?" I whispered. "We can't! They'll turn us out before we put a second foot in."

"No, they won't." Kathleen was annoyed at my country cluelessness. "We can pass for respectable maids. We've perfectly good bonnets—"

"And no more than one petticoat." I argued. Fashionable women in those days often wore a dozen.

"We're *maids*," she hissed. "Now look. We missed two of them." She shot me an annoyed look. "Watch for the next one," she whispered, low but sharp. "We need to be nimble. I'll follow one lady about, and you follow another. We look at what they look at. Just remember, when they buy, you must move away, or the clerk will hand you the parcel."

Kathleen moved calmly into Mr. Stewart's grand store behind an elegant woman in dark-blue silk. I was terrified—I was afraid to do what she had just done, but I was also afraid to be left standing on the street when I already felt like a thief. When a stout woman in an ugly maroon dress and a truly hideous hat lumbered by, I followed her in. She strolled about, with me following at a discreet distance. Although the prices were clearly marked, she asked how much for several bright ribbons, and fingered the fine muslins.

I was so awestruck with the vast array of fine stuff that I did exactly what Kathleen had told me not to. I stood gawping next to the stout lady when she made her purchase, and the clerk handed it in my direction. The lady looked at me, startled, and the best I could do was stammer, "Oh, what a goose I am! My mistress will be livid!" I hurried off, but didn't know where to go. Looking dazed actually suited my purpose fairly well, for when I saw another lady moving toward the door I hurried after her.

Kathleen saw what had happened and met me outside, where we erupted with nervous giggles. As we moved away, she let me have a peek at the laces she had pocketed.

"Well," she said, "I've seen all I need to see here. Let's take a little side trip." She started walking east.

"But that's toward Five Points," I said.

"Oh, little Miss Country Innocent," said Kathleen. "And how do you know about Five Points?"

"Everybody knows about Five Points," I retorted. And it was true. But I was excited to be out seeing the life on the streets, and so I happily walked with her. If she wasn't going to worry about what she'd told her mother, I wouldn't either.

There has been much written and said about the shocking depravity of Five Points. Some of it is true. Anyone with any sense stayed out of Cow Alley, where men and women lay on the ground at any time of day. Sometimes they were drunk, but sometimes they were dead, and it wasn't the sort of place one lingered to ask questions. Still, Five Points, for all its reputation, wasn't really dangerous at midday for two young women, if those young women stayed alert. We both knew how to respond to being accosted on the street: don't act insulted or afraid, simply nod or say good morning, keep moving, and keep a firm hand on your purse.

I think what many people found shocking about Five Points was that races mixed. Black and white mingled freely with anyone just off the merchant ships in the harbor, and with immigrants from everywhere on earth. Musicians played, dancers danced, newsboys hawked the latest news. The eating houses doubled as whorehouses, and the dancing of couples was just a prelude to coupling of another kind. We might sometimes see a rat fight, or hear fiddlers play, or see children dance for pennies.

We weren't stupid. If we heard people shouting, we quickly moved the other way. Gang fights were frequent, and when the brickbats flew, they did not choose their targets. Some of the stories about the gangs have been greatly embroidered, too. We did see men who were clearly Plug Uglies, the gang of hulking Irishmen who made themselves look bigger by stuffing their plug hats with straw. I have often heard it said there were men and women who filed their teeth into sharp points, but I never saw any. The streets were dirty, sometimes ankle deep in dark dust when it was dry and a repulsive sludge when it was wet— but that was true everywhere in the city.

A left turn took us up the Bowery, where we saw a fashion parade very different from the one we saw on Broadway. There were no dove-colored silk day dresses here. The b'hoys and their g'hals of the Bowery wore every color cheap fabric came in. The young women would often wear yellow and blue and red all together, and we saw some wildly original hats. The young men all seemed to wear the red flannel of the volunteer fire companies, whether they were actual fire laddies or not. Some wore gang emblems, and they all greased their long sidelocks with soap or bear grease. It seemed everything surged out onto the street—the garish colors from the cheap goods in the shop, the noise and smoke from the oyster houses, the laughter and pulsing music from the dance halls.

As we walked past the Bowery theaters, which no respectable woman entered, Kathleen nudged me and pointed. One of our bonnets was moving toward one of the "Ethiopian opera" houses, where the minstrel shows played. We assumed the girl wearing it would soon be meeting a man in the balcony, a frequent venue for amorous assignations.

We smiled at each other, and pushed on through the crowd. Some of the men looked us up and down, and there were catcalls and suggestive remarks from some of the b'hoys lounging outside the theater. We nodded to them slightly, as though they'd said good afternoon, and moved on up the Bowery.

CHAPTER 10

*T*HE NEXT AFTERNOON, A GAGGLE OF THE PARLOR GIRLS crowded into the shop, chattering and giggling. They were talking about the latest scandalous presentation at some Bowery theater. "And then," one of them was saying, "the man who came out as the Indian was quite naked above the waist!"

"Where were you naked, dearie?" said another. Laughter. "Didn't you ever see your farm boys like that?"

"Well, they weren't brown the way he was. I really fancied the way that man looked. Besides, farm boys are dull."

Some of these girls had come to the city for an exciting life, and realized the way they could make the most money was by whoring. Some had fathers or husbands or masters who beat or abused them, and all thought this was the best way they had to prosperity. A girl sewing in a factory was lucky to make three dollars a week; a street whore often made ten times that much. These high-priced young women counted their monthly incomes in the hundreds of dollars, and they spent as much as they wanted in our shop.

They squealed about our display bonnet with the dozens of ribbon roses. "Oh, isn't that some pumpkins!" Four of them left orders to have it copied. The six girls bought a total of eleven bonnets and paid us in cash.

As Kathleen and I were writing up the sales and taking the orders, Mr. Grogan came in to settle his wife's bill. Mr. Grogan was a clerk in a counting house, and took his respectability seriously—although not seriously enough to leave when he realized he had walked in among some ladies of the evening. He stood and stared.

As the girls left, they asked him if he'd like to have a little fun. He didn't answer.

"Ooh, I don't think he knows how!"

"Or what with!"

The Creole girl pinched his cheek and said, "Never mind, *cher*. You come to Houston Street for some brown sugar."

They all laughed and romped out, leaving him standing stiffly with his cheeks flaming.

"Mrs. O'Hanrahan." He stopped and cleared his throat. "I had no idea Mrs. Grogan patronized such an establishment."

"Surely you were aware Mrs. Grogan purchases hats."

"But not in a shop that serves such—such depraved creatures as those who just left."

"I'm sorry they upset you, Mr. Grogan. I'm sure they meant no harm. That will be three dollars and seventy-eight cents, please."

"Are you sure? That seems a devil of a deal of money for gewgaws."

"Mrs. Grogan has excellent taste, but she is hardly extravagant."

He fished out his purse reluctantly and paid exact change. "Why do you serve such people?"

"I sell them hats, Mr. Grogan. I do not judge them or any customers."

"Really, Mrs. O'Hanrahan?" He went on. "This is what comes of allowing women to conduct business. Next you'll be owning property, and then you'll want to vote. I can see now that this country will hardly be worth living in."

"We have the greatest respect for you and Mrs. Grogan," she answered, and then said no more, but stood looking at him calmly while he huffed indignantly. Finally, he stamped out.

We stood there for a few moments. Bridget came warily out of the workroom to touch her mother's shoulder. "Ma? Do you think we've lost Mrs. Grogan?"

"I doubt it. She's a clever woman, even if she is married to a self-righteous little twit. Wouldn't be surprised if she talks him into giving her an allowance to settle her own account so he can avoid having his cheek pinched."

"But what if she doesn't?" asked Bridget.

"Well, that's no calamity," answered Kathleen. "Just think about who spent what. He just settled his wife's bill for a season, and it came to the grand sum of three dollars and seventy-eight cents—and at that, he considers himself hard done by. Those girls spent forty-two dollars *this afternoon*, which they paid in silver. Plus, they left orders for another thirty-eight dollars.

"He'll recover," she finished. "Let's close up and have something to eat. I'm famished."

Meals at the shop were not the pleasure they were in the country. There was no cook stove, and certainly not the big cooking fireplace Julia had—only the little potbellied stove that heated the shop and the back room. We had boxty almost every day—just the potatoes, flour, salt, and soda. Boxty can be tasty with milk, butter, or eggs, but we rarely had them. A bit of pepper would have done it a nation of good.

We all knew the Irish rhyme: "Three pans of boxty, baking all the day. What good is boxty without a cup of tay?" Well, we couldn't have "tay" with our boxty since there wasn't room for both the pan and the tea kettle. So we'd have tea before or after. We'd have bread, maybe some cheese or pickled eggs. Once a week, we had sausage or salt meat, and on Fridays, we'd have dried salt cod. Every now and then, we'd have some cheap treat, such as lemonade or oysters. But most meals were dismal.

We could chat while we worked in the back room, and when the hours were long, one of us would read to the others to keep us going a little while longer. It was the easiest work, of course, and it was usually Kathleen or Bridget who was chosen to read, although I was by far the best reader. Sometimes Mrs. O'Hanrahan's girls could get her to agree to let us read a newspaper or even a novel—but more often, it was something from *Lives of the Saints*. I thought it could more appropriately be called *Deaths of the Saints*, since almost every story included a gruesome execution. I was familiar with some of them from Foxe's *Book of Martyrs*, but one evening I learned a hard lesson that showed me the two books were not identical.

Bridget had read us the story of St. Eutrope, a native of Babylon who, after his conversion to Christianity, went back to Babylon and killed all the Jews he could find, since he regarded them as the killers of Christ. I had not heard the story of St. Eutrope and thought the man was misguided. Julia had made me learn enough about antiquity that I knew crucifixion was a Roman punishment. Jews in those days stoned people to death. I opened my mouth to say something. Then I decided I wouldn't, and shut it.

Mrs. O'Hanrahan asked which of the saints was our favorite. Bridget said she liked St. Bridget, of course, who was not only her namesake, but the patron saint of Ireland. Kathleen said she favored St. Catherine because, she added with a twinkle, she was praying to her for a husband. I ventured that my favorite martyr was not a saint, but Hugh Latimer, Bishop of London, because he had been so very brave when he was burned at the stake.

There was silence while they looked at me.

I knew I shouldn't talk anymore, but my tongue wasn't listening. "Well, he was one of the martyrs Bloody Mary put to death."

More silence. Then Mrs. O'Hanrahan said, "Queen Mary

was a good queen. She had to deal with dangerous heretics." She closed the book and put it away.

We worked the rest of the evening in tense silence. I didn't know what to say to make things better, and was afraid anything I did say would only make them worse. That night I lay stiffly beside Kathleen, and was grateful when I heard her steady breathing, and her mother's gentle snoring—the usual signals that everyone was asleep. I was too tired to lie awake long.

The next morning, I went meekly to Mrs. O'Hanrahan to apologize for what I'd said. "I didn't mean to offend," I said. "Please understand I just don't know any better and am willing to learn."

She gave me a long, grave look. "Well," she said at last, "it's good for you that you said something. I had almost decided to send you away."

To live as a hired girl on some Dutchman's farm, I thought. That was close. I thanked her meekly for giving me another chance, and vowed to keep my mouth shut forever.

∽

So for a fortnight, our reading was not the newspapers or novels we all loved, but extra doses about the saints and the significance of the mass. This did not make me popular with Bridget and Kathleen. I found some of the explanations odd: that the bread and wine only appeared to be bread and wine, when it was in reality the body and blood of Jesus. This was one of the nine miracles of the mass, the book explained; even after the transformation, the "accidents abide." They had to explain to me that that meant the flesh and blood looked and tasted like bread and wine—because, as the book said, *It might be great horror, a priest to eat raw flesh and also to drink blood.* I had to agree with that.

The first few times I went to mass, I was completely confused. People stood or knelt, according to some directions I didn't understand. Occasionally, they said something in Latin. At first, I just tried not to look too stupid. Since I was accustomed to long, boring Sundays in church, I was pleased to find this would take only about an hour.

As I became less clumsy and understood more, I began to find the service more moving. *Kyrie eleison*, asking God to have mercy on us, became a sincere prayer from my heart, asking God to forgive me and love me. Then one day, I felt a rush of feeling. I was certain that God did forgive me, and that He did love me, and that I was in a magical and beautiful ceremony celebrating that. Gratitude and joy rushed through me, pushing tears out of my eyes. I felt exalted all that day. The next Sunday, though, I began to think about the priests. I tried to look at them as my mother had. She might have decided they were miraculous beings, and would seek such a man's attention—attention of any sort.

Maybe she never lay with a priest and said she had.

My feelings went back and forth. I was looking for conviction and certainty. Sometimes I was sure I had found it, but the feeling never lasted long. I never got to know any of the priests. I was afraid to so much as speak to them.

☙

I HAD HOPED TO GO home, to Julia, for Christmas, but our work did not allow that. The Christmas season was our busiest time. We worked all the daylight hours, plus early morning and into the night—molding, stitching, stretching, and pressing by the light of a spirit lamp. We had to crowd closely into its little pool of feeble light, and sometimes the fumes gave us headaches—but it was the only way to get the work done. We worked late on Christmas Eve and went to mass at midnight. On Christmas morning, we had a special breakfast with coffee and eggs. By noon, we set back to work, for we had much to complete for New Year's Eve.

The last day of the year was a mad rush, and the dawn of the Year of Our Lord 1851 found us all asleep. That day, we were allowed to sleep until nearly noon. But that afternoon, we went back to work for the rest of the social season, which ran until Lent.

My birthday came and went in January, when I turned fifteen Nobody else mentioned it, and I actually forgot it was my birthday until I got a short note from Julia. My only thought was, *There is one person who loves me.*

We must have been the only young women in New York who looked forward to Lent—when there would be few parties, no social season, and little demand for new hats. At the beginning of Lent, I was allowed to go to Julia—but with the warning that Easter was only six weeks away, when the orders would again be coming fast. When the ferryboat set out across the river toward Brooklyn, I felt a great rush of joy, and I rode the omnibus to Flatbush in a state of elation, in spite of the February drizzle and the seeping cold. I saw only a small, cloaked figure when the bus stopped in Flatbush, and it took a minute to realize it was indeed Julia. I threw my arms around her, and we held each other in an embrace for a moment as I smelled the familiar bitter scent of her tobacco.

"Well," she said briskly, "we'd best set out or we'll be soaked."

As we walked of the neat paths I remembered in Flatbush, I found myself tongue-tied. *I've missed her so much,* I thought, *but she seems different now. There's a lot I want to tell her, but I don't know where to start, and I'm afraid I'll talk too much. She doesn't like it when people rattle.*

The tiles on the kitchen fireplace still gleamed, and she had a kettle of soup keeping hot. It had a rich broth. It even had meat in it.

"Oh, Julia." I sighed after the first savory spoonful. "This is the best food I've had since August."

"Not surprised," she said. "You look pasty."

That wasn't what I wanted to hear, although I had to admit I probably did look pasty. I thought she'd be happy to see me, and was hurt when she just seemed critical.

We spread our wet clothes near the fireplace to dry, banked the fire, and went to bed. I slept very late the next day—too late to go get the eggs from the henhouse.

"Good morning, slugabed. You must be a city girl now, sleeping so late."

"It feels good to be able to sleep. The last time I slept in was New Year's Day."

She nodded. "Today's baking day," she said. "Can you still bake, or are you too citified?"

I wondered if she'd always been this grumpy.

"I'd love to bake. Let me get an apron, and I'll knead the bread dough."

Once we had something to do, we could at least work together. We stitched together a new bodice for me, and we recut and patched my old one, because my shape was changing still and I needed different clothes. I was grateful for that, but I found her conversation odd now. When we stopped in the evening to read *The Universalist*, it seemed tiresome to me—going on about the evils of slavery, and questions of whether people suffer for their sins, and even about how women should have the right to vote. None of it seemed to have anything to do with me or the life I was leading.

The night before I left was cold. We lay down to sleep by the kitchen fire. In the dark, by the banked fire, I told her about the mistake I'd made mentioning a Protestant martyr. I said it was always in the back of my mind that they'd find out whose daughter I was.

There was a long silence. I thought perhaps Julia had fallen asleep. Then she spoke, "Well, if they do, there a'nt much you can do. And not much I can do, either."

I had been hoping she'd have a solution, and now I realized it was a foolish hope.

"I can't figger what you'll do," she added. It irritated me now that she said "figger," like a country woman—though of course, that's what she was. "When they find out, they'll likely have you out on your elbows, and there's little more I can do. We searched the city to find that place. Do you think you could find another shop?"

"I think somebody else might take me. I don't think I'd make enough to live on."

"Well, coming back here a'nt the way out. I'm lonely without you, but I'm only here as long as my brother-in-law doesn't want me out. And if there's nowhere for me, there's nowhere for you but the floor of a farm kitchen."

"I miss you, too, Julia. I know how it is, but sometimes I'd just like to come back here to stay."

"I know. But it can't be the way it was when you'z little. Things change."

We embraced in the dark and lay back down separately to sleep. The next morning I went back to my life in the city.

CHAPTER 11

*C*OMING UP TO EASTER, THE SHOP WAS FRANTICALLY BUSY, and by Easter morning, we were exhausted. That didn't mean we could skip Mass. Mrs. O'Hanrahan wanted her daughters married, and she wanted them to meet their husbands at church. That Easter morning, we all met Finn Malone.

He seemed to materialize in front of us there in the churchyard: a tall, dark-haired young man with flashing black eyes and a wonderful set of teeth, set off by a trim black beard. He swept off his hat, using his right hand, and bowed to Mrs. O'Hanrahan. I thought it odd he used his right hand, since most men used their left, but he held his hat in his right hand behind him.

He stood up, offering Mrs. O'Hanrahan his arm and a dazzling smile. "If you please, Mrs. O'Hanrahan, might you and your daughters be in need of an escort to your home?"

She tried not to smile at him, but fluttered at his attention, and off we set—with Kathleen following close behind them and Bridget and I trailing after, trying to catch what pieces of the conversation we could.

"Mrs. O'Hanrahan, 'tis a beautiful day to be out with your charming daughters, and 'tis lovely you are looking yourself."

Bridget and I rolled our eyes, but Mrs. O'Hanrahan didn't seem to mind he was laying it on thick. "I'm after becoming a policeman," he went on. "'Tis why I've come to New York." He made it sound like "Noo Yarkh"—but then, most Irishmen did.

Well, I thought, *that will make him a catch.* New York City was starting an actual police force. Keeping order had been the task of watchmen, who were sometimes paid by the city and sometimes by business owners—but rarely much. They tended to be old, and most of them slept on the job. If real trouble started, they ran and hid.

But real policemen! They wore uniforms, the work was steady, and their pay was twelve dollars a week! A handsome young policeman was much more desirable than a laborer or navvy—maybe even more than a carter who had his own cart.

Finn had been a corporal in the American army, and had fought in the Mexican War. I heard him say he'd been a brakeman for the railroad, so I tried to get a look at his hand, but Kathleen was in the way.

When we reached our home, the charming Mr. Malone bowed and departed, with an extra smile and glance for Kathleen. We filed silently in, and then burst into a chattering conversation.

"We couldn't hear everything," said Bridget. "Who is this Mr. Malone, and where's he from?"

"He's a Sligo-man, as anyone could tell from his accent," said Kathleen.

"How many fingers is he missing?" I asked. Experienced brakemen were usually missing one or two, but when they lost too many, the railroad sacked them.

"None," she said, quickly. "I got a good look at his right hand. He's only missing the tips of two. He was trying to hide it."

"What do you think are his chances of being a policeman?" asked Bridget.

"He's been a soldier. That's in his favor," answered Mrs.

O'Hanrahan. "And as long as he's missing no more than tips of fingers, they may take him."

"And he is charming," added Kathleen. "Isn't he, Mam?"

Her mother turned her head away, trying to hide a smile.

Suddenly, Finn Malone was a part of our lives—always at the church on Sundays, often staying to have a cup of tea. He'd jam his long body onto a short chair in our little workroom, entertaining us all with his stories of fighting Mexicans and working on the railway. He tried to keep his eyes off Kathleen, and she tried to look modest and unconcerned. They both failed.

He told us how he despised the St. Patrick regiment—the Irishmen who deserted the American army to fight on the Mexican side—and how he'd lost each of his two fingertips. Brakemen had to stand between cars as they came together and guide the coupler tubes together and drop in a pin to link them. If you didn't get out of the way of the moving couplers quickly enough, you could lose fingers or a hand. Do it too fast, and you could be dragged under the cars and killed. It was hard to believe he made us laugh at these stories, but he did. And even though the flash of his eyes was always directed at Kathleen, he was entertaining for all of us.

He wanted very much to be out walking with Kathleen, but Mrs. O'Hanrahan told him Bridget was to be courting first, and soon, the resourceful Mr. Malone had a solution for that, too. In June, he asked Mrs. O'Hanrahan permission to bring around a friend of his. He was already a policeman, and he lived uptown and was "quite bright for a Kerryman." The young man's name was Tom McGonagle.

My stomach tightened in fear. I tried to tell myself there were many McGonagles in the world, and many were likely named Tom. But Tommy McGonagle from Goerck Street would be able to unmask me in an instant as the daughter of Maria Monk. That would cost me my place in the O'Hanrahan's home and shop. And then where would I go?

I kept my fear tamped down until Sunday. I saw Finn Malone in the distance, with a tall man whose hat couldn't hide that McGonagle thicket of red hair. When they approached us at church, I already knew who he was: Tommy McGonagle from Goerck Street, and I knew he'd know me, too. I looked at the ground, studying the toes of my boots as introductions were made, hoping he didn't see my face. I trailed everyone on the way back, then pleaded a headache and asked to be excused. Mrs. O'Hanrahan pursed her lips, but nodded curtly and let me leave.

I lay on our little straw bed during the visit, listening to the murmur of voices and the occasional laughter, most of which sounded awkward. I worried all the next week about what I could do, and still hadn't figured out anything by the time I trailed all of them home from Mass. It was grasping at straws, but when I saw how smitten he was with Bridget, I hoped he'd never pay any attention to me. The knot still stayed in my stomach.

I thought about running away, but where could I go? I was nervous and afraid every time they came to call, and many times in between. Kathleen and Bridget were wrapped up with their beaus, and if they thought about it at all, they probably thought I was jealous, because I had nobody.

Finn progressed toward his goal of being a policeman, and became involved in "polly-ticks," as Tommy was. So far as I could tell, their involvement consisted of going to political gatherings to support their side in a punch-up, which seemed to be the way things got decided.

I learned that most of the McGonagle brothers and sisters were gone. Two boys had headed for the California gold fields in '49, and one sister was in service in Philadelphia, the other at home to help their mother. I prayed Maeve was the one in Philadelphia. I couldn't face Maeve.

But it was Maeve who came, still as bony and beaky as she had been when we were ten. She looked right at me, right through me, with a look that said, *I know you from somewhere. I know you, and it isn't good.*

Mrs. McGonagle was still tall and strong, and didn't look as though she needed looking after. Her resonant voice still carried her heavy Kerry brogue. She squinted at all of us, and I felt a little flash of relief to realize she was too nearsighted to recognize me.

It didn't last long. When Mrs. O'Hanrahan said, "Vera is our apprentice," Maeve's eyes flashed recognition. She watched me as Kathleen, Bridget, and I set out the mismatched cups on the carefully pressed linen cover of our work table, and set down a plate of the best baker's tarts Mrs. O'Hanrahan could afford.

My hands were shaking.

Mrs. McGonagle wanted to talk about how she and her husband had come up in the world. Her husband was a carter, and when he got his own cart, they moved away from Goerck Street. "Thanks be to God," she said. "To be sure, on Goerck Street, there were the worst sorts of people."

"To be sure they were," chimed in Maeve. "Maria Monk lived there! Do you remember her?"

"I do, Maeve," said Mrs. McGonagle.

It's all over, I thought. *I'm trapped. They know who I am, and they're going to tell. I can't stand sitting here pretending everything is fine.*

"We didn't know them well, of course," continued Mrs. McGonagle, trying to hush up Maeve. "That Monk woman stirred up a deal of trouble, though, didn't she? I will never be forgetting the night those bully-boys gathered up the brickbats and stormed St. Patrick's Church. They took the very dead from their graves. They set a fire on Goerck Street. I was terrified for my little ones." She crossed herself at the memory, and everyone shook their heads and murmured agreement. Everyone but me. I was paralyzed.

"It was fine Irish men went to defend St. Patrick's," said Mrs. O'Hanrahan.

Then Maeve spoke again. "And that shameless woman wore the habit of a sister to tell her filthy lies."

Mrs. McGonagle gave her a sharp glance. "That husband of hers was a good man. He tried to help her."

"If he was her husband," Maeve gibed.

"But the devil had her heart—you could just see that. And after he left, well, she just became a wild woman, the worst sort, always the worse for drink and sleeping on the streets. She ended up at the Five Points, to be sure." They shook their heads again and sipped their tea. "'Tis to be hoped the good Lord mended her heart," Mrs. McGonagle finished, piously.

Everyone paused and sipped their tea. I couldn't swallow mine. But then I thought, *She doesn't know. She can't see me.* But Maeve could see me, and Maeve knew. Why wasn't she saying anything?

They chatted for a while about the bishop, that brave and courageous John Hughes who stood up to the Protestants, making Catholic schools available for Catholic children. "Schools ye can send the good Irish children to," said Mrs. McGonagle, approvingly. "Not like the city schools, where there's the singing of the Protestant hymns and reading the Protestant Bible."

As they were leaving, Maeve clutched my elbow and hissed, "I know who you are, missy. I'll tell when it suits me, and you'll be gone."

Then she smiled and held out her hand, as though we'd been talking about the weather, or the delights of silk hair ribbons. "I trust we'll meet again soon," she said, prim as a duchess.

When Kathleen shut the door behind them, there was a pause, and then the O'Hanrahans all gave a noisy sigh of relief.

"Well, I think that went well," said Kathleen, and she gave Bridget a hug. "You'll be married before the year's out."

They were relieved. I was not. I kept silent as we cleared away the cups. They took no notice, of course, with the two girls happily chattering.

"That Maeve's a sourpuss, though, isn't she?" said Kathleen. "You'll have her to put up with."

"Oh, Maeve will be glad enough of a marriage and a sister-in-law," said Mrs. O'Hanrahan. "It will mean she's not the only one left to take care of her mother, and she can make a marriage of her own."

Of course, that was it. Maeve wanted Tom and Bridget married. I didn't have much time left. Time left—to do what?

CHAPTER 12

ONE FRIDAY IN AUTUMN, AROUND CLOSING TIME, MRS. O'Hanrahan came to the back and told me, "You have a caller." She wasn't smiling. "It's a young woman. And I'm not saying young lady."

I wondered who it could be—other shop girls usually came to the back to chat, not into the front. I put down the hat I'd been working on, straightened my hair, and went into the front, where a young woman stood looking at the bonnets. She was dressed like a country girl, with a bright gewgaw or two from the Bowery. Dark hair, cheap bonnet. She turned and faced me, and her face lit with a smile. It was Lizzie.

"Vera!" She leapt forward and flung her arms around me.

I stood a little stiffly at first but put my arms around her and hugged. It was really Lizzie—warm, wiggly Lizzie, but fear of being given away still gripped me inside. "What are you doing here?" I asked.

"A fine, sisterly greeting that is," she teased. "I'm looking for a position."

"I'm sorry, Lizzie," I said, giving her another hug, kinder this time. "I'm glad to see you. But I thought you were working for a shoemaker."

"Oh, he was horrible. He expected more than just working on the shoes." She arched her eyebrows, but I could see a glint of pain in her dark eyes. She went on. "I went from there to stitching shirts, at all of four cents a day. Aunt Betsy said she had given me all the upbringing she was going to give. So ..." She sighed. "I thought it was time this little country girl came to town."

I stood for a moment just looking at her. She was still half a head shorter than I, round and buxom like our mother, with unruly dark hair and sparkling dark eyes.

Mrs. O'Hanrahan, standing in the doorway to the back room, cleared her throat.

"Oh," I said, "I beg your pardon. Mrs. O'Hanrahan, this is my sister, Lizzie. Elizabeth St. John."

Lizzie giggled like some country ninny. I wanted to slap her.

"Your sister?" Mrs. O'Hanrahan's eyebrows arched. "Oh yes, I believe I heard you mention a sister. Raised upstate, were you?"

Lizzie answered, "Yes'm," like a bumpkin.

"Vera, a word with you, please." Mrs. O'Hanrahan motioned me to the back of the shop.

"Oh, yes, don't mind me!" Lizzie waved her hand airily.

In the back of the shop, Mrs. O'Hanrahan folded her arms and said to me, "This is unexpected."

"It's a surprise to me, too. She didn't tell me she was coming."

"Then you weren't angling for a place for her here."

"No, ma'am, I was not. I would have asked you first."

She gave a short sigh and glanced in Lizzie's direction. "And I would have said no."

"I know." I hesitated. "She isn't suitable. But she is my sister. I should help her if I can."

"Indeed," Mrs. O'Hanrahan said and pinched her lips together. "Mrs. Bourget is looking for a ribbon girl."

Mrs. Bourget's would be perfect. She wasn't kind or generous, but she was reasonably respectable, and Lizzie would at least have a place to work, and a chance to learn acceptable manners. She wouldn't need to spell anything, and she could probably learn to measure out eighths of a yard soon enough. I went with her to apply.

As it turned out, the shop was busy when we got there, and Lizzie pitched right in. Within fifteen minutes, Mrs. Bourget had engaged her.

As I walked back, I kept telling myself I should be happier to see her. *What kind of a sister am I?* I was a worried one, that's what. If she acted up, it would reflect on me. Of course, it was only a matter of time before Maeve ruined everything anyway. *I might as well give up now*, I thought. But give up and do what?

Bridget and Tommy set a date between Christmas and New Year's. Mrs. O'Hanrahan tried to put them off until after Easter, because the social season would continue until Lent—and heavens, they couldn't be married during Lent. Finn Malone charmed her into letting them go ahead, though, so he could have Kathleen. For a while, the brides-to-be chattered happily and worked mightily. Toward Christmas, though, we all became more disagreeable by the minute, cooped up as we were in the dark, with little rest and too much work.

Mrs. O'Hanrahan had begun to pay me some actual cash money, and I saved as much as I could against the day they would kick me out.

CHAPTER 13

CHRISTMAS DAY, AT LEAST, THE SHOP WAS CLOSED, AND WE all slept late and rested our sore fingers. We built up the fire in the little stove until the cold back room was actually very warm. Then we had Christmas cakes with real coffee. Christmas night, it snowed, and all of us, Mrs. O'Hanrahan included, went out and threw snowballs, giggling and chasing each other about like children. At the end, when we were all breathless, wet, and disheveled, Mrs. O'Hanrahan flung her arms around Bridget and stood with her silently, her eyes closed. Anyone could see she was feeling how much she would miss her daughter after the wedding. I was worried about that time, too, for I knew that's when Maeve would tell, and I would be out with nowhere to go. As I stood there silently, Kathleen hit me in the back of the head with a snowball, and the chasing and giggling began again.

We all looked very dignified two days later when we were at St. Patrick's for the wedding, and after that, we all tramped through the rain to celebrate at Dooley's. Dooley's Long House was hardly fancy, but it was famous as a gathering place for ambitious Irish lads—and for the brawls they called caucuses.

Finn Malone practically danced his way to Dooley's. He

had his policeman's job, he would soon have Kathleen, and some great friend of his was going to meet him at Dooley's. I listened for fiddle music as we approached. There was none. We entered the smoky gloom and heard the voice of one man at the bar, reciting some poem in Irish.

"Well, won't this be a gay party?" came Kathleen's sour whisper. "He's spouting the coming of the Gael or some other bit of gibberish, and at the end of it, they'll be half of them sobbing, and we'll just have to sit in the smoke and not understand a word."

We each got our bit of small beer and waited quietly for the young man to finish. Bridget snuggled contentedly close to Tom, and Kathleen got as close to Finn as she dared with her mother only a few feet away.

I watched the man reciting poetry, feeling drawn in because he made what he said sound like something moving and important, even though I didn't understand a word. He wasn't handsome. He was short-ish and thin, with sparse light hair. His face shone in the dark as though a beam of light fell on him. His voice was light but clear and strong, and when he finished, there was silence, then a roar of approval. Men wiped their eyes, clapped him on the back, and offered to buy his next drink. Women dabbed at their eyes, too, and one sighed.

"No one speaks Amergin's coming to Ireland the likes of Jimmy O'Dea."

"Oh, so that's your famous friend Jimmy O'Dea," Kathleen said to Finn with a little sneer. "He's a bit scrawny for a lad that built the railway."

"I'll hear nothing against Seamus O'Dea," said Finn, using his friend's Irish name. "He's built the railway all the way to the Ohio River."

"Oh, all by himself?" Kathleen teased.

He looked at her, annoyed and amused at the same time.

"T'was he was clever enough to get them all paid. Sure, and

the bosses who hire the navvies to build have a little trick they like to play on the final payday. They bring out a barrel of the whiskey to celebrate—mind you, before they pay the lads. And when they're all of them away with the band, some Kerryman picks a fight, and in the hurly-burly, the boss slips away with their pay. And they're sat out in the middle of nowhere with the sickness in their heads and nothing in their pockets.

"Seamus got them all to agree they'd take never a drink until they all got paid, even the black ones. He stood and argued with the crew boss and got them all paid, all of them, every red and precious cent. The bastard took away the whiskey, but it's just as well. They'd have all been robbed. They've all come back to New York City with money in their pockets. He's as much a hero as Cuchulain."

Finn went over to greet his friend. Kathleen looked at me, giving a little rise to her eyebrows. "Well, he's a deal shorter than Cuchulain," she said. "He's a bit scrawny for a hero, don't you think?"

I didn't answer. He was beginning to look like a hero to me.

The fiddles struck up, lively and bright. Tom and Bridget led out the first dance, followed by Finn and Kathleen. Then one of the lads came and took my hand and led me in. The music and dancing lifted the weight off my heart, and I started to dance with a joy I hadn't felt since I was a child dancing for pennies. I showed myself off, I admit it. Every time it was my turn to dance a bit in the middle, I kicked my heels high, even doing some buck steps I'd learned from raggedy black boys long ago. I knew it wasn't proper for a girl to dance so, but I didn't care—and nobody else seemed to, either. Men and women whooped, and the fiddlers played their fanciest.

After three dances, I collapsed, laughing and sweaty, back onto the bench near where I'd left my little bit of a drink. My dancing partner and I smiled and shook hands, and he went off to the bar, obviously uninterested in prolonging our acquaintance. Oh well. I leaned back against the wall and took a drink of the warmish beer.

I saw Maeve's face, pinched and angry, the bones in her face sharp as hunger, her eyes glittering at me from across the room. Soon, she would open her mouth to destroy me. Perhaps the dancing gave me courage, for I lifted my chin and returned her stare, thinking she could do her worst and I would survive. I didn't know how. I was trying to convince myself.

"'Tis a lovely dancer you are." It was a man's voice, close to me, in the darkness. I squinted and saw it was Jimmy O'Dea.

Suddenly, the cat had my tongue. I looked at my feet as though I expected them to speak for me. My feet let me know they had already spoken—that dancing was what they did, and conversation was up to my mouth and my brain.

He continued. "When I get up the courage for the dance, I'd like to ask you."

What does that mean? I wondered.

"But before I can ask you," he added, "I'll have to be knowing your name."

I smiled at him, and he smiled back, lighting his whole face. The sparkle in his bright, gentle eyes made my breath catch.

"I'm … uh … I'm Vera," I said, sounding to my ears like a complete simpleton. "I believe you're Jimmy O'Dea."

"I believe I am as well," he replied, still smiling. Silence. The smile dimmed a little. "Is it leaving you'd like me to do?"

"No!" I blurted. "I don't want you to go away." So much for being coy, flirtatious, and seductive.

"That suits me down to the ground," he said, his smile brightening again. "I'll stay here, and happily." He moved a bit closer.

I couldn't think of a thing to say. I looked away. He waited.

"I couldn't understand a word of the poem you recited," I said, "but it sounded beautiful. And I see it makes grown men cry."

"'Tis a lovely bit of a speech." He agreed. "'Tis part of the story of the coming of the Goyl into Ireland."

Goyl? What? *Oh,* I thought, *that's the way he says "Gael."* When I started listening again, he was talking about Amergin, who led the Gaelic people to Ireland.

"He spoke for the gods and said, 'I am the wind on the sea and the eagle on the rock. I am the word of knowledge and the god that puts the fire in the head. I spread light on the gathering of the hills. Who can tell the ages of the moon? Who can tell the place where the sun rests?' And where the sun rests, of course, is the land to the west, sure—and that's when the Irish begin to weep."

"I don't understand why."

"We think of a time when we all had the fire in the head, the inspiration of the poets, when we were all free and noble and not despised as the dirt beneath the heels of the conqueror. And in the land to the west, the trees bow down with the fruit, and all the people are beautiful and forever young. And we keep this treasure of the thought of the land to the west deep in our hearts to give us strength to fight the English. The thought of the lands to the west lifts our spirits and helps us keep the pride in our native tongue. And then, when the famine came, we all thought the lands to the west would be our salvation— the paradise of the Irish people." He paused. "And then, when we get here, everyone is speaking English."

A huge laugh burst out of my mouth.

"And that's why we weep at the 'Coming of the Gael.'"

I laughed again. "I believed every word until you got to the end."

"I know. 'Tis a gift I have."

I don't know how long we sat there that night, talking and laughing. He bought me a drink and told me more Irish stories and a few of the adventures he had had building the railroad. He talked very fast, and once I had to ask him to slow down because I couldn't understand him.

"'Tis that I'm a Sligo-man," he said. "A Sligo-man will tell five lies before a Kerryman can say, 'Good morning.'" That made me laugh, too, but he did talk more slowly.

Then suddenly, Mrs. O'Hanrahan was standing in front of me, with her shawl on and her arms folded. I knew it was time to go.

As we went out the door, Kathleen nudged me and said, "And when is he coming to call?"

"Soon, I hope."

"Oh my, aren't we forward? I had no idea you could dance like that! And I don't believe I've ever seen you laugh so much."

"I don't believe I ever have."

CHAPTER 14

$\mathcal{I}$T WAS A LATE NIGHT WE HAD AT DOOLEY'S, AND WE WERE all groggy the next morning as we slogged through the rain to Mass. By the time we were out, the rain was gone and the weather was clear and cold. Finn Malone swooped Kathleen away as soon as we left the church, and Mrs. O'Hanrahan and I were left to walk home alone.

"We shall be two old maids today," she said. "We'll go tend to a few things and then go for our own walk." It wasn't something I looked forward to, but I nodded and tried to look cheerful.

I was in the back of the shop when the bell sounded, and I heard Jimmy O'Dea's voice greeting Mrs. O'Hanrahan. "And might I go walking today with your daughter, missus?"

What? I thought. *He spent all that time talking to me, and he's just another one after Kathleen?* I felt my eyes prickle with tears.

"My daughter is out." Her tone was flat.

"But, missus, you've more than one."

"My other two daughters are married." I didn't have to see Mrs. O'Hanrahan to know she'd folded her arms.

"Miss Vera is out, then?"

"Vera is not my daughter. She is my apprentice."

She waited for that to sink in, but didn't call me. When

she spoke again, I could tell she was amused. "Many people make the same mistake, Mr. O'Dea. I do have three daughters, but one is grown and gone these three years. Vera is not my daughter, but I do have a care for appearances. You do understand me?"

"Oh, yes, missus, I do. I am ever so humble and proper."

I heard her chuckle. He'd charmed her, too.

She came back. She knew I'd been listening, of course. She gave me her little wintry smile and nodded. "Go," she said. "I'll take my walk with Mrs. Oakley."

A few minutes later, we were walking in the cold wind and sunshine. I had no idea how to begin a conversation. He took my hand and threaded it through his elbow, as a gentleman would for a lady. The rough wool of his coat felt good, and when I looked up to see the smile on his face, I smiled up at him, feeling happiness begin to soar in me in a way I never thought it could. He smelt of soap, coarse wool, and tobacco, and that scent in the cold air made me unreasonably happy.

"Well, Miss Vera," he said as we moved down Bleecker Street. "You heard every word, didn't you?"

I felt my face flush. "Yes," I admitted. "I thought you'd come for Kathleen, like everyone else."

"Ah, no," he answered. "Mr. Finn Malone, the Malone *dubh*, would never stand for that, although he did give me a bit of the bad information. He said you and Kathleen were sisters."

"Malone *dewf*?" I asked, not knowing what that Irish word was.

"The Black Malone, the dark-haired Mr. Finn himself. I suppose I forgive him, since he's another Drumcliffe man, and there are no wise men near Drumcliffe."

"What?" I laughed because what he said was so silly. "Why not?"

"Time for that later," he said. "I'll not get sidetracked again. Your nemm, please, miss, and I'll be having the whole nemm."

Nemm? He wanted my name, I realized. "Vera St. John," I answered.

He stopped and looked at me in mock horror. "Bless my soul, and she's not even Oirish! I feel more foolish by the minute."

"Please don't. I don't think you're foolish. I don't even know whether I'm Irish or not. I'm an orphan, and I was brought up by a cousin in the country, and I really don't know much about my parents." Why was I telling him this so fast? We stepped carefully around a mudhole, as I was trying to step around the question of my mother, and then narrowly avoided an unusually large pile of manure.

"'Tis good to you this cousin has been," he said. "Letting you go learn a trade when he could have hired you out or kept you working about the place."

"*She*. My cousin Julia's a widow lady. She is kind. She had to search out a place for me to work, and she taught me some of the skills herself, and to write and figure."

"A forward-thinking woman."

I paused before I answered, "That's not always considered a compliment."

"I mean it to be. 'Tis no great honor to be backward-thinking."

I had to laugh at that.

"All alone in the world, is it?" he asked.

"Except for my cousin … and my sister. She's come to New York to work. She was raised by other cousins, and we're—we're different."

We were at the Bowery by this time, and stopped to watch a couple of boys dancing for pennies on the street corner. One was black and one was Irish, and they were trading steps just as I had as a child. They had gathered a fair crowd by the time we got there. The spectators were clapping time while the Irish lad flew about in a classic step dance—back stiff, poker-faced, his booted feet flying in a complicated rhythm. The negro lad watched and clapped, and when the Irish lad stepped aside, he put on an exaggerated poker face, held himself stiffly, and duplicated the Irish boy's steps exactly—then began his own rhythmic shuffle, moving his shoulders and hips and clapping his own complicated rhythm. Then the Irish boy imitated him—rolling his eyes and exaggerating the hip movements—and each parody brought a new laugh and maybe a penny or two from the crowd. We enjoyed this entertainment for a few exchanges, and then moved on.

"And they tell us no good comes of the mixing of the races," remarked Jimmy. "They'll not be staylin' apples when they've danced like that all the day."

We walked on toward the East River. "You haven't told me about your family or how you got here," I said. "Or why you said wise men go nowhere near Drumcliffe."

"Ah, well—to answer the last question first, far away in the land of Sligo, in the shadow of the mountain Benbulben, there stand the remains of the Round Tower or Drumcliffe, which in the year of our Lord thirteen and ninety-six was struck by lightning. And the folk around have neither torn it down nor built it up. Oh, no. Being Irish, they have instead made up a story about it. They say it will ultimately fall on the wisest man who passes it. Mind you, they don't even say this must be a *really* wise man—just the wisest one to pass, which is making no sense a'tall.

"And be that as it may, from thirteen and ninety-six until this very day, there has been none walk by that tower that so much as made one of its stones quiver. Some say 'tis very simple, that no man with any claim to wisdom will go where a stone tower is likely to fall on him. Others say 'tis even simpler, that no wise man would ever go to Drumcliffe. The stones of the Round Tower have remained intact for these four hundred and fifty years, utterly unthreatened by the proximity of any wisdom whatsoever."

I laughed.

He put his hand over his heart. "Do I hear the laughter of disbelief?"

"I don't know." I giggled. "I don't know whether to believe that or not."

"That's fair," he replied and shrugged. "Nor do I."

"Well then," I persisted, "what about your family?"

We walked for a moment in silence. Then he said, "We were surplus population."

I looked at him quickly, not sure whether this was more of his fun or the bitter echo heard from so many Irish about the way the British regarded them. He was serious.

We were near the docks now, and we could hear the sailors shouting and singing as they pumped out newly landed ships and made others ready for sea. We sat on a couple of big stones near the water.

"Drumcliffe is near the town of Sligo, in the north and west where there's still plenty speaks the old tongue, as we did. We had both tongues, really, for we spoke the English when the local gentry came into the shop. I suppose it was a shop and a public house and a bakery, for me mother baked the bread to sell, and anyone could stop for a bit of beer and a pickled egg. There were five of us—Da, Ma, Patrick, Mary, and me. I was the eldest.

"T'was a poor enough life, to be sure, but I remember it as happy, until 1847, when the Lord sent the blight and the English brought the famine. They took the food away from us in ships—great ships with grain and sheep, to England, and all with guards on them to keep the starving Irish from stealing the food they'd grown. Da's brother was a guard on one of the ships. Our neighbors started to think we had plenty, when we'd no more than they did. Ma had given food to starving folks as best she could, but then we had so little she couldn't do it anymore, so our neighbors decided my uncle was stealing food from the ship and we were keeping it from them. A good look at any of us would have told them we were eating no better than anyone else, but one evening, when my uncle was visiting, they stormed the place and set fire to it. They barricaded Da and my uncle inside, and they burnt to death."

I was getting cold, but I didn't want to interrupt his story. I put my shawl over my head and huddled into my coat. He put his arm around me. His arm was warm and strong and made me feel happy and safe, in spite of what he was telling me.

He went on.

"They poked through the ashes to find food, and of course, there was none to find. But never so much as a 'sorry' did we hear. We were turned out to beg—the four of us, with me little sister only four. We spent that spring and summer in a scalpeen—that's a hole in the ground to you—with the ruins of a cottage around it to keep out some of the wind. Even if we could have built it up to keep out the rain, some agent would have seen it and we'd have been charged rent, or turned out, so we stayed in shelter as best we could and ate whatever we could dig up, beg, steal, or scrounge—even blighted potatoes. Blighted potatoes are slimy in the mouth and taste like mold and death, and they can make you sick. If you're hungry, the pain in your belly tells you it won't happen this time, but it almost always does. Just thinking about them makes my stomach turn.

"We had bread once, and a bit of cheese, after my mother let a soldier do the upright to her behind the one wall we had. If we'd had any pride, we wouldn't have eaten the bread or the cheese, but no pride did we have, and we did eat it—and sometimes wished another soldier would happen along so she could do it again. To think of it now, though, I think she broke then. And something in me died, too, because I was her boy and I couldn't defend her. Just as I couldn't save my da.

"We knew we couldn't survive a winter there, so we walked to Sligo in the autumn. We'd heard there was a workhouse there, one that might take us in. A workhouse is a terrible place, but we'd heard they fed you once a day, and that they sent people out to Canada and Amerikay. The landlords were doing that, you see, to avoid the paying of the taxes they had on their tenants. Ship 'em off to Amerikay, and 'tis cheaper than having them stay on the land and die.

"It took us two days to walk to Sligo, though 'tis only about five miles. We weren't strong enough to walk fast, and we had to carry my little sister Mary. Most of the time, she was only strong enough to whimper. On the second day, we came to a church, a Protestant church, where they were serving soup to a great long line of skelly-tons with rags on. They all looked ashamed—shamed by being hungry and shamed by betraying their faith for a bowl of soup. We talked about it, Ma and I, and I said I didn't see a difference between Protestant and Catholic that was worth more than a bowl of soup. Ma smiled a sad little smile and said the Lord would understand we were only doing it until the praties grew again.

"We all ate the soup that day. We stayed nearby for several days, maybe a week—I can't remember—walking back and forth between the soup and the workhouse, waiting for the workhouse gates to open so we could get in. We heard they'd sent a ship to Canada, so maybe there was room for more. My mother told us we would all try to get in. But she said if we didn't all get in, those of us inside mustn't cry for those outside. That night, they opened the gates a bit, and we shoved to get in. Patrick and I got through. Our mother and little sister were left outside.

"I can still see my mother's face as the gate closed. She had been such a pretty woman. She was a hag, and her face was like a death's head. That was the last time I saw them."

He took his arm from around my shoulders. I picked up his hand and held it in mine. His fingers lay limp and cold. "Did they die?" I whispered.

He nodded. "Must have done. Don't know for sure, but I've written and never heard back. I know it. I know they're gone."

"You had no choice," I whispered.

He pulled back his hand. "I left them there to die."

It was late afternoon and growing colder, but the day was still beautiful. The sunlight sparkled on the water. The sky was a clear, limitless blue. I watched the ferryboats steaming across the river, belching smoke, and thought about the rye fields of Flatbush shimmering in the sunshine. Nearby, a sailing ship was making ready to leave, and I listened to the clanking of the anchor chain and the hearty singing of the crew.

The old man was a drunken geezer,
Could not sail the Ebenezer,
Learned his trade in a Chinese junk,
Spent his time down in his bunk.

We heard their laughter and their boisterous shouts to each other. Even with their hard life, they sounded happy.

I sat silently with Jimmy, thinking about what he'd said, and thinking the beauty of the world was indeed a cruel thing. I wondered how a day could be so beautiful in such a brutal and blood-soaked place. Then I realized I was shivering again.

"And now we'll stiffen and die where we sit," he said, standing and holding out his hand for mine. "That's enough of that. To be sure, we need to be getting you out of the cold."

I stood up and put my arms around him, and he embraced me. Then I put my arms around his neck and kissed him. Then I kissed him again. I didn't care who was watching or what became of me. He let out a noise like a sob and held me so fiercely I could hardly breathe. He kissed my hair, my face, my ear, part of my collar and hat. I started to cry.

"Here now, we'll have none of that," he said, stepping away and wiping his own eyes. "It's over." He kissed my forehead, and we started away, back toward Bleecker Street, silently for a while. Then he said, "I knew the first time I saw you that you would be the one I told."

"What—how did you know such a thing?"

"That first night in Dooley's. I'm telling a story in the Irish, and in walks the prettiest girl I've ever seen. She's American, and here's me blathering away, and I knew you couldn't have understood a word. But you listened like you understood it all."

"I felt like I did."

He pulled me closer on his arm, and I pressed to him. We had one awful secret in common. We had both walked away and left our mothers to die.

CHAPTER 15

I WASN'T MUCH USE IN THE SHOP FOR THE NEXT WEEK. I made three mistakes in the accounts, handed one customer the wrong bonnet, and twice stitched hatbands to my own skirt—something I hadn't done since I was eleven years old. Mrs. O'Hanrahan complained good-naturedly about what a dead loss all her helpers were, since we were all in different stages of mooning about. It was certainly true for me. I ached for the sound of Jimmy's voice and the touch of his hand.

Just as I'd be deep in reverie, though, I'd get a stab of fear. Maeve hadn't yet told on me, and I dreaded what would happen when she did.

Sunday, when Jimmy and I started on our walk, Lizzie bounced up with other girls from Mrs. Bourget's, and I was actually shocked at the way she behaved. She wasn't just flirtatious; she bumped up against him like a Bowery whore. As she and her new companions walked away, giggling, I was so angry and embarrassed I wanted to scream. Instead, I was silent as Jimmy and I set off on our own.

I glanced sidelong up at him and saw him looking sidelong at me, his mouth twitching. I had to laugh and glanced over my shoulder to make sure she couldn't hear me.

"She's different," he said.

"She was brought up by different relatives."

"And to be sure there's no surprise in that."

I was torn between embarrassment and loyalty to Lizzie. "If she's not careful, she's going to turn out like our mother." The instant I said that, I wished I hadn't.

"Oh? And how did your mother turn out?"

"I'd rather not say."

"I can see that." He gave me another of those penetrating looks. "Perhaps it's time I knew more about your sainted mother."

"I doubt she's sainted." I sighed. "She died in prison."

"And she wasn't there for the robbing of the rich and giving to the poor, was she?"

"No."

"And is that the worst of it?"

"Some would say yes, and some would say no."

He stopped and backed away, holding my hand. He cocked his head to one side, squinted, and said, "Well, you look no different to me. I'm sure you'll look no different to me when I know the rest. And I will know the rest."

I stood and caught my breath, then caught it again, and then couldn't catch it at all because I was crying in great wracking sobs. He put his arms around me and held me while I sobbed. I don't know how long we stood there like that before I became aware that people were staring at us as they walked by. I straightened and said, "I'm sorry, I—"

"And so you should be." He interrupted. "All those nosy people now think I'm a strangler of young hat shop girls."

That produced a laugh on top of the last of my sobs, which in turn almost choked me.

"Let's walk on. These good people should know you're at the least able to walk."

We did. In silence.

We shared a bit of beer from an Irish girl selling it from a barrel. I would rather have had lemonade, but nobody sold that on the streets in the winter.

"I've never told anyone else that."

"'Tis not the sort of thing one boasts about on first acquaintance."

I sighed. "Or ever."

"'Tis what worries you about your sister."

"Yes." *And about myself,* I thought, though I didn't say that.

"There's very little you can do."

"I know."

"I'm just curious, mind," he said after a pause. "Which one of you looks more like your mother, you or your sister?"

"Oh, Lizzie, easily. Our mother was short, with dark hair and dark eyes, and a bit plump, just like Lizzie. Until the end."

"So she became thin in the prison, then?"

Jimmy waited. I knew he was wheedling my story from me. I told myself he could hear it from me or from Maeve.and I thought it would be better coming from me.

"She was in prison because she stole from a customer. My mother sold herself in the Five Points."

"I see."

"She didn't start out that way. It was the drink and us leaving her that did it."

"You left her? You and your sister?"

I sighed and looked down at my hands in my lap.

"My father took us away. My stepfather, really."

"And he left you with Julia."

"Yes, and Lizzie with some other relations."

"'Tis a simple enough story," he said gently.

"But that's not all of it. My mother wrote a book."

"Did she, bedad?"

If I weren't so upset, I'd have laughed. It was a bigger surprise to him that she'd written a book than it was she was a thief and a whore.

"A very scandalous book. She said she'd been seduced by priests and that she bore a child."

It was the first time I'd seen him at a loss for words.

I said simply, "I'm the child."

"You're the child of a priest?"

"I don't even know!" I wrenched away from him. "She told people she was a nun. Maybe she was, and maybe she wasn't. People believed her because they wanted to believe her—because they want to think priests are wicked and Catholics are wicked. She told me so many stories about who my father was that I didn't know which one to believe. I still don't know. But I do know they said that however I was conceived, I was a child arising from infamy. How's that for an introduction?"

"It does mean the meetin' of your family won't be complicated."

I did laugh at that, but not for long. "Jimmy, her story is everywhere. Everyone knows who Maria Monk was."

"Oh." He paused. "To be sure I've heard the name. Didn't think she was even a real person."

"She was real enough. And she's everywhere. We could find her book today if we went to a bookseller's. Here, come into this place and I'll show you."

We did. It only took a few minutes.

"Here it is," I whispered and handed him a copy of *The Awful Disclosures of Maria Monk*.

"Sure. I've heard of this, but I couldn't have said who she was or what she said."

I watched his face as he leafed through the book. He read a passage. Then his eyebrows shot up. He quickly shut the book and replaced it.

"You see what I mean?" I asked.

He nodded, and we left quickly.

"That's strong stuff and no mistake," he said. "Whoof." He blew out a noisy breath.

We walked in silence for a few minutes, and then he said,

"'Tis something to keep quiet. But, pet, how can you be going to the Mass to be seeing the priests and being with the people who believe they are holy men and your mother a monster?"

"I often wonder what they'd think if they knew who I was."

"I'll not be caring what they think. I know what I think."

He put his arms around me and drew me in firmly, gazing at my face. Then he leaned in for a long, slow kiss. Then a smile, another little kiss, and he drew my hand firmly into his arm, and we walked on.

Well, he might have walked. I floated. I had told him. He knew, and it made no difference. Whatever had pressed me to earth had lifted. My heart swelled up and pushed tears into my eyes again.

He turned to me questioningly. "Tears, is it?"

"I'm just so happy."

"'Tis a relief, that is. Can't be having a woman who leaks."

CHAPTER 16

O N A BLOWY, UNSETTLED DAY IN FEBRUARY, JIMMY AND I walked down to the docks where the seafaring ships came in. He pointed to the sorriest-looking old creaker and said, "That'll be carrying some more of the children of the Gael."

"How do you know?" I asked.

"'Tis by the look of her," he answered. "They use the sorriest of old slave ships to carry the Irish. The good ones carry the tay, because the tay is a sensitive cargo, picks up smells and gets ruint if it's wet. Men, women, and children can get wet without getting ruint. We all got wet on the *Ellen Keane,* a coffin ship if ever there was one.

"Think of it, pet. Even the captain of a slave ship cares if his cargo gets there, because he gets no money 'til those poor souls are sold. And while I'm not saying a slave has it better, not by a long chalk, the captain of a coffin ship doesn't have to care if his cargo gets there alive, because he's already been paid their passage. Almost everyone on the *Ellen Keane* died of the typhus, the ship fayver.

"Patrick died of it. They threw his body overboard. So many of the crew died or sickened that the captain needed me to sail the ship, and that was dead lucky. I got crew's rations, even though they weren't much better than those for the passengers. I was on watch, up in the rigging, when we got to Canada. It was night, and we dropped anchor in the mouth of the St. Lawrence. I clung there, looking at the land. I was so glad to see it, so glad to think I could get off the stinking ship, onto land, find work and food. Then I saw this shapeless white thing drift out past the ship, and I saw there were more of them in the water, drifting out to sea. Finally, one floated near to me, and I could see what it was. It rolled over and I saw a dead woman's face floating in the moonlight. All those white things were dead bodies. Other ships were throwing them overboard before they tried to land. T'was my grand welcome to the new world—dead bodies floating by in the moonlight on the St. Lawrence River."

He'd lived in Quebec for a couple years, working as a grocer's boy and living in the shop. "Then I made me way down the Hudson to this grand city, walked to the Five Points, and found me fellow Sligo-man Finn Malone. We got a group of the lads together and went west to work on the railroad."

They learned to stick together, and they still stuck together when most of them came back to New York. They got into the hurly-burly of politics, which was how Finn had been able to get his job as a policeman.

It surprised me, although it probably shouldn't have, that the two of them turned up one Wednesday evening, cut and bruised and in high spirits. They waved off all offers of treatment and said there was a celebration at Mr. Matthew Brennan's new saloon, and would the ladies care to accompany them? Within minutes, we all had our bonnets on and were walking quickly toward Mr. Brennan's on Pearl Street.

Mr. Brennan was fast becoming an important power in politics in the Sixth Ward, which included the Five Points. He had started as a lieutenant of meetings in Dooley's saloon, and was now Sixth Ward police captain. There had been a Sixth

Ward caucus, an almighty brawl, the night before to select a candidate for alderman. Jimmy and Finn had fought for Mr. Brennan's candidate, and his candidate won.

"Finn Malone," said Jimmy, shaking his head in mock disapproval, "you should never have kicked that poor gentleman's teeth out."

"He has more," replied Finn, "and you broke that poor man's fingers."

"I broke no man's fingers."

"To be sure you did. That's the way you break a Kerryman's fingers. You punch him in the nose."

With a few more descriptions of head-breaking, eye-gouging, and other political activities, we soon were walking through the grand polished-wood doors of Brennan's. Although it was early, the place was already filled with cigar smoke and almost as full of people. Political saloons were generous with food, and Brennan's offered banks of oysters, ham, and chicken for the taking. Mr. Brennan himself stood near the door, smoking a cigar and greeting everyone as they came in. He was a tall, barrel-chested man, with curly dark hair and a dark mustache.

"Mr. Malone! You and your friend here acquitted yourselves well last night. You'll make a fine constable." He chucked Kathleen under the chin. "Then you'll marry this beauty, will you?"

"If she'll have me, sir," said Finn.

"Any girl in New York will have a policeman. And you, Mr. O'Dea, well done! You and the ladies are most welcome."

We started on the oysters and got a bit of beer. All around us, the men were talking about last night's punch-up and others they had been in.

Mr. Brennan held up his arms for quiet, and immediately, the whole room was silent and attentive.

"What's the matter with you lads? You look like you've been in a fight!"

A roar of laughter answered him.

131

"Brennan's lads have done some fine work, and I have to say I'm glad it wasn't done at Brennan's."

A ripple of laughter.

"But don't worry, I'll be taking care of Mr. Brannigan's needs to replace his furniture and his drinking jars. Mind you, some of those drinking jars did some good service on some stubborn heads."

An appreciative murmur.

"And this battle won't be the last. You all know that. We're driving these Yankees out of the Sixth Ward, but they'll not be going quietly." He said some things in Irish about the battles of the hero Cuchulain and then went back to English.

"Now, you've heard some of the things they say to get people to turn against us. They say we're taking their jobs. All we're wanting is to live. Yes, every good man wants a job of work. If someone else has got it—well then, maybe we are taking their jobs!"

Laughter and shouts of agreement.

"And they say we're after taking the power from them, the power to run the city, to take care of our own fires and our own policing. And well, listen to me!" He slapped his chest in mock amazement. "Bless my soul, but that's true as well!"

Laughter, applause, and thumping of the bar and tables.

"But you know what they call us: niggers turned inside out. They say we're apes, and worse. And have you seen these?" He held up a couple handbills and pamphlets. "See this? They say we're part of a Catholic plot to bring kings and queens to America, that it's us and His Holiness the Pope doing it together." He held up a handbill showing a hydra with two of its heads wearing crowns, and the third being the ape-like Irishman we saw drawn everywhere.

"And you know who they're bringing back again?" He held up a book. "Maria Monk! If ye've been here as long as I have, you remember her and her lies and her babies. Pretended she was a Sister. Pretended she was wedded to God, and she was wedded to no one. But she still had herself two little bastard children. Said they were children of priests. She was a liar, and everyone with any sense knew she was a liar. You remember the night they dug up the graves at St. Patrick's—remember that night?" A few of the older heads were nodding. "It was all because of her—and she's back."

While I was in a position to contradict his last statement, I felt too sick to my stomach to do anything. Jimmy moved closer to me.

Matthew Brennan went on. "Watch out tonight. We've won this time, but they'll be after us again, and there's no trick so low that they won't use it. When you go to your homes tonight, go in groups—no fewer than four men in any group."

He paused and looked around the room to make sure his order was understood. Then he smiled. "Now then, let's have some music and enjoy ourselves. You're good lads, and you and your fine ladies are welcome at Brennan's."

The fiddlers struck up, chairs and tables were scraped across the boards to clear the floor for dancing, and soon, men and women had formed up in two lines. As I faced Jimmy and the dance began, I still had that sinking feeling in my stomach. The liveliness of the music and the dance, and the sheer joy of being with Jimmy helped lift it for a while.

Jimmy took turns dancing with the other women—including Maeve, whose face lit up when he asked her. Then, when they finished dancing, he escorted her back to her seat and walked toward me.

Maeve shot me a look of pure poison.

CHAPTER 17

THE NEXT AFTERNOON, LIZZIE TURNED UP IN OUR SHOP, disheveled and sobbing. She'd lost her place at Mrs. Bourget's.

"Lizzie, what happened? I thought you were doing so well there."

"I thought so, too. But Mrs. Bourget found a note I wrote to a man."

Well, I thought, *that was probably indiscreet. But it sounds harmless enough.* "What man?"

"Mr. Eckel. He came in with his cousin to purchase some ribbons for an aunt. Then he came back just to talk with me. And he wrote me a note saying how pleasant I was. I wrote him back and said his presence delighted me."

"It was a bit forward, but I don't see why she'd turn you out."

She started to cry again. "I misspelled presence."

"What?"

"I misspelled presence!" she shouted. "It's so stupid! Mrs. Bourget read it, and she thought I meant the kind of presents you give people!"

"Lizzie, didn't she let you explain?"

She gave her head an angry shake. "She didn't believe me."

134

My sister had nowhere else to go. There was nothing else to do but ask Mrs. O'Hanrahan if Lizzie could stay with me. She agreed to one night and one night only. "Her reputation is damaged. I cannot have her indiscretions reflect on us."

That night, Lizzie squeezed in with Kathleen and me and woke up slowly the next morning.

She offered brief thanks to Mrs. O'Hanrahan and gave me a hug. "Don't worry. I'll find something."

How could she be so confident? I was afraid for her and afraid for me—afraid that by nightfall, we'd both be out on the street with nowhere to go, and the happy chatter in the shop just left me feeling so knotted up that I thought something would burst.

That evening at closing time, she was back to let me know she had a place at a shop in the Bowery and would be sharing quarters behind the shop with the owner and another girl. *And who else will share those quarters?* I thought. I was so afraid for her—but the amazing Lizzie just gave a cheery wave and bounced out of the shop.

How could I have been surprised when Mr. Eckel turned up? There he was the next morning, asking for Lizzie. I stood there and actually gawked at him. He said he understood he had a part in her dismissal and wanted to be sure she was well.

He didn't look like much of a rake to me. Maybe I expected some over-oiled gent who twirled his mustaches and sneered. Mr. Eckel was pale and slight, with sad, watery-grey eyes. He hardly seemed like a Lochinvar who would sweep her away to a glowing future, but he appeared harmless enough. He was dressed in gentleman's clothes, and he assured me his intentions toward her were honorable. What else did I expect him to say? I gave him the name of the shop in the Bowery and wished him well.

When I saw Jimmy next, I told him what had happened. But he hardly seemed to be listening. "Pet," he said, "'tis news of my own I'm thinking on. I've had word from a mate of mine from the building of the railroad, and I'm off tomorrow to Balty-more."

"When will you be back?"

"There's the devil of it," he answered. "'Tis that I don't know yet. I'm going to see about a job of work with the Balty-more and Ohio—a good job, mechanic's work. T'isn't me mate that's hiring, but a friend. It may be taking a few days, or a few weeks, to sort it out."

We walked back to the shop in silence. He gave me a distracted kiss, and I stood watching him go, thinking things were changing fast and wondering if that would be the last time I ever saw him. I shook my head to rattle out the thought. *I can trust him,* I told myself.

No, said a nagging little voice inside. *You'll be alone. You'll be out.*

I was so distracted that I walked all the way into the shop before I realized Mrs. O'Hanrahan was standing there waiting for me, along with Maeve and Mrs. McGonagle. Mrs. McGonagle looked upset and embarrassed, which surprised me. Mrs. O'Hanrahan's face was a mask. But Maeve's eyes were blazing, smoky, and triumphant.

Mrs. O'Hanrahan spoke first in a low, steady voice—which, along with her folded arms, told me she was very angry.

"Vera," she said, "there is something important you have neglected to tell me these four years you've been under my roof."

"You didn't tell her your mother was the evilest liar that ever wore skirts, did you?" Maeve burst out. "Nor that she was that drunken whore who pretended to be a holy sister! That you're a bastard from that—"

"Shush, Maeve," her mother said.

"I'll not shush, Ma! You've been shushing me ever since we saw her. She's preened and paraded herself around like she's a queen, good men following her like dogs, like the bitch she is! She's a slut and a liar, just like her mother!"

"That is enough, Maeve," said Mrs. O'Hanrahan without

taking her eyes off me. "Vera, are you the daughter of Maria Monk?"

I knew it was no good trying to avoid a direct answer, so I gave it. "Yes, mistress, I am."

"Why didn't you tell me?"

"I knew you wouldn't take me if I did."

"That's true enough," she said. After a moment, she added, "You know I cannot keep you here."

"Mrs. O'Hanrahan," I pleaded, "I was taken from my mother when I was ten. My cousin brought me up, and she's a respectable woman. I've done good work for you, and I've behaved well. Can't you keep me? Can't you see why I couldn't tell you?"

"Don't listen to her!" Maeve burst out. "Don't you see she's a lying, wheedling little slut? What is Seamus O'Dea going to say when he finds out, little missy?"

"He knows already," I said quietly. "And he's gone away."

"Well, that's why, then, isn't it?" Maeve sneered triumphantly. "He'll not be coming back to you, then, will he?"

Mrs. O'Hanrahan folded her lips together, and then said to the McGonagle women, "I would like to have the rest of this conversation in private, please."

Maeve glared, but her mother pulled her out the door.

"You have made a fool of me," said Mrs. O'Hanrahan, quietly. "Your mother's name is known far and wide to all good Catholics as a woman who did the work of the devil. And you have bamboozled me into sheltering you, teaching you a craft, taking you into my home. And I had to be told by someone else who you are."

"I can't expect you to forgive me," I said. "I'll get my things and go."

"No," she said and heaved a deep sigh.

What? I looked up.

She didn't look forgiving.

"I have one girl just married and one about to marry. And

everyone else in the city, it seems, is about to marry. I can't spare you until Easter is done. But the day after our Lord arises, mark my words, you will arise too, and go out of here. Do you understand me?"

"Yes, mistress, I do. I've tried to be a good worker," I ventured.

"Don't go expecting praise from me, girl. I'm only keeping you as long as I must, and then you're gone."

CHAPTER 18

*K*ATHLEEN SLIPPED INTO BED WITH ME THAT NIGHT, READY
to gossip. "Ma told me about your ma," she whispered.
"Did she really do everything they say she did?"

"I don't know," I whispered back, tears starting to come.
"I've never really known."

"I never thought about doing it with a priest." She settled
back with a delicious shiver.

"Kathleen," said her mother. "Come sleep with me. You'll
not sleep in the bed with that one."

"Ma!" she protested.

"I mean it, Kathleen," her mother insisted.

Kathleen patted me on the shoulder and shuffled in the
dark across to her mother's bed.

I lay alone, tears dripping into my ears.

My head ached the next morning as I sat making rosebuds and lace ornaments for tea bonnets, opera hats, and,
oddly enough, the shifts and corsets of the parlor girls. We did
the work on their undergarments covertly in the back of the
shop, and Kathleen and I had always found the idea of having
one's breasts or buttocks framed with roses very stimulating.
On other days, I'd have held them up to myself when Mrs.

O'Hanrahan wasn't looking, and arch my eyebrows at Kathleen, and we'd stifle our giggles. This particular morning, I didn't feel like giggling.

I met with Lizzie a few days later to see how she was doing, and to see if she knew anywhere in the Bowery that might need a ribbon girl.

"I have wonderful news," she crowed. "Mr. Eckel wants me to marry him! We're being married next week, and I want you to come!"

"And what does his family think?" I asked.

"Oh, that's pretty!" she huffed. "I tell you I'm getting married, and you don't say something nice. You ask what his family thinks because you think they'll disapprove."

"Well, do they?" I asked her.

"They're going to pay for me to go to school and learn to act proper."

"So they do disapprove," I said.

"Why are you being so awful? I'm your sister, and I'm telling you a rich man is going to marry me, and you're just saying mean things." She looked ready to cry. "You're jealous, aren't you? I finally have something good happen to me, something really good, and you can't bear it. Well, let me tell you something, Miss Perfect, with your perfect manners and your perfect speech and your, your perfect—spelling! He loves me. Everybody else always liked you better. But he loves *me!*"

"Does he know who your mother was? Does his family know?"

"No! And you're not going to tell him!" She did cry then—tears of rage and frustration.

"Lizzie, I'm sorry." I tried to put my arms around her, but she pulled away. "Lizzie, please, you're right," I went on. "I should have said that your news is wonderful. I hope you'll be very happy. I do want you to be happy."

She swiped at her cheeks and spoke quietly. "I have a right to be happy. I have a right to have people love me."

"Of course you do."

"Our mother liked you better than me. My own father liked you better than me, and he wasn't even your father. You got to stay with your cross-eyed Julia, and she sent me away."

"Lizzie, you broke eggs. You wouldn't behave. She had to send you away."

"No, she didn't. She could have taken a slipper to me, and I'd have behaved."

I sighed. "Lizzie, that was years ago, and there's nothing we can do about it now. I'm sorry I was hateful. It's just—someone's told on me, and I'm about to be out on my elbows."

"Who told? Who knew about us?"

"You remember the McGonagles from Goerck Street? Tommy married one of the O'Hanrahan girls. You remember hateful Maeve? Well, she's still hateful, and she told."

"You'll just have to work in the Bowery like your low-bred little sister, won't you? You can have my place when I get married."

That was mean. "Lizzie, please—don't let's fight. You're all the family I have besides Julia, and she's not really my family. Can you give me a hug, and we'll talk about Mr. Eckel?"

She let out a heavy sigh and held out her arms. We embraced for a moment and then started to walk.

"You know the first part of the story," she said. "When we first started to keep company, he said something about being a freethinker, and I told him I was one, too."

"You are?" Here was another surprise: Lizzie a deep philosophical thinker.

"Yes, I've thought that way for years. But I have to tell you something strange. Soon after I came to the city, I went by a convent, and I went in and prayed for—for forgiveness, for what our mother did—you know, writing her book of lies. I started to cry, and a nun came over to talk to me. I knew I'd have to tell her about our mother, and I was afraid, so I ran away. I'd love to be forgiven."

"We didn't do anything but be born," I said.

"I know. But we're still being punished, aren't we? Maybe if we got forgiveness, we wouldn't be punished anymore."

"We don't know that our mother did anything wrong," I said.

"Yes, we do! You were either a child of a priest or someone else, and we don't even know who. She still wasn't married when she had me. And she always told lies. You know that. And she was horrible to us. She made us go get her drink, and she beat us. She was horrible, Vera! How can you even defend her? She probably made up lies about really good people, people who were trying to help her. I want to be forgiven. I want to feel I'm not worthless. Don't you understand that?"

"You're not worthless. Don't ever think you are." I sighed. "I'm going to have to get back to the shop. When will you be married, and where will the wedding be?"

"It will be soon, and it will be in the civil registry office because Mr. Eckel doesn't believe in clergy."

⁓

THAT NIGHT AS I LAY by myself on my musty straw pallet, I thought about my sister. I did envy her. She had found a Prince Charming to take her away. A rather weak-looking Prince Charming, with watery eyes, to be sure—but a rich man with his own carriage.

I turned over. It wasn't fair. I had found Jimmy, but he might not be coming back to me. I'd done everything right, everything I was supposed to do. I'd been good and proper, but nasty, stinking Maeve was getting me thrown out on the street. My mother. My poor mother. She really loved me. Maybe all those things did happen to her, and she turned out to be crazy and horrible because those things *did* happen to her, just as Julia said. And maybe I would turn out to be crazy and horrible just like her.

I fell into a restless sleep and dreamed ugly dreams. I came up behind my mother, and when she turned her face to me, it was Maeve's face. Then it was my mother's face again, crying, and I woke up crying, too.

CHAPTER 19

*L*IZZIE'S WEDDING WAS ON A TUESDAY MORNING. IT WAS NO more remarkable than buying a few eggs. In fact, we had fresh eggs so seldom, I would have found eggs more exciting. They were married in a clerk's office with one of Mr. Eckel's friends and me as witnesses. After they had exchanged their vows, and we signed the paper, the friend excused himself, saying he had a business appointment. I went for a tavern lunch with the new bride and groom. And that was that. They were married.

As we walked toward the tavern, I thought ungraciously that my sister's wedding dress was a particularly unbecoming shade of blue—though she was obviously very proud of it.

"Mr. Eckel bought me my wedding dress." She turned around for me to admire it. "He says when I am older, I may wear silk."

I sat across from my new brother-in-law and tried to get used to the idea that I *had* a brother-in-law. His watery eyes and weak chin did not inspire confidence. Perhaps I really wanted evidence that he was a scoundrel and I'd been right about him. He seemed to be neither prince nor scoundrel, but he could hardly take his eyes off my sister. He treated her every serious remark with reverence and her silly remarks with great laughter, which sometimes reduced him to coughing. He seemed besotted with her, which was reassuring. That is, at first he seemed besotted with her—but he drank far too much, and was, by the end of the meal, just besotted.

But what a meal! I ate oysters, cold lobster, roast chickens, and squab; there were meat pies, and sausages, and two kinds of wine. There was fresh fruit, even oranges. And there was as much lemonade as I could drink, all deliciously cold. When I got up to go, my stomach sloshed.

Mr. Eckel paid the score in full, with generous tips, right in front of us. He paid more for that meal than I had earned in six months. He hailed a hansom cab for the three of us. Almost as soon as we were seated, his head fell forward, and he began to snore.

Lizzie didn't appear to be at all embarrassed, but whispered happily, "We're going to live in Philadelphia with an aunt of his while I go to school! Isn't it grand? I know he isn't very handsome, but he is rich and he loves me. He gives me books to read and talk about with him, and he thinks I'm very clever. It's like a dream, isn't it? It's like a miracle!"

"Lizzie, I do hope it turns out to be a miracle for you. And I love you with all my heart." We gave each other a hug and a kiss, and I was out on the street in front of the shop, watching the cab pull away down the street.

I missed Jimmy. *It's been almost three weeks,* I thought, *and I haven't heard from him. But paper is dear. Still, even a scrap would be nice.*

~∽~

KATHLEEN WAS MARRIED THE FOLLOWING Saturday, with ribbons on her bonnet that she'd stolen from Mr. Stewart's shop. I wasn't invited to the wedding, but left to tend the hat shop. It was quiet, and I sat making flowers and bows that would go on fancy bonnets in autumn. *I'll be long gone by then,* I thought, *but I don't know where.*

The shadows were getting long and a breeze was stirring when the shop door opened. And there was Jimmy, out of breath. Before I could even believe he was there, he put his arms around me, picked me up off the floor, and swept me around a couple of circles.

"Oh, pet, we're off to Balty-more," he said, and put me down. "Ye're heavier than you look, you know that?"

I didn't feel like laughing. "I didn't know if I'd ever see you again."

He looked totally bewildered. "And why would you be thinkin' such a thing?"

"I don't know. You didn't write to me. And," I added in a very small voice, "people leave me all the time."

"Perhaps I did, but I'm back. And that's a fine way to treat a man who has come to rescue you and carry you away to be his wife."

"Say that again."

He shrugged, smiling. "Marry me."

"Well, I'll have to think about it."

He took a step back, and looked at me, amazed. I could see him thinking. *I've come back,* he was probably saying to himself, *I have a job of work, I've asked her to marry me, and she has to think about it?*

I could feel my mouth twitching. "It's an important decision," I added. Then I said, "I've thought about it. Yes." My laughter burst out, and he joined me.

"Well, 'tis a load off my mind, that is," he finally said. "Will you close up the shop, the soon-to-be Mrs. O'Dea, and come with me to Brennan's?"

"I'll close up and come with you, but we can't go to Brennan's. That's where the O'Hanrahans are."

"I do know that," he answered. "I arrived back too late for the wedding of my good friend and comrade Finn Malone. But to be sure, I shall dance and wish him well—and I don't wish to give good wishes without you, pet. So put a brave face on it, and let's go."

So we did. All during the walk to Brennan's, my good fortune was sinking in, even though I couldn't quite bring myself to believe all of it. Then, of course, there was my fear of Mrs. O'Hanrahan and what she would say once I brazenly presented myself at the celebration of her daughter's wedding. I hugged Jimmy's arm to me and felt braver. What could she do to me besides dismiss me? And she'd already done that.

We didn't even see them at first. We arrived at Brennan's— always crowded of a Saturday—and Mr. Brennan himself came over to greet us, and pulled us over to a corner to talk with Jimmy.

Mr. Brennan stroked his glossy mustache down by the sides of his mouth and said, "You're a good man to be going to Mob Town." Baltimore was famous for its mobs and its riots. "'Tis a troublesome time to go. They've elected a Know-Nothing mayor."

I laughed, and he glanced at me with some annoyance that a mere young woman had dared interrupt him. "'Tis no laughing matter, miss," he said. "I'm not reflecting on the man's ignorance, but telling your husband something important. The Know-Nothings are dangerous men. They are secret societies, and when they're asked about their associations one with another, they insist they know nothing. But they are sworn to keep all but the native-born and Protestant out of political office and out of good jobs. Their tools are threats, beatings, riots, secrecy, and murder. In Mob Town they have busted up stores and presses and beaten good Irishmen and Germans who try to vote. One of their gangs is called the Blood Tubs because they keep bowls of pigs' blood to mark their victims. 'Tis a smelly, ugly business."

He turned back to Jimmy. "There's a good man named John

Boyle who looks after things around the Mount Clare yards for the railroad there."

"The Baltimore and Ohio," Jimmy supplied. "I've met John Boyle, and I know what he wants me to do."

I glanced at Jimmy in alarm. *I don't know exactly what he wants you to do*, I thought, *but it sounds dangerous.*

Mr. Brennan nodded. "He'll send someone for you when you get to Baltimore. They'll help you out."

They shook hands, and Mr. Brennan nodded to me. "Will you be going as well, miss?"

"Yes, sir, I will."

"We're marrying soon," said Jimmy.

Mr. Brennan nodded. "Well, you've a good man there, miss. Look after him."

"Yes, Mr. Brennan, I shall."

As he moved off, I looked at Jimmy and grimaced to show him I knew I'd put my foot in it with Mr. Brennan. He smiled and took my hand. "The big men do like us to be struck dumb with awe in their presence. Any sensible person would laugh at hearing someone described as a Know-Nothing."

"Jimmy, it's going to be dangerous in Baltimore, isn't it?"

"A bit." He took my hand. "It's what I've done all along, pet."

"But not in a place called Mob Town."

"They say the same things about the Five Points, pet, and about polly-tics here. I've survived nicely all these years, and you've taken a stroll or two around town yourself and lived to tell the tale. Now, let's go congratulate the happy couple and have a dance."

Finn and Kathleen looked beautiful; he had never looked so proud and handsome, and she was radiant. She tossed a defiant glance at her mother and then gave me a hearty hug. "Vera, I am glad to see you. I hated to think of leaving the poor cinder-girl at home."

I gave a glance at Mrs. O'Hanrahan and noticed she looked oddly serene.

"Ma's had a drop," Kathleen confided with a smile. "She'll not behead you here."

The fiddlers struck up, and we lined up to dance a reel. After a minute or two, I saw nothing but Jimmy's smile and heard nothing but the fiddle music, and I lifted up and danced as I hadn't danced since I was ten. My feet flew as I danced and laughed and shouted for joy at my deliverance.

CHAPTER 20

I DIDN'T KNOW THE FIRST THING ABOUT GETTING MARRIED. Well, I suppose I did know the first thing, which was finding someone to do it with. But I'd already done that. I'd heard about marriage licenses, but didn't know how to get one. And what about Julia? I didn't need her permission, but I very much wanted her approval. She'd never met Jimmy. And I'd have to go to Baltimore—how would we live, and, and, and …

And where would we be married? I worried an entire night away about whether he'd want to be married in a Catholic church.

I asked him the next day, and he looked at me quietly for a moment and said, "I took the Protestant soup, pet. 'Tis likely they'll not marry either of us to anyone."

A Protestant church, then? He laughed. "I've never been to one of them, nayther."

So it was the clerk's office for us. I wrote quickly to Julia, and she replied just as quickly. So within a week, we were standing in the clerk's office, with Julia, Kathleen, and Finn Malone for our witnesses.

It was hot in the clerk's office and only slightly cooler at Brennan's. We bought some small beer and had some of the bread and roast beef that came free with the beer. Julia looked very small and sad at the beginning but brightened as Jimmy charmed her. She had brought me a featherbed and a new quilt, all rolled up together—and she'd toted the bundle all the way there on the omnibus, the ferry, and the walk from the ferry. Kathleen handed me a hatbox with three hats in it. Two of them were my own work, and one was a beautiful little bonnet she had made. A few of the rosebuds on it were made from ribbons we'd stolen from Mr. Stewart.

"Ma will want to skin me for giving you wares from the shop," she said, her eyes sparkling. "But I knew you'd need samples of your work. And I wanted you to have a gift."

These gifts were so generous they made my eyes mist over, and I choked up a little thanking them, and then we all laughed. I gave Kathleen a long hug when we said goodbye at the door to the tavern, and Jimmy and I walked with Julia to the ferryboat. I held her arm and talked softly to her.

"Julia, I owe you more than I can ever repay. Thank you so much for coming today, and I am only sorry I'm going so far away."

"Hmp. Well, I'm sorry, too. I am proud of how you turned out, though. You'll be able to take care of yourself, and that's what I hoped for."

Oh, I thought. *Right. Not that I would get married and live happily ever after. Oh well.*

I hugged her arm to me. "I'll write."

"So will I. Sorry you won't be coming to me this summer. Have a whole pot of honey going begging."

"I know. But it can't be helped. We have to be in Baltimore day after tomorrow."

She nodded. We embraced for a long while, and then I watched her—a thin, old woman slowly walking up the gangplank onto the ferry. She didn't look back.

We went back to Brennan's, for Mr. Brennan's wedding gift to us was a private room for the night.

It was dark but still stifling hot when we went up to the

room. We opened the shutters and the window and waited for the room to air out. The practical and obvious thing for us to do would have been to take off our clothes immediately, but I was suddenly too shy.

Still, I was eager and curious. He took off his jacket. I unpinned my bonnet and took down my hair. He put his hands gently on the outside of my shoulders and kissed me—a delicious, soft, lingering kiss. I slipped my arms around him and kissed him back, and then we blended into one wet kiss, and I was panting.

His hands slid down my back to my bottom, and he held me against him while I unbuttoned his shirt and slipped it off. There was much wriggling and giggling as I showed him how to get my bodice off, then slipped off my own skirt and petticoat. I fumbled with the trouser buttons, so he took off his own trousers. Then he moved my shift down off my shoulders and my breasts, and I rubbed against him as he kissed my breasts, and my shift fell down around my feet.

I pulled him to the bed and felt his hand moving between my legs. His kisses were warm and exciting on my neck and breasts. Then suddenly, he was thrusting inside me, and just as suddenly, it was all over. We lay sprawled and sweaty in the dim light, and he fell asleep stroking my hair.

I lay on my back, staring into the dark, feeling surprised, then disappointed, then lonely as my new husband drifted into a sleep beside me. The heaviness deep in my belly and restlessness between my legs kept me awake much of the night. I dozed a little before morning and awoke at dawn.

Jimmy was sleeping with his back to me, and the morning sun on his bare shoulder made it look like a sculpture. His skin was smooth and fair, with a soft radiance under it, with hundreds of little gold freckles. I touched his shoulder—the skin was velvety and soft and the muscle under it hard. Then I kissed his shoulder and smelled his scent—sweet and faintly musky. I moved my hands along his back and kissed him along his back, too. His flesh was delicious, and I began to lick it, for I loved his smell and the salty taste of his flesh.

I became greedier, kissing and licking and smelling and moving my hands and mouth down his back. The shape of his buttocks delighted me; as I moved my hands over them, he stirred and rolled over on his back. I started to kiss his chest, then his belly, licking more than kissing as I moved down his body. His man's tool was erect, and I kissed and licked that, too, then moved up his body to kiss his lips. He rolled me over and entered me, and this time there was a pulsing inside me, a power that made me moan and gasp. This time, too, it was over in a few minutes, but as I lay panting with him still on top of me, it was as if I were landing gently after a flight through the sky.

After a while, Jimmy got up and gave me a strange look. He dressed silently and said gently, "Come on up, pet. We need to go."

I arose and scrambled for my clothes and started to get dressed, too. He was so quiet and preoccupied. What was the matter? Was he angry?

"Jimmy?"

"What, pet?"

"Should I not have done what I did?"

He stopped for a moment. "No, I ... You surprised me."

That was reasonable enough. I had surprised myself. Maybe I would never have thought of such a thing if I hadn't heard the whores talking about it. As we went quietly down through the tavern, not waking anyone, another worry grew in my mind. The way I had behaved was wrong. That was what it meant to be lewd and wanton—and evil. And I had really liked doing it. Maybe the whorehouse was where I belonged.

A heavy revulsion settled into the pit of my stomach and stayed there. We walked silently through the sticky, gray morning to the hat shop.

❦

IN SPITE OF THE EARLY hour, Kathleen and Mrs. O'Hanrahan were awake and in the shop; Finn Malone was there, too, to help us carry our possessions to the steamboat that would, in turn, take us to the railway station. We had a cup of tea in the back of the shop, and I suddenly realized this was probably the last cup of tea I would ever have in this little room—one that had become so cozy and familiar to me. My eyes teared up.

Kathleen appeared not to notice, but chattered away about how exciting it was that I was going on a railway train, and, oh, none of us had ever been on a railway train, and had I ever been out of the state of New York? I shook my head no, and suddenly began to be very frightened. What was I doing? I was leaving everything I knew to cross—how many? Three states? Four?— to go hundreds of miles away to a place called Mob Town, with a man who probably now wasn't at all sure he wanted me.

Kathleen hugged me, and I promised to write as soon as we had an address. Then Finn shouldered the bundle of bedding Julia had made, and picked up my box of hats and the carpetbag that held all my clothes. Mrs. O'Hanrahan glanced at the hatbox and at Kathleen, who lifted her head defiantly and gave her a smile. Jimmy carried his clothes and his tools, and off we went. Once more, I was crossing a river, taking a journey into a new life.

✺

ON THE STEAMBOAT CROSSING THE Hudson, Jimmy struck up a conversation with a German man who was also on his way to Baltimore. "Yah, Mob Town," he agreed. His name was Stahl; he had come from Baden, and, like so many others, had left after the troubles of 1848. He and Jimmy were soon talking about free public libraries, minimum wages, universal suffrage, and other such farfetched stuff.

I drifted into my own thoughts, watching the water grow wider between me and everything I'd ever known.

Mr. Stahl helped us with our bundles across the quay and over to the railway train. The wooden car we climbed into was much like an omnibus—except of course there were no horses, and there was a stove in the middle. No wonder railway carriages often caught fire.

I leaned out the window as I heard the locomotive start, and then was almost slammed to the floor as the train lurched forward. I sat down hard on the seat, and the train car began to rock as the engine gathered speed.

It was terrifying. I had never moved on anything that went faster than a horse could trot. We rocked crazily along, first at the speed of a trotting horse, then galloping, then at a speed surely faster than any horse could ever go. I grabbed Jimmy's arm. He put a calming hand on mine and smiled at me—but then went right on talking to his new German friend as we hurtled forward. Smoke and cinders blew in through the windows, and I hunched down and drew my shawl close around my head. The smoke and fumes from the locomotive made me feel sick.

It was unpleasant, to be sure, but before noon, we were at Trenton, where they unhitched the cars from the locomotive and put them on barges to float over the river. On the other side, the cars were hitched up to another locomotive, and we made a similar trip to Philadelphia. Then a cart ride through some of the town and on to the railway that would take us to Baltimore. Mr. Stahl treated us to a glass of beer—and a great treat it was, too, on our parched and sooty throats. Our faces were flecked with bits of soot, and my hair felt gritty at the scalp. When I scratched it, my fingernails filled with black grit.

The trip from Philadelphia to the Susquehanna River passed in a blur of speed, smoke, and exhaustion. Every now and then, Jimmy looked at me and asked, "All right, pet?" and I would nod, although I was sure my face was green.

He and our new companion conversed off and on. I remember very few of the things Mr. Stahl said, but two have stuck in my mind. One was a bit of outrageous gossip about Vice President King, who had died quite soon after his inauguration. "Ach," said Mr. Stahl, "Mr. King painted his face like a woman! 'Miss Nancy' the other senators called him, and his friend Mr. Buchanan was more than his friend!" Here he tapped a finger alongside his nose. "Mr. Buchanan is now secretary of the state, and he could be president some day!" He shook his head.

I tried to pay attention. I heard him say earnestly to Jimmy, "All the crowned heads of Europe are waiting for this country to fail. Our revolution scared them, and the French troubles made them shit their pants. And Napoleon! It took all of them to get rid of Napoleon and his citizen armies. But we were watching in Baden. Did you know we wrote our own constitution?"

No, I thought crossly, *and why would I care?* A tiny cinder landed on my face, and though I brushed it away quickly, the burn stung.

The two of them were still talking about politics when we reached the Susquehanna River.

The railway cars were again unhitched—Jimmy called it "uncoupled"—and floated across the river on barges. Our train was put back together behind another locomotive and we went on to Baltimore.

It was after ten and dark as Egypt when we reached Baltimore. Mr. Stahl had offered us lodging for the night, in the room above his print shop.

Oh, Jimmy, I thought, *please say no. I'll sleep on the station floor. I can't listen to this man anymore.*

Then a short, potbellied man walked up to us, took off his hat, and said, "Mr. Seamus O'Dea?"

"Me, is it? I'm Seamus O'Dea," said Jimmy.

"Mr. Charles Bump at your service," said the short man. He had a red, scaly scalp fringed by reddish hair and prominent, pale-green eyes. A slight gap separated his front teeth. "Mr. John Boyle asked me to come and meet you."

"Well," said Mr. Stahl, looking at the two of us as though we had somehow transmogrified before his eyes, "if Mr. Boyle is looking after the two of you, you do not need my shelter. I will bid you adieu."

"Mr. Stahl," said Jimmy quickly, holding out his hand, "we have enjoyed your company. We hope to enjoy more of it in the future." Mr. Stahl shook hands, tipped his hat to me, and walked off into the night.

Mr. Bump spoke up in a wheezy voice. "I've brought a cart. We've arranged for you to board at Mrs. Hecker's, over near the Mount Clare sheds. She's expecting your arrival tonight."

"That is welcome news indeed," I volunteered. The thought of our own bed, a good night's sleep, and so much uncertainty gone sounded wonderful to me.

Mr. Bump shouldered our roll of bedding, and we were loaded quickly into the cart. It was a relief to move slowly, listening to the clip-clop of the old horse's feet on the brick streets. We pulled up in front of a narrow house.

"This is our boarding house?" I asked of Mr. Bump.

"Yes, indeed," he said, bustling around the cart to help me down. "This is Mrs. Hecker's. Why do you ask?"

"Well, I ... it's made of brick. Only grand houses are made of brick. I don't think we can afford to live here."

Mr. Bump laughed a wheezy laugh. "Most houses in Baltimore are brick houses," he said. "Baltimore makes bricks, and the city requires their use. I live here. It is well within your means."

He climbed the two stone steps and knocked on the door. A stout, gray-haired lady came to the door with a half-knitted sock in her hand. "Get in," she said brusquely.

Two men sat smoking in the parlor. They nodded at us, but did not get up.

"Put down your bundles and come into the kitchen," Mrs. Hecker ordered.

We meekly obeyed. Her kitchen was large and clean, and a little hot from the enormous cookstove that stood in the middle.

"Sit." She indicated a large table surrounded by chairs. We sat.

She opened a pot that stood on the stove, and a savory cloud of steam wafted out. She ladled portions of dark stew onto tin plates and set them in front of us. Then she put three tin cups, a pitcher, and half a loaf of bread in front of us. "More stew in the pot," she said. "Come out when you finish."

I was famished; the stew tasted heavenly. The bread was stale but served well for sopping up gravy. And the pitcher held lemonade! For a few brief moments, I thought I'd found heaven. I ate greedily.

I looked at Jimmy as he ate, and felt the morning's apprehension come back. *He must be disgusted with me,* I thought.

If he were angry, he'd shown no signs of it. He finished up and looked at me. "Ready?" he said. I nodded, and we went back into the front room.

Mrs. Hecker led us to a room on the third floor. It had a small wardrobe, a bedstead with a straw pallet, and a washstand. She lit a small camphor lamp on the wall. "Four dollars a week," she said. "Two meals. Lunch pail's extra. Privy's down the back stairs, just outside." She poured cold water into the washstand basin, added some hot from the kettle, and strode out the door.

Jimmy and I shrugged at each other and unpacked our few belongings into the wardrobe. We undid the bedding and put the feather bed on top of the straw pallet.

Mrs. Hecker came back in the room with sheets and towels, gave Jimmy a push to get him out of the way, and indicated she and I would finish making the bed. We put on the rough sheets and Julia's quilts. She nodded and strode toward the door. "Breakfast at 6:30."

When Jimmy and I were left alone, we were suddenly shy. Jimmy wanted to let me be first to use the wash water, but I said no. I wanted to wash my hair, too. He took off his jacket and shirt and washed quickly while I slowly took off my bonnet and took down my hair, which was gritty with soot. *My bonnet will need a good shake and a brushing,* I thought absently. Only the front of my hair was gritty. I took off my sleeves, then my bodice. I stank of coal smoke. As I washed out my hair and rinsed my face, I heard Jimmy slide off his trousers and lie on the bed.

I wrapped the towel around my head and sat on the bed. "Jimmy ..." I began. But I couldn't talk while I looking at him, so I stood and turned my back. "I'm sorry about this morning. I'm ashamed."

There was a silence. Then he said, "Come sit back down, pet. I'll not be talking to your back."

I sat down again, and we looked at each other.

"You surprised me," he said. "I thought you were innocent."

"I am. Or I was. I just wanted you so much, and I know it's disgusting."

"I didn't say that. I wouldn't say that. Look at me."

I did. He went on. "Men are more afraid of women than we like to let on. You surprised me."

What? Well, lustful women are scary, I thought. *The ugly old whores yelling at every man who passes by are frightening. I must be like that.*

My throat hurt, and I was afraid I would cry. Then I saw the sparkle back in his eyes. A slow smile lit up his face, and the sun rose again in my heart.

"'Tis fortunate for you, Mrs. O'Dea, that you've married a very brave man."

CHAPTER 21

*W*E MADE LOVE THAT NIGHT, MORE SLOWLY THAN THE first time. We were exhausted, of course, but we were young and just married. Once again, I felt that building passion and powerful release. I drifted off to sleep, snuggled against the warmth of my husband's body, and smiling in the dark.

When Jimmy got up and left early the next morning, I hardly stirred. I sank back into an exhausted sleep and woke only when the sun was high and the room hot. I used the chamber pot, dashed water on my face, and pulled on my clothes. I walked down the stairs to empty the chamber pot, and my steps echoed.

Mrs. Hecker appeared in the kitchen doorway. "You've missed breakfast, missy. It's time to pack a lunch for the men. I'll need your help since my hired girl ran off last week."

"Ran off?"

"With one of my boarders. That's why there's room for you and Mr. O'Dea." She gave me a peevish, squinty look. "How old are you? You don't look old enough to be married."

"I'm of age," I said, meeting her rudeness with a little edge of my own. "I'm seventeen. We're just married."

I thought she might say something nice, but she didn't. I asked her if I might have a bit of bread.

She jerked her head toward a loaf. "Knife's right by it," she said.

I cut off a piece of stiff bread and munched on it with my back to her. I thought she was being a little rude, considering Jimmy and I were paying her for room and board. It then occurred to me that if she wanted me to work, I would—but I wouldn't be paying her for the privilege. I washed down the bread with a dipper of water from a pail, dusted off my hands, and asked her what I could do.

We prepared the lunch pails with slices of bread and butter, bits of cheese, cold meat, and a few dried apples. We put on our hats—hers was a shapeless wad of black felt with a tired-looking rose on it—and carried the pails toward the Mount Clare yard.

Even from far down the street, we heard the clang of metal on metal, and smelled the acrid smoke from coal and the sharp scent of hot metal. Soon, the huge barnlike workshop loomed over us, so sooty black it looked angry. We joined a group of women and children gathered outside the door, who were also bringing food for the men. A couple vendors set up nearby—one with a barrel of beer, others with hot corn or bread and bacon. I peered around the women into the shed. It was a dark place lit only by fires, with dark, shadowy figures swarming around inside.

Out of the darkness walked the most beautiful man I'd ever seen in my life. He was tall and graceful, slim, with broad shoulders and wavy hair that was actually the color of gold. Yes, I know we speak of "golden hair" all the time—but it is usually flaxen or wheat-colored or sandy. But his was the color of the metal.

He stopped to look at me. "A new girl here, hah?" he asked. His eyes were bright green, like bottle glass with the sun shining through.

Two men from our boarding house jostled him from behind. "Oh, sorry, Bill. Didn't see you there, talking to Missus O'Dea. That's *missus*, Bill—as in married. To our new fella."

"Oh? That's how it is, then. So the new lad has a wifey, has he?" He put a hand under my chin. I turned my head away. He snorted, and then spat on the ground.

"The tough little Mick has a tough little wife, does he?" His green eyes looked deep into mine. "And she's a beauty." He moved off, giving me a backward glance, leaving me feeling angry and wildly stirred at the same time.

"Don't pay him any mind," said one of the men from our house. "I'm Danny Fitzgerald, and this is me brother Ralph." They looked like puppies with their big brown eyes and curly dark hair. "Beautiful Bill McCracken thinks he's the best gift the Lord gave the ladies." They took their pails from Mrs. Hecker and moved out into the sunshine of the yard.

The other men started coming out, all looking grimed and sweaty. Some kissed their wives or children; some seemed not to even acknowledge they were standing there.

Jimmy came out. His face was smudged with grease but he was grinning. He didn't kiss me, but took the pail with a squeeze of my hand. "A good morning's work and a pretty wife at the end of it," he said. "'Tis a good life so far."

"What do you do in there?"

"'Tis repairing that great beast we are." He pointed to a huge locomotive on tracks at the other side of the shed. "Crown sheet on the firebox overheated. The explosion from the firebox killed the fireman. They're making a new one over there while we take the old one out. No replacement for the good man, though."

"Why didn't they put a better one in it in the first place?" I asked.

He took a bite of bread and meat. "'Tis that we're just inventing these things, pet," he answered. "And they're devilish tricky machines. 'Tis not like we're making the carts that so many know how to make. These beasts are different every time they leave the shed."

I smiled at him, and for the first time, I was really impressed with what he was doing, and how proud he was of it. But I had domestic things on my mind.

"Jimmy," I said to him softly, "how much is Mrs. Hecker charging us for my room and board?"

"Four dollars the week. Five with the pail. Why?"

"She used to have a hired girl to help her. I'm thinking I'll do part of the work for my part of the room and board."

"Clever girl. Earn your keep." He gave my hand a quick squeeze.

I knew he was proud of me, too, for that.

He finished his food and wiped his hands on his trousers. "See you for dinner, then, clever girl."

He moved off to buy a dipper of beer from the vendor, and Mrs. Hecker and I gathered up the pails. We walked back toward the house, the pails clanking softly into us.

"Mrs. Hecker?"

She gave a short sound to indicate she'd heard me.

"I'm glad to help you with the men's meals."

"Nice of you. One of them is your husband."

Don't let her distract you, I told myself.

"You used to pay a hired girl to help you," I told her.

She didn't answer. She knew what was coming.

"What did you pay her?"

"Why is that your business, missy?"

"Well," I persisted, "why don't I do part of her work for my room and board? My husband can pay you a dollar less each week, and I'll help you with the cooking, cleaning, and carrying."

"What about the washing? It's a deal of shirts and drawers for four men."

I wasn't going to let her saddle me with the laundry. That would be hard work and take at least two days a week—drawing and heating the water, washing the clothes, heating the irons, and probably never done to suit her. A sudden thought: "Don't you have a washerwoman?"

"I do." Mrs. Hecker acted as though I'd trapped her.

"Then you don't need me to do that." I smiled my best shop-girl smile. "So we're set?" I asked, hardly able to believe it.

She gave a quick nod.

We went up the stone steps and into the brick house. After taking off our shawls and hats, we put on our aprons. I couldn't have been more pleased with myself if I'd conquered a country. I'd struck a bargain with my landlady. I'd been married less than a week, and I was already a good and provident wife. I wanted to dance around and cheer, but I kept my face straight.

We chatted a little as we moved around the kitchen, setting up bread dough and peeling potatoes. It dawned on me that the peevish, pinched look her face often showed was probably due to her poor eyesight—although she was certainly not sweet-tempered to begin with. She was short, dumpy, and a little stooped, with one shoulder higher than the other and her thin gray hair scraped back into a tidy bun.

She was twice a widow. Her first husband had been a miner before he was killed in a mine collapse in Pennsylvania. Then she married a German immigrant named Hecker—a cousin of the famous radical—and came to Baltimore's German neighborhood.

"A good man," she said, "but he couldn't keep away from politics."

He had been beaten to death in the street during one of Baltimore's famous riots—a victim of the Blood Tubs, who didn't want Germans or Irish to vote. She had the house, at least, and took in boarders.

Mr. Bump worked for one of the political bigwigs. It was nice they looked after her, she said, but that wasn't going to bring back Mr. Hecker.

Soon, the men were back from Mount Clare and washing off at the pump out back. They were stout, hearty men, most of them—Jimmy was the smallest of the lot. Mr. Bump came in the front door. He looked smaller in the daylight, and his scaly scalp seemed worse. The Fitzgerald brothers came in, from the back, giving each other good-natured shoves and elbows. Danny smiled and winked. Ralph ignored me.

The food wasn't fine at supper, but there was plenty of it: oysters, pigeons, potatoes, cabbage, and cornbread. The men ate quickly and heartily. Then some of them sat and had a smoke while Mrs. Hecker and I ate in the kitchen. We cleaned up quickly, as all the men but Jimmy departed for the local saloon.

Mrs. Hecker sat down with her knitting, and Jimmy and I retired upstairs.

We took off our shoes and lay together on the bed. He told me a little about his first day at work. Then he fell silent, and I heard a soft snoring. I was tired, too. I dozed, waking up when the candle was guttering and I had grown cold.

I rolled over and warmed my arms between the two of us, then slid my hand under his shirt to stroke his chest and belly. His skin was slightly sticky from the day's sweat, and a bit gritty with coal dust—but it was still the same enticing texture. Soon, he began to stir, and his manhood stirred, too. We made love quietly, and afterward, I fell asleep, exhausted and content.

The next morning, I was up early, bustling with the biscuits, bacon, eggs, and tea, eating from what the men left, and cleaning up. I settled quickly into a routine with Mrs. Hecker: tidying up, turning the beds, baking, cleaning, and the endless procession of meals. It was hardly drudgery, especially since we didn't do the washing and ironing. Lunch pails always held bread or cornbread, and usually some kind of meat. Some days, there was cheese or jam with the bread, and, once a week, a bit of cake or pie. Mrs. Hecker was fussy sometimes, and some days silent. She was always tight with a penny, but I don't think she ever tried to cheat us outright.

The men would come back in the evening, wash up at the pump, and come in to dinner. Several nights a week, most of them trooped off to the local saloon. Jimmy rarely joined them. They'd nudge each other and wink at us on their way out—and well they might.

When we came to our bed, every touch seemed to bring pleasure. The scent and touch of Jimmy's skin was only more intoxicating to me, and he enjoyed my body as much as I enjoyed his. He had me try my whore's trick again, and then after some days, he returned the favor to me. At first I thought I wouldn't like it, but then I liked it very much. Simple kisses were rousing, and even now, years later, thinking of his touch and his passion makes me stop what I'm doing, catch my breath, and stare briefly into space while it rouses me again. We would fall asleep exhausted and replete, and our passion infused our life together with joy—such joy that it seemed we could never be harmed or even unhappy.

Baltimore itself was beautiful to me. The black and busy yard at Mount Clare had a fascinating energy. The railroad was new and powerful, and there was something glamorous about the men who created and ran it. Bill McCracken was exciting, too—but every time I thought about him, I'd squelch the thought.

In New York, the streets where the wealthy lived were straight, and laid out in square angles to one another. Rich people's houses were made of brick, while poor people lived in a higgledy-piggledy arrangement of wooden houses—most of which were little more than piles of tinder. In Baltimore, all the houses I saw were brick, and most of the streets were straight and square. Yes, there were alleys running behind, with lean-tos and sheds. But we lived in a brick house. It would not have surprised me if I'd awakened to find the streets paved with gold.

CHAPTER 22

*T*HE GLOW STARTED TO FADE IN AUTUMN. ONE EVENING, the men had finished dinner and went to have their smoke. Mrs. Hecker and I had our dinner from the leavings and then washed up. I went into the parlor, expecting the other men to leave and Jimmy and I to go up to be together—but there he was, putting on his hat and coat, and going out with the other men.

I could hardly say anything in front of the others. He gave me a peck on the cheek and said, "Politics tonight, love. Don't wait up." The door closed, and I stood there staring at it.

"Well, then," said Mrs. Hecker uncertainly, untying her apron. "I suppose it's just us hens."

When Mrs. Hecker and I bustled about with the house-work, we had plenty of conversation. Not now. A heavy silence hunkered awkwardly between us. I sat and listened to her knit. I had no books. In the house, there was only a Bible and a Shakespeare, which did not tempt me. I wanted to read some-thing silly, but that seemed childish. Actually, I wanted to cry, but that seemed even more childish.

Eventually, I excused myself and went to bed. I lay there alone, staring into the dark, feeling my face grow hot as the tears came. Was this what it was going to be like every night for the rest of my life? This wasn't what I wanted.

Well, I tried to tell myself, *you knew what he was when you married him. It's always the polly-tics, and you know why it's important.*

I don't care, I thought as the tears began to trickle down my cheekbones, into my ears, into my hair. *I hate this. I don't want to live this way. If this is married life, somebody else can be stuck with it. But I'm stuck with it.*

I fell into a fitful sleep and barely noticed when Jimmy came in, stinking of tobacco smoke and beer.

I woke the next morning with a headache.

Suddenly, the round of tasks that had seemed so pleasant was instead irksome, tedious, irritating. I hated the cleaning. I hated the washing. I hated Mrs. Hecker. I hated Baltimore. I even hated the potatoes. Most of all, I hated Jimmy. And of course, that night, the men all left, with scaly-headed Mr. Bump in the lead. So I hated him, too.

That night, I asked Mrs. Hecker for pen and ink and paper to write to Julia.

Mrs. Hecker charged me, of course, pointing out that pen and ink and paper were quite dear, and asking would I need her to write the letter for me.

"Of course not," I snapped—and then regretted it, but not enough to apologize.

I sat and poured my heart onto the paper:

My dearest Julia,

Please forgive me for not writing; my new life in Baltimore has kept me very busy. But, oh, Julia! My heart aches. All I want is my husband's company, and he has determined to be out every night to be at the politics. I cannot go with him, and I cannot understand why he has abandoned me so. I do not think I am suddenly unattractive, for the glass tells me the same story it did a fortnight ago. Is it really true that once men have their way, they lose all interest? Whatever am I to do? I am in a strange city with no company but my crabby landlady, and I think I may well go distraught.

I know you have told me I cannot return to you, but is there no hope of that? I remember as the happiest days of my life the times spent walking with you in the grain fields, looking for straw, tending the hens, and learning about bees. Can I not return to you?

And more in this vein.

The next night, Jimmy again went out with the other men, and I sat listening to Mrs. Hecker's knitting needles. Eventually, she said, "You'll have to find something to do in the evenings, you know."

"I'm sorry?"

"Well," she said. She paused, and then continued. "They don't like the—the, um, they don't really like the romance so much, you know."

What? I couldn't believe what she was saying.

"The men," she said. "They make such a deal of bedding a woman. And, you know, I've had two husbands."

That wasn't something I wanted to discuss. She kept going.

"You'd think that since they want it so much, they'd like it when they get it. Well, I just think they don't really like it. It's just something they have to do, you know. To relieve themselves. It's like they're using a chamber pot."

Well, I thought crossly, *that cheers me up no end.*

"I'm not trying to hurt your feelings," she continued, turning her knitting around and starting a new row. "He's as good a man as any, your Jim. I'm just saying that's the way they are. He'll be back, but there will be no more rollicking every night." She knitted her way across the row.

I sat and watched her.

"Well, there," she said. "That's a good place to stop. Would you care for a dish of tea before bed?"

She was trying to be kind, but she wasn't very good at it. I nodded and got up to help her. But it was hard to get the tea past the knot in my throat.

∽

THAT NIGHT I LAY IN bed, stark awake and angry. When Jimmy came home, I pretended to be asleep.

We must have continued this way a week or more. Then one morning I got a letter from Julia.

> My Dearest Vera,
>
> I was very pleased to receive a letter from you, but I must confess I am very disappointed by what you write. Did I teach you nothing? Are you still a child? Did you think somehow that once you were married, you would live in some glorious rapture and never have any troubles again? That's piffle.

Yes, I thought, *of course you told me that. Why do you have to remind me now?*

> You married a good man. You hint that he has already lost interest in you, which I doubt. A marriage has to settle down, and a woman must simply be sensible. It probably wouldn't go amiss if you showed a glimmer of interest in his politics. There may be important reasons he's so interested.

I didn't wish to read that, either. His wanting to make a better world was admirable, but I was finding it tiresome.

170

Why not look around your new city for a way to use what you've learned? I hope I taught you that a woman must have her own means of support if she is to have any guarantee of sustenance, let alone happiness. Men have the best of intentions, but they have a number of inconvenient habits, such as becoming politicians or drunkards or even dying.

As to your returning here, I believe you know the answer to that already. You must make your own way. My dearest girl, you don't need to find the Holy Grail. You just need to find a hat shop.

I crumpled the letter and threw it on the bed. I sat down hard, crying bitterly. Now I hated Julia, too. But it only took a few minutes for a little insinuating thought to pry open my mind.

She was right. As usual, Julia was right. I needed to grow up. I put some cold water on my face and got out my hat box.

The hats I had made in New York seemed to be relics from a long-ago place and time—although it had only been four months since we'd left New York. They were beautiful little hats, really, but I didn't know where to take them. I didn't even know which way to walk.

I spent some time trying them on in the bit of cracked mirror we had by the washstand. I finally decided on the one that gave me the most courage, pinned it in place, and went down the stairs.

"Mrs. Hecker," I called, "where would I find the city's fashionable hat shops?"

She looked up from her mending. "Why, Pratt Street, I suppose," she answered. "Can't imagine you need another fancy bonnet."

"I don't," I answered a little too cheerily, bumping the hatboxes on the doorway on my way out. "I'll be back to help with dinner." And I stepped out into the street.

A new city to explore and a crisp sunshiny day to do it. I pulled my shawl around me, lifted my chin, and set out for Pratt Street. It was only a mile or so. The street was wide and grand and filled with people and carriages, and the road itself was made of brick. Actual brick! Not dirt and dried filth.

After the flatness of New York, Baltimore's hills rising around the harbor seemed romantic. It was even exciting to see the horses pulling the railcars between Wilmington Station—where Jimmy and I had come in—and Camden Station. The dirty locomotives weren't allowed to run through the city, so the horses pulled the cars. Even if the travel through Baltimore was tedious, railroad travel was fast and exciting.

I watched for cutpurses, of course—but mostly watched for where the grand ladies' carriages might be stopping. There were a fair number of ladies to look at, but most of the hats would not have passed muster on Broadway. Many even looked factory-made. The more I saw of this depressing fashion parade, the more downhearted I became. I trudged for what seemed like miles on Pratt Street without seeing a single milliner. I saw only two dressmakers.

I stood outside one of these, wondering if I'd come on a fool's errand, when I heard a low, sweet voice say, "Pardon me, please."

I turned and saw a striking woman's face: smooth olive skin, black brows like perfect semicircles above large, calm, black eyes. Even more striking to me was her hat. It was simply shaped but perfect. The ribbons were good silk, and a few exquisitely placed French flowers made it beautiful.

She seemed slightly amused when she said, "I can go in after you or around you, but I would like to go into the shop."

"Oh, I beg your pardon," I said. I was embarrassed at looking so simple, but I recovered enough to ask, "May I please ask you something first?"

She nodded slightly, giving me an unsettlingly direct gaze with those deep, black eyes.

"I'm a milliner's assistant," I explained. "I'm looking for a bit of piecework or perhaps shop work, and I don't know where to look. Your bonnet is beautiful. I'd like to work in the establishment that made it. Is it in Baltimore?"

"Yes," she replied. "It's mine."

It does save time when people are blunt, I thought.

She looked at the top of my head. "Is that your work?"

"Yes, ma'am."

She smiled slightly at the "ma'am." She could not have been more than thirty years old. "What is your name?"

She had cut right to the meat. She could have asked, "May I have the pleasure of knowing whom I am addressing?" Well, a hat shop girl *was* just a servant, especially to an employer.

"I am Vera St. John—I mean, I am Mrs. O'Dea." *Could I possibly look more foolish?* I thought. "I am newly married."

"Well, Mrs. Vera St. John O'Dea, I am Miss Mary Easley. Please call upon me tomorrow at two o'clock. My shop is on Howard Street, which is two streets east." She extended her arm and pointed in that direction—an inelegant gesture for a lady. "My shop is two streets north of that. I look forward to speaking with you tomorrow. Please be prompt."

CHAPTER 23

I HURRIED BACK TO HELP WITH THE EVENING MEAL AND arrived just as Mrs. Hecker was putting on her apron. "I'm here, Mrs. Hecker," I called. "Let me put away my boxes." I took the boxes upstairs, took off my shawl, and carefully took off and put away the bonnet I was wearing. It had carried the day for me, and I was grateful.

"I may have work," I told her excitedly. "A lady with her own shop has asked me to call."

"Fancy that."

Yes, I thought. *Fancy that, you old witch.*

She gave a little sigh and one of her pinched looks, and said, "Start on the cornbread. Then punch down the bread."

I did. By the time the men came back to wash up, the smell of frying potatoes and onions had mixed with the equally delicious scent of baking bread. But in spite of the enticing food smells, the men all clumped in silently, almost sullenly.

Ralph Fitzgerald had a copy of the *Sun*.

"I don't even know why you buy that fish-wrapper," said his brother Danny.

"I didn't buy it," replied Ralph. "I found it in the street."

"In the gutter, where it belongs," opined Mr. Bump.

"It's worth knowing what they say about us," said Jimmy. "And what the United Sons of America are up to in the legislature."

"Who are the United Sons of America?" I asked. "And what are they up to? And why does it sound like they're sons of something else?"

Conversation stopped. Everyone looked at me, as though I had suddenly popped out a second head. Everyone, that is, except Jimmy.

After a moment of astonishment—a moment that seemed to me to be half of eternity—he smiled a little smile and said—looking carefully at the potatoes—"It's what the Know-Nothings call themselves, pet. This last election, they won the Maryland legislature, and they're trying a good many things to get rid of the likes of us." He indicated all the men at the table and then looked up at me. "They want to make it so you have to be native-born to vote. They want to make all the schoolchildren read the King James Bible. And now they want to appoint state visitors for convents."

That brought a snicker from Danny.

"Why?" I asked, feeling bolder because Jimmy had answered me.

Ralph sighed and unfolded the paper. "For one thing, they claim we're all drunkards." He showed me a drawing in the paper that illustrated an Irishman as a barrel of whiskey and a German as a stein of beer.

"They say Catholics can't be good Americans," Danny added. "These fine fellows put their hands over their staunch hearts and say they must investigate the convents—for the good of the country, and no doubt to impress the good Lord with their good intentions." He folded his hands, raised his eyes, and puckered his lips in a prissy little purse.

"Look at this." He scrambled to another page, with the headline, *No More Maria Monks!* "They're bringing up Maria Monk again. That was almost twenty years ago, and she was nothing but a liar! She said she was a sister and she bore a baby, and said a priest was to blame. Now these … Sons of America say they want to go to the convents so it won't happen again! I think we know why they *really* want to go."

My mother, I thought. *Again. Five years dead and still making trouble.*

Jimmy and I glanced at each other. The other men paid no attention. They talked of the Plug-Uglies and the Blood Tubs and other gangs, and how working folk were sometimes in those gangs. They talked of how they suspected Bill McCracken was one of the Know-Nothings. Even Miss Emma Carroll wrote pamphlets for them, though her family was a fine old Catholic Maryland family.

The next day was hurrisome for me since I had little time between bringing back the dinner pails and two o'clock when I was due at Miss Easley's. Mrs. Hecker was fussier than usual, and I got impatient. When I was finally released, I ran through the streets like a child, arriving at Miss Easley's just in time— out of sorts and out of breath.

There was no missing her shop. In front was a grand window with a display of six fine bonnets. When I entered, the tinkling of the little bell above the door and the smells of glue, buckram, felt, and hot blocking made me feel right at home. Miss Easley came out from the back, dressed very simply in a bodice and skirt of dark gray, and a heavy hatmaker's apron. When she put aside the apron, I could see the fabric of her dress was fine. It hung on her in a way that perfectly emphasized the grace of her slender figure. A small, pink, French silk rose held a bit of Brussels lace about her throat. That tiny bit of color and deli- cacy emphasized the light flush of her white skin and the glossy blackness of her hair.

I had often heard Kathleen talk about "elegant simplicity," but I had never really seen it until I met Miss Mary Easley.

"Mrs. O'Dea, I am happy to see you so prompt," she said

with just enough of a smile. "Please, let me see what you have in those boxes, and tell me about yourself."

And so I did. I opened both boxes, and she went through them, taking out the hats.

"This straw braid is firm and even," she said. "Did you do this or did you buy the braid?"

"Straw braid is one of the first things I learned to do. I was brought up in the country by a cousin who thought I should learn."

"Indeed? You're an orphan?" She picked up a Parisian-style theater bonnet—one with dozens of yellow rosebuds arranged around the wearer's face. It was probably the best bonnet I'd ever made.

"Yes, ma'am. I was brought up by my cousin and then apprenticed to a milliner in New York City."

"An apprenticeship? How old-fashioned." She tried on the theater bonnet and looked at herself in a mirror. "Do you think this looks well on me?"

I decided to be as blunt with her as she had been with me. I took a deep breath and said, "The shape suits you, but I think it would be more becoming with pink or white rosebuds."

"Exactly right," she said, pulling off the bonnet. "Yellow makes me look like a corpse." She looked at the ribbons inside, and then more closely at the rosebuds. "These are stitched in well. Did you make them or buy them?"

"I made them. We would buy one from a jobber, if we could get one, and then copy it. Otherwise, we would copy from pictures, or hats we saw on the street."

"That's a marvelous talent. You say 'we'—are you the person with the good eye?"

"I am not the one born with that talent, but I think I developed a bit of an eye working with the O'Hanrahans."

"Well, I would say you have developed the eye, although I have never heard of the O'Hanrahans. Why are you here in Baltimore? Did you follow your husband here?"

"Yes, madam. He is employed at the Mount Clare yards."

"A clerk?"

"No, madam, he is a mechanic."

"I see." She looked at the bonnet in her hands. "That's just as well. A clerk's wife has no reason to work for her living. I can hardly have a married woman of any description waiting on people in my shop. People wonder what she's doing there." She examined the blue ribbons and forget-me-nots on a little girl's bonnet and smiled. "I don't know you, and I don't know the O'Hanrahans, but I think you've been honest enough with me so far."

Just then, the little bell tinkled, and a large woman with graying hair stepped into the shop, trailing a tidy-looking Irish maid and a young Negro boy. Her tread was heavy, and her clothes, though well-made and of decent fabric, were unbecoming.

She gave the two of us a confused look. "Which of you is the proprietress?"

"I am Miss Mary Easley, and this is my establishment," Miss Easley said. "Mrs. O'Dea was showing me some sample hats."

"Oh." It took the other woman a moment to realize I was not a customer, and that she was the person most entitled to attention. "Give me that one to try on." She pointed to a plain-ish morning bonnet in the window. No "please," no description of the bonnet—just pointing and a demand.

Not well brought-up, I reflected, *but that doesn't mean she doesn't have money.*

The woman took off the bonnet she was wearing—a sad, dark lump with maroon ribbons—put on the morning bonnet, and fell in love with her own reflection. The gray bonnet with its yellow ribbons was a great improvement, and she suddenly looked to be a handsome woman. She was large, to be sure, but more bone than fat.

"Well," said Miss Easley, "that's lovely on you, madam."

There was no reply. Madam was turning her head to see how she looked at different angles.

Miss Easley looked at me. "What do you think, Mrs. O'Dea?"

"I think it's very becoming but would be more so with a dark-blue ribbon," I answered.

"I agree. We can change the ribbon for you in a few minutes, Mrs... .?"

"Plunkett. Mrs. Obadiah Plunkett. My husband is the shipper in the South American trade."

Miss Easley gave me a glance with a little smile in it. There was some meaning there, I thought, but I didn't know what it was.

Mrs. Plunkett sat and waited while Miss Easley changed the ribbon. I asked her, "So it was just chance that you saw that bonnet in the window, madam?"

"Oh my, yes! Never seen such a thing. Golly day, I thought. Hats almost in the street! Well, I need one and should never'a thought of it. It's done, then, is it? How much is it?"

The figure Miss Easley gave her made her eyes widen. "Well, I never thought to be paying so much for a bonnet. But Mr. Plunkett is doing so well; I suppose it's only right I should start paying the earth for frippery."

The bonnet was duly retried and admired and packed into a special box, with the help of the maid, and given to the Negro boy to carry. I saw Miss Easley also slip one of her calling cards into the box.

How clever, I thought, to use her calling cards to bring a chance customer back to her.

Soon, all three were gone, the tinkling of the little bell marking their departure.

"That window of yours must bring in a great many new customers," I remarked.

"Yes, indeed. It's been well worth the money. Now, to us and our business arrangement. Would you do piecework?"

"I suppose that's really the only thing I can do," I answered.

I hadn't thought about that, but my work at home was worth a dollar a week, and I wouldn't get that in the shop. But piecework? Paying high costs for supplies, and getting very little for my work? That might be a lot of work for less than a dollar a week.

She saw my hesitation. "It really is the only thing I can offer you. With fancy bonnets these days covered in flowers, and money coming into Baltimore at the rate it is, I need someone to fashion the flowers and stitch them on."

"What will you charge for my supplies? I have no stocks of ribbon or silk."

"Let's try with one bit of silk. Buy this first one from me, as if you were a customer, and make me some rosebuds like those in your theater bonnet. If I like them, I'll buy them, and then I'll supply you."

Done, then. Even though it was piecework, I believed this would work out well. To keep from dancing about as I packed away my sample bonnets, I did what hat shop girls do everywhere. I gossiped about the customer. "Mrs. Plunkett said her husband is a shipper, but she talks like a farmwife. Do you know anything about her?"

"Her husband is in the shipping trade with South America. Everyone in Baltimore knows what that means."

"I don't. I just arrived here in the spring."

"He ships bird droppings."

I sputtered out a laugh. "What? Why would anyone ship bird droppings?"

"That's all anybody ships from South America. We send out our fine Baltimore clipper ships with grain from up the rivers, and what does South America send back but bird shit?" She glanced at me to see if I was offended at the expression. I was not. She went on. "Farmers spread it on their fields—and some of them have bought into the shipping and are starting to make fortunes. Their good fortune is my good fortune, too."

I felt light enough to fly when I left the shop, and after I turned the corner, I burst into giggles and danced a little jig. I'd found a way to make my fortune. A fortune from French silk and bird shit.

CHAPTER 24

*M*RS. HECKER GREETED MY NEWS WITH A GRUNT. SHE said I still needed to help with the men's mending two nights a week. I smiled my best smile and said I would.

I greeted Jimmy at the back door with a quick kiss and let him know I'd found a way to bring in a bit of extra money. "I'll tell you all about it over dinner."

"So Mrs. O'Dea is clever as well as pretty," he said, holding me close for just a minute. I stood grateful for the feel of his strong body, even enjoying the stink of oil in his clothes. We stepped back and smiled at each other. Then he went to wash up, and I went to get out the biscuits.

As we brought the food in, Mrs. Hecker dumped news onto the table along with the potatoes. "Do you know what your wife has gone and done, Mr. O'Dea?" she demanded.

You old cow, I thought. *That was my news to tell.*

Jimmy shook his head in mock dismay. "I cannot possibly keep up with all the doings of Mrs. O'Dea, Mrs. Hecker." He grinned. "I need a bit of a hint. Animal, vegetable, mineral? Illegal, immoral, impossible?"

"Most men think it important to control their wives."

"Do they, bedad? They must be very clever men. Able to walk upon the water and spit into the wind." He winked at me. "As for meself, I am a simple man from Drumcliffe. If there were ever a clever man in Drumcliffe, the town's tower would fall. I had only enough wit to marry a clever woman." He helped himself to biscuits and smiled up at her. "You must introduce me some day to these clever men you know."

She harrumphed.

The other men dug into their meal and another argument about politics—this time about some strange German idea that workers should have *two* days off each week.

Ralph Fitzgerald took the platter with the potatoes and then started to wave the serving spoon to emphasize his arguments. "There's plenty as would starve if they couldn't work every hour God sends," he argued. "The last thing we need is these crazy German ideas. Didn't they get chased out of Germany for saying such stuff?"

Jimmy said, "I'll have the spoon now, Mr. Fitzgerald. It's too sharp a weapon for the likes of you."

Ralph answered that he considered a potato too sharp for Jimmy but surrendered the spoon and the platter.

Mr. Bump, watching the platter hungrily, said, "We really can't be supporting such radical arguments. We're having trouble enough with our own ideas. We have plenty who can't stop fighting about slavery."

"And what's that to the likes of us?" asked Ralph's brother Danny, helping himself to cornbread. "We're practically slaves ourselves, and we don't need the lot of the darkies coming here looking for work. Some of them have already—that Elijah fellow who was hanging about the yards today."

"I know Elijah Smith from the days of building the line out to the Ohio," said Jimmy. "He's a good man. They ought to have him working on the machines with us. They offered him a sweeper's job. I don't know if he's going to take it. He may just hang about doing the odd bit of smithing."

"Well, we don't need to be using our good offices to get a job for a black man," said Mr. Bump. "Mr. Thorpe is going to need our assistance to get the Democrats a few more city posts and maybe back in the legislature. We'll need some votes in this ward, as well as in the Eighth."

"We know what they do in this ward to the Irish and Germans who try to vote," said Danny. "The Blood Tubs get 'em."

☙

THAT NIGHT, AS WE SETTLED in bed, Jimmy said, "We never did hear your news, did we, pet?"

"No, and it's a good thing you've asked. I thought the Blood Tubs were more important than I was."

He smiled and kissed me, and then asked, "Well?"

"I have work for a hatmaker! It's only piecework, but she's kind and she's clever, and I know this is going to work out well."

"I know 'twill, as well."

After a moment I said, "So who are the Blood Tubs?"

"A Know-Nothing gang, pet. They're the worst kind of thugs. Last time the Germans and Irish tried to vote, the Blood Tubs would catch them and beat them and dump blood on them."

"Where do they get that much blood?"

"Butcher shops. They get pigs' blood and water it down and keep tubs of it at the voting places they patrol. Makes a stink, it does."

"Are you going to be getting mixed up in that?"

"Most likely."

I didn't want to hear that. "Why?"

"Well, for one thing, Mr. John Thorpe helped me get work, and us a place to live. He sent a cart for us when we arrived in

184

this city, not knowing a soul. And more than that, it's something I have to do."

"But why? Why can't we just live in peace? I just—I just want to feel that I belong someplace. Why do you have to get into these horrible tangles of things?"

"Can't you see, pet? I couldn't live in peace if I just left things alone. My family didn't die back home because we spoke out against anything or caused any trouble, but just because we were Irish, and the English had no use for us. These people are no different. They want us gone just because of what we are, which is no worse than they are. We have just as much right to live, and just as much right to live here. And as for belonging, 'tis not the same as fitting in, is it? We belong where we can do some good."

"But if you speak out and get into the fights—"

"I can't *not* speak out. Silence won't buy us safety." He took my hand. "I'll not have us arguing about this."

"I won't argue. But I don't like it. What will I do if something happens to you?" Tears started to come.

He put his arms around me. "I'll not do anything foolish, pet. That's all I can tell you. But I'll not be silent."

He blew out the candle, then settled back with his arms around me, and we lay still for a moment.

I said, "I want to go with you sometimes when you go out."

He took so long answering I thought he was asleep. Then he asked, "Why? Why would you?"

"I want to understand what you care so much about."

"It's not a place for the best kind of woman."

"Oh, all of a sudden we're Mr. Starch, are we, Mr. O'Dea?" I gave him a little shove with my foot. "If Mrs. Hecker is the best kind of woman, then the best kind of woman is the worst kind of company. If I have to stay with her every night, I'll go up in smoke from sheer boredom. You'll come back from your polly-ticks and find nothing but a frock and a pair of shoes."

"I've no use for a frock and shoes without you in them."

He kissed my cheek, and I kissed his mouth. Soon the kisses became wetter, and we made love again.

∽

THE NEXT NIGHT, WHEN I put on my bonnet and bounced to the door with Jimmy, Mrs. Hecker drew herself up, and then pressed her lips together. The Fitzgerald boys looked startled, but they said nothing. Mr. Bump studied his hat. Then he put it on, and we all went out the door.

The saloon was crowded and smoky. There were few females of any description—one or two in odd, mannish clothing; a German wife in plain clothes and a plainer bonnet; a few woozy-looking tarts with bosoms heaving out of their bodices. There were barmaids, of course, and women washing glasses and setting out the cheapest kind of oysters for all to eat.

I saw Mr. Thorpe standing by the bar, smoking a cigar, and watching the room. "Why does Mr. Thorpe come here?" I asked, turning to Jimmy.

"It's his place, pet. Next election, 'twill be the polling place."

A German man with rough side whiskers started to talk to Jimmy right away. So I asked Danny Fitzgerald, "This is where people vote?"

"'Tis," he nodded. "Caucus here, too. But the next election, this place will do for three or four wards."

"Is that because it's so big?" I asked.

"That's part of it," said Ralph.

"It's for the convenience of those who wish to vote three or four times," Danny said, grinning. "And where else, indeed, would the men gather to decide anything important but at a saloon?"

I heard much such talk that night. I learned about "cooping," for instance—how a party would "coop" men by offering them whiskey and taking them about from place to place so they could vote again and again. They'd get their "coops" more and more drunk have them vote in ward after ward. Some coopers were kindhearted and found the coops places to sleep it off. Others left them in the street.

I heard the story of how the famous writer, Mr. Poe, had been cooped a few elections before and left to die in the street. Someone picked him up in time to die in a hospital, which wasn't much better. He couldn't even tell anyone who he was or what had happened to him.

It must have been half past eight or even nine when we left the saloon. The night was black and cold. There was a moon, but the light cast deep shadows, and making our way was awkward and uncertain. I held tightly to Jimmy's arm. We picked our way slowly through the dark city streets, grateful for the few gas lamps. Then, from way down Pratt Street, we heard men singing. The men looked at each other, and we all quickly moved into the darkness of an alley. We saw flickering shadows, then more light, and heard the tramp of feet as the voices grew louder. Then a red light suddenly blazed off the brick walls and a swirl of excitement blew down the street.

Children skipped down the streets in the light, and people suddenly appeared from the houses and alleys and started to cheer. We saw a few men with torches, then many more behind them.

One man at the front was particularly striking—tall, hatless, with his mane of blond hair sweeping back from his face, looking proud and inspired, like a man seeing Heaven in front of him.

The men's voices, deep and strong, rang off the bricks of the streets and houses—all the bricks of Baltimore.

The blond man's voice rang loudest as he led their song. "Our country now is brave and free, few days, few days." Then came the great ringing line of the refrain: "We know the way."

I realized with a shock that it was Bill McCracken from

Mount Clare. He looked like an archangel leading a mighty army. The spectacle was so grand and so unexpected, and the blaze of torches so bright, that it seemed a celestial army was sweeping down Pratt Street to claim Baltimore for heaven.

We hurried along at a safe distance behind them, using the light of their torches to see our own way. When it came time to part, we stood watching them out of sight, and then began to pick our way through the dark.

"What a grand procession!" I gushed. "I've never seen such a thing!" I suddenly realized Jimmy and the others were grimly silent, and I was prattling like a child. "Who were they? What was that about?"

"Know-Nothings," said Jimmy, shortly. "And I'll wager they've been up to nothing good ... or are about to be."

"Probably out to crack some Irish heads," agreed Ralph. "We're lucky they weren't looking for us."

"Or maybe they weren't drunk enough," said Danny. "They just want us to know they're about so we don't start anything."

Jimmy added, "And if you ask them tomorrow morning about a torchlight procession or about who was in it, they'll tell you they know nothing."

"Which means they're ashamed of what they're doing, as they ought to be," said Danny. "But we don't know who's about in the street now, do we? Let's go home."

"Bill McCracken," said Jimmy. "We should have known."

CHAPTER 25

*I*F I HAD TRULY BEEN THE CLEVER GIRL JIMMY THOUGHT I was, I would have kept the Know-Nothings foremost in my mind. But I didn't. Times were good, and we all prospered.

Mrs. Hecker's table-keeping improved. We soon had oysters twice a week, and roast beef on Sundays. Passenger pigeons were cheap, and I used them as Julia had used chickens—to make pies, soups, and stews. Julia would never have used pigeons. She thought they were dirty—and they were. I also learned to use the cookstove to cook big cuts of meat, and to make pies of all the fruit we could have so cheaply in the market. I also learned to shuck oysters—so many oysters! I hope I never have to shuck another oyster as long as I live.

I got a letter every few months from Julia or Lizzie or Kathleen. Finn Malone was a police sergeant now, and he and Kathleen had moved uptown from Bleecker Street, taking her mother with them. So now they made hats in a smaller, more expensive shop, for a "better class of ladies." I wondered if she missed the parlor girls. I did.

Julia's letters made me sad. Her bones often hurt. When her handwriting grew crabbed, I knew her hands were stiffening.

I sent her money when I could and talked to Jimmy about someday having her come to live with us.

In June, I thought I was with child. But in August, I had a great show of blood, both clotted and fresh, and pains I thought would rip my belly open. The miscarriage hurt so much I could hardly walk, much less work, for a week. And I felt so miserable I didn't want to. Mrs. Hecker expressed her sympathy by charging us full rent for the week I could not work.

In autumn, the winds blew cold and the streets grew rougher as the city election neared. I learned to know which gangs were which; some gangs supported theKnow-Nothings and some supported the Democrats. There were Plug-Uglies as there had been in New York—men whose plug hats identified them, even if their faces did not. There were also Rip Raps, Black Snakes, and Rough Skins for the Know-Nothings. The Democrat gangs were Ashlanders, Bloody Eights, Pluckers, Butt Enders, Eighth Ward Black Guards, and the Senior Mount Clares. Some of the fire companies were gangs, too.

Men on both sides carried weapons when they could, although carrying weapons was against the law. Many would carry awls, which were legally tools and not weapons. There were nasty jokes about men who "gave their awl" to support their side. When Mrs. Hecker and I had errands to run or marketing to do, we tried to be done by midday, when we took the men their meals at the yard. After midday, when men had been drinking for a while, brickbats would start to fly and the awls came out. We never knew when we might be safe. That was life in Mobtown.

It got lively early on election day. I walked to the market on Hollins Street, where there was a polling place—or possibly three or four. It made no difference to me, of course, since I could not vote. But part of the street entertainment at the market was a few of the men with a tittering whore, shouting, "Votes for women!"

"Or should we say the ladies?" asked a gap-toothed man with a beery grin. "See here this fine example of the fair sex." The whore dropped an elaborate curtsy. "Would this world not be a better place if she could but vote?" She nodded and grinned to a ripple of appreciative laughter.

I stopped to watch.

"This creature has a fine mind!" bellowed the man. The whore lifted her skirt to show her fine mind.

Howls of laughter.

Then we heard another howl, a man's hoarse cry of fear and other men jeering. A human shape covered in blood ran past us—blood streaming through his hair and beard, covering his shirt. We could not see his eyes, but only an open mouth, howling as he ran. He passed close enough to me that I could smell the reek of the blood, and gobbets of it spattered me.

The men with the whore looked at each other and then walked purposefully in the direction from which the bloody apparition had come. The whore rolled her eyes in exasperation and walked quickly in the other direction.

My stomach tightened. Jimmy was out there somewhere. Election Day was a holiday, and all the saloons were open.

I quickly bought a few eggs and some apples and hurried back home.

❧

WE DID NOT TAKE A meal to the men at Mount Clare that day because we knew they would not be there. We prepared a supper to be served cold, and sat down to knit and read.

I tried to read a Bible, but kept reading the same verse of the same Psalm over and over. I gave it up and tried to knit.

Darkness came, but the men did not. She lit a candle and sat in silence, with me knitting the same row, making mistakes, picking out the row, knitting it again. Finally, we heard their boots scraping at the door and a tired laugh—Jimmy's laugh.

I ran to the door as it opened. The men were disheveled and spotted with blood, but they were all there. The relief swept up from my stomach and into my eyes. I flung my arms around Jimmy's neck and wept.

CHAPTER 26

*T*HE DEMOCRATS TOOK THE CITY COUNCIL IN THOSE ELEC-
tions, and Mr. Thorpe rewarded us well. I turned
twenty the next January. Jimmy and I moved to our
own house, and took the Fitzgeralds with us. It was four rooms
and a garret on Lemmon Street, just across from the yards, in
houses that were rented only to men who worked for the railroad. I thought it a fine Baltimore brick house, even though the
walls between the houses were only one brick thick, and we
could hear everything the neighbors were doing. There was no
proper kitchen or cookstove—just the parlor stove in the front
room, which was big enough for a kettle and one pot.

Mrs. Hecker grumbled about losing so many boarders at
once, but the magical Mr. Thorpe and the railroad soon brought
her more.

Jimmy built a bedstead, and I bought a blue and white-
checked floorcloth. It could have been a Turkish carpet—it felt
that grand to me.

That spring, though, I got a sad letter from Julia, who was
being pushed out of her home. Her brother-in-law had remarried, and his new wife was suspicious of Julia.

The new Mrs. Van Deventer believes I must be her husband's fancy woman—no matter that I am nearly fifty and plain. I'm so arthritic that I couldn't entertain her husband if I wanted to. I must leave all I have here and move into the city, on the sufferance of the Lyles and the other Universalists. I don't think I could even get work as a hired girl. This is a bitter draft to swallow.

I couldn't afford to pay her fare to us, or mine to her. I sent her a little money from time to time to make her life more comfortable and make her more welcome at the Lyles', but I could not rescue her as she had rescued me, and that hurt.

∞

ONE CLEAR AUTUMN EVENING, I went to meet Jimmy. Ralph Fitzgerald pointed me to a small forge at the edge of the yard, where Jimmy was watching as a tall black man hammered. I walked toward the odd little assortment—a mule cart and the essentials for a blacksmith shop as small and portable as they could be made. Sparks flew as the smith hammered a proper curve back into bent tongs.

I walked up beside Jimmy and put my hand through his arm. "This must be Elijah Smith."

Jimmy smiled and said, "I suppose it must be. Elijah, this is Mrs. O'Dea."

The smith gave me a quick glance and a nod, concentrating on his work. This, then, was the man who worked as a sweeper in the engine house, even though he was a better smith and metalworker than most of the white men who got hired. At his forge at the edge of the yard, he would repair tools, and make household things—such as hooks and latches, and he was repairing tongs for Jimmy

Elijah Smith was a lean man—but at his forge, he looked massive. He wore no shirt—just trousers and the leather apron. His skin was the color of burnt sugar, with a few tightly curled black hairs spiraling out on his chest above the apron. His hair bushed out about six inches from his head. His heavy black eyebrows were set in a frown above his large, black eyes—eyes he held expressionless even as the fires from the forge danced within them. With his hammer's dramatic ringing rhythm, he shaped the glowing orange metal, then plunged it into water and set it aside to cool. Only then did he speak.

"Miz OhDay," was all he said, with another short nod.

"Elijah and I have been through heat and cold together," Jimmy said. "We finished off the line to the Ohio together on Christmas Eve. I've never been so cold in my life."

"Don't never want to be so cold again," agreed Elijah. "Never want to be at Roseby's Rock again, neither—Christmas Day or any other."

"My husband tells me how they rolled out the whiskey next morning, saying it was for Christmas," I said. "He thinks the foreman just wanted to get all the men drunk and cheat them of their money. What do you think?"

"I think if it wasn't for Mr. Seamus here, wouldn't none of us been paid," he answered. "Them Irish boys likes they whiskey. Seamus, when you gettin' yourself a better hammer from me?"

"Another payday," Jimmy answered. "But to be sure, I'll be doing it."

The smith fastened the refashioned tongs.

Jimmy paid and took them. "I know that money's going for a good cause," he said. "To be sure, you're getting close."

"Gettin' there," Elijah replied. "Maybe next year."

"Godspeed."

As we walked off, I asked Jimmy what "good cause" they were talking about.

"Elijah's buying his woman out of slavery," he answered. "Bathsheba's in Virginia. He was freed years ago by their master's will, and it also said he'd be able to buy her from the family. He couldn't stay in Virginia as a free man, so he lives here. But he's been working to buy her free as long as I've known him."

I felt queasy as that sank in. I'd known Negroes before, but I never really knew people who had been bought or sold like livestock. Most of the black people in Baltimore were free, and all of them in New York had been free—at least until blackbirders grabbed them and sold them down South. Slavery was something people talked about, but I didn't think of it as something that affected me or people I knew. It rarely even figured in the political discussions Jimmy had with his friends.

"Something else I'm doing, pet," Jimmy said, patting my hand. "We'll have Elijah live in the alley behind us."

In a lean-to or something, I supposed. Probably with his mule that pulled the cart.

"Where does he live now?" I asked.

"He has to move around. He's all by himself. Bill McCracken's threatened to get his papers from him and let the blackbirders get him."

"Why? Why would somebody do that?"

"Billy McCracken's mean," he answered. "He was with us in Roseby's Rock. He joined the crew when we went through western Virginia. They grow them mean out there."

"He hates you, doesn't he?"

"He hates anybody Irish."

That confused me. "But isn't he Irish?"

Jimmy snorted. "Knox Irish. Scots-Irish. They fight with everybody."

A few days later, Elijah was living in a shed in the alley

behind our house. We shared food sometimes, and we and the neighbors kept an eye out for threats.

In the heat of that summer, Jimmy said he'd be going to Virginia with Elijah for a few days.

"What on earth for?" I asked.

"Not sure you should be doing that, Seamus," said Ralph.

"It'll be safer for the two of us," said Jimmy. "Dangerous for him by himself."

"Then why's he going?" I asked.

"To make a payment for Bathsheba," he answered.

Then it dawned on me why Jimmy would go. A black man by himself—especially one carrying money—would be an enormous temptation. Somebody could take his money, steal his papers, and sell him down South. Yes, it was illegal, but a black man without papers on him was presumed to be a slave. If Jimmy traveled with him, they'd be taken for a slave and his owner, and Elijah would be much less likely to be robbed and sold.

"But your work," I argued, even though I knew it was pointless. "You can't just not show up."

"'Tis only a few days' pay."

"Only? There is nothing 'only' about a few days' pay. And you could lose your job," I said.

"Elijah could lose his freedom, pet. Maybe his life. If I have to find work, I will."

He was right. I felt like wringing my hands and crying, but I didn't. I was afraid, but he was right.

∽

THEY LEFT ON SATURDAY. ON Sunday, I crept into the church of St. Peter the Apostle to pray they'd be safe. I didn't really know how to pray, and was too afraid to feel like it might really do any good, but I didn't know what else to do.

∽

MONDAY NIGHT THEY WERE BACK.

I saw them coming down the street in the dusk, and thought at first that Jimmy was some visiting planter—he was wearing a fine broad-brimmed hat. I ran down the street as he stepped down from the wagon and held out his arms.

I flung myself into them with a laugh and a sob. "I'm so glad you're back. It went well?" I asked, looking at Jimmy and then at Elijah.

Elijah nodded and walked his mule around toward the alley.

"'Tis a fine hat, isn't it?" said Jimmy, sweeping it from his head and holding it out to me. I couldn't resist taking it and looking inside to see how it was made. It was beautiful—firmly made, but soft. A gentleman's hat.

"It is indeed," I answered. "Are you sure someone won't try to rob you just because you're wearing it?"

"They didn't try it in the wilds of Virginia," he answered. "A gentleman's hat is a clever disguise for the likes of me. And I like the hat."

"I'm just glad it came home with you in it."

"We had no trouble, pet. We left the mule at the port with a friend of Elijah's and took the steamboat to Aquia Creek. From there, 'twas a walk of three hours to the plantation—as hot and nasty a walk as I ever hope to take in my life. The air was thick—it was that hot—and, after midday, filled with mosquitoes. The young master was drunk when we arrived, and he offered us no refreshment—not so much as a cup of water. I witnessed his signature for Elijah's payment, and Elijah had a few minutes with Bathsheba. In the slave quarters, at least, they gave us a cold drink."

"Did you see Bathsheba?"

He nodded. "I did. I see why he's willing to work so long to buy her out of bondage."

"Now I have to know what she looks like. Tell me more!"

"She's very light," said Jimmy. "She's her master's half-sister."

He watched my face as that sank in. *Dear God,* I thought, *this evil has so many twists in it.*

I put his hat on his head and my arm through his. "I'm so glad you're home. Please stay for a while."

CHAPTER 27

*A*S I WRITE THIS, IT SEEMS ODD I DIDN'T SEE THE shadows cast over our lives by what was going on around us. I grew used to Jimmy and the Fitzgeralds being gone in the evenings, and to the small injuries that resulted from various punch-ups. I grew used to not asking too many questions.

The Know-Nothings flourished all around us. When Mr. Millard Fillmore stood for president as a Know-Nothing, the state of Maryland voted for him. Ralph and Danny speculated that since he'd been president once before, he should have known something. But now he claimed to know nothing. Plenty of folk who knew nothing right along with him held rallies and parades, and fought in brawls all over Baltimore.

With so many Irish and Germans in and about Mount Clare, the church of St. Peter the Apostle was bursting. They'd just started a school, with nuns teaching, so of course the Protestant newspapers denounced this "invasion of the so-called Sisters of Mercy," pleading with readers to remember the awful disclosures of Maria Monk, giving the more lurid details just in case their readers didn't. "Much more is to be dreaded," they thundered, "from the growth of Popery in America than from the Stamp Act or any other acts destructive of civil liberties. Catholics teach doctrines subversive of civil government."

In every country where Catholicism was established, they said anarchy and intolerance held sway. Mind you, they could have said the same of Baltimore "There should be no Catholic church in these United States," they said, "as long as there are no Protestant churches in Catholic countries." And so on, saying anyone who advocated tolerance was a dupe or a liar, and the arrival of the nuns was a test of our "timidity, passivity, and ignorance of history."

It bothered me when I thought about it. But I didn't often think about it. Instead, I enjoyed the long summer evenings when we could walk out or sit on the front step to have lemonade and talk with the neighbors or watch the children playing in the street. The houses themselves were like ovens in the summer. The only windows were at the front, and even opening all of them, plus the back door and the front door, was not enough to coax the slightest breeze through the house. Sometimes it was midnight before it was cool enough to sleep, and the men would have to be up early and out to work.

While I couldn't make real pies or cakes with our little stove, I invented a sort of puffy apple pancake that was Jimmy's favorite. I made it one hot summer day, even though the heat was oppressive. We could afford cinnamon, and the smell of it gladdened our senses even as the sweat trickled down our backs and sides.

I put the cake and pan aside to cool and made to go out, but he caught me around the waist and pushed the damp hair from my forehead. "I never thought I'd be so happy," he said.

I hadn't expected philosophizing, so my reply was a foolish, "What?"

"I don't think I dared dream of having so much," he said. "When we were begging at the hedges or scrabbling for crusts at the poorhouse—even when I was building of the railway, with me body parts freezing off—I never thought I'd be sitting in my own house, married to a beautiful woman, and about to eat an apple cake."

"That was clever," I teased him. "You're not about to eat that apple cake. A *slice*, when it cools, perhaps."

"And perhaps I want something else first." He untied my apron and began to kiss my neck.

"We'd better bar the door." I giggled.

"No, we'll just move away from the window and be quiet, won't we? They won't need to know."

Indeed, by the time Ralph and Danny came in, I was demurely finishing a slice of apple cake. Jimmy told them, with a mostly straight face, it was the best he'd ever had in his life.

❧

ONE NIGHT IN LATE AUGUST was actually cool and mercifully peaceful. Jimmy and I walked up onto Federal Hill, among the fine houses, and stood looking at the city. It looked so serene and beautiful in the dusk, with ships moving through the harbor and the city's gentle hills and steeples glowing in the reddening light.

"It's beautiful, isn't it?" I said. "You'd never think this city was boiling with hate."

"Is it so bad?" He turned to look at me.

I glanced up at him, then looked back out onto the city and sighed. "I worry so much about you," I said. "And it just doesn't seem to me like you can change anything."

"But so much *is* changing, pet. It's hard to see in our short lives, but just think about what's happened since this country started. 'All men are created equal,' they said. An outrageous statement to be sure—and perhaps they didn't really mean 'all men' when they said it. But do you see what's happened? People say it *does* mean all men. And maybe even women."

I smiled and shook my head. "I don't think anybody really believes that."

"There's some that do. They believe it of black men. *I* believe it of black men."

"Some that believe it are crackpots."

"T'was crackpots started this country," he retorted. "But we ask, don't we? Does it mean Irishmen? My answer's yes—and there's others that answer yes, and soon, there'll be enough of us. Does it mean slaves? There's more all the time think it does."

"People who have slaves will never let that happen."

"'Tis true enough. It will probably take a war. But something has to happen, or they must say, 'You know that part about all men being equal? We didn't really mean it, and we're going to have a king now, so you lot just go about your business.' I don't think we'd stay still for that."

"Oh, I think things will just stay the way they are."

He shook his head. "Nothing stays the way it is, pet. Things always change. You can make it change the way you want it to, or someone else will change it to what he wants. Simple as that."

❧

THREE WEEKS LATER, THERE WAS a riot on Federal Hill, of all places, started by people who went up to watch the fireworks commemorating the battle with the British at Fort McHenry. A punch-up started, and then shots were fired and brawls broke out. In the end, two people were killed. Jimmy and the Fitzgerald boys came home that night with cuts and bruises. But they were mightily pleased with themselves for capturing an important trophy: a fancy piece of paper.

"What on earth is that?" I asked.

"This, pet, is a portion of the fortunes of the Baltimore and Ohio railroad," Jimmy replied, settling down with a bit of bread and cheese. "'Tis a certificate for ten shares in the company. As the railroad grows, so will the value of this little piece of paper. It can be traded for gold money at a bank."

"And how did you come by it?"

They laughed and exchanged amused, guilty glances.

"To be sure, Mrs. O'Dea ..." Danny grinned. "A fine gentleman left it behind when he left his coat in our hands, in his haste to be away from us."

"Now the interesting question," said Jimmy, "is how did he come by this beautiful piece of paper? We understand these are being distributed by some disreputable friends of Mr. Thomas Swann, who used to be president of the great railroad, and is now a candidate for mayor put forward by the United Sons of Unknown Fathers. Not to riff-raff the likes of us, you understand, but to more prominent folk. This has no man's name on it, and is ours from this day forward." He tucked it into our little metal box where we kept some cash money. "This is a good night's work, gentlemen," he added.

∽

I STAYED IN THE HOUSE the day of the municipal elections, but I heard nothing. Just before sunset, I decided I didn't want to be cooped up anymore, so I went out the door and walked toward the Lexington Market, where I knew Jimmy and the Fitzgerald boys would be defending the polling place at the Irish Fire Company.

It was getting dark, and as I came nearer, I started to hear shouts. The echoes bounced off the brick houses and streets so I couldn't tell where they came from. I was frightened for myself, but I was more frightened for Jimmy. I stuck close to the houses and inched along, my heart pounding. I heard running footsteps and flattened myself into the shadows.

Danny Fitzgerald came bounding down the street, hatless, with blood streaming from his forehead. He was alone.

"Danny!" I shouted. He slowed, looking around wildly.

I ran out to him. "What's happened?" I shouted. "Where's Jimmy? Where's your brother?"

"I don't know. I've lost them. You can't be out here alone. I can't either."

He tried to hold my arms, but I wrenched free.

"I'll find him," I said and moved to the shadows. Danny ran on.

I inched along the walls and doorways, trying to keep as far as I could from the shouting. I was about to cross an alley, but I heard scuffling, and I peeked cautiously around the corner. I saw a tall man with golden hair run out the other end of the alley, and saw a man lying face down. Fear snatched my breath, and I walked toward the man, too afraid to admit what I was thinking.

It was Jimmy. He was facedown and moaning, with blood all around his head. I turned him over and saw a bloody hole where his right eye belonged.

Someone started screaming. I realized it was me.

I didn't know how long I stood and screamed, but two hands rested on my shoulders, and I turned to see Elijah Smith.

"Miz Ohday," he said, quickly, "you can't stay here. I got my cart. We'll put Seamus in it and go for a doctor."

I stood, stunned, while he knelt. Then he looked up at me. "I needs your help getting him up."

I scrambled to pick Jimmy up and put him in the cart. We set off at a trot, away from the shouting, toward home.

Ralph Fitzpatrick caught up with us. "Don't go home!" He warned. "The Rip Raps are moving this way, and they're setting fires."

"We'll go to Federal Hill," I said. "Go to the house and get

my money box and meet us there. We have to find a doctor."
Ralph ran toward Lemmon Street.

As we moved toward Federal Hill, we became part of a
gathering crowd—some men, but mostly women and children,
carrying whatever they left their houses with. The children
were crying, and the women urged them to hurry, as flames
began to grow behind us. We hurried past the yards and up
Federal Hill, and turned to look at the city.

I held Jimmy's bleeding head in my arms, listening to his
moans, my mind screaming, *No, no, no!*

When we got to Cross Street, the doctor came out to the
cart, took one look, and shook his head.

"But it's his eye!" I screamed. "I don't care if he's half-blind!
I want him alive!"

The doctor shook his head again. "It's not that." He pushed
open Jimmy's coat and shirt. His chest was pushed in. Though
scraped, it was hardly bloody at all. But it was concave and heaving.

I screamed.

The doctor buttoned him back up again. "Bashed in. I can't
help him." Then he turned Jimmy's head and showed me a
small hole beneath his ear. "This will finish him off. I'm sorry.
Now you need to move on. He went inside and I heard him bolt
his door.

Elijah started the mule pulling us up the hill.

Jimmy's breathing became less breath and more rattle. Then
there was no more breath and no more rattle, and he was gone.

I sat in the wagon, sobbing, his head still in my lap, his
blood on my hands and all over my clothes.

I looked down at the city and saw huge fires and running
shadows, and heard the noises of anger and gunfire.

The fires of hell. They were real. They were there in front
of me. Jimmy was gone. My husband was gone. That thought
came to me over and over as I stood there numbly watching the
flames, unheeded tears pouring from my eyes.

Over the flames, over the smoke, over that hell on earth, I saw the clear autumn sky, where the stars were coming out, serene and unmoved. The eternal arch of heaven was beautiful and calm. I couldn't stop crying.

CHAPTER 28

*I*T WAS GRAY, DIM DAWN WHEN ELIJAH DROVE US BACK TO Lemmon Street. My teeth were chattering, and though my arms ached, I could not let go of the body of my husband. It had grown cold. His blood had thickened, clotted, and dried on my clothes. Yet I could not let him go. I kept sobbing, though I had no tears left.

The houses stood calm and still, though smoke hung in drifts all around. Danny and Ralph met us, and walked quietly beside the slow-moving cart, and as we moved down Lemmon Street, the people on the street began to walk after us.

One neighbor said timidly, "The fire spared our houses, missus. But they took—"

One of the other women grabbed her arm and shook her head. "Not now."

They reached up to me. "Come down, missus. Let the men carry him into the house. We can help."

I couldn't let go. Ralph gently pried my arms from Jimmy's body while I sobbed and howled like an animal. The men carried him into the house.

The gentle hands of the women helped me walk in after

him. Someone brought me a cup of tea, and then they gave me laudanum. I fell into a black, miserable sleep.

When I awoke, I was in our bedroom. My bloodstained clothes were gone and some unfamiliar ones laid out. I was on a pallet of straw instead of Julia's feather bed. My head ached, and I was so groggy I almost fell as I pulled the chamberpot out from under the bed. I used it and then washed a little. I still stank of smoke and didn't wash enough to get rid of the smell. I dressed. The room still tilted from side to side.

I was holding onto the dresser when my neighbor friend put her head in. "It's good you're awake, Mrs. O'Dea," she said, softly. "We've laid out your husband, and the priest is here."

The house was full of people. Some I knew from the neighborhood, some from Mount Clare, some not at all. They were all eating and drinking. I didn't know where such food could have come from. There was a ham, a pile of oysters, a small barrel of whisky, and buckets of beer. It was as merry a gathering as I had ever seen, except Jimmy was laid out on the table with candles at his head and feet, and there was Father McColgan.

Father McColgan was the priest from St. Peter the Apostle. I don't think Jimmy ever set foot in the church, but it was generous of the priest to come. He reached out a hand to me and said softly, "Are you the widow?"

I wanted to slap him. Father McColgan looked a good and gentle man, but he had just called me a widow. I wanted my husband to get up off the table and throw all these people out of our house.

A dim shaft of reason entered my head, and I nodded mutely. *Yes, I am the widow. Yes, I will always be a widow.*

He spoke to me briefly about a mass and a burial, all to take place within a day. I agreed to everything.

Ralph had saved our little cash box with our money and the strange piece of paper in it. Rioters had taken almost everything else: my hatboxes, my pot and pan, and Julia's featherbed. They had left one quilt.

I sleepwalked through a blur of a mass at St. Peter the Apostle, and the burial in St. Peter's graveyard. My beautiful Jimmy, the man who had taken the Protestant soup, was laid to rest far from home in a Catholic cemetery. Then I went back to the house on Lemmon Street with Danny and Ralph.

Mr. Thorpe and Mr. Bump were standing outside as we approached. We heard Mr. Thorpe saying, "Within the week, you hear?" Then he strode down the street, passing us, tipping his hat to me as he walked by.

There was an awkward silence as we approached and stood in front of the house with Mr. Bump. He cleared his throat and took off his hat. "Mrs. O'Dea, Mr. Thorpe would like me to convey his condolences."

"That's very kind."

"I trust the food and drink he sent were satisfactory?"

"Oh. It was he who sent the whiskey and oysters?"

He nodded once. "Yes, missus. And the ham and beer."

"I'm sure they were satisfactory. I have no taste for food and drink at the moment."

After a silence, Mr. Bump spoke again. "I have some business to conduct, Mrs. O'Dea, and it is awkward to do so on the street. May I come in?"

I couldn't imagine what business he had to conduct, and I certainly was in no frame of mind to conduct any. But I nodded and said, "Yes, of course." We had no place to sit. Everything was gone but the stove and the floorcloth.

"This is a very delicate matter for me to bring up," he said, "but I must. You will have to vacate the premises within the month."

"What?" Danny spoke what I felt.

"Oh no, not you, Mr. Fitzgerald, nor your brother, um, Mr.

Fitzgerald." He nodded to Ralph and then looked at his shoes. "Just Mrs. O'Dea."

"You'd throw a widow out of her home?" Danny, at least, had words. I was so shocked I could manage none.

"The houses are for workers at Mount Clare."

"But I can pay rent," I said, "at least for a while."

"We can just take in another boarder," said Danny.

"I'm afraid not," said Mr. Bump. "Mr. Thorpe is quite firm on that point. I'm sorry, but you must be out by the end of the month." He waited for a minute. None of us had anything to say, so he nodded and left.

Where could I go? What could I do?

More to the point, what did I have to do it with? The clothes I stood in belonged to someone else. I could spend all the money in the little box on a railroad fare to go back to New York, but I had no one to take me in. Julia had no home of her own now. What would I do there? Kathleen wouldn't take me into her shop as long as her mother was alive.

The month was almost up when I heard Mrs. Hecker's Irish girl had quit, so I went to hire myself to her. I could not think of another place to go.

"Thought you might be back," she said. "Can't board you, you know. You can stay for a while as a hired girl. You'll have to sleep in the kitchen."

So all our dreams, all of Julia's great plans, had come to this. I would have the life of a hired girl after all, sleeping on the floor in the kitchen, scrubbing the floors and emptying the night soil, invisible. I wouldn't be getting decent wages from her. She knew I had no place to go.

I wrote to Julia and Kathleen. Julia wrote a kind letter, but it was short and the writing was crabbed. I even wrote to Lizzie, asking if she and her wealthy husband could help me, perhaps take me in. I got her reply a month later.

My Dearest Vera,

   I do so mourn for your affliction and wish still
I could invite you to live with us. But my husband
insists we maintain the fiction that I am without
other family, and I must abide by his wishes, as you
know. I am entirely without funds of my own and so
can send nothing more than my love.

I wasn't sure I believed her. Not that it made any difference.
There was no place I belonged—no place I could go, except for
the floor of a hard-hearted woman's kitchen. My own sister
either could not or would not make my circumstances better. *At
least her spelling's improved,* I thought spitefully.

Spite was a poor comforter.

How could people think a boardinghouse that wouldn't
board women was more respectable than one that would? The
hired girl sleeping in the kitchen was vulnerable to any man
in the house, and after a few nights of sleeping on the floor, I
thought I would gladly sleep with any of the men just to be in
a soft bed with real covers.

There were dozens of daily humiliations. Mrs. Hecker no
longer called me Mrs. O'Dea, or even Vera, but just "girl." She
had agreed to pay me wages—but only after she had used them
for board or anything I broke or any other excuse she could
find. I could do nothing about it.

Whenever I reflect on that time, it seems to me it lasted
for years. I must have kept Christmas in her house, but I don't
remember it. Then, late one night, I was awakened by someone
breathing beer fumes in my face.

It was Mr. Bump. He had put his hand inside my shift and
on my naked breast. I awoke with a scream, and he said, "I
won't hurt you. I won't hurt you. Please don't. I won't hurt you."

"You won't hurt me? You won't touch me! Get away from
me, you nasty little man. Get away!"

He retreated, stumbling away in the darkness.

The next morning, Mrs. Hecker informed me she would have no more "funny business" from me. "I'm not deaf, you know," she said. "Everyone in the house heard you."

"I didn't do anything," I protested.

"Where there's smoke, there's fire."

"What does that mean?"

"You must have led him on. I've seen what you're like." She glared at me. I glared back. "No use looking uppity," she said. "Any more of this funny business and you'll be gone by Easter. Is that understood?"

What choice did I have? Tears burned my eyes, but I nodded.

"Stir up the stove fire," she said. "I'll get the eggs."

I knelt and raked the fire, and then put kindling in where the embers glowed. Tears made tracks in my dirty, sooty face.

Gone by Easter, I thought ruefully. *Old cow*. But then I realized that meant it must be almost Easter. Jimmy had been gone five or six months. I started to sink into familiar misery, that dark chasm where I'd lived since he was gone..

Then a spark lit my mind.

Easter meant bonnets. I could go see Miss Easley.

No, I can't, I thought. *I don't have ribbons. I don't even have a bonnet of my own. She won't let me in the front door.*

It's the only way.

The only way—where? The only way—to do what?

It's the only way out of here.

I had learned from Julia that I was worth something, and I'd learned from Jimmy not to accept whatever ill God chose to send. Still, I couldn't even dress properly to go see her. I had no bonnet, my clothes were shabby, and I'd have to get permission to go out. What if she turned me away? The possibility of that humiliation kept coming up my craw that day, pushing tears into my throat and sometimes out my eyes.

The next morning, my head ached from my tears and the

smoking of the stove. I had to risk it. She might reject me, but my only other choices were sleeping by the stove or on the street, where any passing man would be free to molest me. I had to do it.

I got permission to go out in three days, so I had time to wash and mend what clothing I could. When the day came, I put my shawl over my head and set my feet toward Howard Street.

I pushed the door open and had only gone in a step, when Miss Easley came striding forward to turn me out. Then she stopped and put a hand to her mouth. "Mrs. O'Dea? I hardly recognized you."

Just hearing my name spoken as "Mrs. O'Dea" started my tears. She took my arm, led me to the workshop, and gave me a cup of water.

"What on earth has happened to you?" she asked. "I haven't seen or heard from you in months, and you suddenly appear, bareheaded as a beggar, and you burst into tears. Has your husband turned to drink?"

"He's dead," I blubbered. "He was killed in the riots."

"Oh, dear God."

"I'm a hired girl in a boardinghouse."

"Oh, no."

She gave me another cup of water and a handkerchief and waited for me to compose myself. "Our belongings were ransacked," I said, finally. "My bonnets are gone, and the silk and ribbons. My bed is gone. My home is gone. My husband is gone." I burst into great wracking sobs just as we heard the shop bell go. She patted my arm and went to attend to the customer, shutting the door behind her.

When she came back, I was spent, dabbing helplessly at my eyes and streaming nose with the soaked handkerchief. She took it from me, rinsed it in cold water, and gently wiped my face.

"Now," she said, "take a good breath." I did, and promptly hiccupped. We both laughed at that.

"You've come to me for work."

"Yes."

"You'll never be able to make bonnets as a hired girl. When will you do it? Your time is not your own."

"I don't know," I said, feeling as though the tears would start again. "I just know I will *not* spend the rest of my nights on a kitchen floor."

"Well, then. Come stay here for a while and work. I can't pay you wages, but I can board you."

It would be starting all over again. That's what I did when I was thirteen. I worked for room and board. Still, it was better than what I had, sleeping on the kitchen floor, waiting for Mr. Bump to come back.

"Go back and tell your missus you'll see her through Sunday," said Miss Easley. "Then come back here Sunday evening."

❧

MRS. HECKER WAS NOT PLEASED. She withheld half my wages for the short notice and let me eat nothing but cold potatoes for the whole week. I didn't care. As I bundled my quilt, my little box, and my few clothes, I felt lighter by the minute. By Sunday evening, when I put my shawl over my head and left, I felt I was floating through the darkening streets.

Miss Easley had a pan ready for me to take a bath—my first hot water bath since Jimmy died. It felt so wonderful to be clean and free, even in my ragged shift.

As she settled into the narrow bed with me, she said, "We'll get that shift washed tomorrow." That sounded wonderful, and I smiled at her.

She blew out the light and gave me a gentle kiss.

215

CHAPTER 29

F OR THE FEW WEEKS UNTIL EASTER, I WORKED ONLY IN the back of the shop, since my clothes weren't fit to be seen in the front. It was agreeable to sit for my work and to stitch at ribbons and flowers, and I wondered how I could ever have thought such work to be hard. Spring was stirring, and I thought something was stirring in me, too.

Late one Monday afternoon, Miss Easley quietly admitted two young women and drew the blinds to show the shop was closed.

They were women of startling beauty, dressed in silk and lace and flowers from head to toe. One was fair, with hair so pale it was almost white. She had round blue eyes, and porcelain pink and white skin. As she came closer, I could see there was pink powder on her cheeks, and coralline paint on her lips. The other woman was a mulatto, with lights dancing in her black eyes and a smile that threw sunshine right into my heart. French silk trimmed their bonnets, Brussels lace edged their parasols, and Italian kid leather gloved their hands. Even without the paint on their faces, even without the scent of the perfume that immediately filled the shop, I knew they must be parlor girls. Expensive parlor girls.

"Miss Emmeline and Miss Delilah are here for their spring

bonnets," Miss Easley told me. "They will want the latest fashion." This was her none-too-subtle code for "the most expensive articles in the shop."

"That's right," said Miss Emmeline, removing her bonnet and patting her perfect cornsilk-colored curls. "We'll want 'em for church." And they both snickered. "We're *artistes*," she explained.

"Musicians?" I inquired blandly, since the high-class parlor houses provided multiple forms of entertainment.

"Musicians," agreed Miss Delilah. "She sings, and I play the pianna."

Miss Emmeline picked up a dark bonnet with red flowers and plunked it on her head. I didn't know how a beautiful woman could make herself look bad just by putting on a hat, but she did it. The colors brought out the circles under her eyes and made her skin look blotched.

I felt Kathleen's skill coming back to me. "Miss Emmeline," I ventured, "those blue eyes deserve some blue flowers."

"I'm tired of blue flowers," she said, pouting. "They're dull."

Hmm, I thought. Next best would be pink or light gray. But if blue was too dull for her, she certainly didn't want to hear about gray.

"We have some lovely, um, *silver* flowers. And some bright roses would be delicious."

I went to the back room to search through the stocks of French silk flowers, wondering briefly if Miss Easley had stolen some of them, as Kathleen had done. Pale gray, indigo, some little deep-pink posies, a little pale straw saucer, silvery ribbon, a spray of Venise lace. I loosely pinned it all together and set it on her head.

"Oh, Emmeline," crooned Delilah. "That's just elegant. Now do one for me."

Up to that point, Emmeline wasn't sure she liked her bonnet. I could have set a gourd on her head and she wouldn't have known the difference. But if Delilah wanted one, then it must be worth having.

I gathered a golden straw saucer, maroon and yellow flowers, a brown ribbon, and held them near Delilah's face. She declared she would be "the prettiest black-eyed Susie you ever saw," when the bonnet was done. So then they wanted more combinations of flowers and lace—corsages, waist furbelows, rosebuds and daisies to go on their corsets and shimmies. By dusk, when they pinned on their bonnets and left, they had paid us an amount worth two weeks' wages for a man at Mount Clare.

"Well," laughed Miss Easley as we tidied up, "that was well done. Silver indeed."

"Can she really sing?" I asked.

"I have no idea. I don't know if it matters. You may have a chance to find out, though, when you deliver their orders."

"Deliver?"

"Yes, deliver." She gave me a sidelong smile. "They do not come to pick up their purchases. I suppose I could hire a boy to go, since a boy would be perfectly happy to go to a whorehouse. But boys talk. I can't have the talk. Oh, don't look so frightened. There's nothing to hurt you there early in the day, and they'll probably tip you. Let's have our supper."

A week later, I had two bandboxes to deliver to an address on Baltimore Street, the establishment owned by a Mrs. Ophelia Fenton. Her name was familiar somehow—it teased at the back of my mind, but I couldn't match the name with any face I knew.

Baltimore Street was quiet at nine in the morning. The sunshine warmed my face and hands, but the street smells of stale beer and urine made my eyes water. I found the place, went around to the alley, and knocked at the back. A tired-looking old black woman let me in and led me to the parlor.

A stout woman with gray threading her dark hair was sitting in a soft chair by the piano, working at something on a lap desk. She looked up, adjusted her spectacles to look at me, and then set aside the lap desk. "Take a pew," she said, cheerfully. "Deborah, have we got some coffee for our visitor?"

Deborah nodded—or at least seemed to nod—and shuffled off.

My hostess waited a few seconds and then said, "I'm Mrs. Ophelia Fenton."

"I am sorry, Mrs. Fenton. I forgot my manners. I'm Mrs. Vera O'Dea, and I'm newly employed at Miss Easley's."

"Missus? You're married?"

"Widowed." My throat closed so hard when I said that word it almost choked me.

"Recent?" she asked.

"Yes, ma'am."

"I'm sorry for that. Of course, if you loved him, you will always miss him."

"Thank you."

My own reply confused me. *Thank you? Why am I thanking her? For telling me I'll always be miserable? Well, it seemed polite. Let it go.*

"You're very well-spoken. Where did you grow up?"

"New York, ma'am. Flatbush."

"Flatbush? Really. I grew up in Flatbush."

Her name finally caught in my memory. "You're the one who—" I clapped my hand over my mouth like a child.

"Yes," she said with a short laugh. "I'm the one who burned down the courthouse."

Deborah came in with a small pot of coffee and two cups.

"Sit," Mrs. Fenton urged again.

I hesitated. Customers did not usually pour coffee and visit with delivery folk.

"Oh, go on, sit," she repeated. "I like to visit, and my girls just want to cry or complain."

Something made me feel that if I sat, I would be trapped forever. But coffee was a treat. And I was curious.

"If it isn't too impertinent ..." I began. "I'd rather stand."

She looked at me skeptically.

"But the coffee smells wonderful," I added. "And I'm very curious about your story."

"Suit yourself," she answered with a sip of her coffee and a shrewd glance. "You want to know what happened with me and John Fenton, don't you?"

"Yes!" I answered. "It's a story everyone in Flatbush knows. I never met anyone famous before."

She gave a short laugh. "So I'm world-famous in Flatbush." She leaned back and sighed. "Well, I didn't do any of it to make myself famous." She took a sip of her coffee, settled back, and began a story she had clearly told many times.

"John Fenton was a handsome man. I never had any man talk so sweet to me—let alone one so good-looking. My pa never had two words for me and took no notice that I was talking to that gambler he'd put in jail. I'd take John his meals, you know. The first time I took him some bread and cheese, he looked up and said, 'They have angels serving the poor sinners here.' It was claptrap, and I knew it was claptrap, but no one had ever bothered to talk claptrap to me before.

"The escape part was simple enough. One night, I just put the key under the potatoes and agreed to meet him late at night. I had horses for us. If he could have gotten a horse himself, he probably would have left me there in Flatbush. I know that. Setting the fire was his idea. He figured they'd be too busy putting the fire out to come after us. He was right. We left the horses in Brooklyn and sent word as to where they were. They'd have chased us all over the world for the horses, but they wouldn't spend much effort on a gambler and a silly, plain girl."

"You're not plain." I gave the expected polite correction.

Another short laugh. "Yes, I am. Always have been. But I'm smart. He was, too. Gambled and won enough to get us to Albany and out along the Erie Canal. We stopped outside of Buffalo, at a little boatmen's inn, and he won the inn from the landlord."

"In Flatbush, they said you'd gone west with the Conestoga wagons."

"Probably would have if John'd had his way. He wanted to sell the inn and keep moving. I said, 'No—let's run this place and let the sheep come to you for fleecing.' That appealed to him. So we stayed there for years, building up the place. It was popular. We had some girls lived there who did good trade, paid us good rent. We had whiskey coming down the canal, and I learned to make beer. John played cards. He promised never to bet the place, and he never did. After a few years, we got married."

She stopped to sip her coffee.

"How did you come to Baltimore?" I asked.

"By way of San Francisco," was her answer, and her glance told me she loved having this part of the story pulled out of her. "We heard about the gold in '48 and sold up and moved out. We travelled a lot fancier than a Conestoga wagon, I can tell you. Coach to Pittsburgh, riverboat to New Orleans, and clipper ship round the Horn. John figured we'd make our own gold strike, only we'd mine the men.

"It happened fast. Soon we had a little place on the water-front, then a bigger place on the hill. We had fine whiskey and brandy and a darkie playing the piano—whores from all over the world. Frisco's where I learned about the high-priced whore business. You get pretty girls, get some music and dancing, make it so everybody's having a good time, and the money rolls in. I even bought a couple Chinese girls. Pretty things. That's right. You can buy 'em just like you can buy a darkie in Virginia. The men always get fascinated with something different. They brought in good money, those Chinese girls.

"So how do you think John died?" she asked.

Of course, this was the first I knew that John *had* died. I had been looking at her clothes, perfectly fitted and good quality fabric. I shrugged slightly, shook my head, and shifted my weight in my shabby boots.

"He got shot in a card game. He just pushed too hard on one man who was drunk enough to shoot and sober enough to shoot straight. He got a bullet right through that handsome forehead."

She paused, sipped her coffee, and sighed.

"I couldn't stand to stay there after that. So I sold up. Sold everything—the hotel, the whiskey, the furniture, the Chinese girls. Sold 'em for gold and got on the first clipper leaving San Francisco. It brought me to Baltimore."

She sipped her coffee. I sipped mine. It had grown cold.

"Can you play music?" she asked.

"No, ma'am. I've never learned."

"Do you sing?"

And right in that moment, I think I decided not to live the life she and her girls lived. My mother had been used, and I would not. The thought didn't form in those words right then, right then, but I know it was there because I answered, "Only in church."

"And you're not much of a talker, either, are you?"

"No, ma'am. I'm only good at making hats."

"Well, there's not much fun in that. Not much money, either. You have a pretty face and a ladylike manner. There's good money in the life. Pays better than hats."

"Well, I know that's true," I conceded. *But I don't want to be used that way.* I thought of my mother, used for pleasure, used for profit, dying mad and drunk in a prison. I wasn't going to do that.

"Well, here's a little something for you," she said, scooping her hand into her purse and concealing the coin as she handed it to me. "I'm sure you can run some errands for us someday."

"I will certainly check with Miss Easley, ma'am," I said, closing my fingers around the coin.

When I got out in the alley, I opened my hand and looked at the coin. I bit it, and it gave a little under my teeth. It was gold.

CHAPTER 30

ONE MAY AFTERNOON, RALPH FITZGERALD CAME BY WITH three letters for me, the floorcloth from the house on Lemmon Street, and Jimmy's hat. He was so kind it made me cry a little. I spread the shabby little floorcloth in our workroom and put the letters down to read later.

I knew right away what to do with Jimmy's hat.

"Are you walking back toward Mount Clare?" I asked Ralph. "I should go see Mr. Elijah Smith. I've never thanked him for all he did."

"He's working in the alley today," said Ralph. "He's reforging a hammer head for me."

As we walked toward Mount Clare, I asked, "Did anyone ever swear out a warrant for Jimmy's murder?"

Ralph sighed, shaking his head. "We tried. We told the magistrate you saw Bill McCracken going around the corner, but McCracken and his Know-Nothing chums all said he was someplace else. Nobody killed in that riot but Irish, so the law doesn't want to know."

That sank in me like a stone in my stomach. I should have known better than to ask, but hope dies hard.

When we got to Lemmon Street, so many feelings rushed

back to me—happy memories and fresh grief combined, so strong I could hardly speak to Elijah Smith when I found him.

"Mr. Smith," I began, as Ralph stood by. "I never thanked you for your help when ... on the night ..."

"Wish I could have done more," he said and sighed. "Seamus O'Dea was a good man."

"He was," I said and held out the hat. "Would you take this to remember him by? I think he would want you to have it."

He hesitated. "Do *you* want me to have it?"

"Yes," I said, suddenly sure. "Because I think it shows you remember him. He liked that hat a lot, and you were with him when he bought it."

He gave a quick, short snort. "Standin' outside the shop," he said, grimly. He turned the hat in his hands, and then put it on.

It suited him. It more than suited him. It showed the dignity in his face and carriage. "It's perfect," I said. "It's yours. Thank you for taking such good care of it."

There was a moment of awkward silence. Then Ralph piped up, "Mr. Smith has some good news."

A wide smile flashed onto the smith's sweaty face. I realized I'd never seen him smile before. "I'm going to Virginia to fetch Bathsheba," he said. He turned and hung the hat on the peg. "Thank you for the hat."

"You're very welcome. Wear it in safety," I said. "That's good news about Bathsheba." I still didn't quite know how such things worked, but knew it must be difficult. "How long did it take you?"

"More'n eight years," he answered. "Old master who died freed me, told his family to let me free her."

"Why didn't you stay in Virginia?" I asked.

"That was part of the bargain. Free man a bad influence on the slaves."

"Why didn't he just free both of you?"

"Family wouldn't stand for it. Sons still tried to cheat me."
He shrugged.

"I'm surprised he hasn't succeeded. Isn't everything set
against you?"

He put the bellows to the forge to start work on a couple
of awls. "The mistress wants Bathsheba gone." His guarded
look incompletely masked his pain and anger, and in a flash,
I understood the whole situation—the white man taking full
advantage of his power as master, even over his half-sister; the
wife wishing the other woman gone; the man who loved that
powerless woman forced to stay miles from her, humiliated and
helpless. Until now.

"Well, congratulations, Mr. Smith," I said, offering him my hand.

He looked surprised, then took it and gave it an awkward
shake. Then he nodded silently and got back to work.

We said good day and walked on.

I strolled silently through the summery twilight back to the
shop, which was cool, dark, and silent. Miss Easley was out, so I
made myself a solitary cup of tea and thought about Elijah Smith.
It was as Julia had said about the priests who had—perhaps—
so abused my mother. "Any mortal has that much power over
another, there are some that will use that power in evil ways."

It was the nature of power. It was probably the nature of
men. And women. After all, Ophelia Fenton had bought and
sold her Chinese girls. Priests had the power to abuse women
and children, and some of them did.

Julia. I had not yet read her letter or Lizzie's or Kathleen's.

Julia's letter was painful to read. Her writing had become
square and shaky, and she was no longer in her home, but staying
with the Lyles, her Universalist friends in New York City.

My dearest, how I long to see you again! Our friends
are kind and loving, but I know I am useless here. My

arms ache to embrace you, and my failing eyes yearn
only to see you again.

My throat hurt. How could I get to her? How far would my
one gold piece get me? Even if I walked the whole way and slept
by the side of the road, I had not the means to purchase ferry
rides or even food, not to mention the danger of such a journey.
I promised myself I'd write her a loving letter.

I opened Lizzie's. She was well and hoped I was the same.

Such an elegant dinner and ball we went to last night!
We dined on lobster and squab and a great plenty of
ices. I was all in silk. Can you imagine?

Well, yes, of course I could. This sister who had told me she
had no money to give me or a place for me to stay was wearing
silk and eating very fancy food. She could now spell "imagine"
correctly, so the education must have done her some good. Why
did she get everything handed to her?

Kathleen's letter was chatty and cheerful, after condolences
from her and Finn for Jimmy's death.

Constable Malone is doing well as a police, and hopes
soon to be Sergeant Malone. He looks fine in his uniform and, if I may say so, makes a fine married man
and is a kind father to our little one.

Speaking of little ones, Miss Maeve McGonagle
is soon to be married, although she and her husband
will be a family of three a week or so after the wedding! Rumor is she got in the family way in a doorway.
Her mother is mortified, and Maeve is the size of a
butcher's cart.

I did feel a pinch of satisfaction at that news—although

what good did it do me now? She'd tried so hard to get rid of me and have Jimmy, and now he was gone forever.

Did I wish it had all been different?

No. I still ached with grief, but the love I had for him came rushing back with such force that I caught my breath. No. While our happiness together had been short, at least I had had it. Maybe that was all I would have in life. Maybe not.

I shook my head and rinsed out my teacup. Miss Easley would be returning soon, and we expected Delilah and Emmeline.

Delilah and Emmeline were in a hilarious mood that evening. They had earned a fat purse that week from a Bostonian who wanted them to perform opera for him, with Emmeline dressed as a page. She sang a little of the music for me. She had a lovely voice, sweet and high, and even though the song was in a language that was gibberish to me, she put on a great show of acting like a young man unable to make up his mind. She and Delilah hooted, and Delilah said their caller became very excited when they told him they were sisters.

"Why did you tell him that?" I asked. "Was he such a fool that he believed it?" After all, Emmeline was one of the fairest women I'd ever seen, and Delilah was clearly a colored creole.

They gave great grins to each other and then to me. "We are sisters."

I looked at Miss Easley, who gave a catlike smile and nodded.

"Don't look at our color," said Emmeline. "Look at *us*."

And as they stood arm in arm, I realized they were the same height with very similar figures, the same smiles, the same noses.

"Daddy was a sailor," said Delilah. "He was white. He said Mama was the prettiest girl he ever saw, even if she was brown. She was a slave in Charleston, and he stole her. Stowed her away on the rice boat and brought her to Baltimore."

"We have a brother, too," said Emmeline. "He's a carpenter, and he passes for white."

"And so do you," said Delilah. She shrugged. "Folks believe what they see."

So I had only seen what I expected to see.

They left in the deepening twilight, having again spent well on hats, flowers, lacy frills, and ribbon furbelows.

I watched them go and realized, from the back and in the twilight, that they were indistinguishable—with the same posture, the same backs, the same walk, and the same gestures. How could I have missed that they were so much alike?

CHAPTER 31

O N A HOT JULY EVENING, AS HEAT LIGHTNING SHIMMERED IN the sky, I sat in the back room, looking through the contents of my little box. There were a dozen gold coins from Ophelia Fenton—for I had made several deliveries and run other errands, and she liked me. I had some lesser coins from other customers—tips and such. I was thinking maybe I could go see Julia before the summer was out.

I also had the fancy piece of paper Jimmy had brought home, saying it was worth a share in the Great Baltimore and Ohio Railroad. I smoothed it out and read it. The language meant little to me.

I became aware that Miss Easley was looking at it over my shoulder. I looked up at her.

"What on earth is that?" she asked. "It says 'redeemable by bearer?' Redeemable for what?"

"I don't know, exactly," I answered. "My husband brought it home one night and said it meant we owned a bit of the Baltimore and Ohio."

"Well, it's a very impressive bit of paper," she observed. "If you own a bit of the railroad, I should imagine you could turn this into gold. How did he come by it?"

I smoothed the paper again and smiled. "I don't think he came by it honestly. He and the Fitzgerald boys came back with it after a rough night on the streets. But he said it was worth money."

"'Redeemable by bearer' means whoever has it can get the money. Still, I can't see you sailing into Mr. Brown and Mr. Flanders's grand bank and having them tip their hats and put gold in your hand. Can you?"

"No," I admitted. "They'd probably call for a constable."

I sat and stared at the paper until the words went out of focus. There was so much I didn't understand. Jimmy had thought this piece of paper was valuable. But he was gone, and I couldn't understand why, or how to make anything out of this blasted thing. He couldn't help me, and Julia couldn't help me, and Lizzie wouldn't help me. I was so bitterly alone.

I started to sob and weep wretchedly. I couldn't help it. Miss Easley patted my shoulder—but even as she did, I knew I did not belong with her either, and felt I would never find any place I did belong.

"Dear Vera," she murmured.

"You're so kind," I choked out. "But I feel so alone. I've had no one to love me but Julia and Jimmy. Jimmy's gone, and I can't get to Julia, and I can't even decipher a way to use what Jimmy left for me."

She knelt beside me. "There are more who care for you than you know," she said softly. "Look at me."

I looked. Suddenly, I was conscious that I was quite unlovely, with my eyes red and my nose streaming.

She handed me her handkerchief and began to stroke my head. "Dear Vera," she said. "Do you think I have shared my house and bed with you and not cared for you?"

It had never occurred to me that she cared for me. I sat sniveling stupidly, her handkerchief clutched in my hand, until she gently took it back, dried my tears, and held it to my nose. I blew and gave an embarrassed laugh.

She softly stroked my cheek and then kissed it. Something loosened in my throat, and I put my arms around her shoulders. She returned my embrace. I didn't know how long we stayed there, awkwardly, her kneeling and me sitting. The room began to darken as the rain began outside.

We separated.

"Water?" she asked softly. I nodded, and she dipped a cup for me. It was tepid and tasteless, but it braced me a little. We went upstairs and silently stripped down to our shifts, brushed our hair, washed our faces, and lay down together.

She put an arm around me, and I embraced her, my head on her shoulder. I had ached for so long for someone to hold me. It was strange, embracing a woman when I had become so accustomed to Jimmy. Her shoulders were small, her neck and arms delicate, her skin inexpressibly soft. Her lips were gentle on my cheek, my neck, and then on my lips.

"Oh, Vera," she whispered. "I have cared for you so much. I'm so glad you're here with me."

Why hadn't I expected this? I had accepted her kindness as little more than a practical proposition, and was overwhelmed to find such a person had passionate feelings for me. She was clever and independent. It was wonderful to have someone treat me so tenderly.

I smiled and said, "I'm glad, too," and I kissed her.

We settled into a melting exchange of gentle kisses and caresses, and I soon sank to sleep in her arms.

The next day passed in a happy haze, and at night, we kissed again, this time more deeply. Soon she slipped a hand inside my shift to stroke my breast. Then her lips found my nipple. I moaned with pleasure as she sucked like a babe.

A few nights later, I explored her body the same way, and found I loved nuzzling the softness of her breasts and soon was sucking on them. There was anticipation as we went to bed on those nights. Soon we explored each others' most intimate parts, probing the velvet and wetness with our fingers and tongues.

I'd had no idea females could pleasure each other so. I knew men pleasured other men—although, to be honest, I hadn't thought much about how they did it or why.

It made the work easy for us to love each other, although I never felt the powerful passion for her that I had for Jimmy, and our way with each other was more affectionate than it was passionate, at least on my part. No one seemed to notice or care how we treated each other, but few people think anything of women walking arm in arm or greeting each other with a kiss.

We still called each other "Miss Easley" and "Mrs. O'Dea" in the shop, but our time together was intimate and pleasant. The days with Mary slipped by gently, and we might have been together the rest of our lives.

I didn't see the storm coming.

CHAPTER 32

O PHELIA FENTON STILL WANTED ME TO BE ONE OF HER whores. She wasn't tiresome about it, but often talked about how much money her high-class girls made. I wasn't fooled. I didn't have the musical talent to be a parlor entertainer, and, while I looked well enough and kept myself neat, I certainly didn't have Emmeline's lush beauty or Delilah's exotic liveliness. She told me about specialties involving costumes, play-acting, or even whips. She even had a hurdle over which a man could be tied to be whipped on the back and pleasured underneath at the same time. I didn't want to do that.

Still, my curiosity about the life drew me, and I danced around the edges of it for a while. Ophelia saw that and would get me to accompany one of the other girls when they went to make a house call. A woman alone, after all, was often assumed to be a whore, which was not desirable even if she were one. I easily passed for a high-class lady's maid and would sometimes accompany one of the girls to a house or even to a place of business to pose as a servant, to stand watch, and perhaps provide a little extra safety.

One customer assumed we were both there for his pleasure. Emmeline told him the bargain did not include me and I would cost a deal more. At first, I was afraid he would agree. Then I was afraid because he became angry. The disagreement put him so out of the mood that he tried to dismiss us both, but Emmeline, determined to earn her money, soon enticed him into the other room and earned the money for both of us.

Mary was tolerant of these escapades. In fact, we often giggled about the scandalous behavior, particularly because we often knew who these gentlemen were.

One was a prominent lawyer. His great indulgence was summoning one of the girls to his office. She had to be elegantly dressed in black and veiled, as a wealthy widow would be. He wanted her to pretend to be mourning the death of a husband, and then he would comfort her with his attentions. What he paid for this elaborate bit of play-acting would have purchased him a fairly good horse, but a horse was not what he wanted. So one bright fall day, I found myself in a smart hired carriage with Emmeline, who was swathed in black silk and practicing her sniffles into a Belgian lace handkerchief.

We arrived at his grand office in late afternoon. There was no clerk in the front area. Emmeline told me to wait there and swept back toward an open door. A very corpulent, red-faced gentleman met her there and murmured a greeting. She entered the room, and he looked around quickly, his eyes lighting briefly on me. Then he shut the door.

I heard Emmeline playing the sobbing widow, then murmuring. The murmuring became less. Then I could hear muffled sounds of movement. A silence. Suddenly, Emmeline was screaming.

"Oh, God help me! Vera! Somebody help me!"

I stood and looked around, uncertain of what to do. Was this part of the game? She kept screaming and calling my name. I ran over and tried the door. After some frantic jiggling of the knob, it opened. I could barely see Emmeline's hair and feet.

She was on the floor with the large man on top of her. He wasn't moving.

"Help me!"

"I—"

"He's stuck in me! He's dead! Move him!"

I went over and gave the man's hulking body a hearty shove. It rolled slightly, and Emmeline screamed again. "He's fucking stuck in me!"

An excellent summary of the problem, I thought even as I knelt next to them and put my shoulder under him.

Emmeline inched herself along her back away from him, grunting with exertion and grimacing in pain. Finally, with a soft "splop" sound, she pulled away, and I saw his grotesquely swollen member bounce onto the dark carpet. Blood trickled from his mouth.

Emmeline sat gasping, her knees up and her petticoat falling open, the light hair on her delta matted and sweaty, the flesh swollen and purpled. I puffed, too, my heart racing.

The deceased released a long, slow, flabby fart.

I started to giggle. Emmeline did, too. Then we couldn't stop. We laughed until the tears ran, and, as we were wiping them away, I said, "His last words." And that started us again. We were laughing like lunatics when the clerk came in.

"Jee—hosephat!"

A thin young man stood in the doorway, his eyes bulging. I hiccupped and smothered a giggle that threated to gush out as laughter.

"What—Mr. James?" the clerk said. He went over and held his hand over the late lawyer's throat. "What happened here? What are you doing?"

Emmeline slapped her knees together and tossed back her disordered curls. "This gentleman arranged for our services. He has met with misfortune."

He gave her a wild, confused look. She raised her chin and

gave him a look that dared him to challenge her. "We had an agreed-upon price for our transaction," she said primly and named a price that staggered me. "In gold. Are you his clerk?"

The young man nodded. He looked from his dead employer to the haughty whore, then to me.

I stood and smoothed my dress and stared at him. "His family would no doubt be distressed if these circumstances became known."

Comprehension dawned in his eyes.

"Do you know how to open his wall box?" asked Emmeline, pointing to the wall. He nodded, walked shakily over to it, and took out a key, occasionally glancing over his shoulder at the scene behind him. As he pulled out a small sack, I saw the fancy papers at the bottom of the safe box—stock papers like the one I had from Jimmy. As he held out the sack to Emmeline, I cleared my throat and held out my hand.

They both gaped at me blankly while I stood with my hand out. Then he took three gold pieces from the sack and handed them to me. He handed the rest to Emmeline, who looked at me sharply, then hefted the weight of the sack and shrugged.

"I would also like some of those papers," I said, pointing to the certificates. He looked at the safe box and then back at me, as blank as if I'd spoken Hottentot. "I like those papers," I repeated, although I still had no clear idea how to use them. The gold pieces could get me to Julia and back. "I can help you tidy things up," I offered.

The clerk handed me a sheaf of the papers and took something else out of the safe and put it in his pocket. He was now a party to our little game, and he was very unlikely to go to the magistrate.

"Don't tidy up," he said. "It should look like a robbery."

We buttoned up the late gentleman's trousers and left.

CHAPTER 33

A FEW WEEKS LATER, I WAS ON A TRAIN CAREENING northward, going to Julia, thinking about all that had happened. Mrs. Fenton demanded her portion of Emmeline's gold, of course, but let her keep most of it. Emmeline was bound for San Francisco in a grand stateroom on one of Baltimore's finest clippers.

Mrs. Fenton wrote her a reference for one of the whorehouses out there. I wondered, *What do you write when you give a character for a whore? This young woman's morals are beyond reproach? She is clever with her hands and many other parts of her body?* Then I started to be fair about it. *I bet it's important that she gets along with the others, and doesn't steal from the people she lives with, and keeps herself clean and tidy.* I can tell you Emmeline was generous; she shared some of her bounty with Delilah.

This journey to New York was much easier than the one Jimmy and I had taken to Baltimore. I never once had to leave the car I rode in. There was a bridge across the Susquehanna, so no getting on a barge to cross. I simply sat and watched the sparkling river fly under me for a few minutes, and we rattled on. In Philadelphia, horses pulled us from station to station. The ride was rough, but I was content to sit, more or less, as we bumped through the streets. Then we careened on toward New York.

It was dark when I reached the Lyles' door and knocked.

Kathleen opened the door and gave me a smile and held out her arms for a hug.

"Kathleen?" I blurted. "What are you doing here?"

"A fine greeting that is." She laughed. "I call on Julia once a week, and I stay with the old folks so Jerusha can go out."

I hugged her. "I'm so glad."

We went into her little parlor, where an oil lamp cast a bright pool of light on her floorcloth. Mrs. Lyle gave me a nod, and over in the corner, away from the light, I could just make out Julia's face. I hurried over to embrace her.

There was almost nothing to her. She was thin and light as a straw pillow. It made tears come to my eyes.

"Well, I must be a sight if I make a grown woman weep," she said. Her voice was slurred, and only a faint echo of what it had been before. But the spirit was still there. I laughed—partly with emotion, and partly with relief.

"Oh, Julia, I have missed you." I held her close and smelled the scent of her again. But it was faint. The shabby dressing gown she wore had none of the smell of straw and fresh air her clothes always held. I pulled myself together, gave her a smile and a kiss, and straightened up.

Kathleen made tea, and when we finished, she said she'd have to go, but could I come by tomorrow evening? Of course, I told her.

Jerusha came in a few minutes later. She was thinner and bonier—just past thirty and looking older.

I offered to put hot water on the tea leaves, and she nodded. While the kettle boiled, I fetched water for the washing up.

"I was sorry to hear about your husband's death," she said.

"Thank you."

"He died about the same time Pa did."

"I'm so sorry. I didn't know your father had passed away."

"He'd been ill. We've been struggling for some time here. The bit of money Julia brought us was welcome."

"I can give you a little. I don't have much either." I frowned regretfully.

Jerusha looked at me keenly, and spoke very quietly. "She won't be here much longer. I think she's been holding on until she could see you again. Let's start supper."

Supper was potatoes fried up with some onion and a bit of salt fish. Neither of the two old ladies wanted more than a few bites. I was famished, but held back because I knew there wasn't much.

We tidied up, and Julia and I got ready to sleep in the tiny back room. We undressed—Julia a little slowly and with help—and put out the candle. I let my exhausted body sink into the straw pallet. We lay awake for a few minutes, holding hands and chatting softly. But I was so tired I soon slept like the dead. When I awoke, the sun was up and the room already hot.

Julia still lay beside me. "Awake now?" she asked.

I grunted an assent.

"I want you to take my family Bible."

My sleep-stupid mind groped to understand this. "What?" No answer. "Why?"

She answered quietly, "I have no other family."

I considered this. I turned my head to look at her. "Julia, we're not even related."

"You have no idea who your relations are."

I had to smile at this flash of her old spirit.

What she said was true. I knew my mother, but I wasn't sure whether Lizzie was my sister or my half-sister. I was reasonably sure my "father" had not been my father and that my "cousin" Julia was not, in fact, any such thing. Yet of all living persons, she was the closest to my heart.

"Julia, I will of course take the Bible and cherish it when the time comes. I hope you will have need of it, though, for quite a while."

"Piffle," she slurred. "I a'nt got long to live. I know that; you know that. Please go pick up the Bible off the dresser."

I rolled over, put my bare feet on the gritty plank floor, and padded, yawning, over to the dresser. The Bible sat between the *Works of William Shakespeare* and a bound copy of the sermons of Hosea Ballou. Her beloved book of Greek stories completed the set. That was all she had of what had once been a good collection of books.

I held the Bible out to her.

"Open it," she said. "To the front."

"Genesis?"

"No, girl. The very front. Where the family is listed."

I did as I was told.

"Read the last few entries," she said.

I saw the entries for Julia, her marriage, her mother, father, her long-dead brother—and her daughter, Vera. She had listed me as her daughter in her family Bible.

I looked up at her, confused.

"It makes as much sense as a lot of family Bible entries," she said. "I raised you."

"You did," I agreed. "And I'm grateful, but ..."

"But nothing. A'nt a fortune in being my daughter."

"But this isn't true." I shook my head.

"I say it is, and it's my Bible. Who knows how many people have listed children who weren't theirs? How many children are listed as children of a man who just happened to be the mother's husband?"

Who knew the answer to that question? Not me.

"Men and women have claimed parents they never had, especially if there was money in it. Sometimes a child is adopted, and the family records say nothing. Foundlings are listed in family Bibles. Families belong in family Bibles. You belong in mine."

"But ... I ... I ..."

"Don't sputter, girl. Either say something or don't." The last word was a whisper. She'd used up her strength.

I knelt by the bed and clumsily put my arms around her. Tears pushed out of my eyes—tears of gratitude, tears of love, tears of pain. I had no words. To this day, I still don't

After a time, she whispered, "Take it with you when you go."

I nodded, pulling away. I washed my face and tenderly washed hers.

That evening, I went to see Kathleen and Finn Malone. Finn was a bit stouter, but had the same merry look in his dark eyes, and the same comfortable manner holding a beer glass in his hand despite his missing fingertips. Mrs. O'Hanrahan had more gray hair and more lines sinking into a permanent frown. A chubby, ruddy-cheeked child sat in the middle of the floor, buzzing his lips and blowing bubbles.

"That's a happy child," I said, laughing.

"That's Seamus," said Finn. "We named him for your Jim."

That made me smile. "So, Mr. Malone," I began, "how goes the work of a constable?"

"It's sergeant now, Mrs. O'Dea," he answered. "And it would be wonderful work if it weren't for all these bloody Irish making trouble."

I laughed, but he said, "I'm serious, missus. I know we did a bit of head crackin', and God knows our lads loved their beer, but this new lot off the boat ..." He shook his head. "Riots! Tearin' up the streets. Burnin' shops and houses. All fueled by whiskey. Then they call us turncoats when we haul them off to jail. Like bein' Irish is supposed to make us all brothers." He snorted.

It was amazing to hear, but I suppose it was no real surprise. Now that he had a family and property and a city to protect, Finn's attitude about a street punch-up had shifted entirely.

What he once considered normal recreation, he now saw as a dire threat. A remarkable change had taken place in—what?—four years.

"He looks so good in his uniform." Kathleen smiled. "Every day when he goes, I give him a pat on the behind and remind him to tell all the hussies he's married."

Soon, little Seamus started to yawn. Kathleen picked him up to put him to bed, and I said I must go. Finn walked me back through the dark streets. I remarked that Baltimore was ahead of New York City when it came to streetlights.

"That may be," said Finn, "but I think the day has come when every city needs real paid police. Watchmen and magistrates can't keep up with all that wants to do evil."

"Well, that's true. If we had police like you in Baltimore, maybe Jimmy's murderer wouldn't still be walking around free," I said bitterly.

"Not if I could make an arrest." He agreed. "Seamus O'Dea was one of the finest men the good Lord ever made. Here we are. Good night, missus."

He watched as I went inside.

⁓

JULIA ONLY LASTED A FEW more days. I stayed with her, talked to her, read a little to her, emptied her chamberpot, combed her hair, braided some straw. One morning, she became still, staring straight ahead. She tried to speak but no words came. Jerusha quickly sent for a doctor.

I lay next to Julia, my arms around her, feeling her breathe—and then feeling her stop breathing. The doctor arrived and held her wrist for a minute and then shook his head and gently closed her eyes.

We had a service in the little Universalist chapel, with Jerusha and a few of her Universalist friends in attendance. Kathleen was there with me, in defiance of her priest. The rest of the family joined us in the churchyard for the burial—Mrs. O'Hanrahan looking grim and disapproving, Finn holding little Seamus.

It was cold and blustery that day, and I think my tears froze as they streamed down my face. I stood hugging Julia's Bible. *Oh, Julia,* I thought, *I only now learned how much you loved me. I belonged to you. Now you're gone, and I belong nowhere.* I stood there long after the ashes had gone on her coffin, watching the shovelfuls of earth thump down. Then Kathleen came up and took my arm, and I looked around at the shivering minister and the people who plainly wished to go. I nodded, and we walked off.

It took only a few minutes to take care of Julia's few possessions. I decided I would keep her Bible, a quilt, her good skirt, and her worn little ring. I would give Jerusha the other quilt, the other skirt, her one bodice; Kathleen could have her two hats (whether she wanted them or not). The book of Shakespeare could go to Finn, and the Ballou sermons to Jerusha. And then all traces of Julia would be gone. This capable, intelligent woman had lived her life on the edges of other people's lives, her presence barely tolerated. If I chose to stay here, I would likely live all my days that way—and I was only three-and-twenty.

No. My situation with Mary Easley might be odd, but it was better than what I would find here.

∽

LATER THAT SAME DAY, I was hurtling southward toward Baltimore with my arms around Julia's Bible.

I thought about how little I had ever belonged anywhere—not with pity for myself this time, but as a simple fact. Still, I had been very lucky. A man who was not my father had taken me away from certain doom on Goerck Street. A woman who was not my mother had taken me in, schooled me carefully, and made sure I could fend for myself. Still, I never felt I belonged anywhere—partly because of my mother, who probably never belonged anywhere herself.

Whoever my father was, he had probably used her and cast her aside. I could be Chinese on my father's side, for all I knew, or African. Did other people always feel a sense of belonging? Maybe a sense of belonging was just a comforting delusion. Like God.

That last thought startled me. I hadn't put that feeling into words before. Well, I certainly knew enough to keep that to myself. Even if God were no more than a comforting delusion, even if I belonged nowhere, it still gave me comfort to hug Julia's Bible with my name in it. So I did.

I thought for the first time about the possibilities presented by the fancy certificates, but also of how distant was the possibility of turning them into something useful. A hatmaker's assistant could scarcely bounce into Brown and Flanders's bank, present the papers, and expect to get the money they might represent. The bankers would, at the least, escort me out for my impertinence and, at the most, escort me to jail for having such things in the first place. Even if they said, "Why, of course, Mrs. O'Dea, you have the proper instruments, and we can see in your clear eyes you're an honest woman, so here is a preposterous sum of money," then I would likely be robbed on the way home.

How to do it? It teased at my mind. Ophelia Fenton. Surely she knew men who could do this. But could she trust them, and could I trust her? And what would it cost me?

We arrived in Philadelphia and stayed on the railway wagon as they hitched up horses to take us across town, and unhitched them again to put us with another locomotive. The train jostled and banged, and then we chuffed away from Philadelphia. The thought of the papers still teased at me. I held something significant in my hands—possibly even a fortune. But I needed a key to unlock it, to make it be more than just a stack of pretty papers.

Dishonest means would be dangerous, but honest means might not work. After all, these papers were stolen in the first place.

I didn't trust Ophelia, and I was afraid to try it myself. I didn't have to do anything right away, I reasoned. I did have a place to live, even if it was Mob Town.

That would soon change.

CHAPTER 34

NOW THAT I LOOK BACK, I WONDER WHY I DIDN'T SEE the direction the country was heading, and my life with it. People everywhere were angry, ready to fight. Baltimore earned its Mob Town nickname over and over in the next year. Whiskey and politics were a volatile mixture, and they exploded with brawls. Sticks, stones, and brickbats flew through the air every day—even in the respectable neighborhoods. Sometimes the gangs could keep a sort of order; the poor night watch certainly couldn't. As often as not, they hid in their stations, which were little more than outhouses. If their stations were in the way of the brawl, they just got turned over.

Men fought over who had jobs and who didn't—native-born or foreign-born. Then the Know-Nothings seemed suddenly to evaporate. They lost the Maryland legislature; they lost the municipal offices. Maybe they became Republicans or Free-Soilers—or "night-soilers," as the wags called them—or perhaps they crept into the walls.

I think Bill McCracken must have flown from a crack in the wall the day I encountered him near Mount Clare. I was walking along, thinking of nothing very important, and suddenly he was standing in front of me.

"If it isn't Mrs. O'Dea," he said. I tried to walk around him. He stepped in front of me. He was still breathtakingly beautiful. He went on: "Or should I say, Widow O'Dea?"

Toe rag, I thought, glaring at him.

"My condolences on your husband's death."

I said nothing.

"You could say he gave his *awl*." McCracken smirked.

If I'd had a gun, I'd have killed him. If I'd been a man, I'd have hit him. As it was, I simply stood there, boiling, glaring at him.

"Oh, now. I'm just a country boy. I don't mean any harm. You were too good for him, you know."

"No, Mr. McCracken, I did not know that."

"And you think you're too good for me, don't you?"

I thought, *Disemboweling is too good for you.* I said primly, "I have never given the matter any thought. May I walk on, please?"

"Yes, for now." He stepped aside and gave an elaborate bow and then took my arm as I passed by. "But you won't get away from me. I'll do anything to have you, and you know that." His green eyes looked deep into mine, and I felt a powerful pull.

I tugged free from him and walked away, my insides roiling with my white-hot anger and my helpless fury at injustice and ... something else. It stirred me that he wanted me. Yes, it did. In spite of who he was and what he had done, he was handsome and impetuous, and he profoundly excited me. What was wrong with me?

I shook my head and walked on. But I had powerful, urgent dreams of him that night—and again on other nights. I would wake up passionately stirred, wet between the legs, and angry with myself.

That was not the only thing that disturbed my thoughts. Although I had a good, quiet place of it with Mary Easley, a letter from Lizzie set me to thinking.

My Dearest Sister,

> I am so saddened to hear of Miss Julia's death. I
> know you loved her grately, although my memories of
> her are not so fond.

I thought nastily that her spelling had slipped again.

> I think I can confide something in you. I am mys-
> tically, deeply drawn to Catholicism. I stopped to
> pray in a Catholic church here in Boston not long ago,
> and I felt a deep peace come over me. I want to be
> a Catholic, and I want to ask forgiveness. My dear
> sister, do you find that so very strange? Mr. Eckel
> would. He is a freethinker. I want to be forgiven for
> what our mother did, for all the lies she told, for the
> evil person she was. I want to be forgiven for hating
> her. Do you ever feel that way?

Well, yes, I did feel that way sometimes, but it never occurred
to me to ask for forgiveness for something I had not done. I did
wonder sometimes if I were being punished for our mother's
deeds. I blamed her some for Jimmy's death, but I didn't hate
her the way Lizzie did.

Her letter went on with some hints at financial reverses and
Mr. Eckel's plans to move.

> We may move to Washington City! Mr. Eckel
> wants to further his business interests, and we may
> journey there soon to see if the climate is good.

Odd. I hadn't recollected that he had any business interests—
but then I was never entirely clear on the sources of his great
wealth.

She wrote that they might stop in Baltimore on the way
to Washington. She gave the name of a hotel near the railway
station—one that probably wouldn't let me in the front door, I

thought bitterly. Still, she wanted me to join them for dinner. I wrote back that I would be happy to see her.

They came through Baltimore in January of 1860, the day after I turned four-and-twenty. The pompous clerk at the desk looked me up and down but told me they were expecting me to visit their room. They had ordered dinner in their room—which was a little odd—but nonetheless, I went up the stairs to see them.

Lizzie met me at the door with a hug and a whispered hello. Her husband was snoring on the bed. Lizzie whispered, "Poor thing. He's exhausted from our journey, and from looking after me."

He was no such thing. He was drunk. Cannon fire wouldn't have wakened him, but we whispered our conversation.

Was her health good? Yes, and she had exciting news. She was expecting a baby! She was a little pudgy and pale, but did not look as though she were carrying a child. She said the baby would likely be born in September. William had such wonderful prospects in Washington City, she bubbled. It was a wonderful time to be going. "We'll be dealing in government contracts," she whispered. "It's so exciting! It all depends on who you know—and William's family knows so many people. Even women can make money. I might be able to do it."

Yes, I agreed, it was probably a good idea to make a little money on her own, even if it would belong to her husband.

We ate a bit of bread and beer, some cold meat, and some very bad mustard. She told me they'd be staying at Brown's Hotel in Washington City. The name meant nothing to me, but she seemed impressed.

"You should come with us," she whispered. I whispered back that we could wait and see.

She was lonely, I thought. As I walked home that cool autumn evening, I thought she was probably as lonely in her marriage as I was in my widowhood. But I didn't want to go with her. It was odd, perhaps, but I didn't feel I belonged with Lizzie.

They did have some good luck. A letter she wrote in May told of contracts solicited and gained, fees paid, and many parties and gatherings. But it also told a story of great loss. She had miscarried her child.

Oh, Lizzie, I wrote. *I am so sorry for your grief—for I know it is a grief. I miscarried a child when I was married to Jimmy, and there has been many a day I have wished I had that child and sorrowed greatly that I did not.*

I kept telling myself I was happy enough to stay where I was. My life with Mary was peaceful. Still, all around me, people were restless and angry, and I thought I should try to see if I could change my pretty papers into gold.

I hinted in a roundabout way to Ophelia that I might know of someone who might need a gentleman's help in obtaining money. She let me know, in a less roundabout way, that she would need that someone's full confidence and a large slice of the proceeds. I didn't trust her, and I didn't want to have to trust her, so I decided to try it myself.

One fall morning, I put on my best skirt and shawl and a fine lady's bonnet from the shop window. I took the paper Jimmy had left, and one other, and walked up to the grand Brown and Flanders Bank. I summoned all my courage to go in the door, and then stood inside a large room. It had fine carpets on the floor and cages with men behind them, handling money. Other men sat at desks nearer the door. None of them looked up.

I stood there for a few minutes, feeling more awkward by the minute, when the nearest clerk arose, walked over to me, and gave me a cold, appraising look.

"Are you waiting for someone?" he asked.

"No, I have some papers I need seen to." My hands shook as I took them from my little bag and held them out.

He did not take the papers, but looked at them and then at me and then at the papers again.

"I do not know you, miss. Do you have a letter of introduction?"

One of the other clerks snickered. I was humiliated. My eyes began to sting and my face began to burn. "No," I said and stuffed the letters back into the bag. I turned and walked from the bank, trying not to cry.

I thought of half a dozen superior responses in the space of half a minute. But I knew that even playing the grand lady, wearing the best bonnet in the world, would get me nowhere in a bank unless I had a husband on my arm or a lawyer at my back. They knew I had no business with such papers, and there was no reason for them to humor me.

My face burned, and it took all my presence of mind not to rush home crying. It was very comforting to get back to Mary and the shop, and a place where I knew I would be treated kindly. I decided then that I could just stay and not try to be too ambitious.

As it turned out, I didn't have a choice.

⚬⚬⚬

I THINK EVERYONE WHO WAS in Baltimore on the nineteenth day of April, 1861, remembers exactly where they were and what happened to them. Marylanders had been talking loudly of seceding from the Union. When the Southrons in South Carolina fired on Fort Sumter, Baltimore's streets were filled with bonfires and cheering crowds.

Mr. Lincoln had been elected president and had been supposed to come through Baltimore on the train. I'm still not certain if he came through in the middle of the night, as some have alleged, leaving his wife and children to be greeted by the mayor—or if he went round the city by some other means. But feelings were so high, for and against the union of the states, that many feared if he showed his face in Baltimore, he would have been killed. I think he might have. We heard there would be soldiers coming through town to occupy Washington—or they might even occupy Baltimore—because feeling for secession ran so high.

April nineteenth was the day of the Battle of Baltimore. I had started the day enjoying a clear, sunlit Saturday morning. I went for a walk around Fells Point, watching a clipper ship set sail and listening to the songs of the sailors soaring over the water. Easter was past and we were not busy, but I knew there would still be ladies in the shop of a Saturday afternoon, and I had to get back. I was thinking about my situation. I was five-and-twenty and living like a child, doing my bits of work, making some money here and there, but without a husband or a place of my own.

As I walked toward Pratt Street, I saw horses pulling the railroad cars through town. Soldiers were on them, and there were soldiers marching with the cars, troops from Massachusetts headed south to protect Washington. There were a few children skipping along behind and a few idlers watching the parade. I walked alongside, avoiding the idlers and enjoying the antics of the children. Then groups of men quickly appeared, and suddenly, I was in a jostling, jeering, angry crowd. I tried to move away but I kept getting pushed back, because more and more people were pouring onto Pratt Street to jeer the soldiers.

"Go back to Trasha-chusetts!" A rock sang through the air and clipped a soldier's shoulder. The men beside him pointed their guns where the rock came from, and the crowd howled and surged around them.

I pushed more desperately, trying to get away. I was slammed against a house, scraping my face. I felt a hand grab at my breast, and I lunged away, tearing my bodice. I finally broke through to a side street and started to run. I heard a shot and felt a splatter on my back, then saw blood on my arm. Men's arms grabbed at me, and I started to struggle and scream. One man's arm knocked away two of the other men, and I was pulled backward and held against my defender's body.

"Get off and let her alone," he said. I knew that voice. The men who had attacked me sneered and muttered, but they walked away. My defender turned me around, and I was looking once more into brilliant green eyes of Bill McCracken.

"Are you all right?" he asked.

I nodded.

"Are you close to home?" he said.

I nodded again.

"Where?"

"That way." I pointed and started walking. He ran up behind me and caught me by the waist, walking me more rapidly toward Howard Street.

"I'll get you there," he said, holding me firmly. And when we arrived, he turned me to him and kissed me, powerfully, urgently, leaving me gasping.

"You're safe now," he said, and ran toward the noise of rioting and shots.

Safe? Perhaps. But I was rattled, and the shouts and gunshots of the riot were coming nearer.

The shop was shuttered and barred. I pounded on the door. "It's Vera! Let me in!"

The door opened a crack, and Mary gasped and grabbed my arm and pulled me in. She held on to my arm. "Here, walk through," she said. "Don't touch anything." And she led me to the back, past pale, wide-eyed women.

I took off my torn bodice and saw the back was covered with blood and grime. I splashed cold water on my face and put the bodice to soak. As I walked up the stairs to get my other clothes, I started to shake. My hands shook so I could hardly fasten my bodice, and it was several minutes before I could brush my hair and compose myself.

I went back down into the shop, where a half-dozen women

and girls sat silently, listening to the rising noise of shouting and shooting.

Miss Easley whispered, "Are you all right, then? You looked a fright."

I whispered back, "It's not all my blood. I'm fine." But I was shaking.

One young woman began to cry. Her mother, looking distracted, patted her shoulder.

"Well," said a ponderous voice, "we're all afeared." Mrs. Obadiah Plunkett was huddled at the back of the room.

I don't know how long we sat listening to the running feet and shouts outside, jumping at every gunshot. Mary made tea, but most of the cups sat untouched. Frothy little bonnets sat on their stands and on the shelves, looking both pathetic and absurd—as though they, too, were afraid and helpless.

But as I sat, I felt an enormous rush of exhilaration and, yes, desire, sweep through me. I felt alive—more alive than I had felt at any point since Jimmy died. Maybe more alive than I had ever felt. I wanted nothing more than to be naked and struggling in a bed with Bill McCracken.

I sat and sipped my cold tea.

Suddenly, there was quiet outside. After it had lasted for a few minutes, we started to speak.

One woman said, "I don't know where we're going to go. All my friends are leaving. All the Southrons are heading south. There's no point in giving fetes or balls anymore because there are so few people left to come. We haven't left because—because we have no place else to go."

"Well," said Mrs. Plunkett, "Mr. Plunkett and I will probably move back out to the country. The city's too dangerous now. I don't want to be here if it's full of soldiers. It will get rough, and nobody will do any business."

"And there's talk that all the important men will be arrested. They even speak of putting Mr. Teackle Wallis in jail," said one lady, naming one of the most respected elder statesmen in Baltimore.

"Mr. Teackle Wallis should mind his tongue if he doesn't want to go," said Mrs. Plunkett tartly.

Heavy silence. We all knew people in the city disagreed with one another, but we were trapped together, and argument would just make it worse. Sweeping from the room in high dudgeon would be foolish and possibly fatal. So we sat or stood in a tense silence for a little while. Then the ladies departed, none of them having ordered anything new.

After they left, Mary closed the door and leaned against it. "There's one mercy in all this," she said. "Easter was early, and we've been paid for the Easter bonnets." Then she sat down and burst into tears. "But I won't be able to pay the rent," she sputtered out between sobs. "I can't keep my shop. I can't stay here. I can't! Half my ladies have left, and more are leaving."

I tried to console her. "I don't think Mrs. Fenton's girls are going anywhere." Even as I said it, I knew some were. Everyone was frightened, and some were restless. We didn't know if the soldiers were really going on to Washington City, or if they would stay in Baltimore to keep order. And if they didn't stay, there would be other soldiers. Soldiers would want whores, but they didn't have money for parlor girls. Ophelia Fenton's parlor girls were already leaving to try their luck in other cities. I had little comfort for Mary. I didn't know where we could go, either. Nor did I know what to do if she went someplace I couldn't follow.

Find Bill McCracken? *No.* I slammed that thought down. *I don't* know *that he killed Jimmy,* my mind wheedled.

I went outside and looked at the scene on Howard Street. There were small groups of men moving toward me, away from the tracks on Pratt Street. Bill was not among them. I stood for a minute, unsure whether I should stand there or go back in and bar the door. The men walked wearily, and I decided to stay outside. Some of them were bloodied, and I was reminded again of the bloodied men who had tried to vote and even, oddly, of the Negro who used to butcher pigs on Goerck Street. I had seen too many bloodied men, and I was tired of it.

I swept some brick shards from the front step and sat down on it heavily. The spring afternoon was still bright with sunshine, but my heart was dark and fearful. Where could I go? How would I get there?

CHAPTER 35

*M*ARY HAD TO MOVE TO PHILADELPHIA, WHERE SHE HAD a brother. He had found a man for her to marry. She did not wish to marry—but it was marry, whore, or starve. She stormed bitterly about it.

I had no brother, and no place to go.

Mrs. Fenton would take me in, but I hadn't wanted to be a parlor girl, and I certainly didn't want to be a street whore for soldiers. I needed money, even if it was just to go to Washington City to live with Lizzie for a few weeks. I had to find a way to use the railroad papers. I would be going to Mrs. Fenton's one way or the other.

Early one afternoon, as people at Mrs. Fenton's were just beginning to stir, I bounced in and said, "Mrs. Fenton, I have a business proposition."

"You'd have the same terms as all my girls," she answered with a sly smile. She had assumed the troubles in town would sooner or later mean troubles for me.

"That's not what I mean," I answered quickly, and pulled two papers from my bag.

"Where did you get these?"

"I can't tell you that."

"I'll wager I know, missy. You got these when Emmeline got her gold."

I hesitated. "I got one from my husband."

"Oh, and where did your Irish boyo get it, eh? Well, never mind. I think we can do business."

"How much will you want?"

"Now that's a question, isn't it? And the better question is how much will one of our gentlemen want, so he can take care of this for you."

I realized she probably couldn't carry off demanding money in a bank any better than I could. She probably kept her money under a mattress in the whorehouse.

I held out my hand for the papers. "I'd like to meet the gentleman who does this for me—for us."

"Oh, would you now?" She looked at me shrewdly as greed struggled with caution inside her. Greed won. "Be back in two hours."

I kept my hand held out. Grudgingly, she returned my papers.

⁓

I WAS BACK IN LESS than two hours. Mr. Bump stood in her parlor. The sight of him made me slightly queasy.

His face and the top of his head turned a deep red. "Mrs. O'Dea?" he blurted.

Mrs. Fenton's eyebrows shot up. "You know each other? Well, that puts a different face on this, doesn't it?"

Yes, it does, I thought. *You don't know how different.* He couldn't look me in the eye. I said, primly, "I will be very grateful for Mr. Bump's assistance."

He was still flustered. I handed him the certificates, and he looked at them and regained his composure in a snap. "How did you get these?"

"I beg your pardon?" I answered coolly. Here was someone I knew I could face down.

"I know that, um, certain persons have received these in gratitude for favors. Um, political favors," he added quickly, reddening still further.

"Well now, it could have been for other favors, couldn't it?" said Mrs. Fenton, who was starting to enjoy this little scene.

"My husband left me one of them," I answered. "The other was given to me. Willingly."

I looked him steadily in the eye. He could think what he wanted. I didn't care anymore.

He blushed and looked away. "Well," he said. "Yes, I can redeem these for you. But I will need a percentage."

"You may have a quarter of the proceeds," I said, having no idea what a quarter of the proceeds would be. "Mrs. Fenton may also have a quarter. I will be satisfied with half." I had no idea what kind of bargain I was making, but I thought it sounded good.

"Yes, well," he said, putting on his hat and hurrying toward the door. "I should have this done by Thursday."

∽

He did. Thursday, I went to Mrs. Fenton's, and she had a small, heavy purse for me.

"Do you have any more of those papers?" she asked.

"No." I lied. "Why?"

"Look in the purse," she said. "That's your half."

The heavy little purse was filled with gold and silver. There was almost a hundred dollars in it. I could go to Washington. I could walk out the door and get the next clipper to San Francisco. I could go anywhere I wanted—for now.

259

CHAPTER 36

J WROTE TO LIZZIE. SHE ANSWERED THAT I COULD COME, BUT she could not afford to give charity. I could stay for a few weeks. It was better than nothing, and better than any other choices I had.

It was bitterly hard parting from Mary. I had come to love her, and knew something in her broke as she was forced into a choice she did not want. The landlord got the hat stands—and the silk, feathers, and other hat-making materials. In other times, those would have been worth three months' rent. But we couldn't sell the hats. On the other hand, there were plenty of takers for a shop space to sell things to soldiers. The landlord could rent it out for five times what Mary paid. Even if I used all the money I'd just gotten, it would have done no good. We'd have had more time together, but no money coming in. We would still have to part, and the money would be gone.

Sometimes we cried together. More often, I held her sobbing in my arms. We kissed and made love in a desperate way that did not ease our sorrow. Then, early one morning, I walked her to the President Street station for her train going north, and we clung together in one last tearful embrace. She walked away without looking back, and bowed her head as she got on the train. Then I walked back to the shop to pack up all I owned.

The building stood quiet and empty. All that had made it a home for me was gone. I gathered up my six hatboxes, a cheap carpetbag with my clothes, a quilt, and the floorcloth from the house I had shared with Jimmy. Within a few minutes, I closed the door one last time, and was on my way.

Camden Station was noisy. Most of the hubbub was caused by a beautiful woman commanding a platoon of porters.

It was Delilah, dressed in bright yellow and creating a huge scene. She had trunks and boxes, hatboxes and bandboxes—all bound for Washington City. I stood with a small crowd and watched how fast and with what terror these men moved. "That go there!" she ordered to a portly Irishman with a handcart. "Don't be crushing that box!"

She stopped briefly in her commands and put a hand over her eyes.

"Delilah?" I said, touching her elbow.

She peeked out from behind her hand, gave a great exhale, and then clutched my arm. "Vera! I don't know how I'm going to do this!"

"Do what?" I asked. "You seem to be getting whatever you want."

"I'm so skeered," she answered. "I ain't never been on one of these." She'd dropped her high-class parlor girl grammar.

"A railway train?" I asked, feeling suddenly much the veteran. "They go very fast, and it's frightening the first time. But where are you going? *Why* are you going?"

"I'm going to Washington City," she replied. "Miz Ophelia says she's going to do fine with the soldiers here, but I think there's bigger times in Washington City for a yella gal. And I think I can get more yella gals." She pulled up tall and threw her chest forward, greatly impressing the male spectators. "I'm going to open me a parlor."

"Well, Delilah," I said, "I think we're both off to seek our fortune in Washington City. Would you like me to ride with you?"

I was rewarded with a smile that would light the way to

heaven. "Oh yes," she said, her molasses eyes bright and seductive, even to me. "Stay with me."

An odd pair we made, I thought—a mousy hatmaker and a magnificent golden whore. When the train started and lurched forward, Delilah shrieked and grabbed my arm. She prayed aloud to Jesus for the length of the trip.

The trip probably took only an hour or so, but it seemed like a year with Delilah clutching my arm and shrieking at every little bump. Finally, the train slowed, and we came into Washington City. Delilah recovered the instant the train stopped. She was soon on the platform, gathering another platoon of men. We waved to each other and I smiled as I walked on.

Washington City stank. The heat slammed the front of my body and the top of my head with a physical force I never knew air could have. I could hardly catch my breath for the stink. The first thing I saw outside the station was a dead dog, already picked over by crows, and home to a Biblical plague of flies, which arose in a buzzing horde as I walked by.

Then I heard Lizzie's voice. "Oh, hallooo! Dear sister!"

She sat waving her handkerchief in the backseat of a shabby trap. An elderly black man sat drowsing in the driver's seat as a rusty black mare stood with her head lowered, resting with one hind foot tilted up.

Lizzie jumped down and held out her arms. She was a good deal plumper than I remembered—and, I discovered as we hugged, quite moist. This sweaty little woman was all the family I had.

"Washington!" she said loudly. "Put Mrs. O'Dea's boxes in the carriage."

The black man dipped his head and sighed a deep breath, then moved slowly down from the driver's seat and shuffled toward my boxes. I started to help him, but Lizzie hissed, "No! Sit here with me! Washington is to manage them."

The old man slowly walked my boxes, two at a time, over to

the trap. I was so impatient to get out of the heat I could hardly sit still. Lizzie sat vibrating an ivory-stick fan, beads of sweat forming on her lip and starting to trickle from her brow.

"He was the best we could afford," she said. "We expect to do better soon."

"Lizzie!" I whispered urgently.

"It doesn't matter if he hears me," she said. "He's like the furniture."

Washington certainly gave no indication he had heard. His eyes showed nothing, and his face was a mask as he slowly walked the hatboxes, then my carpetbag, then my one bundle to the trap. Finally he climbed into the driver's seat.

We sat for a minute. Then Lizzie said, "Home," in a haughty tone that made me want to slap her. Washington picked up the reins and clucked to the horse, which started on a slow clip-clop over the road.

I say "road," but it was nothing like the neat brick streets I had become accustomed to in Baltimore. It was more of a sticky clay track, out past some sagging houses and lean-tos. Suddenly we were into a broad vista with a half-built dome floating above.

"That's the Capitol," said Lizzie proudly. "Isn't it grand?"

"Grand" was not the word I'd have used. The Capitol was an unfinished hulk squatted on a landscape littered with bricks and wood and workers' tools. The big circular part was partially open to the sky.

What are men thinking to do such? I wondered. *This great, grandiose idea that they'll never finish, that they'll never get done—and all around it squalor.*

Below the Capitol building sat a wide green canal. I say "sat" because the water did not appear to flow. Its distinguishing characteristics, besides the stink, were a nasty green scum, clots of horse manure, and a rotting cat.

I held back an urge to gag, and asked, "How far is it to your

263

hotel? And please tell me about your baby and how Mr. Eckel is doing."

Lizzie laughed and crossed her arms across her breasts, almost bumping me with her parasol. "This is only my second outing since Felicity was born in May," she said. "I'm afraid talking about her will make me squirt milk!"

I had to laugh, but was embarrassed for her coachman, or servant—or slave.

"Lizzie." I laughed. "There's no need to tell the world!"

"Oh, I won't. And we don't have far to go. I just didn't want you walking through Swampoodle by yourself."

"It doesn't look any worse than Goerck Street," I said, seeing listless skeins of Irish children in the fetid street. One grimy-faced lad walked beside our trap, trying to catch our eye and perhaps a penny.

Lizzie gave me an exasperated look and continued. "It's been so hard. Did I tell you William lost all his money?"

"No."

She paused and took a breath, going on in a lowered voice. "Perhaps you heard about the sinking of the good ship *Obed Mitchell*?"

I shook my head. She continued. "Well, it was a ship and it sank. It ruined him and cost his family dearly. He didn't tell me for months, of course."

Of course?

"Poor dear, he just drank and played cards. Not that playing cards was all bad, mind you. We have made a great many prominent friends in Washington in this wise, and they have come in handy. He fell ill and thought he was dying, so he told me about it. I wept, and he wept, and I told him more about our childhood than I ever had before, and that I was deathly afraid of being poor. We wept some more, and then I stopped. I said I was tired of being a pretty puppet, and that, as he had stood between the world and me, I would stand between him and the world."

What does that mean? I wondered, looking at her questioningly.

She saw my expression and laughed. "He didn't know what I meant. I probably didn't either. He said if it hadn't been for me, he would have lit a handful of charcoal in his room until it was all over."

She shot me a meaningful glance and went on. "The next morning, I went to see our friend Colonel Bilbo of Tennessee. Colonel Bilbo declared to his friends that I was to be considered his adopted daughter, and his Southron friends were to come to me for his good offices. He found dear William a post at the Custom House, although he hasn't been back to it since Felicity was born."

She paused to let this sink in. I watched Washington's back and listened to the horse's hooves scuff on the clay street. Finally the horse stopped in front of a tall townhouse.

"Colonel Bilbo has left, of course," she said. "All the Southrons are packing up and going home. Speaking of home, here we are."

We had not gone far. We stopped before Brown's Hotel. Washington helped us both alight, and we proceeded through the lobby. As we came to the stairs, I stopped to read a sign: *The Proprietor of this hotel has roomy underground cells for confining slaves for safekeeping, and patrons are notified that their slaves will be well cared for. In case of escape, full value of the Negro will be paid by the Proprietor.*

"Lizzie?" I asked her softly. "Does that sign mean that Washington sleeps in a cell under the hotel?"

She looked at me as though I were suddenly speaking Greek. "Well, of course he sleeps in the slave quarters," she answered. "Did you think he stayed with us in our rooms?"

Lizzie and her husband and baby occupied a suite of rooms on the fourth floor. Her husband was out. We opened the door to a squalling baby, held by a tired-looking young Negro woman.

Lizzie bustled over and held out her arms. "I'll take my little darling, Queen Esther. Show my sister where she'll be sleeping."

265

Queen Esther silently handed over the baby, and led me down a short hall to a small room with a straw pallet on one side, a small table, a ewer, and a wooden box. It was not grand, but I would have it all to myself.

Washington came up with my hatboxes. I stacked them in a corner and sat for a few minutes on the wooden box. I heard Washington walking away and then down the steps. I heard the traffic on the street—horses scuffing, carts creaking, people talking. Occasionally, a child shouted.

Soon Lizzie came in, smiling and radiant, with her baby in her arms. "Look, 'Leecy, it's your Auntie Vera," she cooed.

I reached out a finger, and the infant grasped it and looked at me. "Hello, Felicity," I said and smiled. The child looked at me as if something in its little mind were asking, *What is this?*

"Auntie Vera's come to stay for a while," said Lizzie in a high, sing-songy voice, "Yes, she has! Yes, she has!" And she nuzzled Felicity's face, which promptly crumpled as the baby began to cry again.

Queen Esther came in and, without a word, took the screaming child and began to walk around the front parlor with her.

"She's just colicky," sighed Lizzie. "Queen Esther says it will pass."

"I'm sure it will," I replied. "You see very few twenty-year-old women screaming like that."

Lizzie gave a rueful snort, closed the door, and plopped down on my pallet.

"I'm glad you're here. I don't know quite what we're going to do."

"What do you mean? You seem to be doing very well."

"Well, there's all this uncertainty with the war. Most of my connections were Southrons, and they've almost all left the city. The few connections I have left will be here tomorrow, for my soiree. I understand there's a deal of money to be made supplying the war, but it's not quite the same as building roadways

266

and collecting customs duties, and I'm not quite sure how to go about easing the contracts. I'm sure I shall learn." She sighed. "I shall have to."

"I don't know that I can do anything to help."

"I don't know that you can either. However, a good sisterly hug is certainly in order." Lizzie held out her arms, and we embraced for a good long time.

Then, still in her arms, I said, "Lizzie, I want to know something."

She sat back. "What?"

"Queen Esther. Is she a slave, too?"

"Well, if you must be so crude—she is," Lizzie answered. "We bought her from one of my Southron friends, at a very good price. It's not easy to get a mammy."

"Lizzie, I—I just—I think it's wrong."

"Oh, really!" She stood up and put her hands on her hips, just as she had when we were little. "Then perhaps you'd like to find another place to live. I am doing you a great favor. I'm making a good way for myself in the world, and you just might want to learn a thing or two from me."

And she flounced out, slamming the door. In some ways, Lizzie really hadn't changed very much. Or maybe I had.

CHAPTER 37

WHEN I AWOKE THE NEXT MORNING, IT WAS ALREADY light. The day's heat was beginning to seep into my skin. I lay on my back, listening to footfalls on the street. I wiggled to a cooler spot and reflected how purely delicious it was to sleep in a real bed, alone. It was a privilege I had not had since the days I lived with Julia.

Julia. I thought of my little bed, the henhouse, and the shimmering fields of barley in Flatbush. I thought about happy, simple times reading to each other, braiding straw, sewing. All gone now. No more home, no more little bed, no more Julia.

Jimmy. Jimmy with his bright eyes and brighter hopes, and his smooth, softly freckled, scented, sugary-salty skin. His delicious kisses gone. Gone forever. And as his face faded in my imagination, Bill McCracken's took its place, and I once again felt a rush of desire.

Don't do this, I thought. He might have killed Jimmy. I could see his blazing green eyes and feel how it felt when he kissed me and pressed his hard body to mine. My nipples grew hard, and I got hot and wet between my legs. I tried to find a cool spot in the bed. I slid a finger inside myself and used my thumb to stroke the little button of flesh, as Mary had. In less than a minute, I was pulsing wildly. Soon I felt strong contractions and release.

It was so long since I had a man.

Don't be stupid, I told myself. *He probably killed your husband. He says hello to you a year later, and two years after that, he kisses you. And now you want him so much you can't stand it. You probably won't see him for another two years. He doesn't care anything about you.*

How many people are in this discussion?

There hadn't been many men in my life. I'd worked in hat shop and certainly didn't want to go looking for men in a whorehouse. I told myself to take myself in hand.

Poor choice of words, I thought.

There was a tap on the door, and Queen Esther said, "Coffee here, Miz Ohday."

"Thank you," I answered, in what I hoped was a disciplined and ladylike fashion.

I sat up and took a deep breath, standing on the cool planks of the floor. I poured water into the basin and started to wash the sweat from my face. What, precisely, was my business in moping after worthless scum like Bill McCracken? Nobody owned me the way they owned Washington and Queen Esther. I might be carrying a fortune in my little box. And Lizzie and her friends, whoever they were, might be able to help me.

Maybe you shouldn't count on that, I told myself.

I brushed my hair and pinned it up neatly, stooping and craning to see my image in the dull bit of metal that served as a looking glass. I washed and dried my body. It felt good to clear off the layers of sweat. I put on my clothes and straightened my back. I went to face Lizzie and whoever else was about.

Lizzie sat looking haggard in a morning dress, nursing Felicity. I kissed her cheek and sat down next to her.

"What can I do to make you happier?" I asked. I smoothed her hair behind her ears. "I can trim you a bonnet."

"Oh, nobody here cares about bonnets."

"I do. And you're so pretty." I meant it. Even though she looked haggard, she still had her flashing dark eyes and thick dark hair. "And, Lizzie, I'm sorry I upset you. Let me get a bonnet and make it pretty. It's something I know I can do."

I got one of her bonnets from where they were all tossed higgledy-piggledy into a bandbox, and took out my sewing kit and some ribbons. We sat quietly for a few minutes. Lizzie burped Felicity and moved her to the other side.

"You seem so happy with your baby," I said.

She smiled—a serene smile I had never seen before. "I am. I love her so."

"Do you ever think about our mother?"

"All the time," she answered. "And you?

"Often, I answered, "And at the most unexpected times. Do you think she loved us?"

Lizzie looked fondly at her nursing baby. "I never thought our mother loved us until I had a child." She looked at me and shrugged slightly, although the baby at her breast limited her movement. "Now I think she *must* have loved us. I love my baby so much." The words caught in her throat as her eyes misted up

"What do you think of her story?" I pressed. "Do you think it was all lies?"

"I don't know." She sighed. "Our cousins thought it was gospel, although they never would have had anything to do with her. They thought she told the complete and total truth—even read her book to me. Can you imagine? But they called her a strumpet. She probably was. But, you know, there's something I've never told you. Never had the chance."

Felicity was asleep. Lizzie carefully did up her bodice with one hand. I kept arranging flowers on her bonnet and stitching them on.

She went on talking, "There was a neighbor who put his hand up my skirt when I was twelve. I told my Aunt Dora. She switched me and locked me in a closet for an afternoon, and then made me memorize some more Bible verses because I was evil. I thought about our mother a good deal after that—that maybe what she said was the truth. But even people who believed her thought she was evil. She *was* evil. Don't you think she was evil?"

"I don't think so," I answered. "She did lie. She lied so often about so much that I don't know what to believe. I'll probably never even know who my father was. At least you know yours. I don't know who I am or where I belong. Half the time, I don't even know what I think about anything."

"You were fairly sure of yourself talking about Queen Esther and Washington," she observed tartly.

"I was, wasn't I? Well, maybe I do know what I think about some things." *Change the subject*, I thought. "Now," I said, "tell me what you think of this bonnet. I'll hold Felicity while you look in the glass."

A smile into the looking glass told me what I wanted to know. "You really are good at this, Vera," she said. The coral and ivory ribbon posies brought out the brightness in her eyes and the warm gloss of her dark hair.

"I'm glad you like it. Now what can I do to make this evening a success?"

She yawned. "You could go get us half a barrel of oysters while I take a nap." She gave a little laugh at herself and went on. "I don't make much of a fuss. Men don't really care what you have, as long as there's something to eat and plenty to drink. So I give them have beer and whiskey and oysters and little else—perhaps just bread and cold meat and peanuts. Why don't you go with Washington today to get the oysters?"

An outing—any outing—sounded good, and the task sounded easy enough. The day was already bright and warm. We drove past the big market, where there were plenty of oysters for sale. Washington shook his head and drove on, down to a dismal little waterfront on the Potomac River. A few oystercatchers had put in. I paid for half a barrel and waited in the shade while a bony, sunburnt, tow-headed white man and his two bony, sunburnt, tow-headed sons shucked and iced them.

It was a sleepy, dull waterfront compared to New York or Baltimore. There were only the odd-looking oyster skipjacks for vessels—none of the great clipper ships of Baltimore's harbor, or the belching bustle of steam and sail I remembered from New York. There were no sailors, no ships unloading, no merchants, no whores. Just mud. I sat thinking I had come to a dull little city and would have little to watch outside in the streets.

I changed my mind as we drove back across the pasture in front of the Capitol, because it teemed with human beings—most of them soldiers. One small company marched in a drill, while other men in various uniforms stood in lines waiting for food or outfitting of some sort. Shutters had opened on ramshackle buildings, revealing stores of food and clothing, and other supplies. Tobacco and candy butchers and other sutlers moved through the crowds, selling to soldiers. Children of all colors ran about excitedly. There were a few women, black and white, carrying washing bundles on their heads. At the edge of the pasture, a cluster of horses stood dozing under a couple of trees.

A black man was shoeing one of the horses. I thought of Elijah Smith and wondered where he was now, and whether he had safely brought Bathsheba out of slavery. I craned my neck to see if it was him—but there was such a press of horses and men that I could not tell.

When we were back at Lizzie's, it occurred to me that I would be at a glamorous party that very evening, and I had nothing remotely appropriate to wear. In spite of what she said, I imagined it would be like those grand soirees at the great houses in New York—with coaches and fine carriages, elegant ladies in hoop skirts, and yards of fluttering silk.

I had no hoops and I owned no silk, except for a few flowers. I had always thought hoop skirts to be idiotic, but now I longed desperately to own one. I couldn't save myself with an elegant bonnet, for it would be an evening affair, and bonnets would not be appropriate. I would look like the poor relative I was.

I went to Lizzie to try to beg off. "Lizzie," I said, "I can't be there. I just don't have anything I can wear to a grand party."

"Oh, Vera," she said, "I'm counting on you! These parties aren't grand—and really, in Washington, nobody knows anything about fashion. It's mostly men, anyway. They really won't care how you're dressed."

That was hardly reassuring, since it meant her assessment of my clothing was about the same as mine.

"Lizzie, I've never been to any gathering that wasn't in a church or a tavern." *Or a whorehouse*, I added to myself.

"This will be a lot more like a tavern than a church. I can lend you something I had before the baby was born."

She did. It was hideous—a green frock that made me look like an oddly shaped bush. It brought out every blotch and freckle on my face. I imagined it even put circles under my eyes. I decided at the last minute that I would wear my own clothes. If I could not be impressive, I could at least be comfortable. So I got into my best skirt and bodice, braided up my hair as best I could, and took a flower off a bonnet to wear in my hair. It looked silly, so I took it out and sighed. I would have to do the way I was.

No carriages swept up for the start of this party. Tired-looking men shambled to the door—many of them with grimy collars and spotty waistcoats. They gave Lizzie a perfunctory greeting and ignored me. They lit up their cigars and got to work talking to each other.

They talked about the war—but not in political terms, about who was right or wrong, or even who might win. They talked about who had agreements to make uniforms or provide weapons or supply meat. Soldiers, they said, could wear slops the same as sailors—and cheap salted meat could be sold to the army at a premium.

It had never occurred to me that so much of war was

business, and that there were clearly fortunes to be made. It seemed so ordinary in one way, and so outlandish in others.

The cigar smoke grew thicker. I heard a conversation about railroads, and edged closer to see if I could understand anything that might be useful to me. One of the men noticed me standing by his shoulder and asked me to fetch a spittoon. Another in the group said quickly, "Colonel, this is Mrs. Eckel's sister, Mrs. O'Dea."

"Oh," said the colonel, "my apologies, madam." His speech slurred slightly. "Please pardon a poor-sighted old man."

"You do not seem old or poor-sighted, sir," I said, "but of course I accept your apology." I smiled what I hoped was an ingratiating smile. "I was just ever so interested to hear what you're saying about the railways."

"Hmph. Share your sister's head for business, do you?"

"I hope so, sir."

"Smart little lady, your sister."

"Yes, sir, she is," I said. "Please go on with what you were saying about the railways. It sounded very interesting."

"Oh, yes—well, I was just saying the railways stand to make a pretty pile. We need them to move the troops down and to move supplies around. Damned expensive—beg your pardon, ma'am, *very* expensive—but we can't have an army mired down with carts and horses. Have to have the very best. Can't beat the iron horse."

"Do you think people with shares in the railways will profit from the war?"

"I do, unless the Southrons win. Won't be worth much then. Do you stand to profit, little lady?"

I had asked too many questions. Now I had to answer one. "I have some shares in a railway."

"Your husband does."

"I am a widow, sir."

He was embarrassed, of course, and so I slid away from more questions about the shares.

"Well, you won't be a rich widow this week," he said bluntly. "Shares in the railroads now are just pieces of paper. Might as well use 'em to wipe your—I mean, um ..."

"Might as well use them to wipe the windows, then?" I asked, brightly.

"Exactly," he replied.

"Well then—let me see if we can't find you a spittoon."

So that was that, I thought, lying on the straw pallet that night. There was no fortune in my little box—at least not now, and never if the Southrons won this war. I turned on my side. What could I do? Hats for ladies didn't seem to be in much demand. And even if they were, I had no idea where to get the supplies I needed—unless perhaps I made the flowers out of paper. Would the ladies of Washington want gilt-edged flowers with print on them?

I turned on my other side. I didn't know much about what a war was, not really. I'd certainly seen enough brawling in the streets, with awls and knives and brickbats. I had seen very little done with guns. As it turned out, many other people in Washington City didn't know much more about war than I did.

CHAPTER 38

$\mathcal{G}$ENERAL WINFIELD SCOTT, WHO WAS PUT IN CHARGE OF THE Federal troops, did know something about war, but he'd learned it long ago. He'd been a great hero in the Mexican War, which was now nearly fifteen years past. Lizzie had arranged an introduction to him to smooth the way for her friends, and friends of her friends, to have contracts to sell provisions to the Federals. I went with her on a hot June day to call on the general.

The general's study was a study of the general—it was filled with portraits of him on horseback, or gazing stalwartly into the middle distance. One particularly disconcerting work of art was a marble bust with its shoulders bare and no suggestion that the rest of the body was wearing any clothes. This was a particularly unappealing image for me after the general came into the room—for he was enormously fat, and the mental suggestion of him with no clothes just would not leave my mind.

He wheezed over to his chair and plopped down. "Please forgive my sitting, ladies. I am an old man and request your indulgence."

He couldn't stand on his own feet in his own study, and he was supposed to command troops in the field? He was nonetheless charming to us, and Lizzie was moderately successful in her good offices for her friends, ensuring commission payments for her that would support her household for several months. When it was time to leave, the general's black manservant had to help him out of his chair.

We hired a hack to take us back to the hotel. The driver moved his nag slowly through the muddy streets—past a company of drilling soldiers; past hucksters who came chasing after the hack, trying to sell us apples or sweet corn; past clerks, workmen, washerwomen, pickpockets, whores, cutpurses, shell-game tricksters, and ragamuffin children. On one corner, a few men stood casually about in Zouave uniforms, their full scarlet pantaloons and hats modeled after some French soldiers in North Africa. They looked exotic and exciting, even though I knew they were from New York. I decided the street show in Washington City was beginning to rival the New York of my childhood, and I was thoroughly enjoying it.

I turned my attention to Lizzie. "Well done, sister!" I said. "You make this all look so easy."

"In some ways, it *is* easy," she said. "There's so much work to be done for a war. It's just so difficult to be sure of picking the right side."

"The general's appearance doesn't exactly inspire confidence in a Federal victory, does it?" I asked.

"No," she said, and sighed. "I understand he is actually a brilliant military man, but it takes two men to get him up on a horse. The Southrons have Mr. Lee, who was first in his class at West Point. He can get on his horse by himself."

It was the middle of July when the soldiers marched out of town. Everyone knew where they were going, for the newspapers were filled with troop counts and plans. They were going some twenty miles into Virginia to engage the Southron forces and drive them south to Richmond. There were many people who thought that would be accomplished in a week or two, and the war would be over.

By Sunday, the twenty-first of July, many people had decided a battle would make a jolly Sunday outing, and so drove carriages and toward the town of Manassas with their friends and families. People packed sandwiches and opera glasses, preparing for a great show in the countryside.

Lizzie and Mr. Eckel hired a hack with a smart-looking bay horse and set out early on Sunday. I stayed behind, saying I would look after Felicity. I had some rough tastes in entertainment, but they didn't extend to seeing people killed.

I did take a walk midmorning, and listened as the distant sound of cannon mingled with the nearby sound of church bells. It was quiet in Washington City with so many of the soldiers gone. Any idea of turbulence or violence seemed very far removed from this peaceful world.

That changed in late afternoon. The men on horseback arrived first, having ridden hard all the way into town. They were dirty, bloodied, and terrified. They leapt off their sweating horses at the taverns, telling all who would listen of a terrible battle at Bull Run near Manassas, where a fierce Southron attack had routed the Federal soldiers, who broke and ran. The news spread. A tumult of terrified people poured into the city over the Long Bridge—a pell-mell hodgepodge of soldiers, terrified women, and ashy-faced men. There were stories of soldiers pulling people out of carriages—even wounded soldiers out of ambulances—so they could get away. I began to worry about Lizzie. Ambulances filled with groaning soldiers rolled in as I waited on the street through the afternoon into the night.

The people kept coming into town as I waited. By full dark, it was mostly soldiers on foot. Most of them walked silently, heads down. Still no Lizzie.

Baggage wagons started to roll in around midnight. The horses were tired, with their heads down, pulling wagonloads of supplies or men. Some of the men were chattering. One or two were crying. Many were silent.

I stood all night in front of the hotel, trying to swallow my fear. Just before dawn, it started to rain. I remained outside the hotel, straining my eyes into the darkness. Finally, in the gray dawn, I saw their hack. The once-proud bay horse limped slowly, and his head was so low his nose might have grazed the grass. I ran up to them and held my arms out to Lizzie, who tumbled out and embraced me.

"Oh, Vera, it was terrible! The soldiers just rushed over us. Some of them tried to pull us out and take the hack. I saw a man with his arm shot away." She started to sob.

William paid the hack driver a good deal of money and said, "Thank you, sir, for bringing us back in one piece. I hope you and your horse can get some rest."

The driver nodded silently, and he and his horse moved off into the rain.

CHAPTER 39

J WENT IN AND HELPED LIZZIE UNDRESS, AND THEN GAVE HER
some laudanum and put her to bed. Felicity wheezed
fretfully in her little cot. I tiptoed to my own room,
where Queen Esther dozed on my bed.

Let her sleep in it, I thought. *I can't.*

I went back down to the porch in front of the hotel, where
the rain continued as the dark lightened to gray. I saw a bedrag-
gled group of Zouaves, their fanciful uniforms soaked and
hanging like rags, walking silently and numbly toward their
company headquarters. A cart full of bloodied men—some
groaning, some too silent—creaked slowly by, and then turned
toward the railway station and the infirmary.

I have to do something, I thought. *Perhaps I can help.* I followed
the cart.

A few candles flickered inside the infirmary. Outside were
carts like the one I followed, with piles of bodies and some living
men. The rain was letting up, but it still fell on their unguarded
faces—some of which were contorted with pain, and some
of which were deathly still. I dodged around the carts to the
doorway, and said to the woman at the door, "I've come to help."

She looked at me appraisingly. "You're no nurse." It was a

280

statement of fact. The nurses for the hospitals had to be at least thirty, and plain.

"No," I answered.

"Get water and offer drinks to those that can drink," she said, sighing. "We can't ..." She shook her head and approached the next cart. "Here," she said to the driver, "help me sort the quick from the dead."

I saw no spare buckets and so ran back to the kitchen at the hotel, taking one and filling it at the pump out back, conscious of the restless sleepers in the slave pen. I walked back with my burden, unmindful of the rain. I went to one cart—giving water to those who could respond—then to another. Then I went back and refilled the bucket, taking it to another cart. It was a blacksmith's cart. The driver was on the other side, bent over a soldier he and an orderly were getting onto a stretcher.

I recognized the driver's hat at once. Even soaked with rain, there was no mistaking that hat, and no mistaking its wearer once he straightened up. It was Elijah Smith, and he still wore Jimmy's hat. I dropped the dipper of water and then fumbled to pick it up again. Elijah and the orderly staggered into the infirmary with the soldier on the litter.

I gave a few sips of water to one delirious boy, and then held out the dipper to a sandy-haired man, who grimaced and took it from me. He drank and thanked me. There were three others piled onto the cart—one with his face turned away from me, one with his eyes closed and his breath rasping. One stared straight at the heavens, water falling into his blank, blue, unseeing eyes. I reached over and closed them. His flesh was cold.

"Let us get in here, miss," said a man's voice next to me.

I turned. It was Elijah.

"Mr. Smith," I said. "It's me. Mrs. O'Dea, Jimmy's wife."

He held most of his face expressionless, but I could see surprise and recognition in his eyes. "Miz Ohday," he said, giving a brief nod. "We do need to get in here."

I stepped aside, and he and the orderly took the delirious boy onto the stretcher. I waited beside the one remaining conscious man.

"Ma'am," said the soldier quietly, "I could do with another drink." I wiped the dipper on my apron—why, I don't know, for one was as wet as the other—and gave him the last of the water in the bucket.

Then Elijah was standing beside me again, water dripping from the brim of his hat as he held one end of the stretcher. The orderly at the other end asked the sandy-haired man, "Where you hit?"

"Back," came the reply. He turned slightly so we could see the blood covering the left side of his back.

"Get under his right side," the orderly said. He looked at me and hitched his head toward the man. "Help him on."

The sandy-haired man put his right hand on my shoulder and leaned on me so heavily my knees almost buckled. He inched gingerly toward the stretcher, where he collapsed, face down. I could see the back of his jacket was soaked with blood, even in the rain. Elijah and the orderly carried him into the infirmary.

I stood outside, hearing the screams of men who were having limbs sawn off. I walked through the steaming mud and found another pump. I filled the bucket and gave drinks a dipper at a time. Another trip, another bucket. Then another.

I intercepted Elijah as he made yet another trip with the stretcher. "Where can I find you?" I said. "Are you living in Washington?"

The orderly looked at me, raising his eyebrows in surprise. I realized I might have put Elijah in danger. He hesitated for a moment, and then said, "No."

I knew it was a lie. I nodded and went for another bucket of water.

I worked all day and into the night, fetching bucket after

bucket of water. I don't know that I did anyone any good, but I needed to be doing something. Everywhere there were tangles of bloody bodies and, as the day went on, a growing pile of sawn-off limbs and unrecognizable bloody flesh. Flies covered it—sometimes so thick the pile was just a moving mass of black. It was so hot that my clothes stuck to my skin. The blood and sloshing water just made them wetter. The surgeons gave men whiskey to numb their pain—but even whiskey isn't enough to numb the pain of someone sawing your arm off.

My own monthly flow started, so there was sticky blood oozing down my legs. But there was so much blood everywhere, it didn't matter.

I have heard generals talk rapturously of "the stench of battle." I now know that it is simply the stink of rotting blood—the same stink of a woman's monthly blood flow, supposedly the most repulsive substance on the face of the earth.

My belly ached and my feet hurt, but I couldn't stop. Finally, after dark on the second day, I just couldn't walk anymore. Stiff, sore, and drained, I slumped back to the hotel and left the bucket in the kitchen. I asked for a bath and soaked a good long time in the hot water, dozing off twice and feeling guilty about the groaning men I knew filled the hospital. Everyone in the family was asleep when I tiptoed in my shift to my bed.

From the next morning on, things moved forward in such a confusing way I don't remember what happened in which order. Lizzie and William talked often, and with increasing urgency, about what they were going to do. They were Southron sympathizers and were convinced the Southron side would win. After the terrible battle at Bull Run, many more people thought the cause of the Union was lost. I think I thought so, too—but it was dawning on me that I could not take the Southron side.

Lizzie, like me, seemed to have nowhere to go. They began to talk about Europe, and I began to think they were losing their minds.

Little Felicity cried more and more—and then, one stifling hot day, she began to cough with that terrible gasping sound that meant whooping cough. The poor little girl died within days. Her passing completely unmoored Lizzie. She went and lay down on the child's bed in the nursery, staring at the wall. When I went in and put my arms around her, she moved away from me. William shut himself up in their bedroom with a quantity of laudanum. *Better that*, I thought, *than charcoal*—although I wouldn't have put it past him to leave this earth and take the rest of us with him.

I don't remember how many days we went on like this—but one morning, I went again to Lizzie and put my arms around her. She burst into tears. She shook and sobbed and wept and howled. I wiped her tears and stroked her hair and held her in my arms for a good long while. I had no comfort to offer her, for I did not believe it was all for the best or that Felicity was in a better place. I could only say it was a terrible, terrible thing to happen, and that I was so sorry.

God may be good, as people say, but God, if he exists, does not operate by human standards. It is wrong for humankind to kill, but God does it all the time—even killing children before their parents' very eyes. Burying a child is one of the deepest sorrows humans can suffer.

I thought, after her stormy weeping, that Lizzie would fall asleep exhausted. But she did no such thing. She asked for a drink of water, and then asked me to order her a bath. She bathed and ate, and I helped her dress her hair. Then she said she and her husband had some decisions to make, and she walked into their darkened bedroom.

The next day, she announced they would be moving to Paris. Life for all of us changed very fast. Lizzie seemed suddenly to become a force of nature—a woman concentrating on getting all about her in order. She arranged the journey for the two of them. Since they could not take slaves to Paris, she decided to sell them. I would have to decide what I wanted to do, and do it.

Lizzie spent nearly two days making calls on all her friends, trying to sell her slaves. She couldn't find anyone to buy. She came stamping in on the evening of the second day, her eyes hot and her mouth set in a straight line, glaring at her own reflection in the mirror as she unpinned her hat and took it off.

"Still no luck?" I asked, quietly.

She whirled around at me for a sharp reply, but bit it back. "No," she said, bitterly, shaking her head. "I paid fifty dollars for Washington and two hundred for Queen Esther. I can't get anyone to take them off my hands—not even for fifty dollars for the two of them."

"Nobody wants them?"

"Nobody wants slaves now. They're figuring they'll all be freed. And most of them are afraid enough of the slaves they already have—afraid they'll cut their throats in the middle of the night, or steal the silver and the horses. They certainly don't want to risk owning more."

I didn't think about it. I just said, "I'll buy them from you. I'll give you a hundred dollars for the both of them."

"Gold and silver?"

"Yes."

"Well ..." She paused and looked at me. Then she shook her head as though she would rattle it. "Well," she continued, "of course. Thank you. But I had no idea you had so much money about you."

"It's just about all I do have."

"Then why?"

"I want to free them."

"That's lunacy. But—" She moved her shoulders as if that would help her find words. "Fine, if you want to do it. Of course. Would you mind giving me the money now?"

I nodded and went to get my purse. I had only the briefest

jab of fear. Wasn't this a foolish thing to do? Yes. It was. My sister was leaving Washington, and I had decided not to go with her. She was my only living relative, and I had no way to support myself. But I *knew* this was something I wanted to do. I was more sure of this than I had been of anything in a long time. I got my purse and handed over a hundred dollars in gold and silver, leaving myself only about a week's rent at Brown's.

That night, I lay awake, sweating through the hot September night. The heat was not what kept me awake, though. At first, it was the excitement over what I was doing. Then, very late at night, it was utter fear. What would I do, and where would I go? And how would I tell Queen Esther and Washington? What would they do, and where would they go? They had even fewer choices than I did.

The newly unstoppable Lizzie quickly arranged for proper sale papers and manumission papers for Washington and Queen Esther. On a windy day in late September, Washington loaded Lizzie's and William's boxes on the wagon. I had tears in my eyes when Lizzie and I embraced to say good-bye. Her eyes were dry. I'm not sure William knew where he was or what was happening. I watched the wagon pull out of sight, wondering if I would ever see my sister again. And when Washington came back, I asked him to join me and Queen Esther in the front room of the suite at Brown's.

He stood holding his hat, and Queen Esther stood looking at me with her arms folded.

"Well," I started. "You probably know my sister, um, transferred the two of you to me."

They did not speak. Washington stood waiting patiently. Queen Esther shifted her weight from one leg to the other, but did not uncross her arms.

"I have arranged for your freedom."

They did not move or speak.

I held out to Washington his letter of manumission. "This is your paper. You need to keep it with you so people know you're free."

He nodded and put the letter in his pocket. A moment later, he said, "Thank you, Miz Vera," in exactly the same tone I had heard him use to thank Lizzie when she ordered him to do something, or when she told him he could go get something to eat.

Queen Esther held out her hand, giving me an imperious stare. I handed her the letter and tried to give what I hoped was a magnanimous smile. I don't know what I expected, but her reaction wasn't it. Queen Esther took the letter, opened it, and handed it back to me, saying, "You has to read it to me."

I don't have *to do anything,* I thought. *Neither do you, anymore. Do you not understand that?* But I meekly read it to her and told Washington his letter said the same.

Queen Esther nodded her satisfaction. "Good," she said. "Now what's we s'posed to do?"

"I don't know," I admitted. "I don't even know what I'm going to do. We need to be gone from here by noon on Saturday."

"Then you got nothing for us," said Queen Esther.

"Well," I said, lamely, "that's true. I don't have anything, either—except my freedom, whatever sense I've got, and my immortal soul. Same as you."

Then I returned her imperious stare with the steady polite look I'd so often given difficult customers. I'd given her freedom. Why was she expecting something else? Why wasn't she grateful?

∽

AFTER A FEW MINUTES OF silence, Washington nodded and said, "'Bye now." "Wait," I said. "What will you do?"

Queen Esther spoke for him. "He can stay in the stable

same as he always has, and work with his same horse and wagon. Ain't that right?"

He nodded again. "'Bye now." And he walked away toward the stables.

⌒

QUEEN ESTHER FOUND WORK AS a washerwoman that afternoon. "I be washin' for the soldiers," she said. "Hard work. *Hard* work. But I ain't goin' t'be no maid, and I ain't goin' t'be no mammy."

CHAPTER 40

I NEEDED A PLACE TO LIVE. I ALSO NEEDED A WAY TO MAKE money, since I had none. I didn't know what course to take, so I took a walk. I went out the front door and onto Pennsylvania Avenue.

What had been a dull city of mud when I arrived now offered constant entertainment. Soldiers drilled in the avenue. I saw a fistfight, heard fiddlers and banjo players, and saw children dancing for pennies. Whores lured soldiers, swindlers charmed anyone they could, and I even saw one innocent-looking young couple in love.

Twisters abounded, of course, and there were some twix-ters—people whose sex might have been a matter of a coin toss.

I joined a small crowd watching a carter trying to get his cart out of a mudhole on Pennsylvania Avenue. We were not far from Murder Bay, so I carefully tucked my little purse under my clothes as I watched the carter swear and his horse strain. Others tried to help, grabbing pieces of lumber to put under the sunken wheel. A bright-skinned mulatto walked up and stood next to me, wearing a hat so fanciful it might have been a pea-cock sitting on her head. It was Delilah.

"Delilah? It's Vera. Vera from Baltimore."

She squealed and held out her hands. We embraced happily, briefly attracting the attention of the crowd before they turned back to the carter cursing in the mud.

"Look at you!" I said. She was all in golden yellow, and most of it silk. "You look like a Creole queen."

"I *am* a Creole queen," she informed me, happily. She took my arm. "Come on, honey. Let's move away from this.

"I got me a house," she went on. "I got eighteen girls working for me, all egg-zotics or entertainers. I got Creoles—three girls who sing, one who plays the banjo, and one who plays a guitar. I got twixter boys. I bought a Chinese girl. Emmeline sent her to me from San Francisco. Little Chinee can touch her feet to the back of her head."

"You are doing well."

"Yes, I am. And I don't do nothin' I don't want to."

I smiled. "I think the happier you are, the more down-home you sound."

She laughed loudly at that. "The freer I feels, the freer I talks. What you doin'?"

I took a deep breath and let out a sigh. "I'm looking for a place to live, Delilah." I stopped and looked into her eyes. She appeared wary. "And I need a way to make money," I added. *May as well put the cards on the table.*

"What happened to your sister?"

"She's gone to France. I spent the last of my money buying her slaves."

"Well, sell 'em!" she answered.

"I freed them," I told her.

She gave me an odd look for a minute. Then she put her arm through mine and we walked together down Pennsylvania Avenue. "Come live in my house," she said.

I laughed. "I'm a little old and plain to get into the life."

She laughed, too. "Yeah, you is! Naw, why don't you just come count up my money and do some sewing and some little chores? You gets a bed of your own, and you can eat after the gentlemen eats, and what tips you gets, you splits with me."

So I ended up in a whorehouse after all. And the "little chores" for Delilah turned out to involve keeping on top of a constant hurly-burly of deliveries, payments, surprises, cheats, and illegalities. Every week saw the delivery of three barrels of whiskey, nine barrels of beer, twenty-one barrels of oysters, plus brandy, champagne, sweetmeats, and peanuts. Deliveries of ham, bacon, and beef came in the middle of the night, and I didn't understand why until I learned our deliveries had been diverted from supplies meant for the army. We employed two cooks, four laundresses, six stout Irishmen to keep trouble away, and a dozen women and urchins to keep the place clean and run errands. They all wanted to be paid. Most of them stole what they could, every chance they got.

But what a fine time was to be had at Delilah's! Every evening, the music resounded down the muddy street. I was sure they could hear it at the White House, which was only a few streets away, and in the soldiers' tents—although not many of the common soldiers could afford Delilah's. Generals came, to be sure, and colonels, and a major or two, and some of the men I recognized from Lizzie's.

The women were all beautiful, the piano player was astonishing, and the singers were good. One sassy Scots-Irish girl was a particular favorite. Her name was Rosalie, and she sang bawdy ballads in a demure and ladylike voice, and sweet, sentimental songs with a slyness that brought knowing grins and salacious snickers. She had freckles all over her, and when she said, "Oh, yesss—*all over* me," you could see men switching around in their chairs as their erections made them uncomfortable. Rosalie made a lot of money.

Women came to the house, too—veiled and by the back door, for Delilah also had two rooms for assignations, and those, too, were busy every evening. It was an excellent place for black-mailers, businessmen (licit and illicit), and spies.

One evening I stood near the door to the kitchen, eating a cup of soup, watching the entertainment, and tapping my foot while two fiddlers played a lively jig. Suddenly, my attention caught on a man's back—a slim back, with broad shoulders, topped by a head of flowing golden hair. I heard him laugh, and knew it was Bill McCracken. My heart turned over. I watched for a minute as he teased the two women sitting in his lap. They leaned close to him so he could better see down their bodices. Then all three laughed. I finished my soup and left through the kitchen. I hated the sight of him, yet I too wanted to be sitting in his lap, showing him my breasts.

∽

TWO IMPORTANT THINGS HAPPENED IN April of 1862: President Lincoln freed the slaves in Washington City, and a Miss Jennie Douglas was hired at the Treasury Department to cut sheets of money. I wished many times that Mr. Lincoln could have signed the emancipation bill sooner, because it provided for slave owners to be paid compensation, and it would have been good to have some money. Still, he didn't. I was secretly a little proud for what I had done.

Miss Douglas's hiring turned out to be much more important for me. It wouldn't have happened if there hadn't been a war. War is expensive. Weapons and supplies and soldiers all cost money. The government decided it needed to print lots more paper money. The men who cut the printed sheets into money were needed to fight. And besides, Mr. Spinner, who was the treasurer for the country, thought women were better with scissors than men, so he hired Miss Douglas. She worked out well, so he started hiring more women.

Freckle-faced Rosalie decided one day that she would like one of those jobs, so she put on her most modest clothes and went to apply. She came back in a pet and came to me to sulk. "They're only paying women half of what the men get! Six hundred dollars a year! That's fifty dollars a month!"

Better than what I'm making, I thought.

She went on. "I make fifty dollars in a *week*. Last week, I made seventy-two. Delilah takes her share, but if I left, I'd have to pay twenty dollars a month for room and board. Pfft!" And she flounced out, leaving me thinking.

I finished up that day's accounts, thinking that if I made fifty dollars a month and paid twenty for room and board, I would still have thirty to spend. That was more than I had at the moment. Much more than any other work had paid me. And I could probably go on doing some work for Delilah. I could be a war profiteer. The thought made me smile.

CHAPTER 41

ETTING THE POST AT THE TREASURY WAS AMAZINGLY EASY. I presented myself as a widow, which I was, and said a former employer—a Miss Mary Easley of Philadelphia—could give me a good character. Delilah might actually have had more influence, but I didn't know if they'd figure I'd steal the money after I cut it. It was a turbulent summer, even though I was safely inside a large building—for there seemed to be new cutters every day. The department was growing so fast they were building a new building right around the old one while we worked. Soon, though, I was in a boarding house on F Street, with four other Treasury girls. For twenty-five dollars a month, I had a room all my own—a bed to myself!

Our landlady, Mrs. McInnis, was probably the stingiest woman I have ever known. The porridge she served was a thin gruel, and the bread always seemed stale. How do you never have fresh bread when you're feeding five people? I didn't go hungry, though. I always had pennies to spend on hot sweet corn from a street vendor. I only tried their lemonade once, though. It was a rank, sour-smelling drink that made me sick.

I enjoyed the work, and by September was a copy clerk. The money was no better, but the work was far more interesting. As we copied documents for people to be paid large sums of money for horse blankets or whale oil or carpenter's nails, I learned the business of war. It had never occurred to me that war was so expensive, and how many things were needed to fight it. I noted with great interest the large sums being disbursed to the railway companies in order to carry goods and soldiers, and I wondered how much difference it would make in the value of the gold-edged papers I still kept as treasure.

I worked in a large room at a writing table, along with rows of other women at writing tables. There was a space in the middle of the room, and then, on the other side, rows of men.

Mr. Clancy was our supervisor. He was a portly gentleman who sat at his large, elevated desk at the end of the room, usually smoking a cigar or reading a newspaper. He was very attentive, though, when he checked our work. More than once, he berated some poor girl for the "stupid" way she had left a word out of a copy, or mis-added a column of figures. The rest of us would cringe and stare at the papers in front of us, or our little boxes of pen nibs—anything to keep from looking up.

I escaped this kind of attention from him. He actually seemed to enjoy my questions, and appreciated that I would read the documents for sense instead of just copying word for word. I made very few mistakes.

<hr />

I THINK I MUST HAVE been at the Treasury office for about six months when I got a letter from Lizzie in Paris. Her sad husband had done as he had threatened so many times—lit charcoal in a closed room. She found him dead after she came back from a walk with some of her Southron friends.

She was making her own way, learning French and making some kinds of arrangements for people she knew. I got the sense she was somehow aiding the Southron war effort, but I didn't quite know how.

Her fairy tale had no happy ending. On the other hand, she was the ever-buoyant Lizzie, and she seemed to be happy in Paris.

∽

ONE RAINY SUNDAY AFTERNOON, I was sitting in the parlor of my boarding house, trimming a hat, when the houseboy told me a colored woman wanted to see me. Had Delilah come to call? No. When I went to the back door, there was a sturdy, bare-foot washerwoman with a full basket on her hip. It took me a minute to recognize Queen Esther. How had she found me?

I didn't get a chance to ask. She said, "Miz Vera, I come to see if I can wash for you."

"There's a woman who does the laundry for the house," I answered.

"I'm better than she is," answered Queen Esther confidently. "And I charge you the same. But I ain't gonna do no bloody rags."

I was flabbergasted. First of all, I would never ask any other woman to wash out my bloodied rags, although I suppose some women did. And what was she doing marching in here and telling me what to do?

I looked at her confident face, with her chin tilted up to me. I smiled in spite of myself. I couldn't help it—I liked her.

"All right," I said. "I have nothing now. When can you come by?"

We negotiated a day for her to come back, and I thought we were done, but she stood there looking at me thoughtfully. Then she said, "You know Elijah Smith? The blacksmith man?"

"Yes," I said, "I do. He was a very good friend of my husband. Is he in trouble?"

"No, no." She shook her head quickly. "He just say your husband a good man. Elijah, he a good man, too."

"You know he's married." I teased her.

"*Was* married. You don't know the rest of that story?"

I shook my head.

"Elijah done went down there with the last of his money, and they gave him Bathsheba. When he got to Maryland, they sent the law after her, say she burned down some shack or somethin', and they gon' take her back. They clapped him in jail and took her away. And then the war broke out, and her master took her and run west. She gone. He don' know where."

"Oh, no," I whispered.

"Sorry to be the one to tell you, Miz Vera. But Elijah, he joined up with the First Regiment."

It had taken a while for Congress to decide that black men could be soldiers, or as the recruiting notices had put it, "Black, Copper & Bright." So Elijah had joined the First Regiment, United States Colored Troops.

"I think he'll make a good soldier."

"Uh-huh," she replied. "I be back next Wednesday."

Queen Esther's story about Elijah sat like lead in my stomach. I had imagined him happy these two years. He had worked so hard and had to trust a vile system, and without thinking twice, people who thought it was right to own another human being had taken his wife from him—his precious, precious wife, and a poor man's only treasure. It ate at my insides. Perhaps that was why I caused a man's death.

❧

WASHINGTON CITY WAS FULL OF spies and Southron sympathizers, and everybody knew it. It was easy enough to go into a state that had seceded—for the Long Bridge, with Mr. Lee's house on the other end, was still open, and people crossed it every day. We could see the Confederate campfires across the river at night, and smugglers and spies crossed right along with the country folk who brought in their food crops to sell.

One day, as I jostled along the sidewalk with the soldiers and senators, whores and washerwomen, I heard footsteps behind me.

"Mrs. O'Dea!" someone said. I knew that voice, and turned around to see the brilliant green eyes and wide smile of Bill McCracken. He swept a broad planter's hat from his head, bowing in greeting. "What a purely joyful surprise it is to see you in Washington City."

I caught my breath and my heart sped up. I was sure he had killed my husband, but he had probably saved my life that day in Baltimore. I despised him, but he fascinated me.

"Mr. McCracken. What brings you to Washington City?"

"Why, the war, Mrs. O'Dea, the war—just as it has brought so many others."

"You appear to have prospered." He was no longer in workmen's clothes, but in a fine gray suit and an excellent-looking hat.

"I have, thank you, I have. Would you do me the honor of taking some refreshment with me at Brown's Hotel?" He put his hat back on his head and offered his arm and his bright-eyed, seductive smile.

It annoyed me that he assumed I would accept his invitation. Still, that's exactly what I did. I took his arm, enjoying the feel of his strong body and the soft cloth of his coat.

"Do you know Brown's, Mrs. O'Dea?" he asked.

"I do. I lived there with my sister for a time."

"Is she there now? Perhaps she would care to join us."

"No. She's moved to Paris."

His eyebrows shot up. "Paris?"

"Yes," I answered drily. "The one in France."

"Well, Mrs. O'Dea, if you will pardon a personal remark, I knew you were a person of breeding the first time I saw you."

Ha.

We walked into Brown's, past the sign that had so appalled me when I first saw it.

"Do you find that posting odd now?" I asked him. "The promise to reimburse an owner if their slaves escape?"

"I don't see anything odd about it," he answered. "If they're responsible for a man's property and it escapes, they ought to pay the value."

He'd said "property." Why did I even find that remarkable?

We were seated in Brown's dining room, and he ordered oysters and chops for both of us.

"Aren't you afraid you'll be taken for a spy?" I asked. "You look and talk like a Southron."

"They can't shoot me for that. Besides, anyone who can read the papers knows where the Yankees are and what they're going to do. Anyway, I'd rather talk about you."

He leaned toward me, taking one of my hands. It was easy to enjoy that, and his strong, clean-shaven jaw, and the contrast alongside his soft lips. "You are so remarkable," he said.

"Hardly." I laughed. "I'm just a hatmaker who was lucky enough to get a job at the Treasury."

"You're a very pretty Treasury girl, and your spirit makes you a beauty."

My heart turned over. He had called me a beauty. He was looking at me with a gentle smile and adoration. He wanted me, and now I wanted him.

"You're a handsome man, Mr. McCracken, and I'm sure you charm all the ladies."

"I might." A little self-satisfied smile. "But you are different. I haven't seen you for more than a year, and not much before that. But even seeing you in the crowd on the avenue, I knew who you were. The way you move through this rough crowd—easily, quickly, always with your head up. So many of the ladies walk with their heads down."

He came to call the next day, and the next. On Saturday, we had dinner at the St. Charles Hotel. We had wine, and perhaps I drank too much—but that wasn't the only reason I went to his room with him. I had been wild with thoughts of him, and once we were in his room, I was wild at his touch. His lips on my neck, then on my breasts, had me squeezing and thrusting even before he got my skirt up and my pantalets off. I jumped up and flung my legs around him, putting us both onto the bed.

He felt into my crotch and groaned when he realized how wet I was. After just a few minutes with his finger in me, I came, pulsing and gasping for air. He stroked me calmly and gently for a few minutes and then thrust into me. Soon I came again, and he came too, grunting and powerful. I wrapped my legs around him again, and we lay panting, quieting for a few minutes. Then he rolled off of me and lay looking like a god fallen to earth. He stroked my hair gently, and I looked at him and smiled.

He smiled back, and said, "You're a tiger, aren't you? Worth killing for."

I felt ice form in my stomach and my heart. I'd been telling myself all this time that maybe he hadn't been the killer. Maybe I'd been mistaken. Now there were no maybes. He had killed the man I loved, and now I had betrayed Jimmy. I lay there as Bill dozed off to sleep, my bodice open and my skirt around my waist, wishing I were dead.

∽

THE NEXT TIME I SAW him, I was walking into Delilah's, carrying two hat boxes. He was arguing with her. The Yankees had discovered he was the spy called Golden Bill, who had been selling secrets to the Southrons and taking wagonloads of supplies through the wilds of Southern Maryland. They were hard after him, and he needed an escape.

Delilah didn't want him caught in her house, and she'd ordered her twixter boy Curtis to share his women's clothes so Bill could wear them to get away. She told Curtis to dress in Bill's clothes.

"No!" protested Curtis. "I pay a lot of money for my girl clothes. I'm not going to just give them away."

I cleared my throat. They all looked at me. Bill looked startled to see me there. I offered no explanation. They went back to their argument.

"You can wear his clothes," Delilah snapped at Curtis. "You go with him as a man. Get someplace where you can trade clothes. He'll pay you."

This appealed to Curtis's sense of adventure as well as his avarice. It did not appeal to Bill. "I can't wear petticoats," he said, glancing at me. "I'll die like a man!"

"Think about what you just said," I told him. "Would you really rather die than spend a few minutes in a petticoat?"

They went to one of the back room to change, and came out looking like a tall blonde woman with a small, slender man.

"You make an attractive woman," I told Bill. He did. He was very tall for a woman, to be sure, but his golden curls looked good in the flowered bonnet I had made for Curtis. His lips and cheeks had been rouged, and his face looked sweet and smooth.

"I can hardly breathe," he said.

"Don't speak if you can't speak any higher than that," I told him. I was starting to enjoy this.

"Git on out of here!" hissed Delilah. "Git!"

McCracken's coat hung wide off Curtis's shoulders, but other than that, the clothes were passable—a handsome enough couple, even if the lady was a bit tall. It was dusk, and in the tumult around the avenue, they might not even be noticed.

Once they were gone, I walked across the avenue toward my boarding house, and then changed directions to go into the regimental tent of one of the army units. A handsome captain was lighting a lamp at a camp table when I walked in.

He looked up when I said, "I have information that will help you capture a spy."

CHAPTER 42

O N THURSDAY, THERE WAS A SMALL ARTICLE IN THE *Evening Star*: "Rebel Spy Killed on Long Bridge. 'Golden Bill' Disguised as Woman."

Killed. I hadn't expected that. Or had I? Or did I just think he'd be captured and locked up in the Old Capitol Prison, wearing a corset and skirt?

The article ran:

> William McCracken, a rebel spy and smuggler, was caught on Long Bridge by Federal troops on Sunday last. McCracken, whose clandestine deeds had been uncovered, was attempting to cross into Southron territory disguised as a fancy woman. He was ordered to halt but attempted to run. Being greatly hampered by the women's clothing, he was shot and killed by the Federals. A young man who accompanied him was captured but allowed to depart when it became clear he was but an unwitting accomplice.
>
> McCracken was the mastermind and executor of an extensive smuggling operation, carrying stolen munitions and supplies through Southern Maryland.

He was also a frequenter of saloons in Washington City, where he discovered information on the movement of Union troops.

Something inside me died as I read. He was handsome and strong and I had to admit his attention excited me. But I had held a blazing anger in my heart, and the anger started to die, along with the excitement.

I was sorry Curtis had lost his treasured clothes. His life was difficult enough even without that. I bought him ten yards of black silk to make a fine new gown. In the parlor house, black clothing was code that the "woman" wearing it was not a woman. Curtis was pleased to have silk. I also made him a fine black bonnet.

One evening, about a week later, I was sitting in the parlor of my boarding house when there was a knock at the door. My landlady led in a tall, broad-shouldered soldier. As he walked into the parlor, removing his hat, I saw he was the handsome captain I'd told about Bill McCracken.

"Mrs. O'Dea, Captain Duncan would like a word with you," my landlady said. "You may speak in the entry."

What was this about? We went into the tiny entry room, where a pathetic fire smoked on the hearth.

"Mrs. O'Dea, I want to thank you for the information you provided the Union Army," the captain said, his earnest brown eyes considering mine. "It enabled us to capture a very bad actor."

How kind he looks, I thought. *And how decent.*

He appeared ill at ease, and it suddenly dawned on me that he had not come there to talk to me about the late Bill McCracken. I smiled up at him. "I thought it was the right thing to do," I said.

"Yes, it was," he said, and paused. "Mrs. O'Dea, I would like to request the honor of calling on you at some later date."

I stood there a moment, looking at him. *You're so good-looking,*

I thought, *and you seem so kind. You are expecting a sweet, virtuous widow you can take home to Ohio or Michigan or wherever you come from. I am not that woman. That man killed my husband, and I made him my lover. Where there should be regret, there is only dry, smoking anger. I've tricked people, I've taken things that didn't belong to me, and my best friend in Washington is a whore.*

"Captain Duncan," I said, "I am honored by your request, but I must ask that you not come to call. I would rather not give an explanation."

He waited for me to say something else, but I did not. He nodded, put on his hat, said good night, and went out into the rain.

ॐ

THE WAR DEEPENED, GROWING EVEN more terrible—and then, suddenly, it was over. General Lee surrendered on April ninth, and for a few nights, there was jubilation and dancing in the streets. Then, less than a week later, on Good Friday, President Lincoln was killed—just a few streets over from my boarding house, at Ford's Theater.

The next Monday, when I arrived at the Treasury office, the only people there were Mr. Clancy and me. Nobody else showed up for work that day. The city was in shock, mourning. I had always been accustomed to going to work no matter how I felt—and so, I suppose, had he.

There was plenty of work to do. As I was drawing on my muslin sleeves to start on it, Mr. Clancy came over to talk to me. "I want to give you a word to the wise, Mrs. O'Dea," he said. "You'll need to find yourself a husband or a protector."

I gave him a blank look.

He went on. "You'll not have this post through the summer."

"Why not?"

"Men will need these posts. The soldiers will all be leaving

305

their regiments soon, and they'll need to be employed. Mr. Spinner thinks he can keep you, but I don't think the Congress will let him do that, even if he is the Treasurer of the United States."

Of course. Men need to support themselves and their families. Women have some magical means of supporting themselves. We can be whores or eat grass or live on rainwater and mushrooms. Or get ourselves "protectors."

He jiggled the change in his pocket. I said nothing, but just continued to look at him.

"It's too bad. The girls have been better than the boys are. They're tidier, their work is neater, and I never had a one of you come in drunk."

"But we still have to go," I said.

He put his hands up. That was the way of the world, and he, poor Mr. Clancy, was helpless to change it.

"Will you stay here, Mr. Clancy?"

"Well, now, Mrs. O'Dea, there's a question." He put his hands back in his pockets and rocked back on his heels. "No," he said. "I shall not. This war has been good to me and to everyone else clever enough to purchase railroad shares when it started."

"Really?" Now I was very interested—although probably not for the reason he thought.

"Oh, yes indeedy—really." He smiled. "I scraped together three hundred dollars in April of 1861 and bought myself some shares of the great Baltimore and Ohio railway. Put in two hundred more on the way." He pulled a cigar from his pocket, bit off the end, and spit it into the spittoon by his desk. "Those steel rails went right to a pot of gold. If I play my cards right, I won't ever have to work another day in my life."

I looked down, carefully fastening my sleeves, my mind racing. *Well, Mr. Clancy,* I thought, *it's interesting that when I asked you what to do with my money, you told me to put it in the bank.* So now he'd made a pile of money, and I wagered I'd made more. *How much has he made?* I wondered. *I can't just ask him that point-blank.*

"Why, Mr. Clancy," I said. "How very shrewd of you. You must have doubled your money—maybe even tripled it. You have been very clever indeed."

"Mrs. Clancy thinks so, too." He put the cigar in his mouth and looked hard at me. "She doesn't know how much there is. I could spend it on a fancy lady if I'd a mind to."

"Well, I'm sure you won't have any trouble finding someone to help you spend your money," I said. "Especially if you've made a great deal of it." I gave him what I hoped was a sincere and dazzling smile, even as I took a step away from him.

He paused, jingling the coins in his pocket again. "More than six thousand dollars, missy. Does that interest you?"

It certainly did, but not in the way he obviously hoped. "Oh," I said, moving out quickly. "I didn't mean to be rude. I was just so very impressed, and much too curious. But, my goodness! More than twenty-fold! You were very clever indeed! How do you get the money? Do you just walk into the bank with some papers and cash them in?"

"I could. In fact, I'll do that with some of the stock. But the B&O pays dividends. Do you know what dividends are?"

No, I didn't. At least not exactly. "No, sir, what are dividends?"

"Well, now." He puffed out his chest and his cigar smoke. "As long as the railroad makes money and you own stock, they send you a share of their profits every quarter. That's dividends, and I think they can support me and the missus as long as the railroad keeps running."

"Well, that's wonderful for you and Mrs. Clancy, and I know she's proud of you. Now, if you'll excuse me, I really must get to work."

He snorted. "Well, give some thought about what you're going to do."

I knew exactly what I was going to do. I was going to go back to my room and figure out how much my stock certificates were worth. As I left the Treasury building, the sun was setting in a tepid red sky, the wind was beginning to start up, and it smelled like rain. How could I turn those pieces of paper into gold?

My answer was right across the street: Mr. Riggs's bank. I had an account. I could walk right in. I could tell them I wanted dividends.

How much did I have? I went back to my room, locked the door, and got out the box. I took a deep breath. The writing on the shares added up to more than a thousand dollars.

Mr. Clancy's holdings had increased more than twenty-fold. Mine probably had, too.

So now I had a fortune, as soon as I could get to it. What to do when I had it?

The banks were closed that week, to mourn the president. The chaos of my thoughts matched the chaos going on around me. We heard the news that Sunday. The glamorous Mr. Booth had been run to earth in a barn, shot like a rat as the soldiers burned it down.

CHAPTER 43

*F*IRST THING MONDAY, I WENT TO THE MR. RIGGS'S BANK with my papers. and was met with a very different reception from the one I got in the Baltimore bank five years earlier. After all, I was a different woman.

The bespectacled teller greeted me by name. I pulled out my little money box from my reticule and set it on the counter. I pulled out one of the papers, letting him see clearly that there were others.

"Do I need to see one of the officers of the bank to have this cashed?" I asked.

His eyebrows shot up as he looked at the paper. "Yes," he replied. "You will need to see Mr. Lewis or Mr. Daniels. I will conduct you."

Mr. Lewis was a short, stout young man who kept his face carefully blank as we discussed the papers.

"Mrs. O'Dea, I see you are listed in our records as a widow. May I ask if you are planning to marry again soon? That will, of course, affect your finances."

"You may ask. I am not."

"These represent a considerable sum."

"I am aware of that." *And I can see you are dying to know how*

I came to have these, I thought, *and whose mistress I might be. You're probably starting to think about what I did to get them. May that keep your mind pleasantly occupied.*

"It will take several days to render these into gold or currency," he said.

"I am in no hurry." They'd been nothing but paper for six years, I thought. I could wait another week. Or two.

He sat back in his chair and placed his fingertips together in a steeple. After a moment, he said, "It would be irresponsible for us to simply hand you such a sum of money."

"I am also aware of that." Perhaps I should have said, *I am also aware of that, you weasel. You're trying to get me to take less for them than they're worth.* Instead, I said, "I would like to liquidate ten percent of them, with the proceeds to be deposited into my account in this bank," I said instead. "Can you arrange that?"

"Why, ah, yes, certainly."

"And can you also hold the rest for me and arrange for quarterly dividends to be put into my account?"

Of course he could. He was clearly amazed that I had sense enough to ask the question. He was so ingratiating during the rest of the interview that it occurred to me I might want to marry a banker.

I walked out of the bank and into the heat of the avenue, feeling light all over—almost giddy.

No, I wouldn't marry a banker. No need to settle for such a dull life. *And what do you think you're going to be doing?* I asked myself. *Going west to shoot buffalo? Rob stagecoaches? Take up piracy?*

I decided what I really wanted to do was walk. The day was already so hot that I could feel the sweat beginning to trickle down my sides and between my breasts. I dodged a dead dog and set off north, along the Seventh Avenue turnpike. Horses pulled army wagons slowly through the dust and dirt.

Did I want a husband? No. Not even a rich one. Lizzie's marriage had been like something out of a fairy tale, with a rich husband who, it seemed, would give her everything she wanted. But look how that had turned out. What did I want?

I started to climb toward Vinegar Hill.

I could go to Montreal, to try to find out more about my mother, and maybe even who my father was. *Do I want to? No.* This realization startled me so much that I stopped walking and stood for a moment with my mouth open. A cart creaked by, drawn by a skinny mule, driven by a skinny man with two days' beard growth and a stogie in his mouth. He looked at me curiously and indicated the seat beside him, offering me a ride. I shook my head and waved him off with a smile.

I don't need to know how I was made to know who I am, I thought.

I was a woman who spent all she had to free slaves. That said something about me.

My earthly fortune came from blackmail, and that said something about me, too.

And my poor, crazy mother. What about her? Was she really a martyr, or really a whore? Or both? Would she always keep me from fitting in anywhere? When I was with Jimmy, I had been content, and didn't care about fitting in. I had fit in as a clerk at the Treasury—but soon, I would no longer be a clerk at the Treasury.

My mother's story was part of my story, but it was not my whole story. My mother gave me her love, and she may even have kept me from being killed and buried under a convent.

I stopped to buy a dipper of lemonade from a Negro woman who had set up in the spreading shade of an elm tree. It was delicious, refreshing my mouth and my soul. The woman's little girl and boy offered to dance for me, and I agreed. They danced to their own handclaps and mouth music, with great, wide smiles. It so appealed to me that after a few minutes, I joined in. They squealed with laughter, and I danced with them as I had danced with other children in my childhood, imitating them and doing the best Irish steps I could remember. I was soon laughing and breathless, my hair soaked with sweat, but I felt better than I had in many years. I gave them each a silver coin. I settled my bonnet, and continued on my way. I'd forgotten how much I loved to dance.

I still didn't know what I was going to do. Set up a hat shop? No, that was foolish. Who would buy hats? Mrs. Lincoln ordered hers from New York City, and even she was leaving. Mr. Johnson's wife never left the house, and his daughters sewed their own clothes. The few rich ladies we had here had gone home.

There were few parties, receptions, or balls anymore. Those ended abruptly with the war and Mr. Lincoln's death, leaving Washington City once again a shabby, muddy little town with half-finished efforts at great buildings. It seemed mostly populated by freed slaves.

I could go to Paris. While I wasn't sure of a welcome from Lizzie, she'd be happy to see my money.

I was walking steadily uphill now, and there were only a few houses along the road. Shade from the trees made it cooler than it was in town, and I took off my bonnet to let my hair dry in the breeze. I stood looking back at the city and realized I loved it. Why? It certainly wasn't beautiful. The distance between hope and actual accomplishment was great, as symbolized by the unfinished buildings and the thousands of freed slaves who had no place to go. But I wanted to stay. Perhaps I just wanted to see what would happen next. Perhaps there was something for me to do. Perhaps, as Jimmy had said, we belong where we are needed.

The breeze became rougher, and the skies began to cloud. I realized a thunderstorm was blowing up and knew it would be wise to get down off the hill. So I started walking back toward the city and shelter. I was soaked but exhilarated by the time I got back. I might not know what I wanted to do, but I knew where I wanted to be.

CHAPTER 44

SOLDIERS FLOODED INTO WASHINGTON CITY TO BE MUSTERED out. They brawled in taverns and reveled in the whore-houses, and in late May, they marched down the avenue in a grand review. It took two entire days for all the soldiers to go by. First came the Army of the Potomac, and the heroes of Gettysburg and Antietam. The crowd on the avenue cheered and sang Union songs. One young woman ran from the crowd to give a laurel wreath to the dashing-looking General Chamberlain, the hero of Gettysburg. She spooked his horse and nearly got the good general tossed off into the mud. Sherman's army marched through, trailed by slaves who had followed them from the plantations of Georgia and South Carolina.

I saw no colored troops in the grand review. The war might have ended, but its work was not yet done.

I had my own work to do, starting with finding a place to live, a place where I could be of use. And I thought I might be of use where the colored folk were settling. Several times I walked back up the hill where I had stood, inquiring where I might find a house to purchase. Summer was coming on, and the heat of Washington City was becoming oppressive. I finally found a place to suit me—a wide, low farmhouse on the hillside, near the

Seventh Avenue pike. The owner was a pinch-faced widow whose husband had fought and died with the Confederates in Tennessee.

"I cain't hardly keep the house up," she said, "and I cain't bear livin' here no longer." She was selling up to move to Alabama, to what had once been a prosperous plantation. Perhaps it was odd, but we each thought the other was moving into a difficult and dangerous situation. I ventured that her home in Alabama must also have fallen on difficult times. "Yes," she said, "but when I'm surrounded by darkies there, they're the darkies I know. Around here, we have more of them coming in every day, and they're everywhere. Are you sure you want to live here?"

"It's a fine house," I said, avoiding her question. "The sheds in the back—stables?"

"Slave quarters."

"Oh. Well, I suppose I shall have to tear those down."

"Oh, no. You can rent those. Those people will live anywhere, and that's what they're used to."

"Well," I said, "most people do the best they can."

She pursed her lips and gave me a short stare. "I need five hundred dollars, cash, and you'll have clear title."

"Done."

Things happened very fast in the next few days. All of us women moved out of our boarding houses, and men took our places there, as they did in the Treasury building. A few women were actually able to stay at the Treasury office. Others found places as governesses, and some went with the husbands they'd met in Washington City, to farms and cities far away.

I wrote to Lizzie in Paris, to Mary Easley in Philadelphia, and to Kathleen Malone in New York, to let them know I was comfortable and settled. I received a letter from Kathleen first, letting me know she and Finn were also prosperous—her hat shop was doing well, and her four children (four!) kept her busy.

I received a short note from Mary's husband, letting me know she had died. He did not say how, but I knew she had not turned forty, and I wondered how much a broken heart had to do with her death. I wept as I read the letter, and the thought of her still brings tears to my eyes. This vital, capable woman was forced into a life she desperately wished to escape. I felt deeply that it was wrong, although I know many others would think it wrong of me to feel so.

Lizzie's letter was long and interesting:

> I have fallen in with a group of Americans who call themselves *Les Inutiles*, the Useless Ones. They are very pleasant but are proud they do no work. I don't think I can live like that. I learned yesterday to paint my eyes!

She was enjoying the attentions of an octogenarian French count, and amid her speculation about what it would be like to be a countess, she had taken time to study French law, because there were apparently some obstacles in the way of a marriage.

> In France, my marriage would not be legal and my title could be disputed after his death by anyone who wants to lay claim to it. The French will not recognize a marriage to a foreigner unless the foreigner can produce a birth certificate, and I understand very few Americans can do that. Such chicanery! I discovered there is a way to get a declaration of true birth. I must give my father's name, my mother's name, and my place and date of birth and have seven witnesses to swear to the truth. I got my seven witnesses and gave a declaration, but, as you know, I would not tell them our mother's true name for all the world! I gave her name as Maria de Ville, which just means Maria of the City. They all swore to the truth of this, and I have a certificate!

I explained to my friend the Duke of Morny what I had done, and he laughed and laughed and said, "What is your religion that you can arrange your conscience to suit such an emergency?" I was surprised he should suspect me of having any religion at all, since it is not fashionable, and said I believe in Venus and Mars, love and fight." "So do I," said he, but the next day, he brought me a book on the life of Jesus.

I put the letter down with a smile and a sigh. Lizzie was always interesting. The letters made me think about what my life might have been. If I had given in to Maeve McGonagle, she might have married Jimmy, and I might have continued working in Mrs. O'Hanrahan's hat shop, still trying to hide who I was. I might be an adventuress like Lizzie—but I had a feeling that Lizzie felt lost, especially as her friends were self-styled "useless ones."

I wanted to be use*ful*, and I was beginning to see a way to do it. I had settled near the Freedmen's Bureau, which was set up to provide help and aid to former slaves. What the bureau provided was much less than what they needed, but it did help people find their families.

To do this, freed men and women needed to write a letter, or have someone else write a letter, stating who they were looking for and what they knew about where that person might be. Many of my new neighbors needed help writing these letters and reading the ones they got back. Often, they needed my assurance that the letter was what they hoped it was, or a sympathetic explanation that it was not.

Many more people asked for help than got it, of course, and the procedure was cumbersome. People who couldn't read or write might get someone in the Freedmen's Bureau to write a letter to where they thought their families were. The letters were then carried around to churches in the area—churches were, after all, one of the few places where colored people could gather together—asking for a mother, a sister, a sister's family, or even a stepchild. If they could go in and begin the search with their letter already written, they were ahead of the game. Sometimes the lucky ones got from the Freedmen's Bureau some information on where their family members were. If they were very lucky, they also got a safe-conduct letter from the bureau, asking that they not be interfered with.

It was always a good day when they brought their safe-conduct letters to my house, so I could read them out loud.

The bearer of this letter, the colored man James Redd ...

"Which is it? Which one is my name?"

"Right there, see? This is 'James' and this is 'Redd.' When it's just the color red, it looks like this." And I wrote "red" for him.

"It says you shall not be interfered with," I went on. "See, right there. And down here, it's signed by Mr. Stanton himself."

Those letters were treated like gold. It was a rare and wonderful ray of hope when people were identified and found, but a colored man or woman travelling alone was vulnerable to any form of harm, just as they were in the days of slavery. These letters of passage struck me as no more than permission to travel into the bowels of hell, but they were such good news to the recipients that they wanted me to read them over and over, show them their names, trace the signatures. I have never felt as useful, or as important, as I felt when I read those letters.

∽

SOON AFTER I MOVED TO my new home, I answered an impatient knock at the door and opened it to find Queen Esther on my front porch. I was surprised to see her because I hadn't thought to tell her where I was going. She was not surprised to see me.

"Good mornin', Miz Ohday. You got washin' to do?"

"Well, I ... Yes, of course. I'm back in the habit of doing it myself."

"You can get yourself out of that habit right quick. I does good work."

"I know you do," I answered. "Come on in."

She did, plopping herself in a chair without being invited to do so. Her presumption made me smile, and I was glad to see she had not changed.

"You got yourself a nice house," she said.

"I think so. How are you doing? Where are you living? How did you find me?"

"I be over behind the Willsbys'." Pastor Willsby and his wife were the only other white people nearby. They were earnest folk from Ohio who ran a small school. Queen Esther went on. "They teachin' me to read and write, and I washes for 'em. They told me you'z here." I handed her a skirt, a petticoat, and two shirtwaists.

She nodded. "I have these back to you Tuesday." And she left, leaving me curious about her life and what had happened to her.

CHAPTER 45

O N A BRIGHT MARKET DAY IN OCTOBER, I WAS WALKING
through a swirling, noisy crowd, mostly of black
people, and I saw a smith's wagon and a man bent
over shoeing a horse. Dangling from a peg on the side of the
wagon was a stained and battered planter's hat—Jimmy's hat. It
was Elijah Smith.

I stood watching him for a few minutes. His strong back
was to me, crossed by the straps of his leather apron. His hair
was beginning to gray, and his clothes hung loose about him.

I waited until he was finished with the horse and had taken
the corn his customer paid him with. He was working under
a canopy, at a real forge—not the little improvised one he'd
worked with before. A good-looking wagon was set at the back,
and a handsome mule was tethered nearby. I thought as I walked
up that he had made good use of his mustering-out money.

"Mr. Smith. It's good to see you again."

"Miz Ohday," he replied with a reserved nod and his
familiar guarded look.

"I am glad to see you survived the war."

"Glad I did, too." He stood for a minute, and then added,
"Glad we both did. How you farin', Miz Ohday?"

"I'm well, thank you. I live nearby."

He smiled. "Well, maybe you think I be surprised, but you been surprisin' before."

That made me smile back. "I find I'm useful here."

"How you bein' useful?" he asked.

"I help people write letters and read letters, and I'm teaching some people to read." A sudden thought occurred to me. "Do you think I could help you find Bathsheba?"

"No," he answered. "I found out about Bathsheba. Bathsheba done passed, done gone." He turned his back to me and started working again.

"I'm so sorry. You did so much to have her with you."

He nodded. "Her master died at Petersburg. She had a baby girl. I wants to find that baby."

"Your regiment was at Petersburg," I said. "Is that why you know he died?"

"No," he answered. "Found out later."

"Do you think you might have been the one to kill him?"

He paused for a moment, and then turned to meet my eyes. "Hope so. Don't know so."

"I think that would have been justice," I said.

He nodded.

"Can I help you with letters?" I asked.

"I'd 'preciate that," he answered. "I can sign my name and figure, but I can't write fancy letters."

I gave him directions to my house, and we set a date and parted.

⁂

WHEN THE WEATHER WAS PLEASANT, I would sit on my porch, helping people read newspapers or letters—anything that would help them find someone. I would point out their own names in letters and show them words they wanted to read. I even went so far as to purchase a McGuffey's Reader and other simple books to help me and my new neighbors. Some passages struck me as suited only to wealthy white children: "See this fine pony. He is black and sleek. He can trot and pace and run."

Elijah Smith was willing to read the McGuffey's Reader. He already knew his letters and could sign his name—and soon, he could read the words as though he were speaking them on his own.

"O, how fast can he run! Are not his eyes large and bright? Has he not a long mane?"

I was so amazed when he read that I had to shake myself out of a little trance when he stumbled on a word. It was so different to hear him. I had never thought about his voice, which was fluid and deep when he read. He had usually spoken to me so quietly and in such short bursts that I'd never had a chance to listen—and now his resonant voice, even reading the childish words, stirred in me a mixture of respect and excitement.

In December, he asked me to write his request to the Freedmen's Bureau. He had more confirmation that Bathsheba was dead, and that her daughter, who would now be five, was living in Memphis. I had him come into the parlor while I got out ink and paper. He stood awkwardly, with Jimmy's hat in his hands, and I realized he had never come into the house before. We had done all our lessons on the porch.

"Please have a seat."

He did, on the edge of a chair close by, looking still more uncomfortable.

Of course he's uncomfortable, I thought. *He's alone in a house with a white woman. I'll just do this quickly.*

I wrote to the Freedmen's Bureau in Memphis, Tennessee, reading the letter to him as I wrote. "Would you be so kind," I wrote, "as to have a notice read in all the colored churches in your city, asking for information regarding my child, whom I have never seen, but who was the daughter of Bathsheba

Spottswood, who used to belong to Edwin Spottswood, late of Prince William County, Virginia?"

How can there be even a thread of hope he will find this child? I wondered as I dipped the pen in the inkwell. I looked up at him. "Is there anything else?" I asked. "Do you have any more information?"

A smile lit his face—a smile I hadn't seen since he had purchased Bathsheba's freedom. "She be livin' with people called Harris. Colored people."

That was new. That was important. Maybe he really did have a reason to hope.

I skritched the pen across the paper, writing, "I have understood she is living in Memphis with a colored family named Harris."

As I wrote, the smell of soap overtook the smell of ink in my nostrils. It was different from the acrid smell of smoke and forge Elijah usually bore—and there was another scent, his own, I was suddenly aware of. I wanted to touch him and breathe in that scent. I kept my eyes firmly on the paper and pen as I wrote.

I want to kiss him, I thought.

I finished the letter and swallowed hard before I looked up. "Would you like to sign it?"

He smiled a little and nodded, standing next to me so he could sign his name. He dipped the pen too heavily in the inkwell and pressed too hard on the pen, but wrote in clear block letters "Elijah Smith." When he had stopped, he drew a firm line underneath.

"Your name is Smith," I said. *Yes, Vera, what a brilliant grasp of the blindingly obvious. How long have you known this man's name was Smith?*

"Why isn't it Spottswood?" I asked him. "Who were the Smiths?"

He looked directly into my eyes. "I be the smith," he said. "My name is what I am."

I couldn't move for a moment, seeing for the first time the power in his eyes. Then I concentrated on taking a pinch of the drying sand for the letter and sprinkling it. I sat looking at it as the ink dried, not daring to meet his eyes again. I think my hand shook only slightly as I handed him the folded, addressed letter. "Godspeed," I said, my voice trembling a little.

I held out my hand for him to shake, and he took it. So gently. The calluses felt papery. They might have been the feathers of angels' wings, so much did the touch excite me. "Thank you," he said, nodding and looking down. He moved quickly toward the door, putting his hat on and leaving swiftly.

I watched him go, suddenly savoring the make of his shoulders and back in his plain shirt, the firm curve of his buttocks, and the grace of his walk. I knew it was foolish. I shut the door quickly, leaned against it, and took a deep breath. His scent was still in the room.

It was January before he heard anything from Memphis. I saw little of him in those weeks, largely because I thought it best to avoid him. But I could not keep him out of my thoughts and dreams.

∽

IT WAS THE MORNING OF my thirtieth birthday. I sat at my parlor table, drinking a cup of tea, thinking about growing old alone.

Why hadn't I remarried? Because I wanted a man I admired, and I admired none of the callow soldiers, banal clerks, or various mountebanks. And now I craved a simple blacksmith—a black smith—why? *Because he smells of soap? Because he wears Jimmy's hat? Because he loved a woman enough to risk his life for her?*

Because he had a sense enough of himself to choose his own name? Because I can't have him? Because I've loved him all along?

That was an eye opener. Literally: as the thought hit, my eyes flew wide open and I sat up with a start.

Then I heard a sharp rap on the door, and Queen Esther's voice. "You in here? I got your wash."

"Yes. Come in."

She did, as always, without hesitation. "Hoo-eee. I been walkin' fast to get here, tryin' to beat that rain that's coming." She looked meaningfully at the teapot.

"Would you like a cup of tea?" I asked, smiling more to myself than to her. She was what white people called "uppity"— presumptuous, straightforward, and sometimes downright rude. She was also very free with unsolicited advice. It was part of why I liked her.

She sighed and flopped down in a parlor chair. "Yes, I would. I surely would. It's a long walk up that hill with that heavy basket."

I poured the tea—by now stewed and barely warm—and added cream and several spoons of sugar.

There was another, softer, knock at the door. "Busy morning," I commented and opened the door to see Elijah on the doorstep, a letter in hand.

He had hope in his face, and my heart stopped. "Good mornin', Miz Ohday," he said, taking off Jimmy's hat. "The bureau got this letter from Memphis. I can read some of it, but I wants you to read the rest." He nodded to Queen Esther. "Miz Queen."

"That's Miz Brown to you," she retorted.

Brown? The last time I'd seen her, it was Jefferson. I stammered, "I ... Did you get married?"

She snorted. "I'm just pickin' my best name. Don't want no slave name."

I opened the letter. It was in large, loopy writing. "To the Freedmen's Bureau in Washington. I am pleased to tell you we may offer you assistance in the matter of Sahavie Harris or Spottswood. She is a bright girl living with the Harris family, known to members of this church."

It was signed, *Gabriel Jefferson, Pastor, Mount Nebo AME Church.*

I couldn't resist. "Is Pastor Jefferson a cousin of yours, Queen Esther?"

She sniffed and hitched her bottom around in the chair, taking another sip of her tea.

"So now you need to request a safe passage," I said. "Isn't that what you want?"

He nodded. "I needs that letter to travel in the South. And I never been to Memphis."

"Well," I said, "I haven't either. But I do know what to write."

So I wrote it. "I, Mr. Elijah Smith, have good information that my daughter is living in the city of Memphis in Tennessee. I would like permission to travel and funds to do so." The permission and safe conduct letter were much easier to come by than the money, but the Freedmen's Bureau did sometimes provide money if the proof was strong and the case dire.

They would probably not consider his case particularly dire, since they could easily figure out he had never seen this daughter. But it was worth trying. And, I thought, I could certainly give him money to travel—although I couldn't imagine him asking me for it.

When he stood next to me to sign the letter, I had to close my eyes. I didn't know whether to swoon or curl my hand around his leg. I did neither. I sprinkled the sand, waited for the ink to dry, and folded and addressed the letter. I handed it to him and wished him Godspeed, and he left.

I turned to see Queen Esther looking sharply at me. "You like that man."

"Well," I said, "yes, I suppose I do. I mean, I've known him a long time. He and my husband were friends."

"I don't mean like that," she said. I knew she hadn't. "You better not let him know."

"I know that."

"What you gonna do?"

"I don't know," I said. "Nothing."

"Mm-hmm." Silence. Then she asked suddenly, "Is he why you bought me and Washington?"

"No," I said. Then suddenly I wasn't sure. "I don't think so."

"Then why? I always wanted to ax you that."

I sighed and looked out the window. Then I looked back at her. "I don't know. I thought it was the right thing to do."

She looked at me appraisingly for a minute, her mouth sideways as she chewed on the inside of a cheek. "This whole damn country thought it was the right thing to do. And now they don't know what to do with us. And all these people don't know what to do with theyselves, neither."

Well, that was true enough. That was why all around us were colored folk who had come up from the South, in from the country. There was no work in the city for them to do, but the countryside could be dangerous. Colored folk thought they were getting forty acres and a mule. But which forty acres? Whose mules? Nobody knew.

"Do you ever see Washington?" I asked. Maybe I hoped to change the subject.

"He still sleepin' in the barn at Brown's," she said. "Gettin' tips for holdin' horses, just like he always done. He don't know what to do with hisself either. Doin' the same thing he did as a slave. Only difference freedom made to him is now he got nobody to look after him."

"Did it make a difference to you?" Suddenly, I had to know. "You had easier work before."

"Yeah, and I had a bed to lie down in if I got sick. But it wadn't my bed, and I couldn't pick up and leave. I hated bein' a slave, and I hated the white people who made me do it. You paid a lot a'money for us."

I nodded. "It was all I had."

"Then how'd you get this?" She gestured around the house. "Where all that money come from?"

"I invested in the railroads." I hoped the idea was beyond her grasp and she'd stop asking questions about my money. "Railroad stock bought me this house."

"Hmph. Then what you want with that Elijah Smith? He like an old man—got no juice to him."

"Juice? Is that what you look for?"

"Mm-hmm. And they plenty juicy young men want a black gal." She smiled and stretched her legs. "And if she got money, she gots her pick. And I been pickin' 'em. And you might want to pick you one'a your own. That's my good advice for the day. Pick one'a your own. You got any washin'?" She put down her teacup and stood. Queen Esther's audience was over for the day.

I gathered my laundry, and she shook out each piece and counted them up. "I'll bring these back Thursday," she said. "You 'member what I said. You pick one of your own. Won't no good come of what you thinkin' you want."

CHAPTER 46

I WAS SITTING ON MY FRONT PORCH ON A BEAUTIFUL DAY IN April when Pastor Willsby came to call. Spring was short in Washington City. We seemed to go from the dank, dreary days of late winter to a stinking hot summer in less than a week—but the few spring days we had were so perfect you could hardly believe you were on earth.

I watched the pastor walk toward me. I wondered why so many westerners seemed to look like Mr. Lincoln, rawboned and homely. I put the unflattering thoughts out of my mind and welcomed him.

"Mrs. O'Dea, I know you helped Mr. Elijah Smith write for his daughter." Pastor Willsby got right to the point. "He has a pass from the Freedmen's Bureau to travel to Memphis to fetch her."

"Excellent. I wish him Godspeed."

"They didn't give him no money."

"I see." That was hardly a surprise. "So he sent you to ask me for it?"

"No! I mean, no, ma'am. He ain't that kind of man." The pastor cleared his throat. "He don't know I'm here. I'm askin', ma'am, for some travel money, not just for him, but for me, too. I'll go with him. And we'll need something for the child. It's dangerous for a black man to travel in the South alone, and I'm afeared for him."

"That's only wise, pastor. My late husband once accompanied him on a trip into the South."

"I didn't know that, ma'am."

"No reason you would. It was before the war. How much do you need?"

He swallowed hard and named a sum. "That's if we take the railroad, ma'am. It's the fastest way. We can go by boat or wagon, but both them ways is dangerous and takes long."

"I can have that for you on Wednesday, pastor." I nodded once. "Would you like to sit down? May I offer you a cup of tea?"

"I—no, thank ye, ma'am. I'm a bit 'mazed that you agreed to that amount of money."

"Well, please don't spread the word around. I don't have enough for everybody. Elij—Mr. Smith was a good friend to my late husband, and I admire him." *Goodness, Vera,* I thought. *Just put up placards and let everyone know.*

Pastor Willsby and Elijah left for Memphis a few days later.

A few days after that, we heard about the riots. There were just a few bald facts in the papers. Some colored men in Union blue were pushed off a sidewalk by Irish police officers in Memphis. They resisted, and the riot started. Rioters burned four churches and killed dozens of Negroes. Two white men were injured.

Neighborhood gossip had it that hundreds of colored had been killed, all the women had been raped, and all the babies butchered. I could almost see Memphis in flames, in spite of the fact that I had never seen Memphis at all.

I put on my bonnet and went to the Freedmen's Bureau to find out. What I discovered there was bad enough.

My old friend Mr. Bump was now chief clerk for the military area of Tennessee. His remaining hair was gray now. I recalled he was married, and he looked fat, but somehow not prosperous.

"Well, Mrs. O'Dea," he said in his raspy voice, "it's a little irregular, but I will let you see this report from Memphis."

I read it quickly. On April thirtieth, several policemen forced a group of Negroes off the sidewalk. One fell, and a policeman stumbled over him. The police drew their revolvers and attacked the Negroes. The next day, a group of Negroes gathered—they appeared to be former soldiers. Some of them were drunk and boisterous. Police arrested two of them, and "a promiscuous fight was indulged in by both parties." One policeman accidentally shot himself in the hand, and that was the only injury to a policeman.

Police fired on a crowd of Negroes in another part of town. The *City Recorder* exhorted whites to arm themselves and kill every Negro, or at least drive them all from the city. Negroes were hunted down, shot, and robbed. Their houses were plundered and set on fire. The next night, a white mob appeared in South Memphis, shooting men, women, and even small children. One woman was shot and thrown into the flames of her burning house.

Negroes had gone to General Pickering, the agent of the Freedmen's Bureau. He said he was totally unable to protect them.

Rioters burned eight schools, four churches, and about fifty houses—none of which belonged to white people. There were at least fifty Negroes killed, with about fifty more wounded or beaten. White people who tried to help them were beaten as well. There were no white people killed, and aside from the policeman who shot himself in the hand, the only other white person injured was shot by another white man.

Was Elijah dead? Was Pastor Willsby one of the white men who were beaten? Was Elijah's daughter one of those poor babies killed?

I stood looking at the dispatch, not seeing it anymore. My mind raced, and a hard chill sank into my stomach. "Has it ended, at least?" I asked.

Mr. Bump sat back and put his fingertips together. "It seems to have quieted, for now," he said. "Your friend Mr. Smith is in Memphis, seeking his child."

"Yes," I replied, in my primmest fashion. "And my friend the Reverend Willsby is with him."

I knew what he meant by "my friend Mr. Smith." He knew I knew. He didn't have the courage to make any more of it.

"Well, Mrs. O'Dea, I'm sure you know we can't send an inquiry to Memphis on your behalf to discover what has happened to your friends. Relatives only. You understand. Will there be anything else?"

This officious little man could still infuriate me. He could have shown some compassion. At least he had let me see the report. I walked out into the sultry May day and thought there was but one kindred soul I could call on: Mrs. Willsby. I walked past the line where the threadbare floorcloths and curtains from her little house were hanging to dry, and knocked at the door. I stood looking at its worn, chipped paint as I heard her walk slowly toward the door. She opened it and stood drying her hands on her apron, looking as though she were mesmerized by something a short distance behind me. She was a worn, fair woman whose hair had once been bright and whose intense blue eyes were now rimmed with red. Her cheeks were red and puffy under the eyes.

"Mrs. Willsby, have you heard from the pastor?"

"I have not. And I've scrubbed everything in the house twice, trying to keep my mind from it. Come in."

Everything smelled of lye soap, as well it might; the floors were wet and bare. She offered me lemonade, and I offered to help make it, telling her I was very fond of lemonade. We worked together for the few minutes in silence and then sat to drink. She took one swallow and put down the glass, dropping her head in her hands and weeping.

"I'm so afeared for him," she said, drying her eyes on her apron. "He goes where his own kind turns to animals, and he thinks he'll just walk among them like Daniel in the lions' den.

I keep thinking of all the things that might have happened to him, and to that man Elijah, and I get so torn with worry I can't do anything but weep. Prayers don't help, and the Bible don't help either. Maybe I'm weak in the faith, but I just don't know what I can do."

I told her as gently as I could what I had learned at the Freedmen's Bureau—that the Bureau and the forces of the Union Army could not protect those poor Negroes from a mob. I did tell her, while white men who tried to interfere had been beaten, the dead ones had been identified and neither of them was her husband.

"He'll be back," I said, patting her hand. "We just have to be patient and not lose hope." But what about Elijah? He knew no one in Memphis, and had no place to run if a mob decided to tear him to pieces. A black man, and a stranger to boot, travelling with a white preacher—what had they done to him? Was he among the many unnamed Negro dead?

I said farewell and promised to let Mrs. Willsby have any further information I might glean. She promised to do the same. At home, I sat watching the sunset alone. When I went to bed, I lay staring into the darkness for hours until the warm dawn came. I moved like a sleepwalker through daily tasks.

The next afternoon, I saw a group of children running excitedly toward the Willsbys' house, shouting and pounding on the door. They were followed by a wagon, drawn by a mule, with a driver and one man sitting beside him—Pastor Willsby.

My knees kept threatening trying to buckle as I walked over. The pastor and his wife were embracing each other and weeping. The driver walked around the back of the wagon, and I heard a low moan come from it. I hurried around the back and found Elijah lying in the wagon.

My heart leapt, and it was all I could do to keep from weeping myself. Then the driver and Pastor Willsby moved him, gently, for he had a splinted bandage on his leg and his face was swollen and discolored. One of his teeth was gone—one of his fine, white, beautiful teeth. I started to reach for his hand but pulled back and swallowed a sob.

"What happened?" I asked too loudly, too hysterically. "What happened?"

"Come in the house," said Pastor Willsby. "We'll put him in the bed, and we'll tell you."

"I'll fetch water and a salve," I said and went to do so.

My hands shook as I heated water and prepared arnica, trying to gain some mastery over my feelings.

He is alive! I thought. *Hallelujah! But what happened—what happened? And where's his little girl? But he's alive. Oh, thank God.*

I took a deep breath and a drink of water and steadied myself enough to go back. Mrs. Willsby was giving Elijah a bit of broth, and together we bathed and treated his wounds as best we could, then left him to rest. I fetched bread and some dried fruit from my house, and we sat at the Willsbys' crooked table to hear the story.

"We arrived in Memphis with no trouble," the pastor began, "in just over a day and a half. That railroad is surely a wonder. We asked our way to the church and didn't think anything of the crowds of people standing around. It was Saturday evening. We thought everyone was just out enjoying a warm, fine night. Real sudden like, we heard shouting and shooting, and a group of white hooligans was upon us, hitting us with clubs, and threatening us with guns. Most people ran. We didn't. That was our mistake." He stopped for a minute. "We thought we had no reason to run.

"They grabbed Elijah and beat him. I tried to stop them, and they beat me, too. They'd have killed him, but once he was down, they lost interest, gave him a couple more kicks, and left.

"The hardest thing was finding someone who could set his broken leg. Some women came and helped me move him to a house. No doctor would come, but we finally found a soldier who knew how to set his leg.

"I tried to find his little daughter. I couldn't. I found the pastor of the church, but his church was burned. He didn't know where the Harrises were. Mr. Smith did not want to leave without his daughter, but we rapidly ran out of funds, and the good people who put us up couldn't sustain us for long. So we've returned."

"You're alive, John," said his wife. "I am grateful for that." He patted her hand and nodded distractedly.

I told him I was grateful for their return as well. I walked the short distance home slowly, as the moon was rising. I wondered what could come of this chain of events.

Elijah stayed with the Willsbys as his wounds healed, but he seemed to have little interest in recovering and none in speaking to me about what had happened. I would go every day to take him some broth or fruit, and he would accept as politely as anybody could without saying a word—then turn away.

In a week or so, he started to regain his appetite. I took him some good bread and hot sausage, hoping he would talk to me.

He did say, "Thank you. That's mighty kind." And he fell to on the sausage.

I said, "I want to talk to you about something that has troubled me. Something I did."

He looked at me warily but nodded.

"I think I'm responsible for a man's death. I didn't kill him, but I told the soldiers he was a spy, and they killed him."

He waited a minute, perhaps to make sure that was all I was going to say.

"Rebel spy?" he asked.

I nodded.

"You done right." And he went back to eating.

"I think he's the man who killed Jimmy."

He chewed and swallowed. "Then you surely done right."

I won't tell him I lusted after this man, I thought. *That's just too strange.*

"Did you kill anyone in the war?"

He finished the meal I had brought him and wiped his mouth. "More'n a dozen," he answered, giving me a direct look. "I was a sharpshooter at Petersburg."

"Does it bother you? Does it bother you that you killed people?"

He shrugged. "A little—time to time." He paused, looking back at me. "But not much. It felt good. Felt like every last man I shot was a Spottswood, and I had power to take from them like they had power to take from me. They took Bathsheba. I took their whole damn life."

I waited to see if he had more to say. All he said was, "Sorry for the language, Miz Ohday."

"Don't be sorry about that," I told him. "I think the language was justified."

He gave an abrupt nod. "Then I just be sorry I couldn't get Bathsheba's child. They beat me and took her from me again." He hit the bed in frustration, then leaned back and shut his eyes. "And I can't do nothin' about it. I'm weak again."

"I understand," I said. Our little conversation took all the force he had, but there was a thought forming in my mind, and I had to make sure it was right. "It's important for me to know," I said. "Do you still want her if she's not your child?"

He gave a pained look, and then turned away. "I do. She may be Spottswood's child," he said. He looked me in the eyes. "But she Bathsheba's child, and I prize her for that."

That's when I decided my impulse was right. But I didn't tell him what I wanted to do, because he wouldn't have wanted me to take the risk.

∽

THE FIRST PERSON I TOLD was Queen Esther. "I think I'll go to Memphis and bring his daughter back."

She raised her eyebrows. "You been hit in the head, too?"

"No. I just think it's the only way he's going to get his daughter back. I think a white lady can travel a little more safely there than a black man can. What do you think?"

"I think them paterollers ain't fussy about who they hits."

I sighed. "You're right. Of course you're right. But I think he doesn't even want to live now."

"And there ain't nothin' you can do about it. Just as well, too. It ain't your trouble, and it ain't your bidness, and you got no need to go makin' it your trouble. You got any washin' this week?"

Still, the more I thought on it, the more determined I was to go to Memphis. So I began to make preparations without telling anyone. Anyone, that is, except Queen Esther. When she came the next week, I told her I would be gone a while.

"You goin' to Memphis, ain't you?"

I tried not answering her.

"Ain't you?"

"Yes," I admitted. "That is my plan."

"Well, I been thinkin' about this, too. Take me with you."

"What?"

"I can get answers you can't get. You can pay my way, and I can help you find that child."

Why was she doing this? I told myself not to turn down help, and she was right about being able to get answers I couldn't. "Well, yes, I could probably use your help. Why did you decide to do this?"

She looked uncomfortable. I wished I hadn't asked. But I did want to know.

"I ..." She stopped, looked down, and then back up again, with her chin out toward me. "I wants to do something righteous. Like you done."

I stood amazed, trying to think. She folded her arms and

cocked her hips to one side. "When we goin'? I needs to make arrangements."

Well, of course she did. She had people who depended on her for their washing, and she would need to tell them she'd be gone—probably for a week or so. A quick wave of panic rose in me, warning me this was a dangerous and foolish thing to do. I quelled it.

"I'll ... I'll ... What will I do? I'll check on the train timetables and see when we can best get there."

CHAPTER 47

THREE DAYS LATER, WE CLIMBED ON A SOUTHBOUND TRAIN. We'd be changing at Roanoke, Virginia, for another train—one that would take us across the mountains, along the Tennessee River, and west to Memphis. As the train gained speed on the bridge over the Potomac, I suddenly realized I had lived in Washington City for more than four years, and had never crossed that river.

"I've never been into Southron territory," I said quietly to Queen Esther—or as quietly as I could in that rattling car behind the chuffing locomotive.

"Well, I ain't been here in a long time," she responded. She crossed her arms and looked straight ahead. "I forgot how much I don't like it."

"Do you want to turn back?"

She shook her head, just once. We rode on in silence.

We changed trains just at sunset and rattled west across the mountains. I had never seen mountains before. We sped past scenes of breathtaking beauty as the sun set. Delicate mists wrapped about the mountains like soft nightgowns, and the deep greens and shadows grew stronger against the reddening sky. Night brought a welcome coolness. I watched the stars come out, and then dozed on the slatted wooden seat.

When I awoke, it was already daylight and already hot. We were speeding across flat fields, and all of them and all the trees were the deep, brilliant green of high summer, even though it was only May. The air in the car was oppressive, not only from the smoke of the locomotive, but also from the heavy, wet heat that permeated everything. I was sticky and smelt past ripe. My head ached, and I was thirsty.

Queen Esther lay on the seat across from me. Her eyes were open, and when she saw me looking at her, she sat up, patted her hair, and put her bonnet back on. "We be there soon," she said, setting her mouth in a tight line and looking out the window.

We *were* there soon—our arrival was almost abrupt. Suddenly, we were slowing past dozens of shanties and piles of lumber and timber, and we were at a squat wooden depot. The train stopped, and the conductor helped me down. He did not assist Queen Esther.

We asked about a hotel for ladies, and he volunteered that the Gayoso was a fine place "now that the Forrest boys chased out the Yankees." I looked at him quizzically, which was all the prompting he needed to tell us the story of how Nathan Bedford Forrest had led his cavalry right into the hotel, riding his horse into the lobby. General Forrest's brother had captured the Yankee general's pants, which the Southron general later returned with his compliments. I smiled a wan smile and thanked him, and we walked through the oppressive heat to the Hotel Gayoso.

To our right was the huge Mississippi River—its thick, brown water churned by paddle wheelers, flatboats, and barges. To the left squatted a variety of wooden buildings, none of them attractive or imposing. We walked past two sets of charred ruins—churches?—and were trailed by a small group of children imitating the way we walked. I smiled and walked on.

In the hotel's dim lobby, a young man with very well-oiled hair offered me a "lady's suite," which would provide a trundle bed for my "maid." I started to protest that she was not my maid, but Queen Esther delivered a quick, light kick to my ankle, and I kept my mouth shut. The clerk asked our business in Memphis, and I replied we had come in search of a child. His eyebrows shot up, but I gave him a direct, no-nonsense look, and paid for the room in advance, with gold. He asked no further questions.

Our room faced the river, and the breeze, although slight, was cooling and welcome. We opened the shutters and sat on the bed.

"Well," I said after a moment. "We're here. Now what do we do?"

"Clean up first," said my companion. "And I'll go find the Harrises."

"I'll go with you."

"No." She shook her head. "I been thinking about this. I'll talk to the black folks, and you talk to the white ones."

"The white ones won't know anything."

"Well then, you try to find the preacher. He'll know something."

"It's going to look suspicious if I just walk around by myself," I said, getting a belated glimmer of reality about this enterprise.

She sighed. "Well, then we won't get too far apart."

The first day was fruitless. We were two strangers looking for a pastor whose church had been burned, and for a family sheltering a child. I received only shakes of the head and mumbled answers.

"No ma'am, don't know nothin'."

"Reverend Jefferson, he done left with the rest of 'em."

On the morning of the second day, it dawned on me that I could try the local Freedmen's Bureau. Perhaps the men on site here in Memphis might at least be able to tell me how to find the pastor of the church. So we walked to the Freedmen's Bureau, and Queen Esther waited outside while I went in to transact our business with the white men who ran it.

They confirmed that Mr. Jefferson's church had indeed burned—and while they couldn't tell me where he was, they could tell me where the church had been. Perhaps our search could start there, they suggested. They did not ask me why I would be looking, and I did not tell them.

As I went back outside to Queen Esther, two bright-eyed little Negro boys who had been talking to her laughed and ran away. I told her I had found where the church had been and suddenly realized she was starting to smile.

"Those little boys done told me what we needs to know. There's a family named Harris, lives just a ways over there." She pointed in the direction where I had been told the church would be.

"A lot of black folks left town after the riots," she explained as we walked. "The Harrises didn't go because Miz Harris was about to birth another baby."

The Harrises lived in a real house, although not much of one. It was a shabby frame building with the paint worn off, and it was perched on stones so it was open underneath.

The door was hardly a door, but a frame with a patched wicker screen on it. I stepped away and let Queen Esther knock and go in. I stood outside in the heat and dust, while a small crowd of children gathered around me.

I nodded and smiled. "Good morning."

Some giggled, and they all moved away and tentatively toward us again.

"Miss, what you doin' here?"

"I'm looking for a child."

"Plenty chirren here." Another muffled giggle. "You here for that yellow girl?"

"I don't know," I answered truthfully. "I'm here for a little girl of about five, who is living with a family named Harris."

They nudged each other and grinned. "She here!" one blurted, and the others quickly shushed him.

Queen Esther cracked the door open and motioned me to come in.

A woman and a baby sat quietly in a dim room, the mother rocking gently back and forth with the dozing infant. As my eyes became used to the darkness, I saw a man sitting protectively behind them. "This is Miz Vera Ohday," Queen Esther said softly. "Miz Vera, this is Mr. Joseph and Miz Elizabeth Harris."

I moved close to them so we could speak softly and not wake the baby. The room was stuffy and smelt of human occupation—the sour smell of sweat and the sweetish odor of dried urine. We looked at each other, uncertain how to begin.

"Why you want Sahavie?" Mrs. Harris asked, finally.

"Her father wants her," I said flatly.

The couple glanced at each other. "Her father dead," said the husband. "Killed in the war."

"Well," I said, fumbling out the letters from Reverend Jefferson, and the one I had written for Elijah Smith, "here's what we have about her. Her mother was Bathsheba Spottswood. Our friend Elijah Smith was her husband. He came to get her in May, but he got beat up in the riots."

The couple looked at each other again. "I think she better see Sahavie," said the wife. "Sahavie!" she called softly. "Come on in here, child."

Several children inched shyly out of the back room. Three of them had gleaming dark skin and glowing black eyes. One little girl looked white. She was the one who came forward. I looked at her in the light through the doorway and saw that her skin was a honey gold and her large eyes were a brilliant green. While her hair looked soft and woolly, it was light brown. She had freckles on her nose and a tentative smile on her face. I suddenly remembered the description of her, "a bright girl." Of course.

I smiled at her, and her own smile widened and she gave a little giggle, covering her mouth with a chubby golden hand. I was enchanted.

"You all go outside for a while," said Mrs. Harris to her children. I watched the little girl go, and she glanced back at me and smiled again.

"Hmm," said Queen Esther. "She no more Elijah Smith's child than she a housecat. Now what you gonna do?"

"He wants Bathsheba's child." I knew it sounded foolish, even in my own ears, but it was true. "He loved her. He bought her freedom, and she was stolen from him. I think he'd treasure her child."

"Sahavie is Bathsheba's child," said Mrs. Harris. "Bathsheba was my friend, and her husband Elijah did love her and she loved him. That child is her master's child. He was killed in the war. Bathsheba passed, oh, two years ago and asked me to care for her child, and I said I would." She looked at her husband for a long moment. He said nothing.

"We have five of our own," she added. There was another silence. "Times been hard," she continued, and looked at her husband again.

He nodded.

"We loves that child. I loved Bathsheba." She rocked her baby, and I waited. "Is he going to care for another man's child just because it was Bathsheba's?" she asked.

"I believe he will," I said, "and if he doesn't, I will."

"Why would you do that?" asked Mrs. Harris.

"She'll do it," said Queen Esther. I looked at her in surprise. "She'll care for that baby."

"I'll write to let you know how she's doing. And when she learns to write, she can write to you, too."

"They burned our school here," said Mr. Harris.

"I know," I answered. More silence. "Do you need some time to talk about this?" I asked.

"That'd be good," he answered.

"We'll come back—tomorrow morning, all right?"

They nodded, and we said our good-byes.

We walked back through the heat and dust. "Thank you for speaking up for me," I said to Queen Esther.

"Hmm," she said. "I could see you fall in love with that child."

"Was it so obvious?" I had to laugh a little with embarrassment. "I will care for her—I can care for her. I can get her anything she needs."

"They knows that. But they not the kinda people just sell a child or give her away. 'Course, folks do talk when there's a yellow child in a dark family."

"Should we give them money? Should we just buy them food and leave with the child so they don't have another mouth to feed?" I asked.

"I think that's for you to figure. Right now, I wants to go back to the hotel so you can buy me a bath."

That sounded like a very good idea.

We walked silently back to the Hotel Gayoso, and I paid for baths for each of us. It felt good to soak and relax, although my mind kept spinning through a thousand questions. *What am I doing travelling a thousand miles to fetch the child of someone I never met, to help someone whose child it isn't? What can I give to the Harrises that will say thank you, but not insult them? Will she need shoes to ride the train? What if she has lice? What if she doesn't like me?*

Well, at least I knew what to do about that last one. I hadn't liked Julia when I first lived with her. And Sahavie had been through so much—probably even more than I could imagine. She was probably terrified during the riots. Her mother was gone, and she'd been living with another family. They at least seemed kind.

For me to just swoop in and take her will frighten her, too, I thought. *But going to Julia probably saved me—maybe even saved my life.* I closed my eyes and lay back for a few minutes in the bath. All I could see was Sahavie's little face and her luminous eyes.

When we were clean and dry and rested, I knew what to do. The next morning, we bought food, sheets, some needles and pins, and a Bible. I put a purse with gold and silver in with the sheets, so we wouldn't be handing it to the Harrises. And I told myself I would give them all these things whether they let us take Sahavie or not.

We lugged our bundles to the little house, walking past children playing in the street. They stop their play to whisper, so we knew word had spread about our errand. *They probably know what's going to come of this,* I thought, *even though we don't.* Queen Esther and I just glanced at each other, and kept walking.

When we came to the door, it stood ajar. The couple waited inside with their baby and with Sahavie, who looked scrubbed and tidied, standing with a little bundle of her own and wearing a shabby pair of little shoes. There was no smile this time. She looked uncertain and a little afraid, and when she saw me, she put her finger in her mouth and stood staring down, turning back and forth as though with her whole little body she was saying *no.*

The baby started to wail, and Mrs. Harris walked into the back room with him. Mr. Harris stood with us, putting a hand on Sahavie's shoulder.

"We goin' to let her go with you," he said, and swallowed. "It be a better life for you, baby," he said to Sahavie. "You understand that?"

She turned away from all of us, keeping her finger in her mouth.

"We brought a few things for the family," I said. "Please take them. It's what we can give. And we would have given them whether you let her go with us or not."

He hesitated, nodded, and indicated a place to put the bundles down.

I squatted next to Sahavie. "Sahavie," I said, softly. "I know you're worried. Your mama and daddy are going to let you go with me to live with someone else who loves you. When I was a little girl, I had to go with someone else, too, and I know it's hard at first. I have a little doll for you."

She looked over her shoulder at me.

"This little doll likes you. And I like you. We'd like you to come with us. We want you to get on the train and take a ride with us and go to a place where there are plenty of children to play with. We think you'll like it."

She looked at me for a long moment. I put the doll on the chair near her. She looked at it and back at me. Then she picked up the doll.

"We need to get to the depot if we going to catch today's train," said Queen Esther.

Mr. Harris nodded and stooped down to give Sahavie a hug. Mrs. Harris came back in, and kissed the little girl, holding her fiercely.

"You be a good girl, Sahavie," she said, holding her in a lingering embrace. Mrs. Harris looked up at me, her eyes bright with tears, and nodded.

And we left, with the little girl holding my hand. The clerk at the Hotel Gayoso gave us a quizzical stare as we crossed the lobby, and another as we settled the bill. But he didn't say anything.

When we purchased tickets at the depot, the station master looked at the three of us. "Your girl and her pickaninny will have to ride on the colored car," he said, pronouncing "girl" as "gull," "ride" as "rahd," and "colored" as "cullud." His accent was strong, but his meaning was more than clear.

"The child is my husband's child," I lied, loftily. "I came to Memphis to fetch her. And I would like for us all to ride in the ladies' car."

"Well, ma'am," the man said, coloring crimson, "I do beg

your pardon. I didn't understand the sitcheation, you see. And not many ladies would do that, if I may say so."

I did not answer. He got more flustered.

"The child needs her mammy," he added, trying belatedly to be helpful. He glanced at Queen Esther, who stared back at him impassively. I stood silent and still.

"Um," he said. "The ladies' car is extra, of course."

"Of course," I said, opening my purse.

The time for the train was approaching. Negroes with pushcarts and boxes gathered around the station to sell food to the passengers. We bought some cold fried chicken, three sandwiches, and some lemonade. Sahavie tasted her dipper of lemonade tentatively. After that first sip, she drank with gusto.

I couldn't help smiling at this child who loved lemonade on her first taste, just as I had. "Would you like some more?" I asked.

She looked up shyly and said, "Yes'm," in a high, whispery little voice. It was the first time I had heard her speak.

We bought another dipper of lemonade each, and enjoyed it as the train puffed up to the depot.

We settled into the ladies' car, which was almost empty. There were three other women, all white. Two of them looked like country wives travelling together. The other looked like a schoolteacher. There were spectacles on her nose, and she sat and read and never looked up. The two women gave us an appraising stare and whispered to each other for a minute, then looked out the window.

The chicken was salty and greasy, and tasted wonderful. I ate as though I had only just discovered food. Queen Esther and Sahavie also dug in, with a hearty appetite. We soon tossed the bones out the window. I wiped Sahavie's hands with my pocket handkerchief, and was rewarded with a smile. She sat excited by the window as the train sped up, and the scenes of Memphis began flashing by.

CHAPTER 48

SOON WE WERE CROSSING FLAT GREEN FIELDS NEAR THE TENnessee River. By then it was late afternoon, and as the shadows deepened, the land became more rolling, and Sahavie's eyelids drooped over her eyes. I pulled her close to me, and she soon fell asleep with her head in my lap.

I sat thinking as we hurtled through the twilight. *This beautiful child, breathing so softly, would not exist if it weren't for incest and slavery, or if a powerful man had not been a brute.*

The hills gave way to mountains, pulling nighttime mantles of mist about their shoulders. The air cooled, and Sahavie wriggled to get comfortable. I softly touched her hair, and her cheek.

Yet she's perfect.

And, I suddenly realized, perhaps I was perfect, too, at least when I was born. I thought about my mother. *It's taken me 'til now to understand. We, none of us, would be alive if someone hadn't cared for us when we were helpless. She did the best she could. And no matter what her whole story was, she was crushed by people more powerful than she.*

My mother didn't make me what I am. I did.

I looked out at the stars beginning to prick the dark skies.

It only takes a little light to pierce the darkness, I thought. *I can give a little light. Jimmy always said we belong where we can be useful.*

I put my arm gently around Sahavie. I could make sure this child would be cared for. *Will Elijah want me along with her? Probably not. I still think it's the right thing to do. Other people helped me belong.*

It startled me to think I belonged somewhere—anywhere. But I had belonged with Julia, with Jimmy, with Mary. *Jimmy told me long ago. We belong where we're needed. I don't need to know all about my mother and what she did to know that.*

It's a good thing I don't need to know. I probably never will.

The train sped forward through the shadowed mountains, and the bright light of the evening star gleamed through the darkening velvet of the night.

AFTERWORD

*M*ARIA MONK WAS A REAL PERSON, AND *THE AWFUL Disclosures of Maria Monk* was published in her name, as was a second book in the same vein. *The Awful Disclosures* was the best-selling book ever published in the United States until that time, and remained so until the publication of *Uncle Tom's Cabin* in 1852.

I discovered Maria Monk when I was reading about the Know-Nothing movement in Maryland, and was intrigued to find that her lurid book had so much influence twenty years after it was published. I have been even more intrigued to find it has been published repeatedly since 1836. The copy I have was published by Senate, an imprint of Random House UK, in 1997, with no indication that it might not be true.

Maria had two daughters, and may have had a son, although the documentation is much less clear on that score. A woman claiming to be the younger daughter—Lizzie St. John Eckel—published her autobiography, *Maria Monk's Daughter,* in 1874, and I drew on that for the Flatbush section of my book, and for Lizzie's later appearances in my story.

I am grateful to many libraries and collections for their help in my research—notably the Library of Congress, the New York Public Library, the Freedmen and Southern Society Project and its gracious director Leslie Rowland, the Irish Railroad Workers Museum in Baltimore, Michael B. Roberts (author of *The Cailleach of Sligo* and our guide for a delightful day in Sligo and Drumcliffe), and the library at the National Endowment for the Humanities, which I happily exploited during the year I worked there.

All the research and writing (and re-writing!) that went into this book would have been less well spent without the support and enthusiasm of the people at Inkwater Press. Andrew Durkin has been a sharp-eyed and thoughtful editor. Masha Shubin's work with design and her patience with galley editing have been heartening.

When I first learned about Maria and her appearances on the lecture circuit with her baby daughter in her arms, my question was, "What happened to her baby?" I don't think the historical record gives a clear answer, and *The Monk Woman's Daughter* grew from my desire to give the baby girl a life.

ABOUT THE AUTHOR

*S*USAN STORER CLARK worked as a radio and TV journalist for many years, mostly in Washington, DC. She received history degrees from Rhodes College and King's College London, and continues to enjoy the study of history. She lives in a remodeled farmhouse near Seattle, and writes for the *Washington Independent Review of Books* and the newspaper *Real Change*. She also blogs about history and historical fiction at her website, www.historymuse.us.

CPSIA information can be obtained
at www.ICGtesting.com
Printed in the USA
FFOW02n1436260917
40361FF